FATE OF THE
FREE LANDS

PRAISE FOR THE PILLARS OF REALITY SERIES

"Campbell has created an interesting world... [he] has created his characters in such a meticulous way, I could not help but develop my own feelings for both of them. I have already gotten the second book and will be listening with anticipation."

—Audio Book Reviewer

"I loved *The Hidden Masters of Marandur*...The intense battle and action scenes are one of the places where Campbell's writing really shines. There are a lot of urban and epic fantasy novels that make me cringe when I read their battles, but Campbell's years of military experience help him write realistic battles."

—All Things Urban Fantasy

"I highly recommend this to fantasy lovers, especially if you enjoy reading about young protagonists coming into their own and fighting against a stronger force than themselves. The world building has been strengthened even further giving the reader more history. Along with the characters flight from their pursuers and search for knowledge allowing us to see more of the continent the pace is constant and had me finding excuses to continue the book."

—Not Yet Read

"*The Dragons of Dorcastle*... is the perfect mix of steampunk and fantasy... it has set the bar to high."

—The Arched Doorway

"Quite a bit of fun and I really enjoyed it. . .An excellent sequel and well worth the read!"

—Game Industry

"The Pillars of Reality series continues in *The Assassins of Altis* to be a great action filled adventure. . .So many exciting things happen that I can hardly wait for the next book to be released."

—*Not Yet Read*

"The Pillars of Reality is a series that gets better and better with each new book. . .*The Assassins of Altis* is a great addition to a great series and one I recommend to fantasy fans, especially if you like your fantasy with a touch of sci-fi."

—*Bookaholic Cat*

"Seriously, get this book (and the first two). This one went straight to my favorites shelf."

—*Reanne Reads*

"[Jack Campbell] took my expectations and completely blew them out of the water, proving yet again that he can seamlessly combine steampunk and epic fantasy into a truly fantastic story. . .I am looking forward to seeing just where Campbell goes with the story next, I'm not sure how I'm going to manage the wait for the next book in the series."

—*The Arched Doorway*

"When my audiobook was delivered around midnight, I sat down and told myself I would listen for an hour or so before I went to sleep. I finished it in almost 12 straight hours, I don't think I've ever listened to an audiobook like that before. I can say with complete honesty that *The Servants of The Storm* by Jack Campbell is one of the best books I've ever had the pleasure to listen to."

—*Arched Doorway*

PRAISE FOR THE LOST FLEET SERIES

"It's the thrilling saga of a nearly-crushed force battling its way home from deep within enemy territory, laced with deadpan satire about modern warfare and neoliberal economics. Like Xenophon's Anabasis – with spaceships."

—The Guardian (UK)

"Black Jack is an excellent character, and this series is the best military SF I've read in some time."

—Wired Magazine

"If you're a fan of character, action, and conflict in a Military SF setting, you would probably be more than pleased by Campbell's offering."

—Tor.com

". . . a fun, quick read, full of action, compelling characters, and deeper issues. Exactly the type of story which attracts readers to military SF in the first place."

—SF Signal

"Rousing military-SF action… it should please many fans of old-fashioned hard SF. And it may be a good starting point for media SF fans looking to expand their SF reading beyond tie-in novels."

—SciFi.com

"Fascinating stuff … this is military SF where the military and SF parts are both done right."

—SFX Magazine

PRAISE FOR THE LOST FLEET:
BEYOND THE FRONTIER SERIES

"Combines the best parts of military sf and grand space opera to launch a new adventure series ... sets the fleet up for plenty of exciting discoveries and escapades."

—Publishers Weekly

"Absorbing…neither series addicts nor newcomers will be disappointed."

—Kirkus Reviews

"Epic space battles, this time with aliens. Fans who enjoyed the earlier books in the Lost Fleet series will be pleased."

—Fantasy Literature

"I loved every minute of it. I've been with these characters through six novels and it felt like returning to an old group of friends."

—Walker of Worlds

"A fast-paced page turner ... the search for answers will keep readers entertained for years to come."

—SF Revu

"Another excellent addition to one of the best military science fiction series on the market. This delivers everything fans expect from Black Jack Geary and more."

—Monsters & Critics

ALSO BY JACK CAMPBELL

THE LOST FLEET

Dauntless
Fearless
Courageous
Valiant
Relentless
Victorious

BEYOND THE FRONTIER

Dreadnaught
Invincible
Guardian
Steadfast
Leviathan

THE LOST STARS

Tarnished Knight
Perilous Shield
Imperfect Sword
Shattered Spear

THE GENESIS FLEET

Vanguard
Ascendant
Triumphant

PILLARS OF REALITY

*The Dragons of Dorcastle**
*The Hidden Masters of Marandur**
*The Assassins of Altis**
*The Pirates of Pacta Servanda**
*The Servants of the Storm**
*The Wrath of the Great Guilds**

THE LEGACY OF DRAGONS

*Daughter of Dragons**
*Blood of Dragons**
*Destiny of Dragons**

EMPRESS OF THE ENDLESS SEA

*Pirate of the Prophecy**
*Explorer of the Endless Sea**
*Fate of the Free Lands**

NOVELLAS

*The Last Full Measure**

SHORT STORY COLLECTIONS

*Ad Astra**
*Borrowed Time**
*Swords and Saddles**

*available as a JABberwocky ebook

FATE OF THE FREE LANDS

EMPRESS OF THE ENDLESS SEA

BOOK III

JACK CAMPBELL

JABberwocky Literary Agency, Inc.

Fate of the Free Lands

Cover art by Dominick Saponaro

Map by Isaac Stewart

ISBN 978-1-625675-07-1

ACKNOWLEDGMENTS

I remain indebted to my agents, Joshua Bilmes and Eddie Schneider, for their long standing support, ever-inspired suggestions and assistance, as well as to Karen Bourne and Adriana Funke for their work on foreign sales and print editions, and Susan Velazquez for lots of other stuff. Many thanks to Betsy Mitchell for her excellent editing. Thanks also to Catherine Asaro, Robert Chase, Kelly Dwyer, Carolyn Ives Gilman, J.G. (Huck) Huckenpohler, Simcha Kuritzky, Michael LaViolette, Aly Parsons, Mary Thompson, and Constance A. Warner for their suggestions, comments and recommendations. And, of course, thank you to Steve Feldberg for his strong support.

CHAPTER ONE

L andfall, oldest of cities, had seen many things. But never before a battle on the waterfront between Mages and one of their monsters on one side, and the Emperor's legionaries and sailors on the other. Mages were well-known for their inhuman and arrogant actions, but even they had never launched such an attack outright. Rumor raced through the city faster than the crowds fleeing the waterfront, citizens whispering among themselves that there could have been only one possible reason why the Mages would do such a thing.

She must be in Landfall.

* * *

The cutpurse lurking in the side alley amid stacks of refuse had only a moment to realize that he'd chosen the wrong victim this time, as the woman in the hooded cloak used the folds of her garment to catch and divert the thrust of his knife. Before he could react, the woman's dagger was plunging into his breast, piercing his heart, and ending his criminal career for good.

Jules of Landfall knelt beside the killer's remains, going through his pockets. "I might've spared your life," she commented to his body, "except that your first thrust was a killing move. I only grant mercy to those who show mercy to others."

She found a purse containing enough money to convince Jules that she hadn't been the man's first victim that night. Hopefully the first one had escaped harm. The purse didn't hold a lot of money, though; a couple of silver galleys, and several copper shields, but not a single gold eagle. However, since she hadn't had any money on her at all before this, it represented a welcome find.

Jules pocketed the money, discarding the purse. Looking up past the aged brick walls of the buildings rising on each side of the alley, she could see the sky beginning to pale with the first rays of dawn, the growing light battling against the haze of smoke as waking households and businesses lit coal and wood for fires. On the street she could hear the slow clop of horseshoes and the rattle of wheels on the cobblestones as milk deliveries were made. A quiet, normal, peaceful morning, very different from the chaos of the night before. The rapid thud of horses being ridden fast echoed from the aged bricks. Jules faded back against the nearest wall, catching quick glimpses of Imperial cavalry as they rode past the entrance to the alley, their brightly-polished chest armor dull in the still-shadowed street, their lances pointing upward like a deadly thicket.

The cavalry was headed in the direction of the waterfront. Was the Mage troll still alive and fighting? That seemed too much to hope for. More likely, the cavalry were being called in to help search for her.

The last trooper rode past, the sound of rapid hoof beats fading. Even after all these years, the sight of legionary cavalry tore at her. Her father had served in the Emperor's cavalry until his death while chasing bandits in the mountains known as the Northern Ramparts.

Jules shifted her gaze to the south, where she'd been raised in Landfall's Imperial orphan home after her mother died as well during childbirth. Even if she hadn't hated the place, with its strict rules and harsh guardians and inadequate food and clothing, she wouldn't have considered it as a place of refuge now. It'd be hard enough to avoid being recognized elsewhere in the city. She'd left that orphan home only a few years ago, so there were plenty of officials and others there who'd know her on sight.

Jules smiled slightly, remembering how proud most of the other kids had been when she earned the chance at an Imperial officer's commission. Were they still proud of her?

The camp outside Landfall where she'd received training to become an officer in the Imperial service lay to the east of the city. Another life, when she'd stubbornly sought the right to wear the dark red uniform of the Empire as proof that she, an orphan, was the equal of anyone. That ambition, that goal, had ceased to matter, had become impossible, when a Mage had looked at her and pronounced the prophecy that had upended her life. *The day will come when a daughter of your line will unite Mechanics, Mages, and the common folk to overthrow the Great Guilds and free the world.* Not a long prophecy, but long enough to act as a death sentence in the eyes of the Mages and to make her an obsession of the Emperor.

Jules looked west, to where the Sea of Bakre lay. Somewhere out there, hopefully, the pirate ship *Sun Queen* still sailed. But, she, the *Sun Queen*'s captain, couldn't hope for help from that quarter. The crew had no idea where she was, and even if they knew couldn't hope to fight their way through Imperial forces to reach her. They had a more important task to carry out, anyway.

For a moment, her eyes saw not the brick of the buildings lining the alley, but the limitless waters to the west. For as long as the history of the world of Dematr went back, which admittedly wasn't very far, humanity had been confined to the eastern part of the Sea of Bakre where the Empire ruled. Every chart, every legend, described the west as a deathtrap of hidden reefs and desert shores. But she'd gone there, she'd seen the truth, she'd discovered new lands and a strait that led to another sea and then the ocean itself. The chart made on that journey had to be copied, had to be shared with as many people as possible, so that the knowledge in it could never be suppressed by the Great Guilds or the Empire.

The vision from her memory faded, leaving her once again in the trash-strewn alley. She took another glance at the sky, trying to measure the time. The throng of fearful citizens fleeing the fight on the waterfront had mostly dissipated. Merging with the crowds of work-ers and other citizens who should soon be populating the morning streets would be her only hope of not being quickly spotted by the legionaries and police doubtless already combing the city for her. Not to mention the Mages who'd been disappointed in their attempts to kill her last night.

Down on the waterfront, the wreck of the Imperial sloop that had brought her to Landfall had probably sunk by now after burning to the waterline. Imperial police—often corrupt, but extremely thor-ough when the Emperor's eyes were on them—would be searching the wreckage to confirm that she hadn't died while still chained in the ship's brig. Legionaries who'd caught glimpses of her during the cha-otic battle as the Mage troll smashed the ship, the pier, and anything in its way, would be undergoing interrogation to confirm they'd seen her.

That led her thoughts to something she'd been trying not to think about. Or rather, someone. Lieutenant Ian of Marandur, who'd given her the keys to escape her chains on that ship, and who might've been badly injured (or worse), fighting that Mage troll. Worries about the fate of her once-friend and former fellow officer tore at her. She couldn't afford such a distraction, though, not while being hunted through this city. Jules did her best to put aside her concerns about Ian, which she told herself were after all only based on their friend-ship, so she could concentrate on surviving.

Because in addition to the Imperial forces hunting her, the Mages, putting together their own picture of their latest failed attempt to kill her and eliminate any chance that the prophecy would someday come to pass, would be using their mysterious skills to find her again.

How many times had she wished that she'd never walked into that tavern, found herself face to face with a Mage, and heard the prophecy spoken?

That left the Mechanics, the other Great Guild. The Mechanics would be sitting back enjoying watching the Empire and the Mages in conflict, while also trying to avoid involving their own Guild in that fight. Between them, the Mechanics and the Mages ruled the world, using the Emperor (or Empress) as their agent to control the common people, though saying such a thing outright was treason within the Empire. With the current Emperor chafing at the bonds of the Great Guilds, and the prophecy roiling a world in which change had never occurred, Jules had learned the Mechanics were willing to use her to further their own ends. But that was as far as it went. Plenty of Mechanics would be just as happy as the Mages to see her die, and some of them wouldn't be sorry to be the ones responsible. She couldn't hope to find safe harbor with the Mechanics here in Landfall, even if the Imperial police probably hadn't already thrown up a cordon to keep her from reaching the Mechanics Guild Hall.

Jules jerked about as something skittered through a nearby stack of wooden pallets. A rat, of course. She was so rattled that she was starting at rats, despite having become well-acquainted with them while in the orphanage.

She leaned back against one of the buildings, slowing her breathing to calm herself. There hadn't been time to think since she left the waterfront, all of her attention centered on looking like one more citizen fleeing the melee. Now her thoughts skittered about, trying to organize everything that had happened since Mages had attacked her ship not far from Dor's Castle. She'd been knocked overboard during that fight, and the Imperial warship had captured her to bring her unwilling self back to the Emperor. Then—as she'd warned the captain of the Imperial ship would happen—the Mages had attacked to try to kill her when the ship reached Landfall.

Hopefully the woman she'd stolen this cloak from had been all right once she regained consciousness.

Hopefully Ian was still alive. And hopefully not under arrest for giving her the keys to unlock her manacles. It had been the only way to keep the Mages and their troll from killing her, but would the Imperial authorities give Lieutenant Ian any credit for that?

Hopefully she'd be able to figure out where to go from this alley.

Jules tried to center her thoughts. The waterfront, even if it hadn't been the site of the recent fighting, was the most obvious place for an attempted escape. There'd be legionaries and police stationed a lance apart along the whole waterfront and every pier. She'd have no chance of getting through there.

South offered some chance of escape if she could get through the gates of the city in that direction, but the land south of Landfall was fairly flat and open, the bread basket of the Empire. It wasn't the best terrain for someone who couldn't afford to be seen.

North offered the best chance for finding an unguarded boat in one of the towns along the coast. But the Imperials knew that as well as she did. They'd have extra guards on the north gates of the city, and along the roads, and would be watching everything that could float between here and Sandurin.

Which left going east, but that was the last direction that Jules wanted to go. East would take her along the heavily-traveled Ospren River toward the Imperial capital at Marandur, where the Emperor sat, eager to get his hands on her for a forced marriage and equally forced production of royal heirs who could claim the legacy of the prophecy for the Imperial line.

And no matter which direction she went, she had to worry about the Mages knowing it as soon or sooner than she herself did, and laying another ambush for her.

What do I do, Mak? Jules often missed the man who'd become a second father to her, but she felt it especially now, trapped within a city full of enemies. What would Mak suggest?

He'd always said the best way to fool people was to show them what they expected to see. So, what did the Imperials expect her to do? Try for the waterfront, of course. If not that, try to go north, or maybe south if north looked too risky.

The one direction they wouldn't expect her to go was east. Because east was the last direction she should want to go. East was where the Imperials had planned on taking her in chains.

She knew the east gates of the city, though. She'd even stood guard at one of those gates while in her early training.

Jules took another glance upward, seeing the sky a bit brighter. By craning her head slightly, she could see a growing number of people walking past the alley where she was hiding. Was it enough? The longer she waited, the more Imperial police and legionaries would be on the streets searching for her and putting up checkpoints to screen everyone going past.

Jules settled the cloak about her, gathering together the part where the thief's knife had cut the fabric so it wouldn't be noticeable and ensuring the hood was settled to block a view of her face except from close in front. Walking to the street, she stepped out onto it as if this was the most normal thing in the world.

Aside from passing side-glances from those who saw her leave the alley, no one appeared to take notice. Jules went down the street, wondering how long she'd be able to keep the cloak on and the hood up as the day warmed before people would start to notice.

A waft of delicious scent took her thoughts in another direction, reminded her that the last time she'd eaten had been a long time before, and that she'd had nothing but bread and water while a prisoner of the Imperial sloop. A quick look around identified the source of the smell, a food cart selling hot breakfast pastries.

Buying anything would require some interaction and the chance of discovery, but if she didn't get something to eat and drink her body wouldn't keep going. Jules altered her path to reach the cart, waiting impatiently until she reached the front of the line of customers.

"Three," Jules mumbled in a deliberately hoarse voice, grateful that for once what the wanted posters called her 'lower class Landfall accent' would help her blend in. "And a flask of sang."

The young girl serving the customers didn't take any special notice of Jules, passing over three hot pastries that Jules slid into a pocket of the cloak, and a flask of the wine, water, and fruit pulp called sang. Knowing she'd have to return the flask when she was done with it, Jules took the risk of staying by the cart. Hastily eating one of the pastries containing a common Landfall recipe combining pork and apples, she washed it down with gulps of the sang.

Three Mechanics, two men and a woman all wearing the unmistakable dark jackets, walked past the food cart. One of the men reached out and snagged a pastry, making no move to pay for it. The owner of the cart glared at the backs of the Mechanics as they swaggered away, but knew better than to object. Mechanics did what they wanted, and common people endured it because they had no other choice.

Jules' gaze lingered on the Mechanics as they walked off. One of the men had a weapon at his waist, the one Mechanics called a revolver that no sword or crossbow used by common folk could match. The Mechanics Guild had loaned a revolver like that to Jules in the hopes that she'd kill Mages with it, but the last she'd seen of that revolver it had been lying on the deck of her ship after being knocked from her grasp. What if she had that weapon now? But there had only been one or two cartridges left in it, and using the revolver would make a noise so loud every legionary and Mage within earshot would come running for her. A dagger was the safer option for someone trying not to be noticed.

Seeing a Mechanic openly armed was unusual. Were the Mechanics in Landfall worried about Mage attacks? Surely, despite what Jules had overheard Mechanics say to each other, they weren't concerned about the Imperials turning on them. That would be unheard of, and incredibly dangerous for the Empire. No common person knew how the mysterious technology of the Mechanics worked—though everyone knew trying to learn those secrets would result in death at the hands of the Mechanics—and no common person knew everything the Mechanic devices could do.

The other patrons of the food cart waited until the Mechanics were far enough off that they couldn't overhear before resuming gossiping among themselves as they wolfed down food before heading to work. "Already on her way to Marandur," one man said confidently. "I've got a cousin in the legions. He said they got her away from the Mages and she'll be with the Emperor soon."

"Then why are the police and the legions still ransacking the city?" another man demanded.

"Maybe they're looking for those Mages that attacked the Emperor's soldiers!"

"They're looking for the girl," a woman chimed in. "My brother is with the police. Find the girl of the prophecy. That's their orders."

"Why wouldn't she turn herself in?" the first man asked.

"Maybe the Mages were able to do something even though they couldn't kill her," the woman suggested. "Take over her mind. Mages can do that."

"Why not just kill her?" the second man said.

"Are you asking me why Mages are doing one thing and not another?" the woman demanded. "Nobody knows how they think."

Jules, resisting the urge to ask all three why it didn't occur to them that the "girl" might not want to end up in the hands (and the bed) of the Emperor, drained the flask and pushed off into the morning crowds. At least she'd learned that the police were definitely searching for her.

Holding a second pastry next to her mouth as if nibbling it as she walked, which served to hide the lower half of her face under the hood , Jules took a wide main street heading east. A secondary street might have been less likely to be watched, but the crowds were bigger here and easier to get lost in.

Wagons, coaches, and carts traveled both ways down the center of the street, the horses pulling them looking resigned to their fate as they ignored most of the people walking past. An occasional carriage bearing a high-ranking Imperial official or rich merchant stood out due to the high-stepping pair of horses drawing it. Chickens and pigs in cages on some of the carts and wagons eyed the people in the street, unaware that they were headed for a butcher shop and eventually the kitchens of some of those people. People called to each other in the Landfall accent that Jules had grown up hearing. The air held the mingled scents of manure, massed humanity, sweaty horses, burning coal and wood, and the occasional waft of food cooking. It was all enough to make Jules a bit homesick for the city even though she'd never wanted to return here.

Any growing feelings of being home vanished as a wagon carrying Imperial police rattled through the crowds, bypassing the other horse-drawn conveyances, the people on foot scattering to make way. Because that was part of the bargain that Imperial citizens had to live with regardless of whether or not they liked it: the Empire gave them stability and rules and security, and in return the citizens were expected to follow all the rules and do as they were told.

She'd gone three long blocks east before Jules spotted legionary armor ahead and the dark red of an Imperial officer's uniform. Looking through the crowd, she saw the legionaries moving portable barriers into place to establish a checkpoint. Citizens were already obediently forming into a wide queue to pass through, knowing that trying to avoid the checkpoint would attract attention from the Imperial soldiers.

Jules glanced around, seeing that the side roads were also being blocked off. The legions were efficient in all they did.

I'm not trapped yet. Stay calm and think. She paused as if reading a sign in the window of a business, trying to decide whether she could hide inside one of the nearby buildings until the checkpoint was moved.

Maybe she could still unobtrusively start walking the other way.

But when Jules turned about she saw four Mages coming down the street, easy to spot not only because of their distinctive robes, but because of the wide, empty area around them as every common person tried to avoid getting too close to or in the way of the Mages.

As the old saying went, she was trapped between a brick wall and a bull.

Did the Mages already know she was on this street, or were they looking for her? Jules saw the Mages paying an unusual amount of attention to the people around them, making those people extremely nervous. It was a search then. They hadn't spotted her yet.

Jules took another look at the checkpoint in the other direction, seeing the orderly queue formed by the citizens moving forward at a snail's pace. She'd never get past that checkpoint undetected by the legionaries.

Unless the legionaries had something else to worry about. Something big.

Maybe the best way out of this was to let the Mages see her.

Knowing her chances were dwindling by the moment, Jules turned to fully face the oncoming Mages, who were still a ways down the street. Partly lowering the hood of her cloak, she looked directly at the Mages.

No common ever looked straight at a Mage. No common wanted the attention that might attract from a Mage.

The Mages noticed, two of them pausing to look back at Jules across the distance separating them.

She didn't think the Mages could recognize her from this far away, but had learned that Mages could somehow tell she was the woman of the prophecy just by laying eyes on her. Some Mages could do that, anyway.

And at least one of these Mages must have had that ability, because all four suddenly began moving fast, running toward Jules as frantic citizens scattered out of their path.

Hoping she hadn't just doomed herself, Jules turned and bolted toward the Imperial checkpoint, weaving through the thickening crowd so that the Mages could no longer see her. *If a Mage can see you, a Mage can kill you,* the old warning went. She didn't have to make it any easier for them by staying in sight.

Ducking under the noses of a pair of horses who snorted in surprise, their heads snapping up to search for danger, Jules shoved her way forward, drawing angry comments from those waiting stoically to get through the checkpoint. With the crowd thickening, forcing her way through was getting harder.

Shouts of alarm sounded behind her, warning that the Mages had reached the rear of the crowd. The shouts changed to screams as the Mages pulled out their long knives and began hacking at anyone in their way. The crowd convulsed like a single creature, waves of fear rolling through it, those closest to the checkpoint looking back to try to see the source of the screams.

"Mages!" Jules cried, pitching her voice high like someone badly frightened. "They're killing everyone!"

The front of the crowd wavered, caught between fear of the Mages and Imperial rules.

Jules saw a couple of legionaries climbing up onto the wagon they'd come in, crossbows tensioned and at the ready, trying to get a view of what was happening at the back of the crowd.

One of the legionaries made the mistake of pointing his crossbow in the general direction of the Mages.

Lightning ripped through the air above the crowd, accompanied by the deafening boom of thunder. The legionary's crossbow exploded into splinters as the lightning hit it, knocking the legionary back off the wagon.

Jules only had a moment to wonder if the Mage who'd sent that lightning was the same one who'd tried to kill her off the Bleak Coast. An instant later the entire crowd went from uncertain and fearful to erupting into wild panic.

Clamoring in fear, the crowd rushed the checkpoint, overwhelming the portable barricades and ignoring the swords the legionaries drew to try to intimidate them. Jules stayed with them as the mob of citizens stampeded down the street, swamping the legionaries and their officer as she tried to call out orders. Horses squealed in fear, bolting forward and plowing paths through the people ahead of them. The barricades blocking the nearest side streets vanished under the tide of fleeing men, women, and draft animals, Jules picking one of those side streets and trying to stay with the crowd. She felt as she were caught in a rushing river of humanity, the current of frightened bodies too powerful for the efforts of one person to fight.

Working her way to the edge of the crowd, Jules managed to duck into another street, feeling the pressure around her lessen as fewer people surrounded her. Most of those on the street were still running, so Jules dodged again into the next street over, slowing her pace to a fast walk. The buildings around her blocked a lot of noise, but she could hear legionary horns sounding streets away as the alert spread, an alarm bell being rung, and the rapid clacking of Imperial police rapping out coded messages to each other by striking the cobblestones with their hardwood clubs. Under all of those distinct sounds continued the indistinct rumble of frightened crowds shouting and running.

Realizing that she'd lost her sense of which direction she was going, Jules ducked into an alley to catch her breath and orient herself. Just inside the alley was a small pile of bricks against one wall where someone was repairing it, so she stopped beside the bricks.

She'd only taken two deep breaths when a Mage turned the corner and was upon her in an instant, the Mage's long knife sweeping toward her.

CHAPTER TWO

J ust about every common facing a Mage, including Jules herself not so long ago, would've been at least momentarily paralyzed with fear. Just about every common would've died. But Jules had confronted enough Mages by now to not succumb to the fear.

Pulling out her dagger and bringing it up in a frantic parry, Jules managed to partially divert the Mage's strike. But the tip of the long knife sliced into her upper arm, the force of the blow knocking the dagger from Jules' grasp.

Her free hand already coming up, Jules' fist slammed into the Mage's face.

As her attacker staggered back, Jules bent enough to grab a brick.

The Mage lunged forward again, knife raised for another blow.

Instead of flinching away, Jules ducked inside the attack, swinging the brick she held against the Mage's head.

The impact slammed the other's head back to strike the nearby wall, the thud of the brick hitting followed almost immediately by the thunk of the second impact. The Mage fell like a rag doll, dropping into a limp heap on the floor of the alley.

Her breath coming fast and harsh, Jules eyed the Mage warily for a moment to be sure the Mage was unconscious. Pausing only to pick up her dagger, Jules quickly stepped out onto the street, searching for any other Mage that might have followed her.

Despite her fears, no other Mages were in sight among the laggard citizens fleeing the earlier fight. Stepping back into the alley and dropping the brick, Jules checked her injury, seeing that the Mage knife had torn a wide slash in Jules' cloak. The cut in her arm wasn't too deep, fortunately, but it was bleeding badly.

Jules picked up her dagger and ripped a length of fabric off the cloak, wrapping it around her upper arm where the cut was, using her teeth and one hand to manage a knot. Having done all she could to stop the bleeding, Jules glared at the Mage, her dagger at the ready.

But after killing this one, what chance did she have of getting out of this city now that the cloak was torn and slashed? Its ragged state would attract more attention than her not wearing it, and there wasn't anything else she could use to disguise her appearance.

Except…

Jules looked down at the Mage, wondering if she dared do what she'd thought of. No one disguised themselves as a Mage. Aside from no one wanting to be shunned as Mages were, the danger of what the Mages would do if someone was caught pretending to be one of them was sufficient to keep anyone from even thinking of doing that.

But every Mage already wanted to kill her. And so far they hadn't done any of the other things to her that rumor claimed Mage spells could do, from making parts of her disappear to changing her into a small animal or insect. Or taking over her mind, for that matter.

She fought down a shudder of revulsion as she pulled off the Mage's robes. They stank, because most Mages never seemed to bathe, so that Jules felt ill at the idea of wearing them. But avoiding being killed, or captured and put into chains again, was more than enough motivation to override her squeamishness.

Jules turned back to the Mage, knowing that every living Mage was one more person trying to kill her. She hated killing a helpless opponent, but such scruples were an unaffordable luxury at the moment.

But her hand holding the dagger didn't move as Jules stared at the Mage. With her robes pulled off, the Mage was revealed as a young woman, perhaps within a few years of Jules's own age. Senseless from the blows to her head, the Mage had lost the carefully maintained lack of feeling or expression that made common people tremble at the sight of what they called dead faces on living Mages. Instead, the Mage's loose features resembled that of any other girl her age lost in sleep. Except that with the robe removed Jules could see the myriad of scars on the Mage's face and body, scars that every Mage seemed to share in permanent record of whatever brutal treatment changed them into Mages.

Jules knew she could, reluctantly, kill an unconscious Mage. But she couldn't kill an unconscious young woman with marks of abuse all over her.

Growling in frustration, Jules knelt by the Mage, whose long hair had apparently rarely been cut. It was a tangled mess, but Jules got some long bundles of hair sorted out and cut them loose to use as rope, binding the Mage's hands and feet. Hair didn't take to knots nearly as well as rope did, but Jules tightened the knots enough that hopefully they'd hold.

Jules pulled on the robes she'd just stolen over the remains of the cloak she'd stolen last night. She wanted to minimize the amount of her skin that would touch the Mage robes, and she thought it would help hide the shape of her body. Anything that made her look less like Jules would be good.

The robes weren't quite her size, but close enough. Jules pulled up the cowl to cover her head and make it hard to see her face. She couldn't manage the Mage dead-face expression, instead trying her best to look impassive, but since everyone avoided looking directly at Mages no one should notice.

Of course, if she ran into more Mages her imposture could get very ugly very fast. And the legionaries would be on high alert for further attacks from Mages, so her disguise would get a lot of attention.

But there weren't any better alternatives.

Jules, having decided on which direction east lay, stepped out onto the street.

And nearly darted away as every person nearby jolted with surprise and fear, hastily putting distance between themselves and her.

It took her a moment to realize that this was the result she wanted and should expect. She'd gone from trying to avoid being noticed to being someone who'd be very much noticed. But not as herself. As someone everyone else would try to avoid.

Jules started walking east, hearing the tumult on nearby streets of the earlier fight and panic beginning to subside. She didn't have to weave her way through any crowds, because people kept opening a clear path for her, frightened of blocking or inconveniencing a Mage.

She'd never paid that much attention to how Mages walked, because like everyone else she kept her eyes averted. Jules tried to maintain a steady pace, not too fast but not slow, walking with a firm stride that she hoped didn't display any un-Mage-like emotion. She had to constantly remind herself not to look around, because Mages rarely showed any obvious interest in their surroundings.

Her gait almost faltered when two more Mages came into view, heading in the other direction, on the other side of the street. Did Mages use their powers to exchange greetings unseen and unheard by common people? If so, she'd soon find out. Resting one hand on her dagger under her pilfered Mage robes, and trying not to wince at the resultant pain from moving her injured arm, Jules maintained her steady, unvarying pace.

As far as she could tell, the Mages didn't look her way as they walked past. Jules followed them as long as possible through the corners of her eyes, but the edge of the cowl blocked her vision before the Mages even passed her. And she couldn't turn her head to look without acting oddly for a Mage.

Sweating under the robes, Jules held her dagger tightly, listening for any hint that the Mages might've turned and were approaching her from behind.

It finally occurred to her to watch the common people in front of her. Their worried eyes avoided looking toward Jules, but as far as Jules could tell they weren't reacting to anything behind her. And they didn't seem more alarmed than usual around a Mage, as they should've been if two more Mages were coming up fast. It was a tenuous reassurance at best, but it was all she had.

Jules kept walking, gradually relaxing as no attack came.

It felt increasingly odd, though. Not having to worry about wending around other people left plenty of time to just think and notice her surroundings. On the one hand, everyone avoided looking at her. Not in the usual manner of people not really paying attention to those around them, but in a very obvious I'm-not-looking-at-you way. She'd never thought about how such a thing would seem to a Mage.

Then again, Mages didn't seem to see such things in the same way as typical people. Perhaps they didn't even notice how other people reacted around them.

At the same time, the way everyone cleared a path for her was something she could definitely get used to. It made the simple act of walking so much easier. This must be how Mechanics or Imperial princes felt too, when they were out on the streets. If she were a Mechanic, how easy would it be to accept this sort of thing? It set her apart in a different way than the Mage robes did, apart in a manner that would easily reinforce any feeling of superiority over others. Was that why people like the Mechanics and Imperial princes insisted on others always deferring to them? Not just because it made them feel special, but because it provided a constant reassurance that they deserved such special treatment?

Jules almost badly broke character by laughing at herself. These people weren't clearing a path before her because she was Jules of Landfall. It wasn't about *her.* They were giving her special treatment because she was wearing Mage robes, and they'd do the same if she wore the jacket of a Mechanic, or had the retinue of an Imperial prince with her., And people weren't acting that way out of respect, but because they had no choice or feared the consequences of not clearing a path for her.

Did Mechanics or Mages or princes ever think about that?

Probably not.

In the west, common people wouldn't be ruled by princes or emperors. Not if she could help it. There wasn't much she could do about

Mechanics or Mages, though. The Great Guilds were something the daughter of her line would have to take care of someday.

Usually she'd feel resentful when thinking about that daughter who'd upended her life and dominated how just about everyone else thought of her. But thinking of how that daughter might humble the rulers of the world cheered up Jules, and made her happier that someone descended from her would accomplish such a thing.

Or, rather, would accomplish such a thing if Jules herself lived long enough to have any children.

A group of legionaries marched past, heading in the other direction. None of them looked at her, but Jules didn't need Mage skills to see the tension in them as they avoided even glancing her way. More than one of the legionaries had a death grip on the hilt of their sword. Word must have gotten around about Mages attacking the crowd at the checkpoint, and that Mages were sometimes attacking Imperial soldiers. But the legionaries at least weren't going to start a fight.

Had anyone yet figured out that each of the attacks had involved Mages trying to get at Jules? Imperial officials must be scrambling to come up with a proper response to the unprecedented attacks by Mages on Imperial forces. Certainly, in the past, Mages had occasionally struck out at individual soldiers or officials who had the misfortune to attract their attention. But there hadn't been anything like these repeated group attacks.

At least, none she'd ever heard of.

Jules again had to resist the urge to look around in a way no Mage would normally do. How much of what she knew of her world was true? The charts and accompanying legends claiming that the western half of the Sea of Bakre was a death trap had been lies. And she'd overheard Mechanics saying the Empire had been "set up" that way. Set up by who? The official history of the Empire claimed that the first Emperor, Maran, had risen out of a period of barbaric anarchy to establish order, had founded the first cities of the Empire, and then constructed Marandur as a new capital. Had it happened that way?

Where had the Mechanics been during that supposed period of anarchy? And the Mages?

She had no way of discovering the answers to questions she'd never imagined while growing up or in training as an Imperial officer. But her enforced association with Mechanics and encounters with Mages had rattled everything she'd once thought she'd known.

Another checkpoint loomed ahead.

Jules put her head down to further hide her face, slowing her pace slightly to give the citizens waiting in the queue at the checkpoint time to shove themselves to either side, leaving a narrow but clear aisle for her to walk down, the fear of the men and women closest to her so strong as to almost feel like a physical pressure.

It made her feel ill. She wanted to be respected. She wanted people to treat her right. But not this kind of dread at the sight of her. She'd met people who seemed to enjoy creating such feelings in others, and never understood why they found happiness in it. As she walked that narrow lane between terrified people the miasma of fear almost choked her.

How could Mages live, feeling such reactions from others? Maybe their lack of emotion meant they really didn't care.

She was almost to the opening in the portable barricades, the legionaries giving their officer frantic looks for guidance, the officer waving at them to move back. Jules walked through as if unaware of their actions or their presence, her back itching in anticipation of a sudden attack that didn't come as she left the checkpoint behind her.

Jules kept walking, common people clearing her way as quickly as possible, legionaries waiting with obvious fear as she went by them, occasional other Mages coming into sight but continuing on their way without any attempt to interact with her. She'd begun recognizing some of the streets, a welcome sign that she'd reached the eastern parts of Landfall. But she was still a distance from the eastern gates of the city, and the afternoon was well along. Her legs and feet ached from the steady trudging on the cobblestone streets, but stopping to rest seemed too dangerous to try.

Could she reach the gates before they closed late tonight? The Mage she'd knocked out and stolen these robes from had probably awakened by now, perhaps had already gotten free of her bindings. That Mage would tell other Mages, and the hunt would be on. If she was still in Landfall when the gates closed, she'd have to shed these robes and take her chances with some other form of disguise.

Her plans dissolved into nothingness as Jules spotted four Mages striding down the street. All four had the cowls of their robes lowered so that their heads and faces were exposed

And they were bending their paths to meet hers.

Jules turned to face the building she was passing, as if about to enter the door there. A glance in the other direction revealed another Mage, cowl also down, walking toward Jules.

Without another moment's hesitation, Jules pulled open the door and walked through the room beyond. It was a bank. Commons who'd been withdrawing or depositing cash, tellers who'd been working with them, all froze into immobility as Jules walked past.

There had to be a back door. Every place had a back door. Jules slammed open door after door, heading in what she hoped was the right direction, finally reaching a door reinforced with metal strips that had a large bar holding it closed on the inside. Pulling the bar loose, Jules dropped it, yanking the door open and finding herself in an alley running behind the block of buildings the bank belonged to.

Pushing the door closed, she pulled off the Mage robes as fast as she could, balled them up and shoved them into a nearby trash receptacle. She headed down the alley at a run, slowing when she reached a cross alley leading back to the street she'd been on. Pausing to catch her breath, Jules darted a glance back at the door she'd left the bank through, seeing that it hadn't opened yet. Straightening her torn cloak and raising the hood, she walked at a steady pace back toward the street she'd left.

Coming out onto the street, Jules noticed two things. Commons gathering to look inside the bank from a safe distance outside the door, and a column of legionaries that looked to be at least forty strong coming down the street at a fast pace, pedestrians, horses, and wagons scattering out of their way. Had someone figured out that sudden outbursts on the part of Mages were related to Jules being somewhere nearby?

Jules walked across the street and into the alley on the opposite side, moving as fast as she dared. Just before entering the alley, she spotted more Mages converging on the street from the opposite direction that the legionaries were coming, as well as coming out of the alley that she'd just left behind.

Inside the next alley, Jules broke into a run, bolting for the next cross alley and taking it so fast that she bounced off the wall on the turn. This alley ended in piles of trash against a wall about a lance high. Without pausing, Jules ran up the trash piles, launching herself over the wall. Despite trying to roll when she landed, she hit hard. Getting to her feet despite the protests of the places on her body where she was accumulating bruises, Jules ran to the end of the next alley and out onto the street.

She knew she looked frantic, but fortunately everybody else on the street did as well. People were dashing off in all directions, mothers picking up their children to run faster, shouts of warning and alarm rising on all sides. Should she run with them? Or would the Imperials already be setting up blockades on connecting streets to sweep in everyone fleeing this area?

Spotting a sewer drain, Jules made up her mind. Kneeling, she pulled the metal grating out as people rushed past her. Turning to slide feet first through the drain, a tight fit but one she could manage, Jules pulled the grating back into place behind her, hanging in space for a moment as she used one hand to shove the grating back into the right spot. Looking down, she saw her feet were about half a lance from the bottom of the drain tunnel. Letting go of the grating, she landed in the muck and moisture, letting her knees bend to absorb the impact, tottering for a moment but staying on her feet.

Grateful that she hadn't fallen full length into the stuff on the bottom of the drain, Jules took a look around in the light filtering in through the grating. The sewer walls were covered with unpleasant looking slime and molds. The angle of the sunlight falling on the brick gave her a rough idea of which direction to go, and she began trudging through the drain, grateful that her boots were able to keep out water and whatever else was in the city sewers. The noise of the tumult above gradually grew less.

At least if the Mages came after her down here she'd be able to hear them coming.

The farther she got from the drain, the murkier the light got, and the worse the smell. Jules had started to feel herself getting light-headed when she spotted the light growing again as she neared another drain. Stopping to breathe deeply in the relatively fresher air near the drain, she went onward, her boots squelching through the muck.

Reaching a spot where another tunnel joined this one, Jules paused to orient herself, then turned into the new route.

She found it hard to judge how far she'd come without any above-ground landmarks to guide her. The noise filtering in through the drains as she passed them had subsided to normal city levels, but between the foul air, her worries, and her growing fatigue, Jules found no comfort in that.

Finally the tunnel she was in dead-ended in a wall of brick. Jules stood for a moment, trying to clear her head, wondering why she hadn't seen the wall until she was almost touching it. Looking up, she spotted a drain opening, but the light coming in through it was dim.

Outside, the sun was setting. If she didn't leave these sewers now, she'd be stumbling around them in total darkness.

Jules felt the wall beneath the drain, finding handholds left in the bricks to form a permanent ladder. Dizzy from the foul air, she had to pause twice in her climb even though it was only about a lance and a half up to the drain. Hating the feel of the slime on the bricks under her fingers, Jules finally made it up to the grating. She hung there for a long moment, gasping for cleaner air and listening for any clues as to where this drain was in the city. From the rapidly dimming light outside, the sun had almost set.

The grate wouldn't budge the first time Jules tried to move it. Bracing herself, she shoved hard, and the grating finally jolted open. Pulling herself out of the drain, her breaths still coming fast as she gratefully pulled in air without poison in it, Jules lay still as she took in her surroundings.

She was on a street ending at a strip of parkland, beyond which she could hear a low rushing sound. Jules saw only a few figures far down the street, none coming this way. Getting to her feet, she realized that the sound came from the waters of what must be the mighty Ospren River where it rolled past the town.

Heading into the parkland, Jules reached a platform where boats could tie up. Sitting down, she lowered her feet into the water so the river could wash the sewer muck off of her boots. Once satisfied that was done, Jules lay on her stomach to reach down and wash the residual slime off of her hands.

At least now she wouldn't smell like someone who'd been walking through the city sewers. But why was a city street almost deserted so soon after sunset? This was Landfall. The evening should just be getting started.

Walking those almost empty streets would make her stand out. But she couldn't stay here. Imperial police loved to snag people trying to sleep in parks or other public places, so they'd be sure to come by at some point. She had to find a better place to hide.

A short distance up the street light glowed beneath a door. Jules checked the sign, advertising an eatery. Wobbly on her feet from tiredness and lack of food and water, Jules still hesitated before pushing open the door, worried about being trapped again.

Inside was one of the hole in the wall type eateries the city boasted, dimly lit by a few candles. A counter ran lengthwise down the middle, on one side of it chairs for customers whose backs would be to the wall, and on the other side the small oven, grill, and supplies for the elderly cook and owner who was sitting glumly in the otherwise empty place. She perked up when Jules entered, waving her to one of the seats.

Jules sat down gratefully as the owner started throwing together a meal. These sorts of places didn't have menus, only serving one kind of meal each day based on whatever the owner had on hand.

"Wine or beer?" the owner asked.

"Watered wine," Jules said.

"Got it."

"Not very busy tonight," Jules said, hoping for information on why the streets were so empty.

"People are scared," the owner said as she stir-fried meat and vegetables along with some kind of noodle. "Checkpoints and blockades all over, the legion is out and all over the city, police are everywhere, and the Mages have been starting fights. Heralds came down the streets warning everyone to stay home unless they had urgent business, and for once people listened."

"I'm glad you didn't stay home," Jules said before taking a big drink of the watered wine.

"I did," she answered with a wink, pointing up. "I live on the second floor. Why are you out?"

"There's somewhere I need to go," Jules said.

"Ah." The elderly woman turned from the grill for a moment to look at her. "And that's not to Marandur, eh?"

Jules' hand went to her dagger. "Excuse me?"

The owner piled food on a plate, setting it in front of Jules. "Marandur. Don't want to go there, do you? I don't blame you."

"I don't know who you think I am—"

"Someone wearing a hood at this hour, who's still letting enough face show to tell she's a match for all them posters." The owner sighed, leaning back against a shelf, her eyes on Jules. "As for me, I'm someone whose family got ruined by a princess some years ago. I couldn't leave the Empire, not back then, but I stopped loving it after that. It looks like you've had a hard day of it."

"Yes," Jules said, cautiously digging into her food, almost dizzy again from the scent of it after not eating since early this morning.

"You shouldn't stay here. Late shift police usually stop by about midnight for their break." The old woman eyed Jules. "So it's true about the prophecy? The Emperor wouldn't be trying so hard to get you unless it was."

Jules swallowed and took another drink before answering. "It's true."

"Why'd you come back here?"

"No choice. I was chained in an Imperial ship."

"And you got away?"

"While Mages were destroying the ship," Jules said.

"Ah." The woman watched while Jules wolfed down her food. "Don't try the river. I heard they've got boats out, with torches on 'em. And guards along the bank as you near the harbor. Not even a mouse could get through that way."

"Thanks," Jules mumbled around another mouthful.

"Here." The woman offered a travel flask. "It's full."

Pulling out her coins, Jules offered the woman a silver galley, but she shook her head. "You keep that. Might need it later."

"Thank you," Jules said, reluctantly getting up from her chair and feeling her entire body protest. "You could come out west. There are good places there."

"I'm too old, and the rest of the family is passed on," the elderly woman said. "No sense in me moving now. Good luck, girl."

"Thank you," Jules said again, not knowing what else she could say. She slipped out of the doorway, opening the door just enough to get through, finding the street still almost empty as far as could be seen.

She stuck to alleys as much as possible, trying to head east with a vague idea of finding one of the eastern gates and spotting a way to get through. The fact that the east gates, as difficult as they'd be, were her best option was almost too depressing to consider.

Twice, Jules stopped, breathing as quietly as possible and hiding in the shadows of the night, as Imperial patrols went by. Luckily for her, the Imperial police had been worked hard for the last day and a half, and were as tired as she was.

After the second near-encounter, Jules had to go out on a street, hastening down it in search of the next side street or alley to duck into. She spotted three people standing on the street corner up ahead, two women and a man. They weren't police, so she kept going. As she drew close, Jules could tell by their clothing and the way they were loitering that the three were street walkers in search of customers.

Someone like that would know as much as anyone about what the Imperial police were doing in this part of the city. It'd be worth the risk to see what she could find out.

Jules walked up to them, keeping the hood of her cloak up and her face mostly hidden. "Good evening. How's work going?"

"Awful," one of the women said. Middle-aged, her make-up, hair, and clothing tried to make her look more sophisticated than the other woman, who was at least a decade younger. "The legionaries are all on duty, the police are everywhere, and the citizens are afraid to leave their homes."

"Police?" Jules said. "Where-?"

"Everywhere," the man said, flashing a winning smile. "Are you interested in a good time?"

"No," Jules said. "I'm broke."

The interest of the three in her vanished as quickly as the light from a blown out candle. The first woman sighed, staring down the nearly-empty street. "This night's a bust. Even if someone shows up, they'll go for the youngest of us."

"You'd think they'd value experience," the man said. "But, no, it's always the younger ones."

"That's not my fault," the second woman said.

"No," the first woman agreed. "And you should take advantage of it while you can. Me, I need to get out this line of work."

"What else have you got?" the man asked.

"Sewing. I'm good at it. Embroidery." The woman grimaced. "But the clothing shops and tailors aren't hiring. I can't even get a license for a street cart because they're sold out. I've been thinking of maybe heading up to Centin and trying my luck there."

The man shook his head. "Centin's worse than here. Too many people and not enough jobs. I've got a cousin there who's a teacher. She finally found a job as a part-time tutor and is grateful for it."

"What are people supposed to do?" the older woman complained. "Marandur, Alfarin, every city is straining at the seams."

Jules had been listening, hoping to hear anything useful about the police presence. "There's always the west."

"The west? You mean outside the Empire?"

"Yes," Jules said. "There's a lot of land out there. New towns. Cities being founded, with every job open for anyone who comes."

The younger woman spoke up again. "I have a friend who's doing that. Going west. She was supposed to be on a ship leaving today with a lot of people being smuggled out of the Empire, but with the waterfront locked down they had to postpone until things get quiet again."

"What's out west?" the man asked. "Those small islands, and some little places along the coast?"

"There's a lot more than that," Jules said. "The western coast of the sea is full of places where cities could be. And there's a strait that leads to another sea, and beyond that the ocean, with amazing lands bordering them."

"Where'd you hear that?" the older woman asked, skeptical.

"I saw a chart."

"You saw a chart." She laughed.

"It was made by Jules of Landfall," Jules said, knowing she should drop it, but wanting to tell others what she'd discovered. "Signed by her. Her ship found those places."

"Jules of Landfall?" The man gave her his full attention for the first time since hearing that Jules didn't have any money. "The Jules of the prophecy?"

"Yes," Jules said, thinking that she really ought to be leaving, but since opening her big mouth not sure how to do it without attracting too much interest from these three.

"She's in Landfall," the younger woman said. "That's why everything's so crazy. The legions out and police everywhere and the

Mages…" She looked around to ensure none were in sight. "Attacking people and looking all over. Did you see her?" she asked Jules eagerly.

"I've seen her," Jules said.

"There's really nice places in the west?" the older woman asked. "Places with jobs?"

"Yes. Any kind of job," Jules said.

"Do you know where she is?" the younger said. "The prophecy girl?"

"No," Jules said. "I have no idea."

The man had been looking at Jules, saying nothing else, but now abruptly leaned close. "Listen. You're broke, and it looks like my chances of earning anything tonight are very low. But you'll have money later on, won't you? Why don't we work out a deal on credit? That way we'll both have a decent night."

Jules began to shake her head. "I'm not—"

"Listen to my offer!" He looked at the two other women. "Let's move over there to talk. I hate negotiating prices in public."

The two women laughed, talking to each other as the man led Jules a little way down the street, stopping right next to a building. She followed, not wanting to cause a ruckus that might attract the attention of Imperial police, legionaries, or any nearby Mages. But her hand stayed on the hilt of her dagger.

"I'm not interested," Jules said in a low voice as they stopped.

"I know." He gazed at her for a long moment. "I also know who you are."

"Do you?" Jules poised herself for a strike, wondering if she could kill this man silently enough that the two women wouldn't notice right away.

"If you stay here, one of those two will figure it out as well," he added, nodding toward the two women who were still on the street corner. "They're not bad people, but their lives are hard. They'd turn in their own fathers for a thousand gold eagles. That's what you're worth, you know. A thousand gold eagles for anyone who gives information resulting in you being found by the police."

Jules inhaled slowly. "And to think some people said I'd never be worth anything. Why won't you turn me in?"

He shrugged. "Because I'm a nice person."

"Sure."

"Not really." He hesitated. "Long story short, my father was a Mechanic, my mother a common. Mother brought me up with stories of how I'd be a Mechanic someday and then my father would marry her. But... I failed their tests. I got kicked out of my home, and after that the Mechanic father pretended he'd never heard of me. It would make me very happy to see the Mechanics humbled when that prophecy comes true."

"It could be generations before that happens," Jules said. "It'll be a daughter of my line."

"That's all right. As long as I know I helped make it happen. That's worth a thousand gold eagles to me." He turned and pointed, his hand held close to his body so the two women on the corner couldn't see. "There's a sally gate that way. You know about those?"

"I know they're kept locked," Jules said.

"Not that one. Four blocks that way, then three blocks left. You'll see the wall. The gate is where a small street ends, hard to see. That's why smugglers like it. They pay off the police in this area to unlock it and look the other way. If there's a path out of this city tonight, it's that gate."

"Thanks. I owe you." Jules gestured toward the west. "If you leave the Empire, look me up. I'll see you rewarded."

He smiled, shaking his head. "Me? In the west? I'm a creature of the city streets." Stepping back, he spoke louder. "No deal! I'm a professional. I don't give it away!" Turning, he walked back to the two women who were laughing again.

Jules walked in the direction he'd indicated, trying to look stiff-backed with affronted pride. As soon as she'd lost sight of the three on their forlorn quest for customers this night, she dropped the act and edged close to the nearest buildings, trying to blend in with the shadows under front awnings and entrances. The moon hadn't yet risen, so the night was comfortingly dark, but she still felt horribly exposed.

As she turned left, Jules wondered if the man was going to betray her after all. Perhaps she'd been directed into a dead end, and would find legionaries blocking her exit. Poorer neighborhoods had fewer street lanterns than more well-off areas, and this looked to be one of the poorest. There was only a single forlorn lantern on this block, the street ahead showing nothing but the pole of an occasional unlit lamp.

Only one block left to go, the darkness unrelieved except by the occasional pale glow of a candle behind an upper story window. The neighborhood seemed to be a mix of tenements and dilapidated warehouses. The lack of any police patrols for the last few blocks seemed to confirm what she'd been told about smugglers paying off the police to stay clear. On this night, though, there might be legionary patrols in the area, so Jules tried to stay quiet and unseen as she headed down the last block toward the wall.

Despite moving carefully, she wasn't as adept at hiding on a darkened street as those who'd been practicing that skill for years as they plied their trade. A figure suddenly stepped out in front of Jules from a shadowed alcove. "Where are you going?" he asked, starlight glinting from the naked steel of a knife he held in one hand.

A lookout. Of course the smugglers would have a lookout. "I must be lost," Jules said. "It's so dark."

"Hold it." Before she could react, the lookout opened a masked lantern, the light flaring out to fall on Jules' face. She heard the exultation in his voice. "I know you! You're going to make me rich!"

Most people would've fled at that point, and she could tell by the way the lookout shifted his stance that he expected her to run. But Jules had been running all day. Instead of fear, she felt anger.

Ready to pursue her, the lookout was off-balance when instead she attacked.

The folds of her cloak wrapped around his knife hand, encumbering it for a precious moment as Jules stepped in. He flung up his arm to try to block her thrust, but too late. The dagger went into his heart, backed by all of her strength.

He fell back, the dagger pulling from his chest as she held on to it.

That freed his blood to flow from the slash in his heart. The lookout managed to open his mouth to shout but never got the sound out. He collapsed onto the cobblestones, his lantern rattling loudly enough to echo down the quiet street.

Jules grabbed the lantern, closing it as fast as she could so its light wouldn't betray her. She paused for a moment, listening for any signs that the clatter had tipped off anyone. Those most likely to hear would be the smugglers, and the last thing she needed was for them to be alert.

The rattle of armor and the stamp of feet came from behind her, though. Jules spun about to see a patrol of legionaries coming onto the street a block away, the soldiers already moving fast as they sought the source of the noise.

Jerking about to look toward where the sally gate should be, Jules spotted shadowy figures coming her way, from their movements some of the smugglers checking on their lookout. They hadn't yet seen the legionaries, but they would at any moment, and like their lookout if they caught Jules would be more than happy to turn her over to the Imperials for the reward and to keep the soldiers from investigating the sally gate.

Caught between a hammer and an anvil, Jules bolted in the only direction that offered her a chance.

CHAPTER THREE

The smugglers caught sight of Jules at about the same moment they saw the legionaries charging down the street. In the dark they must have assumed she was their lookout who'd carelessly made a lot of noise and attracted the soldiers' attention, because one growled "you idiot" before they all turned and sprinted back toward the sally gate. Knowing her only chance was to get through that gate, Jules ran after them.

"Halt!" one of the legionaries shouted.

The smugglers responded by increasing their speed, Jules doing her best to catch up. Reaching the end of the street, Jules ran into the rest of the smugglers amid some stacks of small crates, everyone beginning to scatter as they realized the legionaries were coming at them.

Some of the smugglers vanished against the dark mass of the city wall. Jules angled toward that spot, reaching the inner sally door before it could be pulled shut. Those smugglers already inside were trying to yank the door closed to protect themselves, while those still outside were struggling to get inside. Shouldering her way through the desperate knot of men and women, Jules stabbed and slashed with her dagger to clear enough room to get in the door.

She barely made it into the tunnel through the wall before those inside managed to get the door shut. It had been dark before, but inside the tunnel with the inner door shut it was now pitch black. The city wall was about three lances thick at its base, Jules remembered from her training as an Imperial officer. The feeble starlight coming in through the open outer door couldn't reach as far as the inner door.

The door shut, the knot of smugglers began to unravel, a few still trying to hold it shut while the rest headed for the pale glow of the outside opening. Jules heard the thud of hooves and the clatter of a wagon as some of those outside the walls took off. Running out onto the cleared ground outside the wall, Jules felt a moment of immense relief that was immediately shattered as torches flared on the top of the wall and harsh Imperial trumpets sounded an alert.

The remaining smugglers were scattering, trying to lose themselves in the countryside before legionaries could reach this area. Jules scattered as well, angling to her right. The main eastern gate of the city and the road it served should be off to her left. That was where the on-call legionary cavalry would be coming from as they rode out to run down the fugitives.

Fortunately, her tattered cloak was dark enough to help hide her in the night. Jules ran, trying to put as much distance as she could between herself and the city wall, searching ahead for any signs of the scattered buildings that existed outside the cleared area beyond the castle walls. She knew the clear area extended for twice the range of the ballistae on the walls, which was about three hundred lances. If she could get that far...

The thunder of hooves and the clinking of harness warned of cavalry approaching. Fighting her instinct to keep running, Jules dropped to the ground, covering herself as best she could with the cloak before lying still.

Moving fast, in the dark, the cavalry could spot a moving figure. She'd been told that during training, and warned that someone lying still would be a lot harder to see. Hopefully these cavalry hadn't recently been reminded of that.

Heart pounding from the exertion of her run and fear of being caught, she heard horses passing behind and in front of her as the cavalry searched along the cleared area, the occasional yelp of a smuggler being run down piercing the night. The urge to jump up and run as well was almost overwhelming, but she held herself unmoving as the search went past her.

They'd be back, quartering the area again. She had to get out of the cleared area and as far as possible from the city before daylight came.

Coming up to a crouch, Jules peered into the darkness. Off to her right, the receding sounds of the cavalry search line could be heard. Far to her left, where the main gate and the road were, she could see torches flaring as legionary search teams gathered to scour the area on foot.

For the moment, the night ahead of her held only darkness and silence.

She didn't run, fearing that would make her motion more obvious. Moving at a fast walk, keeping low, Jules headed east, the lights on the city wall behind her looking far too close for far too long.

The moon finally rose, casting more light across the land. Jules breathed a sigh of relief as she saw buildings coming into clearer relief. Barns. A stable. Storage sheds.

Despite her extreme tiredness, Jules kept going, trying to put as much distance as possible between her and the city. She reached fields of crops and pastures, crossing trails and side-roads, heading steadily east. As the sky ahead began to pale toward dawn, she sought some place to hole up for the day. A field dotted with tall haystacks offered what seemed the best option. Picking a stack near the edge of the field, not far off a small stream meandering its way toward the Ospren River, Jules paused only to drink her fill before she burrowed into the hay to hide herself.

Exhausted, she passed out rather than fell asleep, one hand on her dagger.

* * *

The only person who'd recognized her among the smugglers had been the lookout, and he'd died before he could tell anyone else. As far as the Imperials knew, she was still in Landfall.

Mages were another matter. In the past, they'd known she was going to be someplace before she herself had known it. All she could do was to try to avoid predictable routes and keep her eyes open.

The second night after escaping the city, she went through a small town in the middle of the night. Moving like a ghost among the slumbering citizens snug in their homes, Jules had stolen a broad-brimmed hat and a light coat, as well as two loaves of bread. The possibly-betraying and much the worse for wear hooded cloak she wrapped in a stone and tossed into the town's garbage pit.

She traveled by night the first three days, but after that the risk of being caught forced her to shift to walking during the day. No one traveled by night except soldiers or police on forced march or patrol, couriers on horseback, and criminals. During the day, she could blend in with other travelers, though at the risk of someone looking beneath her hat and recognizing the woman wearing it.

Keeping to side roads, Jules didn't see any Mechanics passing by. They'd be on the main road, riding in carriages, or using their "train" that ran between Marandur and Landfall. A couple of times she heard a far-off, piercing wail that sounded frighteningly like a Mage monster, but turned out to be a noise made by the Mechanic train.

Odder was the lack of Mages. At first on edge, expecting to encounter them at any moment, Jules didn't see a single Mage as she trudged east. They couldn't all still be searching for her in Landfall. But where were they?

Heading east, the least expected direction, had gotten her out of the city and the legionary search parties near it, but she couldn't keep heading toward the Imperial capital at Marandur. Escaping the Empire meant finding a boat or a ship, and the best chance for that would be somewhere along the coast well north of Landfall. Hoping she'd gone far enough east, Jules finally turned north. Another half-day's walk took her to the south bank of the Ospren River. That also meant reaching the main highway running east from Landfall, which followed the path of the river, and all of the traffic that used that road. She'd tried to time her arrival at the river for not long before sunset, so that there'd be less chance of her being identified in the fading light.

It was still unnerving to see the many wagons, carriages, and individuals riding horses along the road. Jules joined those travelers on foot walking along the verge of the road, doing her best to blend in. Somewhere up ahead there'd be a ferry she could use to get across the river.

Her nerve almost cracked when a column of legion cavalry came riding past from behind her, her first sight of them happening when the head of the column rode by not much more than a lance to her left. Jules concentrated on keeping her pace steady and trying to calm her racing heart as the ranks of riders rode past her, heading east. But the cavalry took no notice of her, riding with the stoic indifference to their surroundings of men and women who'd already spent a long day in the saddle and would probably be doing the same tomorrow.

As the cavalry rode on ahead of her, Jules watched them, remembering her father. He'd worn the same uniform and armor as those legionaries. Maybe some of the older ones had known him.

What had he been like? The faded, fragmentary memories of her five year old self offered few clues. Would her father approve of what she was doing? Or had he been a loyal legionary who would've insisted her only honorable course of action lay in submitting to the Emperor?

Her line was supposed to someday produce the daughter who'd free the world. But she knew nothing of her own mother and father. Was that irony? Or just life?

With night falling, Jules had to wait until the next morning to cross. This far from a city there were no bridges crossing the river, and only a fool would try to swim across the wide and swiftly flowing Ospren. That left ferries, which only operated during the day. Blending in with the morning traffic across the river should allow her to cross without being spotted.

She gazed at the passing boat traffic, wishing she could safely hitch a ride on one of the boats or barges riding the river's current west to the sea. But as she looked across the river, Jules saw two figures in Mage robes pacing along the north bank. They weren't looking her way, and probably would have trouble spotting her amidst all the other traffic on the highway, but Jules still hastily looked away and as she kept walking tried to keep other people or wagons between her and the river.

The sun had set by the time she reached a ferry crossing, and the inns gathered along the road to cater to those who had to wait through the night for the morning ferries to begin conveying people and wagons over the river. Jules sized up the inns, discounting the well-lit exterior of what was clearly the most expensive. A covered carriage already stopping there bore a small flag on a post to indicate it was transporting Mechanics. She didn't want to risk encountering any Mechanics. But the cheapest inn, barely illuminated, offered its own potential hazards to her health and safety if she slept there.

That left the in-between inn, which seemed nice enough to trust the food and lodgings, but not so nice that common rooms would be brightly lighted and cater to the sort of Imperial officials who'd love to spot Jules and turn her in.

Despite hoarding the money she'd taken off the thief in Landfall, there was little left. Setting aside enough to pay for ferry passage the next day, Jules had enough to pay for the meal in the inn's great room. She sat in a corner, gnawing on beef that had been roasted so long it was dry as well as tough. Some farmer's ox had probably given up the ghost recently and ended up on a roasting spit. But for someone who'd grown used to salt pork on ships, a type of meat that could be easily mistaken for hardwood, the beef was good enough, especially when there was plenty of cheap watered wine to wash it down.

Keeping her hat pulled low to discourage anyone from trying to talk to her, Jules listened to the conversations around her, much of it concerned with mundane issues like a broken wagon, the price of a trained plow-horse, the latest Imperial household scandal, and griping about Mechanics and their treatment of commons.

"I don't know where they're selling them, but they're buying all I can make," a metal smith commented, one of her reddened hands raising a celebratory beer. "Used to be hardly anyone needed new ones."

"Sounds like a lot of building going on somewhere," her companion commented. "Is the stuff going north?"

"No. I send it down the river to Landfall. Where it goes from there doesn't matter to me." The smith frowned, her expression growing unhappy. "But both of my apprentices are making noises about heading west. Why, I ask them? And they give me some nonsense about being able to decide things for themselves."

"From all I hear," the companion said, "the Great Guilds are in the west, too. Why go there when they'll just lord it over us the same as they do here?"

Jules noticed a large woman in traveling gear come in with a snort of disgust that filled the room as she sat down. "Beer!"

"What's it this time, Lil?" one of the wait staff asked, greeting her like a regular customer.

"Mages," Lil grunted.

A large portion of the room fell silent, other conversations stopping to hear what Lil said. "Mages?" one asked. "I haven't seen any here for a few days."

"They're all north of the river," Lil said. "I crossed over on the last ferry of the day, and had to walk past a handful of Mages watching everyone. If you're going north across the river tomorrow, count on having their eyes on you."

After a pause, someone else spoke up. "I thought they'd taken over Landfall. What're they doing here?"

"Looking for her," Lil said, gesturing toward a poster on one wall. "What do you think?"

Jules looked, seeing one of the wanted posters with a drawing of her face on it. Fortunately, this room was dark enough and crowded enough that no one was bothering trying to look under the brim of her hat.

Whatever else Lil had planned on saying was interrupted by other new arrivals, three men whose leather armor, short swords, and whips at their belts advertised their occupation as Imperial prisoner guards. Jules, like most of the others in the room, covertly watched the three take a table. Imperial citizens who were neither wealthy nor powerful learned early in life not to attract attention from even such minor servants of the Emperor.

Conversations slowly began to build again, still a low murmur. Jules tackled her beef, wondering if she should pay for another flask of ale and leave herself broke except for the ferry fare.

"Pirates."

Jules almost jerked her head up at the word, catching herself barely in time and raising her gaze just enough to view the big man who was the leader of the prison guards.

"Hauling pirates to Marandur," he boasted to one of the wait staff.

"Pirates?" she repeated, not seeming all that impressed. "Why didn't they just hang them in Landfall?"

"I dunno. We're just delivering them."

Pirates. Prisoners on their way to Marandur. Jules chewed her meat slowly, realizing that they could be from her ship, the *Sun Queen*. What if they were? But they were being guarded, and were probably chained. And on the north side of the river, watching all of the traffic crossing on the ferry, were Mages. They'd apparently once again gained some foreknowledge of where she was going. But not enough foreknowledge to bring them to this inn, fortunately.

The only route that offered a decent chance of escaping was still to the north, though. This side of the Ospren River offered too few ports aside from Landfall itself. Getting through the Mages wouldn't be easy, but if she didn't she'd be trapped between the desert Waste and the river. That was a big area, but there'd be a lot of Imperials looking for her, as well as Mages once they realized she hadn't crossed.

Nonetheless, the only smart thing, the only prudent thing, would be to leave this inn and head south, away from the Mages and the eyes of Imperial servants who used the main highway. Surviving another encounter with Mages wouldn't be easy. And she shouldn't risk everything to help pirates who very likely weren't from the *Sun Queen*.

As she thought about that, she realized that she'd already made up her mind. Jules dropped a few coins on the table to cover her meal, standing up not too fast and not too slowly. Aside from a couple of glances her way, no one else in the great room seemed to notice or care that she was leaving.

Hunching her coat around her as if cold, Jules walked out into the courtyard and past the lantern at the inn's door. She stood in the starlit open, looking about.

Over by the stables, a wagon stood, its distinctive shape unmistakable even in the dark. Two thirds of the wagon's bed was given over to a cell of crisscrossing iron bars just tall enough to hold prisoners inside if they sat rather than stood. Two horses which must have been pulling the wagon had been unhitched and were at a water trough.

Jules walked toward the prison wagon, taking out her dagger and sliding it up one sleeve where she could get at it very quickly. Her arm that had been cut by the Mage's knife back in Landfall was still stiff and sore, but not enough so to hinder her movement too much.

What was she doing? Stupid. Don't take the risk.

But she kept walking, as she got closer seeing two more prison guards at work on the horses, probably rubbing them with curry combs to remove the mud and dust of the road. Two guards outside, three inside. A hand of five, just as the legions liked to do things.

She could also see the vague shapes of the prisoners still inside the cell on the wagon, packed in closely. It looked like the guards weren't planning on letting the prisoners out during stops like this.

Make a plan, Jules told herself. But how? She had to take out both of these guards without making enough noise to be noticed.

One of the guards noticed her as Jules came closer, watching her with an expression unreadable in the dark. "You need something?" he asked, sounding as if he didn't care about the answer.

Jules kept walking at a steady pace, one hand cupped to keep her dagger up the sleeve of her coat. "I hear these prisoners are pirates," she said.

"Yeah."

The second guard came over, wiping one wrist across his forehead to clear sweat. "You shouldn't get too close to the cell. They can reach out a little," he warned Jules.

"They're not eating?" she asked.

"Nah. They ate before we left Landfall. They'll live until we reach Marandur."

"Animals," the first guard said, spitting to one side.

Those words both decided her on what to do and gave Jules an idea. "I hate pirates. They... killed my father. Can I spit on them?"

"Sure."

She walked a few more steps, both guards coming close to her. Jules saw one of the male guards eye her body up and down and then grin at his comrade.

Pausing about half a lance from the cell on the wagon, Jules saw the prisoners gazing back at her. The dark made it hard to see any detail, but she could still sense their apathy born of exhaustion and lack of hope. None of them looked at all familiar, an immense relief since that meant they weren't off the *Sun Queen*. But now that she'd seen them, she couldn't just walk away.

One guard stood on each side of her.

She let the dagger drop into her hand, gripping it ready to use.

"Why does that prisoner have that?" Jules asked, pointing toward the cell with her free hand.

"What?" Both guards took half-steps closer to the wagon, peering at the cell. "Which one has what?"

Jules side-stepped a little, so she was behind the guard on her right, her hand coming up and around to draw the dagger blade across his throat.

She stepped back toward the second guard as the first fell, clutching at his throat. Prison guard armor didn't have neck protection, allowing Jules to ram her dagger blade into the second guard's throat, who had turned toward her while he was still trying to grasp what had happened to the first guard.

She got her free hand across the guard's mouth, muffling his frantic gasps as he died.

The nearby horses raised their heads, their upper lips curling, as the scent of blood reached them, but aside from shuffling about a little stayed quiet.

Lowering the guard's body to the ground, Jules looked about, seeing no one else in the courtyard.

Now what?

"Where are the keys?" she whispered to the prisoners.

They were staring at her, their eyes shining in the dim light cast by the stars. "The boss has them," one said. "He's inside."

The other three might come out at any moment. Her only chance of taking them out quickly and quietly was by surprising them as she had the first two. Jules sized up the two dead guards, hauling one around to the back of the wagon. Stooping to lift the body, she sat it back against the cell. "Hold it up so he looks like he's taking a break," she told the prisoners.

They could only reach out their lower arms between the bars of the cell, but that was enough. Jules yanked the short sword and dagger from the guard's belt and passed them to the prisoners. "Use these if you get a chance."

She went back to the other body, hauling it around so the wagon was between her and the entrance to the inn. This guard had been about her size, so the armor and clothes should fit. She pulled off the armor, shirt and pants, peeling off her own clothing and hastily donning the prison guard attire.

Setting the leather helm atop her head to help hide her face, Jules came back around to the other side of the wagon, trying to get her breathing back under control.

"Who are you?" one of the prisoners whispered.

"I heard you're pirates," Jules murmured in reply. "Is that so?"

"Yes. We were on the *Evening Star*."

"The *Evening Star?*" She'd heard of that ship. "Captain Orin?"

"Orin was our captain, yeah. He was killed when the Imperials took our ship. So were a lot of others. We're all that lived."

"Why didn't they kill you, too? Why are they taking you to Marandur?"

"I think it's about that chart," the prisoner said. "We picked it up at Dor's. They wanted to know where we got it. It shows lands out west, and another sea."

"I know," Jules said.

"You—?"

The prisoner fell silent as the door to the inn opened and the leader of the prison guards came strolling out, picking at his teeth with one finger. "The other two'll be out and then you go eat," he said. "You finished on them horses?"

Jules nodded, not saying anything.

The leader's eyes fell on the body sitting in the wagon. "What the blazes are you doing, stupid? Never put your back to 'em that close to the cell!" He walked quickly toward the wagon.

Jules followed. Just before they reached the wagon, she jumped, hitting the leader in the back and sending him stumbling into the side of the cell, his head hitting one of the bars.

"Wha—?" the leader got out, before Jules pinned him chest first against the cell, her free hand going over his mouth, her dagger going into his back.

She wasn't able to hit his heart from behind at this angle, and worried the leader might struggle, but he jerked a couple of more times, shuddering before going limp.

Stepping back, Jules saw that the prisoners had made good use of the short sword and dagger they'd been given, stabbing the leader in the front as she held him from behind. Stooping, she found the ring of keys at his belt.

"We've got two more to worry about," she hissed at the prisoners as she fumbled for the right key and got it into the lock of the cell. Opening it, she pointed to the prisoner who'd done all the talking so far. "You're about the size of that guy. Get his outfit on you. And you, strip this one and put on his armor."

"Manacles," the first prisoner said, pointing to his ankle.

Cursing, Jules got the manacles loose, tossing the keys to the other prisoners. "Get yourselves free, but stay inside that cell until we get rid of the last two guards."

The two newly released prisoners came around the side of the wagon, still fastening their sword belts, as the last two guards exited the inn.

"Go on, then," one of them said as he got close. "Hey, you're—"

His words choked off as a short sword went into his gut and an arm came around his back and across his neck to stifle any sounds he made.

That left Jules to handle the second guard. She thrust at him, but to her surprise instead of fighting or fleeing, he dropped to his knees, waiting for the blow.

She halted her attack, watching him. "Do you want to die?"

"I'm tired," he said.

The first prisoner, wearing the armor of the guard leader, came over. "He was the only guard who was decent to us," he told Jules. "Seemed like he didn't enjoy his work."

The guard looked up at them defiantly. "I got in debt, and was sentenced to Imperial service to work it off. It would've been fine if they'd made me a legionary, but instead I got this job, hauling people to work gangs who'd had the same misfortune as me but hadn't been as lucky."

"How'd you like to live?" Jules said. "And go somewhere that doesn't have work gangs?"

"Don't play with me. Who are you to offer such a thing?"

"None of your business," Jules said. "Get out of your armor. You," she told the first prisoner. "Find one of the other pirates to wear his outfit. He'll have to ride in the cell. What's your name, anyway?"

"Artem." He eyed her, then saluted. "My name's Artem of Sandurin, Captain. I don't know why you ran this risk to save us, but our lives are yours."

"Get the bodies into the cell on the wagon," Jules said. "We'll need to haul them somewhere we can dump them so they can't be found. Can any of you handle horses?"

The pirates responded with embarrassed silence. Not that Jules could blame them. She hadn't much experience with horses, either.

"I can," the last guard said as he pulled off the rest of his clothes.

"Then you can earn that life you still have," Jules said. "Change of plans. Put your clothes and armor back on. Artem, take his sword and dagger. What's your name, guard?"

"Nico. Nico of Landfall."

"Artem, keep someone close to him, with a dagger in hand, as he works," Jules said. "We need those horses harnessed to the wagon again. Let's move it, people. We can't hang around here."

The horses weren't happy to be brought back to harness so soon, but Nico calmed them enough to get the pair ready to pull the wagon again. Jules found a bag and stuffed her clothes and boots into it. "Anyone not in a guard uniform has to be in the cell," Jules said as they got ready to leave.

"But the bodies are in there!" one protested.

"You want us to be stopped by the first group of legionaries that sees prisoners outside their cell on the wagon?" Jules snapped. "The five of us in uniforms ride outside because that's where we're supposed to be. The rest get in there."

"Who the blazes do you—?"

Artem stepped in, glowering at the complainer. "If not for her we'd all be in that cell until we got to Marandur and the Emperor's torturers started going over us. As far as I'm concerned, she's our captain, and we're going to do what she says."

"But—"

"And she killed three men tonight before they could make a sound," Artem added. "I wouldn't be giving her any trouble if I was you."

The cell was even more cramped than before, because with Jules making up one of the five guards the size of the group had grown. Of the ten total prisoners, six of the pirates were men, and four were women. Three of the pirates, two men and one woman, were in guard armor and could ride outside, but the other seven had to wedge themselves back into the cell along with the bodies of four guards.

Jules walked next to Nico, who was stroking the neck of one horse to calm it. "I remember that a cell wagon like this would travel at night sometimes. Is that right?"

"Yes," Nico said. "If we needed to be somewhere quickly enough. We were just supposed to suck it up if we had to travel all night. But if we do that, we'll have to change the horses sometime during the day tomorrow, or let these rest for a long time."

"I'll decide how to handle that later. I'm going to ride beside you on the front of the wagon, and if you do or say or even think anything that might betray us, you'll feel my dagger before you finish. Understood?"

"Yes. Where are we going?"

"Back to Landfall."

Nico frowned. "The guards at the gate will recognize the wagon."

"I'm working on that. Let's go."

Nico got up onto the seat at the front of the wagon, Jules climbing up beside him, while Artem and the other two disguised pirates sat in the back where the guards would be to keep an eye on the prisoners. Flicking the reins, Nico got the wagon moving back toward the road.

"Hey!"

Jules tensed at the angry hail, turning to see one of the inn's staff had run out of the doorway.

"You didn't settle up!" the woman yelled.

"Tell her Emperor's service," Jules said to Nico.

"Emperor's service!" he called out.

The woman growled an inarticulate cry of anger, making a very rude gesture toward the cell wagon. But that was all she could do, since those in the Emperor's service could demand free of charge things like meals and rooms from inns. "We didn't usually claim Emperor's service," Nico said to Jules, "because we knew we might have to stop there again, and inn keepers have long memories. The next time we visited they'd find ways to get even without giving us enough cause to report them."

They fell silent then, moving down the road, which was almost deserted at this hour of the night. The wagon moved at a slow but steady pace as Nico tried to get the most he could out of the horses. Jules listened to the waters of the Ospren River rushing alongside, wishing she was riding them in a boat rather than on the uncomfortable seat of this wagon, a dagger in one hand ready to stab Nico in an instant.

A low rumbling sounded, growing in volume.

Nico slowed the horses even more, bringing them and the wagon to a halt. "It's best they're not moving when a Mechanic train goes by," he said. "They can panic and bolt otherwise."

Jules saw one of the unnaturally bright and steady Mechanic lights growing in size as it drew nearer at an amazingly rapid pace, the rumbling sound growing louder and louder, a rattling of metal on metal becoming apparent as well as the train got closer.

Yesterday she'd walked over the "tracks" the train used, twin strips of steel set into rectangular lengths of wood that supported them. Tonight, Jules watched with awe as the Mechanic train thundered past five or six lances from the highway, the first part of it puffing out smoke, roaring in a way that reminded her of the Mage troll she'd fought in Landfall, the impossibly bright light shining on the front. The ground itself seemed to be trembling from the movement of the Mechanic monster, and the horses harnessed to the cell wagon shifted nervously.

Jules watched it go past, feeling an odd sense of familiarity. Of course. "That smoke. It does look like the smoke that comes out of the chimney on Mechanic ships."

"I wouldn't know," Nico said.

A moment later an incredibly loud, piercing scream tore the night. Jules clapped her hands over her ears, staring at the Mechanic train as it rumbled off into the night.

The horses snorted, heads high and their eyes wide so the whites seemed much bigger than they should. Nico worked to calm them, finally getting the pair to relax enough to be urged back into a walk.

"They probably did that on purpose," Nico complained as the wagon rolled slowly west.

"The Mechanics?" Jules said.

"Yes. That noise. They probably did that on purpose to make the horses panic."

She nodded. "You're probably right."

Nico glanced at her. "You sound like you've dealt with them."

"Much more than I've wanted to," Jules said. "You?"

"Yes. That's why I was in debt. Mechanics simply took my stock. They said they needed the furniture. I was left with bills and nothing to sell to pay them with."

"That's Mechanics," Jules said.

"Do you think it's true?" Nico sighed. "The prophecy? I'd like to think that someday the Great Guilds wouldn't be able to do whatever they wanted."

"The prophecy is true," Jules said.

"You're sure?"

"Yes." Jules looked over at the Ospren River, grateful to hear the natural sound of its waters rather than the roar of the Mechanic train. "Someday, a daughter of... her line will overthrow the Great Guilds and free the world."

"It can't come soon enough for me," Nico said. "Do you think she made it out of Landfall? That was the gossip when we left, that she'd slipped out somehow, because no one had seen her for a while and most of the Mages were leaving. We saw a lot of Mages on the north side of the river today. Maybe they thought she was there, or was going there."

"If so," Jules said, "something might have happened to change her mind. How far are we from Landfall on this road?"

Nico frowned in thought. "At this pace, only a little more than a day."

"Really?" Her days and nights of walking across the countryside had added up to a depressingly small distance from the city.

"I doubt we'd reach the city gate tomorrow before it closes for the night," Nico added. "The horses won't take it."

"That's fine," Jules said. She looked over at the river. They were passing a stretch where the river banks were high. In this time between midnight and dawn, no one else was visible on the road. "Stop us here. Hey, back there! We're getting rid of the bodies."

Those confined to the cell came out gratefully, hauling the four dead guards with them. "Fasten manacles on their ankles," Jules said. "For the weight."

Once that was done, pairs of the pirates grabbed each former guard by the head and the feet, swinging them one by one out over the river to fall and vanish with a splash. The pirates confined to the cell got back inside with much more cheerfulness than before now that they had room to breathe. "There's still blood back here," one warned.

"Nobody will worry about that," Nico said. "It wouldn't be the first time a prisoner didn't make it to the end of a trip."

"Captain?" Artem said from the back. "I know we're heading back to Landfall. What's the plan when we get there?"

"We'll get through the city and get onto a ship heading out to sea," Jules said.

"How we gonna do that?"

"I'm working on it."

"All right." Artem and the others seemed to be satisfied with that response. She wondered if that was based on a natural desire to believe in someone who seemed competent, or on the fact that so far she'd managed to avoid getting them caught again. Either way, it didn't give her any good ideas of how to get this group through Landfall.

Traffic on the road began slowly picking up as dawn approached. By late morning, Nico didn't have to be careful to drive slowly. There wasn't any other choice as other wagons clogged the road this close to Landfall.

Jules kept her leather helm on and pulled as low as she could to help hide her face, but fortunately no one bothered looking closely at a prison guard. She kept an eye out for Mages, but the only ones she saw were on the other side of the river. The Mages seemed have known that Jules had been planning on crossing the Ospren somewhere around here, but not that she'd changed those plans at the last moment. Other times, the Mages had known where she'd be, but not exactly when. Prophecies were always supposed to come true, but whatever insight was allowing the Mages to predict her movements was less accurate.

Fortunately. Otherwise, she'd have long since been dead.

A column of legionaries appeared ahead, marching from Landfall. Jules slumped in her seat, her dagger hidden but ready in case Nico tried to betray them. However, Nico did nothing as the legionaries tramped past the wagon with the long-suffering attitudes of soldiers who knew they'd be marching a lot farther before the day was done. Jules followed with her eyes the movement of the officer riding at the front of the column. Dark red uniform, insignia gleaming in the sun, straight sword at his side. About two years ago, that could've been her. About two years ago, being that Imperial officer had been her only long-term goal in life, because it had seemed the highest an orphan like her could aim for to prove herself. The prophecy had changed that, and as much as she hated what the prophecy had done to her life, Jules had to admit that she was happier as a pirate and explorer than she ever would've been as an officer in the Emperor's service.

Traffic on the highway slowed even more as the legionaries crowded other travelers to the other side of the road and the wagon even stopped at one point, but their pace slowly picking up again after the soldiers had marched past.

Nico suggested they stop at noon to rest the horses, pulling the wagon to the side clear of other traffic. Jules walked a bit to stretch her stiff legs. Why was it that traveling by wagon or by walking both had to hurt her legs? At least walking didn't also make her butt sore.

The pirates in the cell had to stay there, because letting them out to move around would've spoiled the illusion of them still being under guard.

As they waited, watching the riders and wagons and travelers on foot using the highway, Jules noticed another line of travelers walking off to the side of the road. As they grew closer, she could see the manacles on their wrists and the chain running between them that held the entire group together. About thirty, she guessed. Five guards dressed and armored just like Jules walked along with the line of prisoners, one guard in the lead and two on each side, the last pair near the end.

Nico saw her watching. "They've probably been sentenced to labor."

"Why are they heading toward Landfall?" Jules asked. "Aren't the big farm estates north and south of here?"

"They could be intended for work gangs in the city," he said. "Digging out basements and foundations for repairing buildings, clearing old debris, that sort of thing. But from the look of these they're probably going to be put on a ship and taken north to one of the estates north of Sandurin. There's been several groups sent north like that lately. I heard it was because one of the Imperial princesses is expanding her estates around Umburan and needs the workers." Nico paused. "Supposedly, a lot of the prisoners sentenced to labor in the north have been escaping into the Northern Ramparts. But a lot of others are probably dying. They get worked hard, I hear."

Jules watched the column of miserable men and women shambling west toward Landfall. "It's not all that surprising that so many people want to escape the Empire."

Nico shrugged. "People are cheap and plentiful. So they get used up. These days it's less expensive to run a man into the ground than it is to lose a horse, or so I've heard."

"You said Mechanics ruined you?"

"Yes." He dug into the grass beside him with one hand, frowning. "That was bad enough. But then Imperial law came after me for my unpaid debts. They should've understood, right? We're all victims of the Great Guilds. But no. No mercy, no bending, no exceptions. The Mechanics ruined me, and then the Imperial bureaucracy enslaved me to pay off my debts. I have a lot more in common with those in chains than I do with those who guard them. I guess the fact that I ended up a guard makes me lucky."

"I guess that's so." Jules watched the end of the column of prisoners pass, a sudden thought catching her. "They won't make it to the city before the gate closes tonight, will they?"

"Huh?" Nico shook his head. "No. Not at that pace. They won't even come close."

"And you say they might be on their way to a ship to be sent north?"

"Likely, yes."

Jules smiled. "Hey, Artem, how much money did that guard leader have on him?"

"Money?" Artem asked, looking over from where he was sitting a couple of lances away.

"Yeah. Money. I didn't bring it up before now, but we need it. How much?"

Artem sighed. "Three silver galleys."

"What was that?" Jules asked.

"Did I say three? I meant five. Five silver galleys."

She paused. "Are you sure?"

Another sigh from Artem before he spoke. "Six. Six silver galleys."

"See those carts selling food and water alongside the road? When we pass one selling booze I want you to buy some bottles. Cheap wine or brandy."

"Are we going to have a celebration?" Artem asked.

"Sort of," Jules said. "Because I know how to get us into and through Landfall."

CHAPTER FOUR

Once they got going again, the wagon rolled along at a sedate pace suited to the weary horses, Jules watching the sides of the road as the afternoon wore on. Artem picked up four bottles of wine at a cart, as well as some food for everyone. Jules let the rest eat, but forbade any from touching the wine. "That's for later."

The sun was close to the western horizon, glaring into her eyes, when Jules finally spotted what she'd been looking for. About twenty lances off the road to the south was the group of prisoners she'd seen pass by earlier. Their chains still in place, they'd been sat in a circle, all thirty slumping with fatigue. One guard stood watching them, the other four sitting to one side. "Pull us over next to them," Jules told Nico.

The wagon rolled to a halt a few lances from the chained prisoners, Jules directing Nico to take care of the horses before she called aside Artem and the two other pirates dressed as guards. "The sun's setting. As soon as it's dark, get out the wine. Don't drink any yourselves, or just a little. When I give the word, I want those five guards to die as quickly and quietly as possible."

"Why are we freeing these people?" Artem asked. "Isn't it going to be hard enough for us to sneak into Landfall as it is?"

"We're not freeing them. They're our ticket into Landfall. We're just replacing their guards with us."

As night fell, Jules led the three pirates to where the four prisoner guards were lounging. The real guards had shed their leather armor while they relaxed. "You guys want a drink?"

The one who must be the leader of the new group laughed. "I wondered what you were up to. Sure. What've you got?"

Jules nodded to Artem and the others, each of whom picked a guard to sit by. She sat down next to the leader, who grinned at her.

Jules raised her wine bottle, pretending to take a big drink but only wetting her mouth. Passing the bottle to the guard, she watched him guzzle down several swallows before pausing to catch his breath.

"That's not bad," he said before belching. "You guys have got it easy, riding in that wagon. We've gotta walk."

"The job still sucks," Jules said. She'd kept her helm on to partially hide her face, but in the dark that probably didn't matter.

"It's got its benefits," the leader said, laughing. "We've got some decent looking women in this bunch. Not as good looking as you, of course!"

"Thanks," Jules said, offering the man another drink.

He took a few more swallows, lowering the bottle afterwards with a contented sigh. "There's a couple in this lot who act like they were high class. Every time I pass them I get in a grab, and there's nothing they can do about it. How about you? You like getting grabbed?"

"Depends on the guy," Jules said, wondering why any man would think a woman would be attracted by that kind of talk. "Come here."

He grinned and leaned close, but before their lips came into contact Jules clapped one hand over his mouth. Her other hand drove her dagger into his heart.

She watched his eyes widen with shock, felt his body tremble, then shifted her grip as he died to keep him from collapsing. Looking over the dead man's shoulder, she gestured to Artem and the others nearby.

One of the guards managed a strangled yell before he died.

"Cas?" The fifth guard, standing watching the prisoners, had turned their way, his silhouette only a vague shape in the dark.

Artem strolled to the fifth guard, holding out a bottle. "Choked on the wine a little," he said, slurring his words a bit. "You want a swallow?"

The fifth guard died with a mouthful of wine that blocked his cry of pain.

Jules went over to the cell wagon, opening the cell. "There're six of you," she told the pirates inside. "The five closest in size to these guards take their clothes and their armor. Be quiet about it."

Nico came over, gazing toward the huddled circle of prisoners. "What're are we going to tell them?"

"Not a thing. Tomorrow, they'll have ten guards escorting them into the city. Get rid of the horses."

"Get rid of them?"

"Can't you make them run away?" Jules asked.

Nico unstaked the horses and pulled off their harnesses, but afterwards the tired animals refused to escape. He managed to shoo them off a little ways, but they wouldn't move any farther. "They should wander off by daylight," he said. "Are we just going to leave the wagon here?"

"We're going to burn the wagon," Jules said. "Get everything we want to save off of it. Artem! Get the others and let's move this thing into that hollow. Who's got a flint?"

It took a while to get the flames going, but by the time the moon rose the wagon had become a bonfire. Other groups camped alongside the road for the night had their own fires for cooking and warmth, so the blaze stood out only briefly for its size. The old, dry wood burned quickly, leaving glowing ashes amid the grass, the iron bars of the cell in the center, bent a bit by the heat of the fire. Once the iron had cooled enough, Jules had eight of the pirates pick up the remnants of the cell and carry it across the road to the river, where they dumped it. The portions remaining above the surface were masked by reeds growing along the river bank.

Totally worn out, Jules divided her group into two to get what sleep they could in what remained of the night, putting Artem in charge of the second group of pirates disguised as prisoner guards.

"But I'm just a sailor," Artem protested. "I've never run things."

"I think you can do it," Jules said.

"All right, Captain. If you say so. I'll do my best."

She managed to stay awake until it was time for Artem's section to take over, passing out almost the instant her head touched the grass.

* * *

The next day dawned with a red sky that worried Jules as she stood up and stretched.

"Got a storm coming in," Artem commented.

"Looks like it," Jules agreed. "Maybe that'll be a good thing. Let's get everybody over here." She waited while they gathered, several yawning. Nine pirates, including herself, in the leather armor and helms of prisoner guards, plus Nico in his own guard outfit for a total of ten. The tenth pirate, lacking guard armor as a disguise, would walk alongside the prisoners as if part of their number. "Here's the deal. We don't tell the prisoners anything has changed. We don't know them, so we don't know if any of them would betray us in hopes of getting a pardon for themselves. As far as they're concerned, the guards changed last night, but their fates haven't."

"Here are the papers the, um, former guards were carrying," Nico said, offering them to Jules.

She looked them over, feeling a burst of hope. "All right! They're supposed to go aboard a ship in the harbor. We'll take them there. If we can get everyone on the ship, we'll do that, and take over the ship once we're out of the harbor."

"We've got a little experience with taking over ships," one of the pirates said, grinning.

"Let's get the prisoners up and start marching. Don't brutalize them, but don't act too nice. We have to pass as prisoner guards until we reach that ship."

As it turned out, a few pokes from short swords were necessary to get some of the prisoners on their feet. The prisoners noticed the change in guards, but none of them said anything, perhaps having already learned not to draw any extra attention to themselves. Jules got the column going across the road, still nearly empty this early, so the prisoners could drink from the river. Then they had to be herded back across the road and a little distance to one side just as they'd walked yesterday. After sending Artem aside to buy some bread loaves from a cart they passed, the guards ate as they marched. Stale bread from the day before was cheap enough to be passed out among the prisoners. Nico walked in the lead, Jules not far behind him on the side away from the road.

Traffic built quickly this close to Landfall, most of it coming from the city, heading east. Jules pulled her leather helm as low as she could and kept her head lowered as if tired, sneaking looks at the road and across the river.

She couldn't see any Mages on the north side of the river.

Great. Had they figured she wasn't going to cross?

"Captain," Artem said in a low voice. He was guarding the prisoners from the side nearest the highway, marching along about even with Jules. "Reefs two points off the starboard bow."

Her eyes went to a spot a little ways to the right of the front of the column, seeing Mage robes among the travelers. Two. No, three. Walking along steadily, apparently not looking around, everyone clearing a path.

One hand grasping her dagger, Jules kept changing her pace slightly, just enough to keep at least one fake prison guard or prisoner between her and the Mages.

"Mad," Artem said. "Get out a little toward the road."

"They'll notice me easier," the female pirate objected.

"That's the idea."

"Oh. I got it. You're gonna owe me, Art."

Jules, not wanting to risk speaking with Mages so close, watched Mad stroll a little closer toward the road as if unaware of the Mages.

And saw the Mages suddenly veer off the road as they came even with the column, planting themselves directly in front of Mad. The female pirate stumbled to a halt, a look of terror on her face that was all the more convincing for being genuine.

The rest of the column kept moving, ignoring what was happening, as commons always had to when Mages decided to single out one of their number. Jules had no choice but to pretend to ignore what was going on as well, consumed by guilt at the thought that Mad might be killed by the Mages. But she noticed Artem had dropped back to keep himself between Jules and the Mages' line of sight.

However, the Mages seemed interested only in Mad. For a long moment, the Mages looked her over. Then as quickly as before they turned, heading back onto the road and striding on toward the east.

Mad, visibly shaking, trotted to rejoin the column. "You owe me *big*," she hissed at Artem.

"I'm the one who owes you," Jules said.

"No, Captain," Mad said. "I already owe you my life. At worst this balances things. But that lug is another matter," she said, pointing at Artem.

Jules slowly exhaled. The Mages might've been looking for a woman in armor like that of the prison guards. Since she'd kept out of their line of sight, it hadn't occurred to them that there might be more than one such woman with this group.

And it seemed Artem might suspect who she was. If so, he'd been discreet about it.

She glanced back to ensure the Mages were still going east, seeing their robes among the other travelers heading that way. But as she looked back, Jules got her first good look at two of the prisoners.

Unless she was very much mistaken, they were the two "high class" women that the former guard leader had boasted of molesting.

Ian's mother and sister. Apparently Ian's father sacrificing his life at Western Port hadn't been enough to turn aside Imperial wrath at Jules' capture of the town. Did Ian know they'd been condemned to a labor sentence?

She didn't even know if Ian was still alive, or if he'd died at the hands of the Mage troll and the Mages who'd attacked the *Hawk's Mantle* to try to kill her.

Or if Ian had been arrested for freeing her from her chains, and already been executed.

That thought made the day darken about her, the bread in her stomach turning into a hard lump.

Ian's mother and sister might know, but she couldn't ask them. Those two would turn her in to any passing Imperial soldiers or police out of spite. But she owed Ian a life debt for her escape from the *Hawk's Mantle*, and a second life debt for his father. Even if he was dead (and please let him not be dead), she had to try to save his mother and sister, even though both doubtless hated her with an intensity hot enough to melt steel.

Facing forward, she called to Artem. "Thanks. Let me know if you see any more of them."

"Aye, Captain," Artem said. "Don't worry. Mad'll be here if we see any more Mages."

"Mad is gonna skin you alive once this is done," the female pirate muttered.

The sky had been clouding over since the sun rose, and now rain began pattering down. Jules' emotional relief at the way the rain helped hide her from being recognized was tempered by physical misery as the cold water fell and turned the ground beneath her feet into mud.

The prisoners faltered in the muddy path, but the pirates proved more than capable of playing the role of remorseless guards, keeping everyone on pace.

Jules watched the city wall of Landfall grow ever taller as they approached it, thinking about how hard it had been to get outside that wall a few days ago, and how she was now marching of her own volition to get back inside it.

There were two Mages standing at the gate. They were watching everyone leaving, but paying no attention to those entering the city. The Mages might have had some warning that she was coming this way, and wouldn't be crossing the river, but they didn't seem to know she was going to use this gate.

Maybe they were also short on numbers. If they'd sent a lot of

Mages north of the river, they'd all have to get back across in order to search for her on the south side. That would take time.

Jules increased her pace to come even with Nico. "You take the lead on getting us through the gate," she said, giving the former guard leader's paperwork back to Nico.

He gave her an alarmed look. "But I thought you'd handle that."

"I can't afford to have the gate guards noticing me," Jules said. "Aside from me, you're the only one with us who can fake being the leader of this group of guards."

"But… I…"

"You've seen this done, right? Just do it."

Nico licked his lips nervously. "All right."

They neared the gate, the rain still coming down just hard enough to make everyone uncomfortable. One of the legionaries checking those entering the city walked over to Nico as the column of prisoners reached the gate.

"Prisoners," Nico said.

"Yeah, I could see that," the legionary responded. "They really do scrape the bottom of the barrel for you prisoner guards, don't they?"

"Um… we're taking them to the harbor." Nico offered the papers.

The legionary looked them over, glancing at Nico as if wondering whether it'd be fun to give him a hard time. Maybe because it was raining, he passed the papers back without any objections. "Don't let any of them get loose. Get going."

The Mages, Jules saw with a quick look, were still watching everyone leaving. Nico looked back to give the command to start walking again.

"Hold on!" The voice was loud, authoritative, and angry.

Another legionary came walking up to Nico. A centurion, Jules saw, bearing an impressive scowl on his face. She glanced at Artem, and saw him looking to her for guidance.

The centurion didn't seem alarmed. Just angry. She shook her head at Artem, motioning for him not to do anything.

"What is this mess?" the centurion demanded of Nico.

"It's… a group of prisoners…" Nico repeated, quailing in the face of the centurion's wrath.

"You know what I mean!" The centurion pointed toward some of the fake guards. "Look at those mangy excuses for servants of the Emperor!"

"It's, uh, raining—"

"I know it's raining! If it wasn't, they'd look even worse! They all need haircuts, their clothing is sloppy and ill-fitting, and their armor isn't being kept up! What the blazes is that on his armor? A bloodstain? Buff it out! I don't care that you're not legionaries! You're still expected to maintain a decent appearance. You get these guards in shape before you try to leave this city, you hear me? If I see them looking this shoddy next time I see them on the streets, or when you try to use this gate again, I'll see that all of you regret it! Am I understood?"

"Yes, sir!" Nico said, his body gone stiff in a desperate attempt to stand at attention.

"Don't call me sir! I'm a centurion!"

"Yes, centurion!"

The centurion stalked off, leaving the gate guards grinning at Nico.

Giving Jules a shaky look, he managed to call out a command. "Let's… let's go."

*　*　*

They spent most of the day walking through the city, heading for the waterfront, Jules wondering every step of the way what security might be like there. After a week's time, would the number of legionaries and police have been reduced? Would the Mages still be watching the waterfront closely?

The rain came and went, the sun once peeking out for a few moments before deciding to hide behind the clouds once more.

As they walked, they passed businesses and pedestrians and riders and wagons going about the daily business of the city. None of them paid much attention to the prisoner guards and the prisoners. Jules knew that etiquette from being raised in the Empire. Any interest in prisoners might indicate sympathy. Indifference was the safest reaction. Why had she accepted that way of thinking for so long? Just because there hadn't been any alternative? Why hadn't she thought more about creating an alternative, another place where citizens didn't have to fear their own police?

They passed a café, the windows open to let in the breeze, a group of Mechanics eating. Normally, Mechanics were notorious for laughing loudly as if intent on showing how happy they were compared to everyone else. This time Jules noticed they were engaged in what looked like debate and arguments. What was going on? She couldn't hear.

But as the prisoners went past, the debate paused and Jules could hear one of the Mechanics talking loudly to his companions. "Why do commons stink so much?"

A lot of passing people heard, as they were supposed to. Jules saw their upset expressions turned away from the Mechanics. No one rebuked the Mechanics. Because no one wanted to attract their attention, either.

She didn't recognize any of the Mechanics in the cafe. It didn't matter; if any of the Mechanics had recognized her, they wouldn't have acted any nicer.

But something seemed to be going on among the Mechanics, and that might involve more danger for her. In her prior meetings with Mechanics, Jules had gotten the impression that various factions in their Guild were jockeying for power in a political debate that could be deadly. And at least some of those factions hadn't approved of the idea of the Mechanics Guild letting Jules run free. "Avoid the square around the Mechanics Guild Hall," she said to Nico. There would be a lot of police still posted there, very likely. And Mechanics going in and out. No sense risking being recognized by any of them.

They took only brief breaks to drink water at public fountains, walking through the afternoon. Between the crowded streets of the city and the slow pace of tired prisoners who had no desire to reach their fates any faster, they didn't make good time. And Landfall the Ancient was big, not only the oldest city in the world but also the largest until surpassed by Marandur. The sky had begun to darken by the time they reached the waterfront, a thin drizzle still falling from leaden skies.

Plenty of legionaries and police were visible, watching the water and the streets, paying particular attention to anyone traveling alone, especially women, but none of them giving more than passing glances to the prisoners and their guards. One finally waved Nico over, looking at his papers as Jules waited nervously.

Nico came back. "He said the ship we're looking for is on pier seven."

Jules searched the waterfront, seeing no Mage robes. "Let's go." The ruined pier where the *Hawk's Mantle* had been destroyed was in the military section of the waterfront, on past the piers usually used by merchant ships. She wouldn't have to worry about passing that spot tonight.

Marching by a chalkboard protected by an awning, where the names of ships visiting the harbor were posted for merchants or those seeking passage, Jules stumbled to a stop, staring at one of the names.

The *Prosper*.

Maybe she'd make it out of the city again.

"Nico, when we get to pier five, head down it."

"But the ship we want is on pier seven."

"No, the ship we want is on pier five. The *Prosper*. Do it!"

Posted at the head of each pier was a poster with Jules' face on it. They moved past the piers, their progress feeling agonizingly slow to Jules. So close. Just a little farther, and she might have the best chance at survival and freedom since being captured by the *Hawk's Mantle*.

Nico turned down pier five, but stopped as a pier inspector stepped outside of her shed and blocked him. "What's your business?"

"Uh, prisoners," Nico said, waving back at the column. "We're taking them to a ship."

"I wasn't told to expect that. Where're your papers?"

As Jules hung back to avoid being recognized, and Nico fumbled with the papers that identified another ship as the destination of the prisoners, Artem stepped forward. "Here they are," he said, holding out two silver galleys.

The inspector gave him a dispassionate look. "I need better papers than that."

"Of course." Artem brought out two more silver coins. "Here. See? All's in order."

"I guess so," the Inspector said, pocketing the bribe. "Get." She went back inside her shed.

Jules shoved Nico to get him moving again, the line of prisoners and fake guards walking down the pier. "Where'd you learn that?" she asked Artem.

"Watched my captain do that a few times," he said. "Kept my eyes open. Guess that was smart, huh?"

"Very smart," Jules said. They'd passed two other ships tied up the pier before they reached the *Prosper*, her wooden hull, masts, and furled sails wet with the rain. "Let me take the lead here."

She walked up the boarding plank, not surprised when a sailor stopped her. "Where are you going?"

"We've got prisoners for passage," she said.

"Not for us," the sailor said, shaking her head.

"Get your captain. Aravind, right?"

"That's right." The sailor scratched her head. "Hey, Daki. She says we're supposed to take some prisoners."

"The blazes we are." Jules saw a familiar man come up to the boarding plank, shaking his head. "Whoever told you that was wrong."

"You should take us aboard, Daki," Jules said. She raised the rim of her leather helm, sweeping hair from her forehead so he could see her.

Daki frowned, looked closely, and his mouth fell open. "Oh. Oh. I… Captain Aravind. Get Captain Aravind," he told the first sailor. As that woman ran off, Daki leaned close. "It's really you?"

"This time I'm the one who could use a rescue, Daki," Jules said. She'd risked her ship to save him and the other survivors of the crew of the *Merry Runner* after their ship wrecked on the reefs of the Bleak Coast, and later arranged them jobs on this ship. Unless she'd seriously misjudged Daki, he'd honor a debt like that.

He didn't hesitate. "Yes, Captain. What about these others?"

"The guards are mine. The prisoners are really prisoners, though."

Aravind came striding up, looking perplexed. "What's going on?" Daki grabbed his arm, whispering to him. Turning a shocked look on Jules, Aravind took one step closer to peer at her. "It is you. Yes. Get aboard."

Jules beckoned to Nico. "Bring them up."

As the prisoners and fake guards came aboard, Jules smiled at Aravind. "When are you leaving port?"

"I was planning to do that tomorrow on the evening tide," Aravind said. "We were waiting on one more shipment. But I think maybe we should take tonight's tide out."

"Yeah, I think so, too."

Jules stood aside, trying not to be recognized by anyone else, as the last of the prisoners came up the plank and Daki told the grumbling sailors of the *Prosper* that they'd be getting underway right now instead of enjoying one more night in the taverns of Landfall.

Artem came up to her with a grin, rendering a passable salute. "At your service, Captain. All of us from the *Evening Star*. You gave us life and freedom when we thought both were lost forever."

"We're not out of Landfall yet," Jules told him, watching nervously as the *Prosper*'s crew started taking in lines and going up into the rigging to unfurl the sails. "Where are the prisoners?"

"Daki told us to take them below so they'd be out of the way," Artem said. "Nico and the rest of ours are still watching them. They're going to have a big surprise before long, eh?"

"Yes, they are," Jules said, smiling.

The smile faded as she looked toward the head of the pier. More legionaries had come into view. Probably just a shift change, but still worrisome.

Captain Aravind had noticed as well. "Move it! Take in all lines and the boarding plank!"

The last lines came off the pier, a couple of sailors scrambling aboard just before the plank was pulled in. Sails unfurled and spars were shifted, catching the breeze beginning to come from the land as the sun sank behind the clouds.

The *Prosper* swung out into the harbor.

Jules watched the legionaries at the head of the pier look toward the *Prosper*, but none of them moved as the ship drew away from the pier. Lights were springing to life around the harbor as night fell and lanterns were lit ashore and on ships, and the big beacon on the harbor's headland flamed to life to guide ships.

On the best pier in the harbor, she saw bright, steady lights flare against the darkness. Two of the Mechanic metal ships. The Mechanics only had four of those monster ships. Why were two here? Did it have anything to do with her?

It wasn't until the *Prosper* cleared the harbor that Jules finally felt herself relaxing. She walked up the ladder to the quarterdeck, nodding to Captain Aravind as she finally pulled off the leather helm and ran her hand through her hair. "Where are we bound, Captain?"

Aravind shrugged. "I thought you'd tell me. Officially, Imperial records show we're supposed to be headed for Sandurin, but I was planning to go to Dor's."

"I'd love to go to Dor's," Jules said. "Thank you."

"No need to thank me. You owe this to a certain pirate who instead of taking my last copper coin instead gave me and this ship a new chance." Aravind looked her over. "No disrespect intended, but you look like you've been dragged under the keel a few times."

"I feel like I've done just that," Jules said.

"My cabin is yours. Get some sleep. I'll have some food sent in."

"Thanks. My companions, the ones wearing guard outfits like this. They're mostly pirates, off the *Evening Star*. They're taking orders from me."

"All right. We'll see them fed, too. And the prisoners?"

"They're real prisoners," Jules said. "Tomorrow they'll find out their fates have changed for the better."

Afterwards, she vaguely recalled making it down the ladder and into the cabin before passing out.

* * *

She woke to a day that seemed far along. Food was set on the table, so she ate and drank, grateful for the reassuring feel of the ship as it rolled across the waves.

Stripping off the prisoner guard clothing with a sigh of relief, Jules got her own clothes out of the bag she'd been carrying since the wagon was burned. Her clothes weren't exactly in great shape after her confinement on the *Hawk's Mantle*, the battle that destroyed that ship, her escape and subsequent travels from and back to Landfall, but they were hers.

She paused before dressing, looking at the strange fern-like scar running down one side of her body, her legacy from a Mage lightning bolt that hadn't killed her, and thinking it was lucky that scar didn't extend to her face. That was something even a passing glance would have spotted.

Walking out on deck, Jules felt her heart leap as she breathed the salt air.

"Good, um, afternoon, Captain," First Officer Daki said, nodding to her.

"I slept that long? What are we doing?" Jules asked, squinting up at the sails. She saw the other members of *Prosper's* crew eyeing her with awe or respect, the first of which bothered her but the second of which felt good.

"Tacking west toward Dor's." Daki pointed to the ladder below decks. "Can we get them out of their chains now? It's been hard to see it."

"Yes, let's do that," Jules said.

The pirates she'd brought aboard had only their prisoner guard outfits to wear as they came on deck, smiling and waving at Jules. "At your service, Captain Jules," Artem said. "I was told it was all right to say that now."

"When did you figure it out?" Jules asked.

"On the road. It was Mad recognized you first, and when she spoke to me I saw it. And it all made sense. Who else could've got us out of there but the woman who fought a Mage dragon and has killed Mages?"

"You got yourselves out of there," Jules said. "I just helped. Are the prisoners free?"

"Not yet. Mad's bringing them up. We figured it was better to take their chains off on deck where no one could get too excited and cause trouble, you know?"

The thirty prisoners were brought up the ladder, looking beaten down and forlorn. They sat still as their chains were unlocked, looking about as if fearing a trick.

When all were free, Captain Aravind stood before them. "I'm the captain of this ship. You are no longer prisoners, though you will be required to follow my orders as long as you're aboard this ship. We're on our way to Dor's, a western settlement, where you'll be set ashore, and where you'll all be free to live your lives."

"You can't do that," one of the prisoners said, his voice quavering. "Don't lie to us. Only the Emperor can pardon us."

"The Emperor doesn't rule here," Jules said. All eyes went to her. "You're free because the west is free. It'll stay free if we all fight to keep it that way."

"Who are you to say such things?"

Artem laughed. "Don't you know her? That's Jules, you clods! Captain Jules of Landfall. The woman of the prophecy. She's the empress of the sea, she is! Not all the Emperor's horses and legions and ships, nor all the Mages in the world, can keep her in chains. And someday a daughter of her line will free this world of the Great Guilds forever!"

Jules saw hope come into the eyes of the prisoners, hope and unlooked-for joy in faces that had expected nothing but suffering, and she thought that maybe it made all of her fear and struggles worth it. Because no one had ever come for her when she was an orphan, but she could come for people like this, and give them hope and freedom.

But two of the former prisoners stared at her with rigid faces.

Jules walked over to them, past men and women babbling with joy to each other while the sailors of the *Prosper* looked on and grinned.

"I didn't kill Colonel Dar'n," Jules told Ian's mother and sister. "He sacrificed himself so the Emperor wouldn't fault him for the loss of Western Port."

Ian's sister glared at her. "Lies. To think our family has been brought down by a gutter rat like you."

"You're free," Jules said, shrugging off the insult despite an urge to slap the young woman. "You can make any life you want outside of the Empire. I don't expect you to thank me. I owed it to Ian to free you if I could."

"When Ian finds you again—!"

"He's alive?" Fears that had been riding her since the Mage attack on the Imperial sloop suddenly shattered, leaving relief and happiness in their wake. The intensity of her feelings surprised her, but she put that down to the stress of recent events still weighing on her.

Ian's sister got the look of someone who'd inadvertently revealed something important and wished she could take it back. "No! He's... his ghost. I meant when his ghost finds you."

Jules smiled slightly, relieved at the news even while aggravated at Ian's sister. "You're worse at lying than Ian is."

Whatever else might have been said was interrupted by a hail from the lookout high on the maintop. "Sail three points off the starboard bow! Looks to be heading for us!"

Jules looked in that direction. With the winds as they were, the other ship had the weather gage and could run down the *Prosper*. If it was an Imperial warship, a fight was inevitable.

As if sensing her thoughts, Ian's mother smiled. "You haven't escaped the hand of the Emperor. Whatever happens to us, we'll still have the satisfaction of seeing you hauled back to the Emperor in chains."

CHAPTER FIVE

J ules started to head for the shrouds and ratlines to climb up to
the maintop, but paused to look at Ian's mother. "The last time
the Empire tried that, they lost a warship. Stay out of my way. Try
anything to harm this ship and you'll be the worse for it."

"You can't give us orders," Ian's sister snarled. "Fatherless, mother-
less—"

"Shut up." The ice in Jules' voice stopped the flow of insults and fear
came into the girl's eyes. Jules couldn't help herself. "Ian was adopted,
wasn't he? There's no way the blood of your family runs in him."

She left without waiting for a response, but swung by where Nico
was standing gazing past the starboard bow. "Those two," she said, indicating Ian's mother and sister. "They need to be chained again before
we encounter that ship. They'll betray us if it's an Imperial ship of war."

"I'll take care of it," Nico said, grateful to have something to do
since he knew as little of sailing as the pirates had known of horses.

Jules hoisted herself into the rigging, climbing rapidly until she
reached the maintop. The sailor there was one she vaguely recalled
from when the *Sun Queen* had first encountered the *Prosper*. "Over
there," the sailor said, pointing.

Narrowing her eyes and shading them with a flat hand, Jules gazed
at the masts and sails coming into view over the horizon. "That's not
a war galley."

"No. Maybe a sloop, though."

"Maybe."

"Can you tell what he is?" Captain Aravind called up from the quarterdeck.

"Not yet," Jules called back. She raised herself a little more, trying to spot any more details on the oncoming ship. "He's seen us for certain. He is coming for us." The *Prosper* rolled over the top of a swell, for a moment raising the maintop a little higher. "There's a third mast. Do you see it?"

"Yes," the lockout said.

"He's not a galley or a sloop of war," Jules called down to Captain Aravind. "He's got three masts."

"That'd mean a merchant ship," the lookout said. "But the way he's coming to meet us isn't reassuring."

"Maybe a pirate," Jules agreed. Would she be able to identify the *Sun Queen* from this distance? But something didn't feel quite right, making her think that ship wasn't the *Queen*. "Artem! Come up here!"

He scrambled up the rigging, coming up onto the now-crowded maintop. "Aye, Captain?"

"Can you tell who that is?" Jules asked, pointing toward the other ship. With the *Prosper* still holding her course, the two ships were closing fairly quickly.

Artem raised himself up, staring toward the other ship for a long moment. "I think it's the *Bright Morning*," he finally said. "See that missing yard on the foremast? That was the *Bright Morning* last I saw her."

"The *Bright Morning*?" Jules felt her expression hardening. "That ship has a bad reputation."

"Aye," Artem agreed. "There are pirates, and then there are pirates. Last I saw of the *Bright Morning* she was running off, leaving us alone to fight that Imperial warship. If the *Morning* had stuck by us we might've had a chance, but they ran."

"Tora's the captain of the *Bright Morning*, right?"

"Aye. He and Captain Orin talked the morning before the Imperial warship showed up. Like Mad said after that, Tora looked like a fine enough man until he opened his mouth and spoiled it."

Jules nodded. "Let's go down. Get our people in their armor, swords at ready."

She and Artem went back down the rigging to the deck, Jules heading for the quarterdeck and Artem to gather the pirates from the *Evening Star*.

"He's a pirate ship," Jules said. "The *Bright Morning*."

Aravind looked relieved. "He'll leave us alone, then, once he knows we're your ship."

"Not necessarily," Jules said. "Captain Tora of the *Bright Morning* has a bad reputation. If he doesn't know I'm aboard, he might ignore your claim to be working with me."

"Then why not tell him you're aboard?"

"Because he might want to collect that Imperial reward for me, and kill any witnesses to his treachery," Jules said. "I'll only expose myself if he doesn't accept your warn-off. We can handle him if he tries anything. We've got ten pirates with leather armor and swords to help defend this ship, plus your crew, and any of the freed prisoners who want to fight to ensure they don't get sold back to the Imperials by the *Bright Morning*."

Aravind gazed unhappily toward the approaching ship, whose sails were now visible from the quarterdeck. "I don't favor fighting, but it seems we'll have no choice if he won't be warned off. And we also have you. If anything will stiffen the spines of our defenders, it's having you lead them."

"You're captain of the *Prosper*," Jules said.

"And I thank you for deferring to me in that," Aravind said. "But when it comes to fighting pirates, you should be calling the shots, I think."

Jules grinned. "Let's try to do this the easy way. But if he wants a fight, he'll find himself in trouble."

By the time the *Bright Morning* came about to match the course of the *Prosper*, Jules had her defenders ready but still hidden. Once settled on the same tack, the other ship veered close. The pirates on the *Bright Morning* crowded the railing facing the *Prosper*, waving their weapons to intimidate the crew of the other ship. "Heave to for boarding!" Captain Tora yelled across the gap between the ships. Tora wasn't a large man, and perhaps to compensate for that he wore an outsized hat adorned with feathers that fluttered in the wind.

Captain Aravind called a reply from his quarterdeck. "This is the *Prosper*, a ship working for Captain Jules of the *Sun Queen*. Our cargo and profits are shared with the *Sun Queen*."

Tora didn't hesitate in his response. "Jules is either dead or in the Emperor's bed! Even if she was here, she doesn't give us orders! We'll take our share of your cargo! If you fight, it'll be the worse for you and your crew!"

She'd been standing on deck, but now Jules climbed up onto the rail facing the *Bright Morning*. Tora hadn't left her any choice. "Jules is here, you sorry excuse for a sailor! And I'm telling you to break off! This ship isn't yours to take from!" Jules had to admit to feeling some satisfaction at seeing the reaction of the *Bright Morning*'s crew to her appearance.

Captain Tora was obviously surprised as well. Instead of another quick reply, Jules saw him talking to a woman who was probably the *Bright Morning*'s first officer.

Finally, Tora called back to her in a voice whose friendliness was too exaggerated to feel sincere. "Jules! It's wonderful to see you well! I've been wanting to meet with you. Will you let my ship come alongside so we can speak and share a drink?"

"He's lying," Artem said. "He means to come alongside and attack us by surprise. He's done that more than once to other ships."

"I've heard," Jules said. "He's one of those captains who thinks no one's going to expect him to do the same thing he's always done. Daki, Artem, line up our armed pirates beneath the rail here, the other armed sailors beside and right behind them. Keep them all low. Then line up as many of the former prisoners as we can behind them, where they'll look like more ranks of armed defenders. When I give the word, I want them all to stand up."

She waited as those on the *Prosper* followed her directions. The crew of the *Bright Morning* would notice some of the preparations, but not all of them, and wouldn't expect nearly that many defenders on the *Prosper*.

When all was ready, Jules called over the gap between the ships. "All right. Come alongside for a meeting."

As the *Bright Morning* put her helm over and slid across the gap to come alongside the *Prosper*, Jules raised the short sword she'd taken off a dead prisoner guard. "On your feet and look ready to fight!" she called to those on deck.

The pirates from the *Evening Star*, the crew of the *Prosper*, and most of the freed prisoners stood up. In the center of the defenders stood the pirates and Nico wearing the armor of prisoner guards. The great majority of the freed prisoners in the back had no weapons except marlinspikes, but that couldn't be seen from the *Bright Morning*. What they could see was that the size of the defending force easily exceeded the number of pirates on the deck of the *Bright Morning*.

Grapnels were already coming across, hurled by the crew of the *Bright Morning*, but as the two ships came together with a thump Tora's sailors hesitated, already thrown off by seeing Jules herself facing them, poised to charge but frozen by the sudden appearance of so many opponents.

"What's the matter?" Jules called to Captain Tora, who on his own quarterdeck was only a few lances from where she stood on the railing of the *Prosper*. The two ships were locked together by the grapnels. "Aren't you coming over?"

"I didn't expect betrayal!" Tora called back.

"Betrayal? None of my crew have left the deck of this ship. But if you want to talk betrayal, let's speak of the *Evening Star*." Jules was close enough to see the ripple of unease among Tora's crew at that ship's name. "You left them, didn't you? You left them to die on Imperial swords and swinging from Imperial nooses. But such acts have a way of coming back on those who commit them. Raise your swords, sailors of the *Evening Star*! Show these brave pirates where you stand."

Artem, Mad, and the others raised their swords.

"Have you nothing to say to them, Captain Tora?" Jules called. The more she thought of the *Bright Morning* sailing away and leaving the *Evening Star* to its fate, the angrier she got. She'd had to hold a lot in over the last few weeks. And every time she thought of Imperial officials and Mechanics and Mages mistreating anyone they wanted because no one could stop them, the heat inside of her grew worse. Maybe it was time to let it out. "Your reputation comes before you, and it fills the air with a foul smell. You're a coward, a cheat, and a liar, not fit to command a boat hauling garbage from the cheapest tavern in Beldan."

That was as close as anyone could come to calling out someone else. And she'd done it in front of Tora's crew, the insults heard by all of them.

Tora's face formed a mask of rage. "Brave words from someone hiding behind a big crew!"

"Clear a space and I'll say it within sword's reach of you," Jules yelled back. "Or do you fear to face me? Will you run away again as you did when Captain Orin and his crew had need of you? How many have you stabbed in the back, you spineless worm?"

Tora's hands were gripping the railing of his quarterdeck so hard that Jules wondered they didn't splinter the wood. He said nothing, his mouth working but no words coming out.

Jules noticed someone climbing up beside her on the rail of the *Prosper*. It was Artem, glaring at Tora.

"Captain Orin was a good man, who died because you ran," Artem said. "I lost a lot of shipmates because you ran. Maybe you fear to fight Captain Jules because she has a destiny that arms her, but I'm just a common sailor. Nobody special to anyone but my friends, many of which are dead! Face me, Captain Tora! I demand you face me to pay for your betrayal."

Jules glanced at Artem. "He might be a good fighter, and he'll be desperate. Are you sure you want this?"

"Aye, Captain, I do want this." Artem's mouth tightened. "I owe it to my friends who died."

"What do you say?" Jules called back to Tora. "Face this sailor. Or face me."

For the first time, one of the other pirates on the *Bright Morning* spoke up. "If our captain fights that man and wins, will you call it a fair ending?"

"Aye!" Artem shouted before Jules could reply.

The pirates on the *Bright Morning* were looking at their captain now. "Our ship and our captain have been insulted," the same pirate said. "Will you take a stand?"

"Their words mean nothing," Tora shouted. "I laugh at their slurs."

"You won't defend the ship's honor?" another pirate of the *Bright Morning* yelled. "I didn't like leaving the *Evening Star* that way! A lot of us didn't. And now you won't even stand up for us?"

"He's nothing!" Tora cried. "Just a worthless deck—" Too late, he realized that he was insulting his own crew with his words.

"Clear a space," a pirate on the *Bright Morning* ordered the others. They moved away from the railing, leaving an open semicircle over two lances across, the edges lined with pirates. "You'll face this man from the *Evening Star* or we'll put you across and let them do with you as you will."

"You can't give such orders!" Tora yelled.

"I call for a vote! Sailors of the *Bright Morning*, shall Captain Tora face this sailor from the *Evening Star* in a fair fight, or else give up command and leave the ship he has shamed?"

"Aye," many voices said.

Artem jumped down onto the deck of the Bright Morning. He pulled off the leather helm of a prisoner guard, then sheathed his short sword and removed the leather chest armor as well. "A fair fight," he said. "I've only ever fought with a cutlass, though."

A pirate from the *Bright Morning* stepped forward, offering a cutlass to Artem, who nodded and took it before facing Tora. "Come on, then."

Tora, with the look of a cornered rat, pulled a cutlass from the rack on the front of the quarterdeck, then after hesitating yanked a second one free with his other hand. Ignoring the murmurs of disapproval from his crew, he came down the ladder to the main deck, his crew opening a lane into the semi-circle cleared for the fight. For a moment Jules lost sight of Tora as he was surrounded by his crew, his over-sized hat gliding along as if moving on its own until Tora stepped out into the cleared area.

"Is it to the death?" another sailor on the *Bright Morning* asked, her voice easy to hear in the silence that had enveloped both ships. Only the wind in the sails and the rush of water alongside the two ships and the creaking of their hulls as they touched could be heard in the quiet after the question.

Artem finally answered. "To the death, or he yields his weapons and admits to his cowardice."

"To the death," Tora said, his face a rigid mask. Even before the last word had finished coming his mouth, Tora hurled himself at Artem, both cutlasses slashing.

Using his cutlass to fend off Tora's attacks, Artem fell back fast until he hit the edge of the cleared area. Unable to step back any further, he leaped to the side, swinging a cut at Tora.

Tora tried to fend off the blow with one cutlass while slashing with the cutlass in his other hand and pivoting to keep facing Artem. An expert might have managed all of those moves at once, but Tora lost his balance, falling sideways, his big hat falling off and making him seem much smaller without it.

Before he could get up, Artem planted a foot on one of Tora's cutlasses, pinning it to the deck. As Artem stabbed at him, Tora let go of his second weapon, rolling away until he hit the rail and scrambling to his feet. He barely made it before Artem caught up and swung at him again. Pressed back against the rail, crowded by Artem, Tora swung back his remaining cutlass for an overhand blow. But his blade caught in the shrouds behind and above him, snagging for a critical moment.

Artem's cutlass went completely through Tora, nailing him to the railing.

Pulling back the cutlass, Artem let Tora fall. He didn't look happy or triumphant. "I can't bring back the others, but I've avenged them."

The *Bright Morning's* healer ran forward, kneeling beside Tora and shaking her head. "Bring me a bottle." She popped the cork, offering rum to Tora. "Anything I do will keep you alive only a little longer and in pain the whole time. Drink as much as you can to make it easier."

Tora's eyes searched about, finally resting on Jules where she still stood atop the rail of the *Prosper*. "See you die as well when the time comes. I'll be waiting," he said, his voice thin and high with pain.

"You'll have a long wait," Jules said. "And if I were you, I'd be more worried about who's been waiting for *you*."

Tora didn't answer, shuddering as rum spilled from his mouth, his eyes closing.

The pirate who'd called the vote on the *Bright Morning* stepped forward. "Captain Jules, we need to elect a new captain. Is it done between us this day?"

"It's done between us," Jules said. "I wish you fair seas."

"Fair seas to you as well. It's said that you always play straight. You saved those sailors from the *Evening Star*?"

"She did," Artem said as he prepared to climb back aboard the *Prosper*. "Killed five guards, set us free, and got us through Landfall and every Mage, Mechanic, and servant of the Emperor who tried to stop her."

"Then we owe you thanks for doing what we did not," the pirate said to Jules. "Is it true about the lands to the west?"

"It's true," Jules said. "Free lands. The Emperor's hand will never fall on them."

"Who will stop him?" the pirate asked. "The Great Guilds?"

"No," Jules said. "I will. With the help of free men and women like those on these two ships. If I ever call for help, I hope you'll come."

The pirates of the *Bright Morning* exchanged glances. None said yes, but none said they wouldn't, and she couldn't ask for more than that.

"Have you seen the *Sun Queen*?" Jules asked.

"She was in Caer Lyn," one pirate answered. "But left before we did, and wouldn't say where they were bound."

The ships finally separated, Jules watching the *Bright Morning* veer off to the northeast.

Captain Aravind nodded to Jules as she came down off the railing. "They might tell the Imperials where they saw you."

"I don't think so," Jules said. "But if they do it'll give me their measure."

She saw Mad walk up to Artem and punch his chest. "You're lousy with a sword, as always," the female pirate told Artem. "Lucky for you that scum was worse."

"I love you, too, Mad." Artem turned to Jules. "Thank you for letting me take that stand," he said.

"It was yours to take," Jules said. "What are your plans now?"

Artem and Mad looked at each other, then back at Jules. "We haven't got a ship any more, but we've got a captain," Mad said. "Wherever you go, Captain, we'll be there."

"Like those guards the Emperor has," Artem said. "The Eternals. We could be them to you."

"The Guards," Mad said, gesturing to her prisoner guard outfit. "I mean, something better to wear than this, but that'd be a good name."

"Don't be ridiculous," Jules said.

"Hey, Nico," Artem called. "Do you want to serve the captain from now on?"

"Can we do that?" Nico came up, grinning. "I was wondering what to do with myself. I've never been happier than since she almost killed me."

"I don't need a little army following me around," Jules said. "And there's the Mages. Have you louts forgotten the Mages?"

"I've faced Mages," Mad said. "Once. It wasn't so bad."

Jules looked them over, reluctant, but thinking how useful such a group might be in the future. She'd gotten used to having people like Ang and Liv at her back. Being alone in the cell of the *Hawk's Mantle*, and while fleeing afterwards, had been rough. Looking back, she realized how much easier things had felt once there were others with her. And the former pirates of the *Evening Star* had every reason to be loyal to her. "We'll talk later. It'll take us a while to get to Dor's. None of you are committed to anything until we get there."

* * *

They sighted other ships occasionally as the *Prosper* continued on toward Dor's over the next several days, but to Jules' disappointment none were the *Sun Queen*. The other ships did serve as an indication of how quickly trade was growing between the established cities of the Empire and the new settlements in the west, despite such trade being forbidden by Imperial law and decree. Like the metal smith Jules had overheard, artisans in the Empire needed new markets for their goods.

"It's odd," First Officer Daki said as they passed another merchant ship on its way back to Imperial waters. He and Jules were standing on deck watching the other ship sail past. The sun was setting at the end of a lovely day, the winds fresh and strong but not too strong, the sea playful but not dangerous. "For so long, everything was the same. And then things started happening. Why do you suppose the Great Guilds allowed that?"

"I'm not sure the Great Guilds could stop it at any price they were prepared to pay," Jules said. "From what I've heard Mechanics say, they don't know what to do, so they're trying to control what they can't stop."

"I never heard of Mechanics admitting they can't do something," Daki said.

"They didn't say it to me," Jules said. "They talk in front of commons like you and me as if we're not there."

"So they're just letting things change?"

"For now," Jules said. "I think they're debating what to do, and so far the ones that want to avoid killing too many commons like us are winning the argument because they want to keep the Empire off-balance. At some point, they're going to realize how much stronger commons are going to become, and try to put a stop to it."

Daki gazed morosely out to sea, one hand resting on the nearest shroud line. "What happens then?"

"I try to make a deal that will work out to our best interests in the long run," Jules said. "Not that I want to make such a deal, but I don't think anyone else will be in a position to do it."

"I never knew Mechanics to do anything except it profited them," Daki said.

"Yeah. Whatever deal we get is going to cost us," Jules said.

Daki made a face. "I've thought sometimes about being a captain, and always decided that I wouldn't want it."

"You could do it," Jules said.

"Maybe I could, but I don't want that. Having to make those decisions. I've worked hard to get where I am, and I'm happy as a first officer. I wouldn't want to face what you have to do. Deciding deals like that. I'm glad someone is doing it, but I'm glad it's not me."

Jules shook her head, frowning, her eyes on the dwindling shape of the passing ship. "You have to step up. Everyone has to. You have a voice in what happens. We don't need another Empire on this world. We need free lands."

"I like the sound of that," Daki said, giving her a sidelong look, "but I also like knowing we have an Empress to face off against the Emperor."

She made a rude noise, waving off his words. "If a leader is needed, and if that prophecy forces the role on me, I'll do it. But I'll never be an empress. If that's what you want, find someone else."

"There's no one else," Daki said. "No one else the common folk would look to."

Not for the first time, Jules wondered how much the prophecy itself influenced what happened in ways that made the prophecy more likely to come true. Whether that ever happened or not, there wasn't any doubt that her own efforts had barely kept her free and alive. It'd be nice to think that some unseen force was protecting and guiding her, but if so that force had a tendency to cut things mighty fine. Better that she assume it was all up to her, no matter what others thought.

* * *

The sky and the wind promised stormy weather as the *Prosper* reached Dor's, standing in to port with a brisk wind at her back. Jules stood on the quarterdeck, off to one side to give plenty of room to Captain Aravind, feeling a strange sense of dislocation. So much had happened since she'd last been on a ship here. It felt as if too little time had passed or too much had taken place.

"The *Storm Rider*'s in port!" the lookout called down as the *Prosper* rounded the last headland.

"That's good," Captain Aravind called to Jules.

"Yes," Jules said, trying not to look disappointed. If only it had been the *Sun Queen* waiting here for them.

* * *

"Blazes!" Captain Erin of the *Storm Rider* said, staring at Jules as if she were a ghost. "How?"

Jules and Dor were already in the small, private room at the back of the tavern. , Erin standing in the doorway. Jules, seated with a mug of wine before her, smiled. "My enemies managed to foul each other's course," she said. "The Mages kept trying to kill me, the Imperials to capture me, and I slipped away while they were fighting over who'd have me."

Erin shook her head, closing the door and taking another chair. "And how's his highness the Emperor doing in his palace in Marandur?"

"Since I declined his invitation to visit, I really couldn't say," Jules said before taking a drink.

"Are you sure you're not really that Mara person? What was it, the unkillable?"

"Undying," Jules said. "Mara the Undying. And no, that's not me. I doubt the Emperor would want me in his bed if I was."

Erin nodded, waiting as Dor poured her a drink. She took a long draw, sighing afterwards. "Who was that lot who came off your ship, Jules? They didn't look like the usual escapees from the Empire."

"Former prisoners," Jules said. "They were on their way to Umbu-ran."

"Didn't pay for their passage, then, eh?" Erin shrugged. "Are they going to be trouble?"

Dor shook his head. "None of them were violent felons. All sentenced for crimes like poverty, petty theft, and the like. It's funny how people who are starving end up stealing food, isn't it?"

"I can understand their motivation," Erin said. She glanced at Dor. "So, Jules, has he told you?"

Jules shook her head. "Only that there was something important that had to wait until you got here."

"There's an Imperial sloop of war off the coast."

"This far west? It must be looking for me."

"No," Dor said. "They stopped in a few days ago and informed us that the Emperor was pleased with our progress, but we were behind in our taxes."

Jules sat down her mug, staring at Dor. "They made a claim to this place?"

"They did."

"After what happened at Western Port," Erin added, "the Empire must've decided to try grabbing an already established town."

"I didn't see any legionaries," Jules said.

"There are none here," Dor said. "But the sloop is supposed to return in a couple of days for the demanded taxes or tribute, as well as our oaths of fealty." He spat into the corner. "They wanted to give us a few days to realize we couldn't fight."

"I take it the *Storm Rider* wasn't in port," Jules said.

"Nah," Erin said. "We came in the day after they left."

"What are they thinking?" Jules said. "The Mechanics have made it clear that they won't accept the Empire expanding control to the west. They don't want the Emperor gaining any more power."

"I don't see any Mechanics about," Erin said.

Jules frowned, remembering something. "There were two of the Mechanic ships in Landfall. And the Mechanics we saw seemed to be... tense. Arguing. Maybe the Mechanics are engaged in some kind of debate that has their attention, and the Empire picked up on that and decided to make a move."

Dor sighed. "So there's no hope for us there. At least no Mages have wandered by since your last visit."

"What were you planning?" Jules asked him.

"That's the question." He looked toward one wall of the room as if seeing beyond it. "We're not ready to fight. Not if legionaries show up."

"You said it was just one sloop."

"Yes, but..."

Erin turned a speculative look on Jules. "Not a lot of people have fought the Empire. The idea scares them. Before I showed up, everyone here was getting ready to cave. What're you thinking?"

"I'm thinking we should kick that sloop in the teeth," Jules said. "Tell the Emperor's servants they're not welcome here, and they'd better not come back."

"The wall isn't done," Dor insisted.

"The wall won't do you any good if you're not ready to fight," Jules said. "Erin and I have beaten legionaries. We captured Western Port."

"You had two of those Mechanic weapons," Dor said. "What do you have now? One pirate ship."

"And the *Prosper*," Jules said. "She's a merchant ship with a regular crew, but there are... extra people aboard." She felt embarrassed to say any more.

But Erin pressed her. "Extra people?"

"My, um, guards," Jules said, taking a drink to cover her discomfort at discussing it. "Eleven."

"Guards?"

"They have leather armor, and short swords."

"Do tell." Erin raised her eyebrows.

"They're from the *Evening Star*," Jules said. "The ship was captured by the Imperials and most of the crew killed. Ten were captured and were being taken to Marandur."

Erin took another drink. "And, what, you just decided to pick them up and bring them along when you escaped the Emperor's hospitality?" She paused. "You said eleven, and then ten."

"The eleventh was one of the prisoner guards. He, um, chose our side. The point is," Jules said, trying to change the subject a bit, "we have eleven extra swords. And there are probably other people in this town ready and able to fight. We bring them aboard *Prosper* as well. That gives us two ships able to fight if that sloop tries to force its way into the harbor."

"Can't a sloop outsail either the *Prosper* or the *Storm Rider*?" Dor asked.

Erin nodded, adding, "But that won't matter if the sloop tries to enter the harbor. He'll have to stick to the channel, so he couldn't dodge us when we tried to close. He'll know that, and see the odds against him."

Dor rested his chin on one hand, thinking. "Is this my castle or isn't it?" he finally said.

"Does that mean we're going to meet that sloop and tell him to gaff off?" Erin said.

"I can't demand it of you, but I ask that you use your ships to defend Dor's Castle," he said.

"I'm getting used to being free," Erin said. "I'm willing to fight for it."

"Me, too," Jules said. "Dor, find us some volunteers, and some weapons for them to use."

"We've got a lot of crossbows for hunting," Dor said.

"Good. Let's start defending what we're building out here."

* * *

It seemed very unlikely the Imperial sloop would try entering the harbor at night, but just in case a lookout was posted on the edge of the harbor along with the materials to start a warning fire if needed.

But the sun rose with no sign of Imperial sail on the horizon. It wasn't until Jules was finishing breakfast on the *Prosper* with Captain Aravind when First Officer Daki stuck his head into the captain's cabin. "The lookout is flashing signals."

Going out on deck, Jules shaded her eyes to see the bright flashes on the edge of the harbor where the lookout was using a mirror to reflect the light of the rising sun. "Looks like we didn't have to wait long."

Captain Aravind nodded. "Take good care of my ship, please."

"You'll be aboard, won't you?" Jules asked, looking at him in surprise.

"Yes. But in a fight, you'll be giving the orders. I'll help with the helm."

"Thank you, Captain Aravind. Artem! Get the volunteers! We need them aboard." She called across the pier. "Ahoy the *Storm Rider*! We'll be ready to sail when we get our extra fighters aboard."

"We'll be taking in lines pretty quick," Captain Erin yelled back. "See you just outside the harbor!"

Jules waited impatiently for Artem to return with the group of volunteers from Dor's town, or Dor's Castle as he now called it. Over thirty had stepped forward when asked, twenty of them hunters with crossbows, the others armed with an assortment of swords and axes. They'd slept ashore due to lack of space on the *Prosper*, but came jogging down the pier in Artem's wake without any signs of misgiving or second thoughts.

Jules watched them come, hoping all of them would make it safely back home.

The *Storm Rider* got underway, her sails filling with a brisk morning breeze, as the volunteers were boarding the *Prosper*. By the time Captain Aravind ordered the last lines let go and the *Prosper* also swung away from the pier, the *Storm Rider* was halfway across the harbor.

"The ship is yours, Captain Jules," Aravind said.

"Thank you," Jules said. "If we're lucky, the Imperials are trying a bluff and will shear off when they see we're willing to fight."

"Sloop in sight just off the port bow!" the lookout in the maintop shouted. "He's standing in toward us!"

Prosper came out of the harbor with nearly every sail set, her bow bursting through a swell with a spray of white foam, momentary rainbows appearing in the mist before it blew away in the wind. *Storm Rider* was already sailing east along the coast, so Jules brought *Prosper* over to head east as well, trimming sail when they got close to *Storm Rider*. "We want to make it obvious to that sloop that we're sailing together," she said to Aravind.

By now the sloop's sails were in sight from the quarterdeck. Jules walked to the front rail, calling to the volunteers. "Arm yourselves! He's still coming in toward the harbor."

"Your guards are ready, Captain!" Artem cried. He, Mad, Nico, and the other eight guards were already in their leather armor, swords at their sides. Jules had to admit they looked impressive on the deck of the *Prosper*.

"*Storm Rider* is coming about," Daki called.

"Bring us about, matching course with *Storm Rider*," Jules ordered.

The helm spun, *Prosper* swinging to port as *Storm Rider* sailed past on that side, sailors hastening to shift the sails to catch the wind on the new tack.

Captain Erin had timed her maneuver well. The sloop's hull appeared over the horizon as the *Prosper* and the *Storm Rider* sailed back toward the entrance to the harbor. If all three ships held to their current courses and speeds, they'd meet up in the tight waters at the harbor entrance, where the sloop's superior ability to turn would be of no use.

The sloop didn't seem to be impressed, continuing on steadily. He was well off the starboard bow of both the *Prosper* and the *Storm Rider*, growing in size as the distance between the three ships decreased, but holding the same relative position. "If he has any bearing drift at all," Captain Aravind said, "it's very small. It looks like he'll collide with us if no one changes course."

"It looks like that," Jules agreed. "On deck! Line the starboard rail and wave your weapons where those servants of the Emperor can see! Let them know what they're going to face if they keep on!"

Forward of *Prosper*, Jules saw *Storm Rider* doing the same, the pirates aboard her lined up along the starboard rail brandishing cutlasses. Some of the crew were up in the rigging though. "*Storm Rider's* taking in some sail," Jules said. "Captain Erin's going to reduce speed enough for the gap between our two ships to lessen."

"Could the sloop have been thinking of trying to slip between our bow and *Storm Rider's* stern?" Aravind asked.

"Possibly," Jules said.

"He's not fast enough. If he keeps on, we'll collide."

"Stand by!" Jules shouted to the crew on deck. "Ready your weapons!"

A line of swords stood ready at the rail, behind them a line of crossbows that had been tensioned and loaded with bolts.

It felt a little odd to be going into a fight without a revolver. Jules didn't feel happy about that. She shouldn't have become dependent on having a Mechanic weapon to feel confident.

Aravind didn't seem confident at all. "If he doesn't turn soon-"

Just then Jules saw the helm on the Imperial sloop of war being spun, the sloop's bowsprit swinging to starboard.

The sloop steadied out on a course matching that of the *Storm Rider* and the *Prosper*, only about twenty lances away, close enough for Jules to make out details on the Imperial ship. The dark red uniforms of the officers, the armor of the legionaries aboard, the ballista mounted amidships, loaded and pointed to port, toward the *Prosper*, the ballista crew standing ready at their stations.

The captain of the sloop was a tall, thin man who yelled across the gap between the sloop and the other two ships in a surprisingly robust voice. "You are hindering the work of the Emperor's servants. Both of your ships are to proceed into port, tie up, and await inspection."

Captain Erin called a reply. "Say again all after *you are*."

"You are hindering the work of the Emperor's servants! Both of your ships are to proceed into port, tie up, and await inspection!"

"No, still didn't get it," Erin cried. "Your ship is not authorized to enter this port. Stand off and leave the waters of the independent town of Dor's Castle."

Jules saw the captain conferring with his officers, doubtless trying to find out what "independent" meant. She wouldn't have known, wouldn't have been able to tell pirates like Erin about the word, if the Mechanics hadn't told her. Before now, there hadn't been any need for the word "independent" on the world of Dematr.

But that would never be true again.

"Why aren't you also warning him off?" Aravind asked Jules.

"Because if he knows I'm here he might attack immediately to try to get me," Jules said. "We want him to go away."

"This is your final warning!" the captain of the Imperial sloop shouted. "If you do not follow my orders I will take your ships and hang the captains of both for treason against the Emperor."

"He doesn't really think we'll fight, does he?" Captain Aravind said.

Erin must have decided the same thing. "We freed the town of Western Port from Imperial rule, defeating the legionaries in the garrison. We'll defeat you as well if we must. Break off and go back to Imperial waters!"

"All waters are Imperial waters!" the sloop's captain cried.

Jules saw orders being called on the sloop, and the ballista being swung to target the *Storm Rider*. "It's a fight they want," she said. "Helm! Come hard to starboard! On deck! Ready your weapons!"

CHAPTER SIX

The *Prosper* yawed to starboard, suddenly closing the distance to the sloop.

The sloop, wanting to avoid coming to grips with either of the two ships, had to also swing hard to starboard, turning more quickly than the fairly ponderous *Prosper* could. The quick turn threw off the aim of the ballista, the crew of the weapon trying to pivot it around to bear on the *Storm Rider*.

Knowing her chance at coming alongside the sloop was gone, Jules kept the *Prosper* turning all the way around and onto a new tack angling southwest. The maneuver cost a lot of speed, but left the sloop charging north, opening the distance beyond effective range of the ballista.

Erin had adjusted the course of the *Storm Rider* only slightly, angling a little north of west.

"Where's she going?" Aravind asked Jules.

"She's getting into position upwind of us," Jules said. "If the sloop comes after us, *Storm Rider* can come after them. If the sloop comes after *Storm Rider*, we can try to close on the sloop again."

The sloop, realizing that neither of the slower ships would be fooled into chasing it, came about again, heading for *Storm Rider*.

Storm Rider tacked, swinging to pass south of *Prosper*.

Jules brought *Prosper* a little closer to the wind, losing some speed but angling to get north of the sloop as it pursued *Storm Rider*.

The morning wore on that way, the sloop making repeated attempts to close on one of the other ships, usually the *Storm Rider*, only to be frustrated by the remaining ship positioning to put the sloop in peril. Neither *Storm Rider* nor *Prosper* could catch the sloop, but the sloop couldn't engage either of them without risking the other trapping it in a dangerous position. Occasionally the sloop's ballista tried a shot, but without any hits, though *Storm Rider* did get a hole through one of her foresails.

"The crew's getting tired," Aravind warned Jules. "We've been shifting tacks fairly often all morning. They're willing, but if they keep on at this pace they'll start making mistakes."

Jules nodded, her eyes staying on the sloop. "I noticed they're beginning to drag a bit. I can't blame them. The crew on that sloop should be getting worn out, too, but I'm not seeing it yet."

"They've got some legionaries aboard to help haul on the braces."

"Yes, but he can't afford to wear out the legionaries. Right now we're in a battle of endurance. Sooner or later he's going to have to haul off, or he's going to make a mistake."

As it turned out, neither happened. As the three ships danced around each other and the sun rose toward noon, the wind dropped, turning the dance into a crawl as the speed of every ship fell toward bare steerageway.

That allowed Jules to rest her crew, because it took much longer between maneuvers. But it also increased the danger, because the sloop could move faster with the light wind than the other two ships.

The crew and the armed fighters on deck ate a lunch of bread, cheese, and watered wine as they stood watching the sloop glide toward *Storm Rider* once more. By the time Jules could tack again, they'd finished eating and were ready to keep going.

The day might have ended that way if not for a sudden call from the lookout. "Sail in sight off the starboard quarter!"

"Someone coming from the northeast," Aravind said, gazing that way. "Another Imperial ship of war?"

"Let's hope not," Jules said. "If it is, we'll head into harbor along with *Storm Rider* and make them come in after us."

But as the other ship drew closer it became obvious it wasn't a war galley or a sloop of war. Three-masted, it was similar to the *Storm Rider* and the *Prosper*. While continuing to maneuver around the sloop, Jules had the lookout keep track of the new arrival as it drew closer. If he was a merchant ship bound for Dor's, he'd veer off once he realized there was a confrontation going outside the harbor. There wouldn't be any profit in getting involved in a fight. But if he was another pirate…

"He's tacking to stay north of us," Aravind told Jules. "Either he's going to stay out of the fight up there, or he's positioning to run down on us."

"Can we tell who he is yet?" Jules asked, her eyes staying on the distant shape of the sloop's captain to provide some warning of when he began to shout another order.

"No. Definitely not an Imperial warship, though."

"Why hasn't the sloop done anything?" Jules wondered. "He keeps trying to trap one of us. He should be worried about that third ship."

"Should he?" Aravind said. "How many times have Imperial warships been attacked by pirates?"

"We captured the *Storm Queen*," Jules said. "And the sloop at Western Port. That's it. Otherwise we've just defended ourselves. You're thinking that sloop captain is overconfident, right? He's encountered two ships willing to defy Imperial authority. He can't conceive of running into a third, even though he's this far west of the Empire."

As the middle of the afternoon approached, Jules could see the sails of the third ship to the north. She saw them swing about, and the ship begin sailing toward the three combatants on a swift beam reach.

"He's coming in!" the lookout called. "I can see crew in his decks! He's got too many for a merchant ship."

"Another pirate," Jules said, grinning.

As the third ship came in, Jules tacked *Prosper* to block the sloop from running toward the east, while Erin bore down with *Storm Rider*, turning away from the wind and gaining speed as the sloop made another attempt to close on her.

The sloop finally realized his peril, coming around to try to sprint north past the third ship. But that ship swung across the path of the sloop, forcing it to turn back east, where Jules had *Prosper* coming in. "All on deck to the port bow!" Jules shouted. "Use the grapnels!"

The *spang* of the sloop's ballista shooting sounded just before the port bow of the *Prosper* rammed into the starboard bow of the sloop. The projectile tore through the air past *Prosper's* quarterdeck as metal grapnels were thrown to lock *Prosper* and the sloop together.

Legionaries on the sloop ran forward, hacking at the lines holding the grapnels. The men and women wielding crossbows on the *Prosper* began shooting, applying the skills learned in hunting deer to hitting Imperial soldiers. Jules saw officers on the sloop gathering crew and legionaries for a charge at the *Prosper*, which she knew her defenders would have a hard time stopping.

Both *Prosper* and the sloop jolted hard enough to cause everyone on both ships to stagger as the *Storm Rider* came up against the sloop's starboard quarter near the stern.

The ballista crew, who'd been reloading to hit the *Prosper*, swung their weapon about on its mount to engage the *Storm Rider* before her crew could board the sloop.

Some legionaries were trying to force their way aboard *Prosper*, but Jules' "guards" were holding them back while the crossbows behind Artem and the others shot into the attackers.

Another jolt, this time all three ships jerking from the shock as the third ship made contact on the port bow of the sloop, throwing grapnels across.

Jules looked over the sloop's deck to the third ship, her heart leaping. "*Sun Queen!*" she shouted. "About time you got here!"

"It's Jules!" someone yelled on the *Sun Queen*. She heard her name picked up, chanted by the crews of the three ships as the crew and legionaries of the sloop retreated to form a tight shield wall around the ballista, leaving many of their number already fallen in the fights against the *Prosper* and the *Storm Rider*.

The three ships locked to the sloop were too close for the ballista to hit their decks without shooting lower than the height of the shield wall about it. But the ballista crew were swinging it about again, aiming toward *Prosper*. Jules, realizing what the Imperials would do, raced down from the quarterdeck to the crossbows. "They're going to open a gap for the ballista to shoot through! Aim toward that ballista and be ready to shoot when the shields move aside!"

The crossbows on the *Prosper* leveled, their shots pausing as each man and woman aimed where Jules had directed. Crossbows on both the *Sun Queen* and the *Storm Rider* were still shooting, but the bolts were only lodging in the legionary shields, not penetrating through to hit the legionaries.

The shield wall facing *Prosper* suddenly swung open, giving the ballista a clean shot at the deck of *Prosper*. But before it could fire the crossbows twanged, sending their bolts into the ballista crew and the backs of legionaries facing the other way. The shield wall closed again.

How to break this stalemate without hurling sailors against legionary swords?

One of the women with a crossbow pointed up. "Can some of us go up a mast? That'll let us shoot down over the shields."

"Yes," Jules said. "Brilliant idea. Captain Aravind! Some sailors to help some of these crossbows up the mainmast!"

As those with crossbows climbed the rigging, Jules went to the railing facing the sloop. "You're beaten!" she yelled at the sloop's defenders. "Surrender!"

"We'll kill all of you first!" someone yelled back from behind the shield wall. It wasn't the captain of the sloop. Jules wondered if the captain was dead or only wounded.

Crossbows released over her head, their bolts slamming into the legionaries unprotected against blows from above. Some of the legionaries tried to raise their shields to protect against the crossbows on the mast, but that opened gaps in the shield wall that crossbows on deck could fire into.

The Imperial formation fell apart, sailors dropping their weapons, legionaries forming small knots of resistance that found themselves surrounded by cutlasses. Jules saw the ship's centurion lying dead and one of the last Imperial officers fall in a fight with pirates off of Erin's *Storm Rider*. The sloop's remaining defenders didn't surrender all at once, but in ones and twos as hope fled.

The clash of metal on metal and the shouts of fighting dwindled as Jules found herself standing on the deck of the sloop with the last fighting ending.

People came charging at her, Jules instinctively raising her sword before she saw who they were.

Gord, Marta, Kyle, and others from the *Sun Queen*, laughing and cheering as they slapped her on the shoulders and back. "We knew you'd be back," Gord said in the relieved way of someone who'd harbored fears of the opposite.

"I couldn't leave you fools wandering around without proper leadership," Jules said, grinning at them.

Her smile faded as she saw Keli the healer had left the *Sun Queen* and was tending to the injured aboard the sloop. The healer from *Storm Rider* had also boarded the sloop. "Did your healer survive?" Jules yelled at some of the surviving legionaries.

One pointed to a woman in legionary armor already at work next to Keli.

Looking about, Jules saw Artem and the other guards close by her. "Artem, have someone stand by the legionary healer so no one interferes with her work thinking she's just another prisoner."

"Aye, Captain."

Captain Erin came striding up, looking about her at the bloodstained decks of the sloop. "As far as I can tell, every officer died before the crew surrendered."

"This one's still alive!" one of her crew called.

Jules followed Erin to a spot near the mainmast where a man in the dark red Imperial officer uniform lay. He'd been turned to lie on his back, but his eyes were closed, a lump visible on his forehead. Only his breathing confirmed that he hadn't died.

Jules heard an inarticulate noise, realizing it had come from her as she stared at the fallen officer. "Ian?"

* * *

The four ships had made their triumphal entrance into the harbor, the inhabitants of Dor's Castle gazing with amazement at the spectacle of an Imperial warship wrested from the Emperor's control and Imperial legionaries made prisoners by free people.

Jules had ridden in on the *Sun Queen* after tearful reunions with the rest of the crew, but she'd been preoccupied the whole time, worrying about Ian. She did, after all, owe her life to him.

But, having seen him lying as if dead, she'd finally realized there were other reasons for her concern for him.

Blazes, why? She thought of the dying Mage's reply to that question. *"There is no answer to why, but the answers are so many they are beyond number."* The last thing Ian needed was for her to have strong feelings for him. The last thing any man in the world needed was that, because she was a walking death sentence to anyone who got too close to her.

Not that he was likely to want her, not after she'd caused the death of his father and the imprisonment of his mother and sister.

And even if he did, the prophecy lay between them. To the rest of the common people in the world, the prophecy was a promise. To her, it often felt more like a curse.

What do I do, Mak? Jules silently asked the *Sun Queen's* former captain. She'd sometimes felt as if Mak was still here, his spirit stopping by his old cabin to check up on her. But if Mak's ghost was here this day, he gave no sign of it.

She gained a brief distraction by examining the Mechanic weapons that Ang and Liv had kept safe for her. The revolver she'd left in the cabin, with one cartridge remaining in it, hadn't been touched. The other revolver, the one she'd dropped from the mast while trying to fight the huge Mage birds, didn't seem to have broken. At least, everything still moved as it had before. She couldn't try a test shot, of course, not when she had only two cartridges left in this Mechanic weapon. Two Mechanic revolvers and a total of three shots between them. Not exactly an arsenal, but possibly life-saving if more Mages showed up.

Would one of these Mechanic weapons have been able to kill the Mage troll that had destroyed the *Hawk's Mantle*? Remembering the creature, and how crossbow bolts had barely nicked it, Jules didn't think it would've helped nearly enough. But then the revolver she'd taken up the mast hadn't been able to destroy the huge Mage birds, either.

A knock on the cabin door offered a welcome break from her brooding. "Captain Erin to see you," Artem announced.

"Send her in. Are you guarding that door?"

"That's our job, Captain."

"Not on my own ship, it's not. Find Ang and tell him you and the other guards are part of the crew now."

"Aye, Captain."

Erin came in, grinning. "Sentry at the door, eh? Getting up in the world, you are."

"Very funny." Jules sighed, looking about her. "I'm still getting used to knowing I'm back here. More than once I didn't think I'd ever see this cabin again. Have a seat."

The other captain sat down, stretching out her legs before her and adjusting her knife sheath so it didn't dig into her side. "I came by for a couple of reasons. One was to let you know *Storm Rider* will be sailing out tomorrow to look for any rich merchant ships around the Sharr Isles that could benefit from us lightening their money chests. But that means we must resolve the matter of the sloop we have acquired thanks to the Emperor's generosity."

Jules nodded. "The sloop needs a new name, a new captain, and a new crew."

"Just so." Erin canted her head toward the town. "There's a woman who washed up here, name of Kat. She was captain of the *Fair Chance*."

"Kat of Severun?" Jules said. "I've heard good things of her. What happened to the *Fair Chance*?"

"A sudden squall ran her aground on the rocks a little ways east of here. Kat saved most of her crew and salvaged enough of a raft from the wreck to sail along the coast until they got here, but she's been stuck since."

"And you think she'd be a good choice for captain of the… um… *Second Chance*? Could she be counted on to give us a cut of whatever her ship takes?"

"*Second Chance*?" Erin laughed. "That's a good new name! Yes. Kat could be counted on for that. More's the point, she'd pay us back in other ways if we ever need her to back us in a fight. Kat's like that. She might need some more crew, though, to handle that sloop."

"I brought about ten new sailors with me to the *Sun Queen*," Jules said. "This ship can spare some of her crew if any want to join Kat's ship."

"I can spare a few as well," Erin said. "Shall I make the offer to Kat, then?"

"Yes," Jules said. "What's your other reason for stopping by?"

Erin turned serious, her eyes on Jules. "The other reason is to make sure you understand what it is that you've done."

"What have I done this time?" Jules asked, smiling.

Erin shook her head in reply, looking somber. "This is the first time in the history of this world that an Imperial order to common folk has been met with defiance and victory. Such a thing was unthinkable not long ago. I wouldn't have even considered it if we hadn't taken Western Port. But people could claim that we only attacked Western Port because we were told to by the Mechanics, and that we only won because we had those two Mechanic weapons. But, here, we made all the decisions. And, here, we won with only the tools available to the common folk.

"Jules, you've changed the world."

A thousand emotions raced through her, culminating in a self-mocking laugh. "It's the daughter of my line who's going to do that, remember?"

"Don't play dumb," Erin said, thumping one fist on the table. "Up to now, every common person served the Emperor and did whatever the Empire demanded of them. But now we have this independent thing, this idea that commons can make their own decisions about who rules them. Without that idea, how could that daughter of your line ever succeed? We have that idea, and we've shown that the Empire can be fought and defeated. We're never going to give up either of those things. And you made them happen."

Jules looked away, trying to think, reluctant to claim credit for what others had helped make happen. But if there was one thing that Erin could be counted on to do, it was speak her mind. She wouldn't be saying this if she didn't believe it and think it needed saying. "There's a lot left to do," Jules finally said.

"Aye. I didn't mean to imply the work was done." Erin bent a questioning look at her. "Or are you thinking of some specific thing yet to do?"

There was no one she could really talk to about this. But she needed to say something to someone. "I need to have a child." Erin raised her eyebrows at Jules as she rushed on, her words tumbling out. "I realized it while I was captured and escaping the Empire. About how angry I'd be if the Emperor forced me to bear his children and stole the prophecy. About how terrible it would be if the Mages succeeded in killing me and destroying my line before it began. I've been avoiding it, because I didn't want to be forced into it. But I can't keep pretending it doesn't matter, pretending that I have all the time in the world to decide and to act."

Erin listened, her expression solemn. "The decision is yours, but I can't fault your reasons."

"But how can I have a child?" Jules asked.

"Girl, you do know how that works, don't you?"

"Of course I know how that works!" Jules glared off to one side. "It's just… who."

"There's no man you'd want that with?" Erin asked. "That fellow Shin we left up at Western Port thinks the world of you."

"Shin is my brother in every way but blood," Jules said. "I couldn't even... ugh. Too weird." She paused, reluctant. "There is... If I had to... I don't know."

"I can't help you there," Erin said. "Ships and the sea are far easier to deal with than a woman's heart, and I should know having had my own troubles there. What about that Imperial officer? The one who survived? You seemed strongly affected by the sight of him."

"What about him?" Jules said, hearing the sudden stiffness in her voice.

"Ah, it's like that? You know him?"

"It's not like anything." She relented in the face of Erin's polite but obvious interest. "Ian and I were friends, and he wanted to be more but I wasn't ready. And then... things happened. Anyway, I only survived Imperial captivity because he gave me the keys to my chains when the Mages were coming for me. But he's only a friend."

"Only a friend? A friend who broke his oath to the Emperor to save your life, you mean." Erin sighed as she stood up. "For all you've done and been through, you're still young. Do you know how rare a thing a true friend is? You can fall in love as quick as the snap of your fingers, but to become a friend takes time and work and caring. Many a woman has married the man she loved, only to realize as the flames cooled that she needed a friend. If it were me facing your choice, I'd take a close look at that friend."

"He won't want me now," Jules said.

"Have you asked him? Never mind. None of my business." Erin headed for the door. "I've a lot do, including running down Kat with what'll be the best offer she's received since that Imperial prince took a liking to her. Mind you, she didn't take *that* offer."

"Captain Erin?" Jules said as Erin opened the door to the cabin to leave.

"Yes, Captain Jules?"

"Thank you. I do know a friend when I see one."

Erin grinned. "Mak would want me to keep an eye on you, wouldn't he?"

She went out, leaving Jules alone again with her thoughts and the ghost of Mak.

* * *

Some time later Ang stuck his head in the cabin. "Cap'n, that Imperial officer you were worried about is awake. He seems all right. Maybe has a headache, but he can walk and talk."

Jules closed her eyes for a moment to control the leap of joy inside her. "Please have him brought here."

"I'll get some of your guards to do that, Cap'n."

She flinched. "Ang, it's not that big a thing. If it bothers you—"

"Not at all," Ang said, looking serious. "Shame about the *Evening Star*."

"Yes," Jules said. "I guess we got some revenge for them today."

Ang grinned. "Yes, Cap'n, we sure did."

The afternoon far along and light fading, Jules lit the storm lantern in the stern cabin. She paused by the stern windows, facing the land, seeing lights begin to come in the windows of the buildings of Dor's Castle. Well behind them, the wall rose against the sky. Dor wasn't fooling around. That would be an impressive wall when completed.

Then all she could do was wait, nervous, until someone knocked on the cabin door again.

Ian came into the cabin, escorted by Artem on one side and Mad on the other. They both had swords out, and Ian's hands were bound behind him. He came to a stop in the middle of the cabin, his body rigid, staring into a corner as if Jules didn't exist. His dark red Imperial uniform bore rips and scuffs, a large wet patch on one leg marked bleeding from a shallow sword cut, and a large bruise mottled one side of his forehead where the lump was still visible.

If she'd hated Ian, it would have been a fine moment to gloat. As it was… it hurt. "Unbind him."

Artem sheathed his sword and went to work, unknotting and removing the rope around Ian's wrists.

Ian let his hands fall alongside his body, the marks of the ropes standing out stark against his skin, but otherwise didn't react.

"Leave me alone with him," Jules said to Artem and Mad.

"Captain?" Artem questioned.

"I'll be fine." She brought out her dagger and sat it on the table within easy reach.

Reassured, Artem and Mad left, closing the door behind them.

Jules sat looking at Ian, who still didn't move, his eyes still looking elsewhere. "Ian."

Nothing.

"Ian, I told you I didn't kill your father. That's the truth."

Nothing.

Jules let out a loud sigh, unsure whether to be angry or exasperated. "Your mother and your sister are here. In the town."

That finally got a reaction, Ian's gaze fixing on her, his expression disbelieving.

"They'd been sentenced to field labor," Jules said. "I don't know what they were charged with. They won't talk to me except to threaten me with dire fates. I was able to rescue them and the others with them who were going to be transported north to estates around Umburan." Explaining that the rescue had been entirely inadvertent wouldn't serve any purpose. "You don't have to believe me. You can go see them. All you have to do is swear not to harm or cause harm to this town or anyone in it. Or you can choose to remain a prisoner and be returned to the Empire along with the others."

He finally spoke, his voice sounding rusty with strain. "Why should I break my oath to the Emperor on your word?"

Her mood settled on anger. "Your oath to the Emperor? The Emperor whose minions were sending your mother and sister to labor and die growing crops on the estates of a princess? The Emperor who forced your father to take command at Western Port knowing the Mechanics would very likely crush that settlement in one way or another? How about asking why you should honor an oath to an Emperor who has betrayed you at every turn?"

Ian looked down at the deck, clearly fighting for control, his hands flexing in a way that made her place one hand on the hilt of her dagger.

But he didn't attack her, breathing deeply like someone engaged in a mighty struggle. "How did he die?" Ian finally said.

"Your father?" Jules felt her anger dissolving into regret. "We had no idea he was in command at Western Port. I went to the commander's home to try to capture him and force the garrison to surrender so as to limit loss of life." She paused. "What? No scoffing?"

"I don't doubt what you say so far," Ian said in a low voice.

"When I discovered the commander was Colonel Dar'n, I resolved to capture him. We fought. He was at a disadvantage, because his orders meant he couldn't kill me or seriously hurt me, so I was about to defeat him." She paused, recalling the awful moment. "He knew what would happen to you if he surrendered, what the Emperor would do to your family, so he surprised me by seizing my dagger and killing himself."

Silence, that felt full of not emptiness but of unsaid things. "Ian, that's the truth. I never would've killed your father. No matter what you were told, I didn't boast of it, or claim it."

He stood, silent, his eyes still on the deck.

"Blazes, Ian, talk to me. I've never lied to you. I'm not lying now."

Ian finally nodded, his gaze rising to look at her. "No, you never lied. You've destroyed my family, my life, my career, and my future, but you've told the truth every step of the way."

Her anger returned in a flash. She came to her feet, glaring at him. "I chose none of that! I didn't choose the prophecy, or how anyone else reacted to it. I've done what I had to do, because I didn't want to die and I will not submit to being a slave to anyone. Blame me for that if you want, but I couldn't have done otherwise."

He nodded again, the emotion in his eyes unreadable in the light of the cabin. "No, you couldn't have done otherwise."

"Give me your word and you can go from here free and speak to your mother and sister and assure yourself that they're fine."

"No." Ian kept his eyes on her, his voice level and strong. "I want to speak with them before I make such a decision."

"Ian—"

"You owe me that."

She glared at him. But he was right. Jules remembered how she'd felt when he tossed the keys to her in the brig of the *Hawk's Mantle*. "Promise me, then, that you'll do nothing but find them and speak to them, and then return to me with your decision."

He hesitated, then nodded. "I promise I will only find my mother and sister and speak to them, and then come back to this ship to tell you what I've decided."

"All right. What happened after I escaped the *Hawk's Mantle*? I saw you tossed aside by the Mage troll, and saw Captain Kathrin also knocked down. How'd you end up out here again?"

"Shouldn't I ask you that?" Ian said. "How'd you end up out here again?"

"It's a long story. I was worried that you'd been killed."

"Thank you." He paused. "Once the authorities realized that you hadn't died on the *Hawk's Mantle*, they thought the Mages might have taken you. But since the Mages kept attacking people and searching everywhere, that obviously wasn't so. There wasn't enough left of the brig area on the ship to tell how you'd gotten out, and the legionaries who'd been guarding your cell were both killed by Mages, which left people guessing everything from you using some Mechanic device to you using Mage powers yourself."

"Seriously?"

"You should have died a long time ago, Jules. That you're still alive makes people wonder about what powers you might have." Ian shrugged. "Since suspicion hadn't fallen on me, and I was in good enough shape to be reassigned to another ship, I was. Captain Kathrin was injured but recuperating." Ian looked at her. "When she finds out you're still alive, she'll be coming for you."

"If she's lucky, she won't find me. I'm not inclined to let her live next time we meet." Jules looked at his leg. "Has the healer seen your sword cut?"

"I don't need—"

"Yes, you do. You've lost enough because of me. I won't see you losing a leg as well." Jules walked past him, leaving her dagger on the table, and opened the door. "Can you find Keli the healer?" she asked Artem and Mad. "This prisoner has need of him."

As she went back to the table, she saw Ian watching her. "Who are they?" he asked, jogging his head toward the outside. "Those ones in leather armor. I've never heard of a force like that aboard pirate ships."

"They're... my guards," Jules said.

"Your guards." He shook his head at her, his eyes intent. "You're forming an army."

"An army?" Jules laughed. "I have eleven guards, who are just men and women who I happened to help rescue and who think they owe me. That's not an army."

"It's the start of one."

"What if it is?" She picked up her dagger, looking at the play of light on the blade. "If people out here are going to stay free, they'll need an army to defend them from the Empire. Just like we defended Dor's Castle today."

Ian watched her as if trying to see into her mind. "I wondered if you were planning on attacking the Great Guilds, but instead you're only deciding to go to war with the Empire."

His sarcasm stung, though she tried not to let it show. "I'm not going to war with the Empire. No one is. We're just defending ourselves against anyone who tries to control us."

"Anyone? You mean like the Great Guilds?" Ian asked.

"Yes, like the Great Guilds!" Jules shouted. "Someday that daughter of my line will come, and on that day she'll need an army! And she'll have one, thanks to me! Maybe she'll be the one to overthrow the Great Guilds, but she'll do it with what I've handed down to her! Free, independent people who can fight for their freedom!"

Ian stared at her as if he'd never seen her before. "Stars above. You really believe it's true that you'll do those things."

"Does that scare you?" Jules asked.

"No. What scares me is that when you said it, I realized that I believed it, too."

Jules was still searching for a reply when Keli arrived. The healer fussed over the sword cut, daubing on a salve before bandaging it. Then he checked the bruise on Ian's forehead, peering into Ian's eyes. "If you start getting very bad headaches or find it very hard to stay awake, get to a healer fast. The healer probably won't be able to save you, but there'll be a chance."

"Thank you," Ian said. "Can I leave now?" he asked Jules.

"Yes, you can leave the ship."

"If this one is going into town," Keli said, "he should either get a new outfit or have an escort. Trouble could find him otherwise if he parades about in that Imperial uniform."

"That's right," Jules said, annoyed that she'd missed such an obvious thing. She was so used to seeing Ian in uniform that it hadn't occurred to her how dangerous that could be for someone walking around Dor's. "Since he hasn't made up his mind about his allegiance, an escort will have to do. Artem! I need two guards to walk with this officer through town to make sure no one gives him any trouble."

"I'll do it myself, then," Artem said. "Me and Mad."

Ian gave Jules a troubled look, nodded in silent farewell, and walked out of the cabin, the two guards following him.

"He'll be all right?" Jules asked Keli before the healer left.

Keli shrugged. "After a blow like that to the head, the only answer is maybe. You're worried about that one, aren't you?"

"I worry about a lot of people."

"Sure you do."

Unwilling to wait in the stern cabin, which had begun to feel too much like a prison of another kind, Jules went out on deck. While many of the crew were ashore celebrating their victory, others had remained aboard to keep an eye on some of the prisoners. She was happy to see that Gord, who had a tendency to drink too much and then do something stupid while ashore, had volunteered to stay on the ship. Gord was a solid sailor who might be able to rise to command someday if he could stay sober.

They sat around the mainmast while Gord and the others brought her up to date on what had happened while she was off the Sun Queen. "We had a vote," Gord said. "And that was to make sure we got copies of that chart out to as many places as we could. We figured while we were dropping off copies in different ports, we could also try to hear anything about you and where you might be."

"That was a good plan," Jules said. "I'm glad you got those copies out."

"We ran out of ink and parchment more than once. So what all happened to you?"

"Oh," Jules said with a dismissive wave of her hand, "Mages attacked the ship that had captured me so I was able to slip away, and then I hid for a while and ran for a while, and after a bit I managed to get on the *Prosper* and out of Landfall again."

Cori, one of the other sailors on the *Sun Queen*, laughed. "We been talking to those pirates off the *Evening Star*, you know. They been telling some stories about you that make things sound a little more exciting than you let on."

"Hey, are you calling your captain a liar?"

"Is it true that Artem fellow killed Captain Tora?" Gord asked.

"Yes. In a fair fight."

"Good for him. I never liked what I heard of Tora. Maybe with him gone the *Bright Morning* can turn into a decent ship."

"They seem like a good bunch," Cori said. "With the *Evening Star* gone they need a ship, and they're pirates, so they understand how a free ship works."

Ang came by, nodding to everyone. "Are you telling lies to the Cap'n?"

"We're just talking about the new guys from the *Evening Star*."

"The Cap'n's Guard?" Ang said, drawing a pained look from Jules and laughs from the others. "It's all right, Cap'n. To be honest, I think we're all glad that you have someone following you around to protect you when you try to get yourself killed." He paused, a shadow crossing his face. "After we lost you, we felt a lot of guilt. I think every sailor aboard the *Sun Queen* blamed themselves for you being captured."

"Truth," Gord said.

"It wasn't anyone's fault," Jules said, leaning her back against the mainmast. "Except those Mages on their giant birds who were trying to kill me. It was definitely their fault."

"We saw you fall," Ang said, "and wanted to turn, but the Mages and those monster birds kept at us. Liv said, they think she's still aboard, we should draw them off, so we sailed into a storm to lose them. But when we came back to where you'd fallen, you were gone."

"That was a good decision," Jules said. "I can't fault Liv for that. Is that why she's been avoiding me?"

"Yeah. Thinks it was mostly her fault."

"I'd better find her. Excuse me." Jules got to her feet and went below decks, finding Liv sitting talking to Keli. When Liv saw her, she started to get up to go, but Jules blocked her. "I've got something to say to you, Liv."

Liv looked away. "I'm sure I've said it all to myself already."

Jules reached and wrapped her arms around Liv, holding her tightly. "You did nothing wrong. Your decisions were the right ones for what you knew. I'm grateful that you and Ang took good care of the *Sun Queen* and her crew. At my darkest moments, I knew if you were all right then the ship would be as well."

"Liar." Liv laughed, holding her tight as well. "Thanks."

* * *

She'd eaten dinner and was sitting in her cabin, a single lantern lit, when Artem poked his head inside. "We're back, Captain. He wants to see you."

"Send him in. You and Mad take off for the rest of the night. Get something to eat."

Ian came in, looking oddly forlorn in his battered uniform. He stood before her, uncertainty and weariness in every line of his body.

"Why don't you have a seat?" Jules asked. "Do you need something to eat?"

"I'm all right," Ian said in a dull voice, but he sat down facing her, his eyes lowered. "Tax evasion, and oath breaking," he finally said. "That's why my mother and sister were condemned to labor."

"I'm sorry," Jules said.

"It's not your fault. Really." He looked up his eyes meeting hers, and she was surprised to see anger there. "The thing that mattered most to my father was his personal honor. His word mattered. He never lied or falsified anything. But when the Imperial authorities went after my family, they chose charges that claimed my father had lied. He devoted his life to serving the last Empress and the current Emperor, and his reward was to be accused of being faithless and a liar."

"They expected him to die at Western Port," Jules said. "The Emperor knew the Mechanics would respond when he tried to establish that settlement."

"So you said earlier." Ian lowered his face into his hands. "Was this how it felt, Jules? When the Mage spoke that prophecy to you, and you realized that everything you'd lived for was gone?"

"Sort of," Jules said. "I was lucky, though. I met Mak, the former captain of this ship, and he told me I could make a new future for myself. The old future I'd dreamed of was gone, taken from me by the prophecy, but I could make a new one."

"You spoke of that Mak before," Ian said, his eyes still lowered. "I guess he was very important to you."

"He was a father to me," she said, unbending and explaining in the face of his distress. "Nothing more than that, but as important as that."

Ian finally looked up, meeting her eyes. "Why didn't you tell me that before?"

"Why did you assume anything else? And since when do I need to explain myself to you?"

He surprised her with a short laugh. "You never change." Then he fell silent again, his eyes lowered.

"What are you going to do?" Jules asked. "And, before you answer, there are plenty of opportunities out west for a man of your skills and character. I'd gladly help you with any of them."

Ian shook his head, frowning. "My first obligation is to my mother and my sister."

"What are their plans?" Jules asked, trying not to sound harsh when speaking of those two.

Some trace of her feelings must have come through, because Ian glanced up at her before replying. "Their plans are fairly vague, and all seem to revolve around ensuring that you meet an awful fate. I still have an obligation to them. They can't go back to the Empire. Even they realize that."

"Unless they trade me for pardons," Jules said.

He nodded, his mouth tight. "Yes. But they can't do that because they don't know where you'll be and when. They're…"

"Hoping you'll tell them," Jules said.

"Yes."

"I'm not planning on telling you, so you won't have a moral dilemma in that regard." Jules got up, walking to look out the stern windows, her back to him. Part of her wondered why that didn't worry her at all. "The people out here need someone like you, Ian. The Empire is reaching west, I think the Mechanics are partly paralyzed by internal disputes, and the Mages just want me dead. What none of them realize is how close everything is to splitting wide open."

"What do you mean?" Ian said.

She watched the light from a torch on the pier dancing on the surface of the harbor waters. "I felt it when I was in the Empire. How many people want to escape, find new opportunities and new lands. Captain Erin commented to me today that the Empire has been all there was for commons for all of history. I've realized what that meant: that no matter how corrupt the Empire got, no matter how badly its people were treated, no one had anywhere else to go. But now they do. When they come flooding out—and it will be a flood when enough find out about those lands to the west I found—they'll overwhelm the ability of the Empire to stop them. No matter what the Emperor wants or what the Mechanics want, new cities are going to spring up in new lands."

"The Empire can change, fix some of its worst elements," Ian said.

"Maybe, but it'll take a major shock to cause that, and in the end it'll remain the Empire." She turned to face him again, trying to speak what she felt. "I'd... I'd like..."

"Jules, I can't," Ian said. "I have to see to the welfare of my mother and sister."

"Of course."

Ian stood up, looking about to avoid setting his eyes on her. "You have my word that I won't harm anyone here, and will no longer serve the Emperor. I'll need some new clothes."

"Ang can find you some," Jules said. "Come on." She led the way out of her cabin, realizing that she had no choice but to once more betray Ian. And she'd have to do it soon.

CHAPTER SEVEN

Two days later, after Captain Erin and the *Storm Rider* had departed, Jules was speaking with Ang and Liv about where *Sun Queen* should go next when the lookout at the harbor entrance flashed the mirror warning that ships were coming from the east. A period of frantic preparations and anxiety followed until the lookout added the quick flashes that meant the ships didn't seem to be Imperial warships.

What finally reached the harbor early that afternoon was a good-sized merchant ship, followed by a string of five large fishing boats like ducklings following their mother. Ship and boats were all packed with escapees from the Empire, crowding the decks and eyeing the new world to the west with fear and hope.

"New taxes, and then a lot of their land and homes got taken for another Imperial hunting preserve," the captain of the large ship, the *Fair Traveler*, told Dor and the other captains. "That new chart is being passed around. Never saw something circulate that fast. They all decided to head out for those new lands to the west."

"That's a lot of people to take in all at once," Dor said, eyeing the crowded ship and fishing boats.

Jules spoke before she realized what she'd decided on. "There are other places. Captain, would those people be willing to go farther west, and start a new city?"

He frowned, skeptical. "How far west?"

"South of the Strait of Gulls. There's a beautiful harbor and fine land around it."

The captain brought out a much-copied version of the chart Jules and her crew had first made. "Where at?"

"Here," Jules said, pointing. "Julesport. There's no city there yet. But they can begin it."

"You'd need to ask them," he said. "Are you... Jules of Landfall? Herself?"

"Yes."

He smiled. "Then I think all you'll need to do is ask them."

* * *

"The *Fair Traveler* and the fishing boats are taking on fresh water and more food," Jules told Ian. "They're leaving with us tomorrow on the dawn tide."

They were in a private room in what passed for the best inn that the town of Dor's Castle could boast. Jules had managed to get Ian there by saying she had certain things to discuss with him, plans for the future that needed his input. She hadn't told him what those plans were, or what she needed him for.

"I'll be sorry to see you go," Ian said. He wore the clothes of an average person, looking somewhat awkward in them in the manner of someone used to other clothing.

"Are you sure you won't come along?"

"I can't. You know that. I need to find steady work, though my skills are a bit limited, and a better place for my sister and mother to stay. They're in one side of a partitioned tent right now."

"Are they?" Jules said, trying and failing to muster any sympathy. "There's steady work on the *Sun Queen*, Ian. Work as a sailor, which you already know."

"With you," Ian said, looking aside. "Jules, if there was ever to be anything between us, that time is long past."

"Of course it is," she said, smiling, and hoping her nervousness didn't show. "I can't get married. Not any more. Any man I married would be doomed. The Empire would stop at nothing to kill him, the Mages would do the same, and the Mechanics would at best make him a hostage."

He turned his head away, looking distressed. "You could only marry someone whose fate you didn't care about."

"Right. If I did care about someone, I'd have to keep it secret. But it wasn't always like that. Let's toast to the past when we could both still dream." She poured drinks from a full bottle, the best rum available in Dor's. His glass was clear. She'd deliberately chosen a goblet made of ceramic.

"To the past," Ian said, touching his glass to hers. He downed the shot.

She took a drink, but not the full shot, quickly refilling their glasses. "And to the future."

"All right." He downed that one as well, as she pretended to do the same but only drank a bit.

Jules refilled his glass, topping hers off in a way that made it seem she was refilling it as well. "And to tonight."

"Tonight?" Ian asked.

"Just two friends. That's all right, isn't it?"

"Sure." He downed the third shot.

When she was much younger, Liv had worked for a short time as a bar girl, learning the art of getting men to spend as much money as possible on booze while she herself avoided getting drunk. She'd told Jules how to do it. The trick was to stay in control while not allowing the mark to realize that he wasn't in control.

But Jules needed some of the rum herself, because the closer she got to the purpose of this night the more nervous she became. "A table needs four legs," she said, filling the glasses again.

This time she drank her whole shot.

"Why did you need to talk?" Ian asked. He'd begun moving and speaking in the exaggeratedly careful manner of someone feeling their booze and trying not to show it.

"I told you, there's something I need to do," Jules said. "Aren't there five islands in the Sharr Isles?"

He frowned in thought. "If you count that rock near the center as an island."

"Then let's count it! To the five Sharr Isles!"

By the time they toasted the Eight Founding Cities of the Empire, Ian's eyes were having trouble focusing on her.

Jules looked at him, pushing aside the bottle and glasses. "Hey, Ian. You know what's a shame? We never even kissed."

"Can't now," Ian grumbled.

"Why not?" She came out of her chair, sitting in his lap before he could stop her, her lips seeking his.

After the barest hesitation, he returned her kiss with growing fervor.

And then one thing led to another.

* * *

The lantern lighting the room had long since gone out. Jules got up carefully, gazing with fondness and regret at Ian, who was snoring as he slept off the booze.

If she cared for a man, she couldn't let the world know.

And if she took steps to fulfill the prophecy, she couldn't let the world know of that, either.

No matter how much it hurt.

She dressed quietly and left, walking through the nearly silent, pre-dawn streets of Dor's Castle.

Liv was standing by the boarding plank as Jules reached the *Sun Queen*. She gave Jules a raised eyebrow. "Where've you been all night?"

"None of yours," Jules said. "I told you I'd be back before dawn. Are we ready to sail?"

"Yes, Lady," Liv said sarcastically. "Captain Kat stopped by and said she wants to sail along with us, if that meets your approval."

"That's fine," Jules said. "It'll give her a chance to break in her crew on the *Second Chance* and to learn the waters to the west."

Naturally, the new settlers on the *Fair Traveler* and the fishing boats proved hard to get organized and counted, so the sun was rising before the ships left the pier. Jules tried not to look nervous, tried not to glance too often toward the town, but caught Liv noticing more than once.

But if Ian had yet awakened he didn't make it to the pier before the lines were finally cast off, sails set, and the ships began heading for open water. The *Sun Queen* took the lead, followed by the *Fair Traveler*, then the five large fishing boats. Bringing up the rear was *Second Chance*. Captain Kat had suggested that arrangement so the sloop could keep an eye on the fishing boats in case any got in trouble. "More likely," Liv said, "if those reefs the old charts show are really there Kat wants to be sure we'll hit them far enough ahead of her she can turn her own ship about."

"When did you become such a cynic?" Jules asked, leaning back against the quarterdeck rail as the *Sun Queen* cleared the harbor and began rolling in the swells parading across the sea.

"I was born that way," Liv said. "Are you sure there's nothing you need to talk about? Whoever you were worried about chasing you down didn't make it to the pier on time."

"You've got quite an imagination," Jules said. "Maybe I was worried about Mages trying to kill me. You know, like happened after the last time I left Dor's?"

"Sure," Liv said.

Once well out to sea but still in sight of land, the *Sun Queen*'s helm went over, swinging her bowsprit across the horizon to point west. A brisk wind coming from north of east let her sail on a broad reach, sails billowing to catch the breeze and send the ship gliding up the side of each swell and down the other into the trough. The seas were running lively but not too spirited, the waves only about a half a lance high, the sun shining down through a sky marked by only a few fluffy clouds. "It's as fine a day at sea as I've ever seen," Ang said, smiling, but wary in the way of a sailor who's seen the sea change moods too often and too quickly.

"A good omen for our voyage, perhaps," Liv said with a nod. "Let's see how far it lasts."

Over the next few days they made it nearly to the Strait of Gulls, only slowing to match the pace that the *Fair Traveler* and the fishing boats could manage. But once again as they neared the strait the weather closed down, low clouds sending down a continuous drizzle and banks of fog coming and going to hinder their view ahead.

"Seeing this again," Ang commented to Jules as they peered through the light rain, "it's little wonder the crew got so spooked the first time we came through here."

"It's as if the world made a place to scare off sailors," Jules agreed. She noticed some of the crew growing nervous again despite knowing the fabled reefs of the west didn't exist, but no one objected this time as the *Sun Queen* continued on.

Those on the *Fair Traveler* and the fishing boats, as well as the *Second Chance*, were probably a lot more worried, but with the *Sun Queen* leading the way they continued to follow, the gaps between ships narrowing as the weather closed in to limit visibility.

The weather cleared enough one day for them to spot the cape that marked the eastern side of the strait. Jules took them out to where the center of the strait should be before turning nearly due south, the line of ships creeping through the murk of another misty night, only the lanterns on the bow and stern of each ship allowing them to keep together.

As the following morning dawned, Jules saw the streamers of fog shredding. "Cape Astra to starboard!" the lookout called.

Ahead, the land fell away, the broad expanse of the Jules Sea opening before them.

The *Second Chance* came bounding up the side of the line of ships, every sail set as she glided alongside the *Sun Queen*. "Blazes, girl!" Captain Kat shouted from the sloop's quarterdeck. "It's all you said and more! I bow before the finest sailor on two seas!"

"Wait'll you see Julesport!" Jules called back.

Keli the healer had come on deck to enjoy the view. "Sometimes life ain't so bad, huh?" he said to Jules.

"Sometimes," Jules said.

* * *

But life still held some surprises.

When they finally reached the harbor where Julesport would be, Jules was surprised to see another ship already anchored.

She brought her convoy into the harbor, eyeing the stranger with concern until Ang gave a grunt of satisfaction.

"It's the *Star Seeker*," he said.

Sure enough, when the first boats came ashore, Captain Hachi was waiting. He offered Jules an elaborate salute. "Welcome."

"What are you doing here?" Jules asked.

"Exploring," Hachi said, watching the *Fair Traveler's* longboats ground on the beach and the fishing boats come in close to drop off their passengers. "My experience as an Imperial official makes me skeptical of grandiose claims, so I thought I'd check what that chart showed."

"You thought I was a liar?" Jules said, smiling as she saw people wandering about, gazing at the new land which would hold their homes. Some had run as far as the scattered groves of trees that grew into a forest in the near-distance.

"I didn't know that you'd actually made the chart," Hachi said, "especially given your name splashed on various landmarks. You didn't strike me as being that egotistical."

"I'm not. This city will be Julesport, because I want the Great Guilds to see it and be reminded that someday that daughter of my line will be coming for them. But my crew insisted on naming the Jules Sea after me."

A burst of noise, voices raised in argument, interrupted their conversation. Hachi looked toward the sound. "There may be trouble in your new paradise."

Jules looked as well, seeing a group clearly divided into two factions. A big man backed by about a half dozen men and women who had the look of bodyguards or enforcers faced a larger group of mixed ages. She began walking that way. Artem and Mad, who'd insisted on coming along to the beach, noticed and followed her.

She walked to the edge of the confrontation, one group to her left and the other to her right, as the argument continued. "What's this about?" Jules asked, using the voice she used to call out orders in high winds and heavy seas.

"Who are you?" the big man asked, in tones that reminded Jules unpleasantly of the way Mechanics spoke to commons. He obviously thought he was talking down to someone.

One of his followers leaned close to him, whispering.

The big man's expression shifted from disdain to respect that didn't feel sincere. "Jules! Of course!"

"*Captain* Jules," she said. "What's this about?"

"We're simply discussing how the town should be run. Administrative matters."

"He wants to take over!" a woman facing the man insisted. "Synda ran the black market in our town back in the Empire and now he wants to run this place!"

"I'm stepping in to meet a need," Synda said, smiling at Jules. "People need leaders."

"Was there a vote?" Jules said.

"A... vote?"

"Like we do on free ships. Every person gets a voice in who the leader is."

Synda looked about, seeing the reaction to her words. "We can do that. Later. When—"

"It'll be done first off," Jules said. "I won't run Julesport myself, but I will insist that it be a free town."

"I know these people and I know how to get things done," Synda said, his voice still agreeable but a hard glint appearing in his eyes.

"He's lying," the woman said. "He even told us that once you'd left we'd start calling this place Synda's."

"I never said that," Synda said immediately.

"That's right!" one of his backers said.

Voices erupted on both sides in volleys of accusations.

"Enough!" Jules yelled. "There will be a vote tomorrow for your leader. I'll make sure some sailors from my ship talk to you about how it's done. This will be a free town." She lowered her voice, looking at Synda. "I have no trouble with those who work the edges of society. I'm a pirate myself. But you have lied to me at least twice in a very short time. You will go back out to the *Fair Traveler* on the next boat, and when that ship leaves this harbor, you will still be on it."

"And if I don't?" Synda said, all pretense of respect dropped, leaning toward her in a threatening way that had the polish of an often-used tactic.

"Then I'll kill you."

Whatever Synda had been expecting to hear, it hadn't been that, especially not in a matter-of-fact voice. "You… you can't do that."

"Yes, I can," Jules said. "This will be a place of laws, but it will also be a place that will help fulfill the prophecy. You've heard of it? You're a danger to it. You and everyone like you, because to you freeing the world means removing any limits on how you can treat other people. So, you have two choices. One, get on the next boat back to the ship that brought you here. Or two, I kill you if you're still here after the next boat leaves."

A couple of Synda's flunkies made abortive moves that halted when both Artem and Mad drew their short swords.

Captain Hachi came strolling up, looking unconcerned. "If I were you, I'd leave. She will do it."

Synda looked about him, then back at Jules. "Fine, then. Have this place. I'll find another. You don't own every place in the west. I don't need this one."

"If your speech is done, get going," Jules said, stepping to one side so Synda had a clear path to the *Fair Traveler*'s boat.

Synda looked to his half-dozen supporters before turning to walk to the boat with exaggerated dignity. Four of the flunkies followed him without hesitation. A fifth paused, then hastened to catch up.

The sixth wavered, then faced Jules. "Can I stay?"

She looked him over. "As long as you play by the same rules as the other people here. If you're found to be spying or working for that one, you'll be sorry." Looking at those who'd been confronting Synda, and were now gazing at her with stunned expressions, Jules gestured to Artem and Mad. "These two understand how votes are carried out and captains, or leaders in your case, are chosen. They'll explain."

She walked back to the beach, keeping an eye on Synda as he got into the boat with the exaggerated dignity of someone pretending that he wasn't being run out of town. Hachi walked with her, gazing inland. "They may never love you," he said. "They may decide that being free also means not letting you decide their fates."

Jules looked out across the harbor, to the sea beyond, wondering how far it was across the ocean. "Good," she finally said. "That's good."

* * *

The vote next day was not exactly decisive. "There are three of us with about the same number of votes," the woman from yesterday told Jules.

"Can you work with the other two?" Hachi asked.

"Work with them? Yes." The woman made a face. "We don't agree on everything, though."

"Then I suggest a council, such as the Emperor has," Hachi said. "Three of you in charge. If there is dispute on what to do, majority rules."

"Two out of three," the woman said, nodding with a look of understanding. "I get it. We can... talk about things. And then take votes among us on what to do. Is that all right?"

"Why wouldn't it be?" Jules said.

She smiled. "I'm Anna, Lady Jules."

"Jules is fine."

"A couple of those with us were trained in building arts. They've drawn up a plan for the city. Would you like to see it?"

"Yes," Jules said.

Anna led the way to a group laboring over a large sheet of paper set on a fairly flat rock as a makeshift table. "Show her your work," she urged the others.

A young man with a quick smile pointed to the drawing. "It's just a start."

Jules looked, seeing a line indicating a city wall, piers and docks along the harbor, straight streets along the coast that meandered a bit once they got inland where the land was rougher. "That's good," she said. "Keep in mind that the Great Guilds will show up here. The Mechanics will want room set aside for their Guild Hall, and so will the Mages."

"You'll permit Mages here?" Anna asked, startled.

"I can't keep them out," Jules said.

"But we've heard you've killed some Mages."

"A few," Jules said. "But I can't stand against a Mage dragon. Or a Mage troll. Or those giant birds of theirs. If we try to keep Mages out of this city, they'll come here and destroy everything. It's the same for the Mechanics. For the time being, we have to accept that they can do what they want. Someday, that'll change. But, for now, build this city. Make it strong, for your children and children's children. And someday that daughter of my line will come, and this city we're creating will help her free the world."

They smiled, proud and determined, and in that moment Jules realized that she really did believe her own words. What had once seemed impossible to her had somehow become a dream she'd determined to help come true.

* * *

Hachi's ship sailed the next day, heading north to explore along the coast west of Cape Astra. The *Fair Traveler*—including Synda and his followers—headed out to sea the day after that, having offloaded everything it had brought and taken aboard fresh water and some of the fish the fishing boats were already bringing in each day.

This large group of escapees from the Empire contained a lot of skilled workers who'd despaired of finding work at home. "We could see no future in the Empire," Anna told Jules. "Now there's so much to do we can't work hard enough to make it happen."

Following the sketch drawn up for the beginnings of Julesport, the three new leaders arranged the settlers into groups to harvest and cut timber so that buildings could be put up. No one knew the weather here, how bad storms might be or how cold it might get in the winter, so along with a sheltered harbor it seemed wise to get shelter built for the people as soon as possible.

Jules watched a group bringing in one of the newly-cut trees that would form a post for the first pier, a mixed batch of men and women trudging along with the trunk resting on their shoulders.

And had an odd moment of recognition as one of the men passed, his face lowered.

Jules waited until the group dropped the trunk to the ground with a thud, then approached the man, who seemed to be doing everything he could to avoid Jules' attention. "Excuse me."

"Yes?" the man replied in a hoarse whisper, his face averted.

Having used similar means to hide her own identity, Jules felt her suspicions rise. "Look at me. I don't want to attract a lot of attention to you, but I will if I have to."

After a long moment, the man turned to face Jules. His face was dirty, and drawn with the sort of sharp edges that long-term tension engraves on a person's features. Jules eyed him, wondering why he seemed familiar. "Have we met?"

"No." The answer came out short and sharp, the way someone in authority would say it. The tone contrasted oddly with the man's humble appearance.

Jules studied the man, wondering why he kept evoking memories of stress and a storm. "We have met. Where?"

"You're wrong."

That voice, the snap of authority coming into it again, sounded vaguely familiar as well. But the clothing the man wore didn't go with Jules' memories. She was sure of that. This man should be wearing… a dark jacket. "We met in Sandurin." She'd gone to rescue a woman held by Prince Ostin, and on the way back to the *Sun Queen* discovered that the Mages were blocking her way to the pier. This man had been a Mechanic in a covered carriage, and had smuggled her past the Mages. Later, he'd been one of the Mechanics who met her at Jacksport, where she'd nearly been killed by both Mechanic weapons and a Mage dragon. He'd saved her at Sandurin, but she didn't know whether he'd been one of those trying to kill her at Jacksport.

"No," the man said again, looking away.

"Yes. And at Jacksport. You're… Hal? Sir Mechanic Hal?"

Hal's eyes swung up to meet hers, filled with fear. "Don't tell anyone."

Hal was either a very good actor, or he was terrified at being recognized. But any Mechanic alone among the commons might well feel that way, given how many common people had serious grudges against the Mechanics Guild. "Why are you here?" Jules said in a low voice. "Why are you pretending to be a common?"

"I'm not… I'm…" Hal sagged with despair. "I can't… whatever."

Jules rubbed her chin, wondering why a Mechanic would be in this state. "We need to talk. Will you come somewhere private with me to do that? Or balk and force me to make it a public matter?"

"Private," Hal said.

"Come on." Jules led the way along the beach. She'd found a small cove the first time the *Sun Queen* had been here, a place that wasn't that far from everywhere else but felt private and secluded. Noticing one of her guards giving her a worried look and starting to follow, Jules waved him off. "I'm just catching up with an old acquaintance."

Once they reached the cove, any noise made by other people in the area sounded muffled and distant. Jules stopped near the water to face Hal. "All right. We're private. Talk to me. Are you spying on us?"

"No," Hal insisted, shaking his head and looking about like someone seeking a path of escape.

"I'll need more than that," Jules said. "What's going on? Why do you look like a fox that's been hunted all day by a pack of hounds?"

Hal sagged again as if exhausted or despairing, abruptly dropping to sit on the edge of the water, his gaze on the little waves rippling up and down the narrow beach. "I'm hiding from my Guild," he whispered. "And from the commons. If they know who I am, what I am…"

"Hiding?" Jules sat down as well, facing him. "I know why a Mechanic would want to hide who he was among us. But why hide from your Guild? Did you do something wrong?"

"No!" Hal's hands grasped at the air as if seeking to pluck the right words out of the space before him. "Do you know how hard this is? Talking about Guild matters with a common?"

"I don't," Jules said. "But I do know this is a really bad time for you to be arrogant."

"I'm… sorry. I remember you of course. A lot of Mechanics thought the Guild was playing a dangerous game by working with you. They said you were smarter than you let on."

"I guess that's a compliment."

"Yes," Hal said, dejectedly gazing at the water. "I told them we needed someone smart. Trying to work with someone who isn't bright is what causes problems. Like the current Emperor. I've talked to people who've met with him. He's not very smart at all, but like many people who aren't very smart he thinks he's really smart. He *is* devious and ruthless. But that's worked against us." He grimaced. "I mean, against the Guild."

Jules studied the tense, taut features of Hal's face. "At Sandurin, you were arguing with the other Mechanic about things your Guild was doing. Lady Mechanic Gayl, right?"

"Yes." Hal looked over at her from the corner of his eyes. "I always suspected you were listening a lot more than you let on."

"Thanks for not mentioning that to other Mechanics. I remember that Lady Mechanic Gayl was worried about you."

Hal made another face, one hand digging at the sand he was sitting on. "Politics in the Guild can get… dangerous. There are some… fundamental things being debated, about how to deal with what's happening. Everything in the world was set up to keep things stable and controlled, but now it's breaking down."

Jules nodded. "I heard some other Mechanics say that the Empire was created to control the commons so your Guild wouldn't have to do that. They'd just have to give orders to the Emperor."

"Yes," Hal said, "that's— Wait, somebody talked about that in front of you?"

"How does someone set up a world?" Jules asked. "How did that happen?"

"I don't know! I know Mechanics came from the stars. We're supposed to have come from the stars, anyway. Maybe when we got here there wasn't anything except commons wandering around, and we got things organized." Hal ran one hand through his hair. "But it's breaking! The system set up back then can't handle what's happening. And we're not sure how to fix it. There's too much pressure inside the Empire."

"Pressure?"

"Like in a… Never mind. I mean, too many people. Not enough land. And the Empire has become so…"

"Corrupt?" Jules guessed.

"That's part of it. It only keeps functioning because there hasn't been any competition. Setting up a single state to control the commons must have seemed like the simplest solution, but with no rivals the Empire hasn't been forced to stay effective or care about its own people. And that's why commons are leaving the Empire and making problems!"

"Is that why the Mage Guild exists?" Jules asked. "To be a rival to the Mechanics Guild and keep it from collapsing?"

Hal pivoted his head to stare at her. "What? No! That's…" He looked down, his forehead furrowed in thought. "I don't really know where the Mages came from. I know my Guild would prefer they didn't exist. But without them…" Hal's eyes went back to Jules. "We have no outsider viewpoints like that. Like what you just said. No Mechanic would dare say that. Even saying what I've said to you is dangerous."

Jules nodded. "I'm guessing statements like those are why you got in trouble with your Guild?"

"Yes." Hal spread his hands, looking out toward the sea. "Some Mechanics want a big crackdown on the commons, to try to shove you all back into your proper places. Even those in favor of doing that admit it might well devastate this world, but they accuse anyone who proposes accommodating the changes in the world as being naïve or treasonous."

"Were you accused of treason?" Jules asked.

"I think so." Hal sighed. "Idealism and engineering make bad bed-fellows."

"Engineering?" How many strange words did Mechanics know?

"Forget I used that word. I got a tip that I'd be arrested." Hal looked down again, rubbing the back of his neck. "Sometimes, people just… disappear. There's no official acknowledgment that they were arrested. They're just gone. Supposedly to the Guild prison at Longfalls, but Longfalls isn't supposed to be very big and a lot of people have been disappearing."

"So what happened?" Jules said. A bird began singing somewhere in the trees overlooking the cove, the sweet birdsong offering a strange contrast to the stress visible in Hal.

"I was an idiot. I told Gayl I was going to go to the Guild Hall Supervisor, to explain why I wasn't a traitor." Hal stopped speaking for a moment, staring out across the water. "Before my appointment, I discovered that Gayl had already gone to talk to the supervisor, to defend me. But when I got to the supervisor's office I was told she'd never been there that day, and no one knew where she was, and why was I asking?"

His gaze stayed fixed on the horizon. "It was my fault. I don't know what happened to her, but I knew what would happen to me. I didn't want to disappear. I ran." Hal finally looked at her again. "I was a coward. Instead of staying and fighting, instead of trying to help Gayl, I ran and hid among the commons. I deserve whatever fate you intend for me."

Jules shook her head, picking up a small piece of driftwood and twisting it between her fingers. "It sounds like you're living with a worse punishment than I could inflict. You don't think your own Guild killed Lady Mechanic Gayl, do you?"

"It's possible. There are things people whisper when they're sure they can't be overheard. Why should you care? The last time we met, you said you wished every Mechanic would die."

"They can't all die," Jules said, her eyes on his. "The prophecy says the daughter of my line will unite Mechanics, Mages, and common folk to overthrow the Great Guilds. So there have to be Mechanics when that day comes."

He laughed. "The prophecy? You know that's nonsense. Mages can't really do anything."

"Why do Mechanics all say that?" Jules asked. "I've fought a Mage dragon, and a Mage troll nearly killed me in Landfall." She rolled up her sleeve to expose her arm and the fern-like scar on it. "And Mage lightning left this mark, though luckily it didn't kill me."

Hal frowned at the scar. "Lightning occurs naturally. As for Mage monsters, it's impossible to create a dragon or whatever out of thin air. "

Jules shook her head, perplexed by his attitude. "I've had Mages appear out of what you call thin air. Right in front of me. I was chased by a dragon that nearly bit me in half, almost plucked from a mast on my ship by a huge bird being ridden by a Mage, and barely got off a ship being sunk by a troll. Why do you dismiss out of hand what I've seen and felt?"

"Mechanics know how the world works," Hal said as if speaking to a child. "We understand all the fundamental forces, and how to use them. Which is how we know the Mages can't do what they claim. Commons just aren't bright enough to see through the simple tricks the Mages use."

"We're not bright enough?" Jules said, not sure whether to be angry or exasperated. "I've gone from wondering what I should do with you to wondering why no one else has killed you yet."

Hal looked at her, then away. "I haven't learned to keep my mouth shut, but among commons I say as little as I can. I've told you the truth about why I'm here. I'm at your mercy, and from what I've heard, you don't have a lot of that."

"That reputation helps keep me alive," Jules said. "But I actually do show mercy to those who deserve it. You saved me at Sandurin. Maybe you didn't do it out of the kindness of your heart, but I owe my life to you. That debt means I won't betray you, unless I find out that you've lied."

"Why would I lie?" Mechanic Hal asked, his expression growing haggard once more. "Why would I put myself through this?"

"I don't know. I've always had trouble understanding Mechanics," Jules said. "If you're among commons now, and your Guild wants to kill you, can't you share some of your secrets with us?"

Hal's eyes widened with fear. "No. They'd be able to spot that. The materials you brought in, the furnaces you would have to build to alloy metal… there are a million ways to tell if commons start trying to duplicate Mechanic secret arts. The Guild would realize what was happening, and they'd come in here and kill everyone and destroy everything to ensure the secrets were safe again. Why would I help you do something that would make my death certain? And yours as well!" He shrugged, looking down at the wavelets rolling up the beach. "Besides, I don't have the tools I'd need, and even if I did commons can't use that knowledge. Only Mechanics can understand our technology."

"I see." Jules looked inland this time, thinking. "I owe you a debt, and you did treat me as decently as any Mechanic has. I don't know if you tried to shoot me at Jacksport—"

"That was Gin. Lady Mechanic Gin. She'd been hoping for an excuse to kill you."

"I see. All right. I won't tell anyone who you are. Unless I discover that you are still working for your Guild. And if I happen to hear anything of Lady Mechanic Gayl, I'll try to get word to you, because I owe her as well. What are you planning to do here at Julesport?"

Hal looked down at his hands. "I'm good at making things. I was planning on learning carpentry. There should be a lot of demand for furniture and other things made of wood."

"There should be," Jules said, getting up and brushing sand from her pants. "If anyone asks what we were talking about, say we once met in Sandurin and I was asking about some people you might've known."

"I'll do that," Hal said, standing as well. "I don't how to thank you for this."

"I already told you that you earned it by your past actions," Jules said.

"Jules… that's the name, right? There's something else." Hal hesitated. "Things are changing in the world. They're not supposed to change, but they are, and the Guild doesn't know how to stop the changes at a cost it's willing to accept. I think, when things settle enough, the Mechanics Guild is going to do its best to make sure nothing like this happens again. They're going to want to ensure they can control any situation, and they're going to do their best to stop any more changes from happening."

"What can I do about that?" Jules said.

"If you talk to Mechanics again, emphasize that you represent a means to help them control things. If the Guild wants commons to help control commons, they need stable governments in the new cities and states that are going to form in the west. I heard and watched while you dealt with that Synda fellow. You're already trying to create stable governments. Just tell Mechanics that's what you're doing, and they'll believe that whatever you create, they can control."

"Thanks for the advice," Jules said. "Do you believe that? That the Mechanics can control whatever is created out here?"

Hal looked about him, then back at Jules. "I think they'll be able to control things for a while. Maybe for a long time. But whatever they make will start to break someday. I don't know what'll happen then."

"Maybe that daughter of my line will figure out what to do," Jules said. She walked past him while Hal was still groping for a reply. Ahead of her, timber was still being gathered for the first structures of what would someday be the city of Julesport.

* * *

Pirates were like sharks. They had to keep moving, even if they were doing legal work such as hauling cargo or passengers. Sitting in port didn't make money for the ship and the crew. In addition, Jules had to worry that staying in one place too long would bring Mages to that spot. Their uncanny ability to forecast her plans, to know where she'd be, could imperil Julesport if she didn't leave it.

So, after several days at Julesport ensuring the new settlers were making a good start of things, Jules took the *Sun Queen* out of port. They'd noticed when sailing along the eastern side of the Jules Sea that a haze was barely visible sometimes in the west. That haze might be the top of a mountain range, so the ship headed west to find out for certain. By the time the sun dawned on the second day out of Julesport it was obvious there were mountains ahead.

"Looks like Altis, doesn't it?" Ang commented as the *Sun Queen* drew near to the land. There some low areas visible, but most of the land was rocky, with mountains rising from the coast and on inland.

"Let's head south and see how far it goes," Jules said. "From the feel of the ocean waters, this land must come to an end not far south of here."

Sure enough, another couple of days brought the *Sun Queen* to a place where the land curved west. Past an area where a big river flowed down from the inland mountains, the land began curving north. Over the next week, their course confirmed that what they'd found was a large island, with a smaller island north of it. Rounding the northern coast of the smaller island and heading east, they reached the coast and ran south to Cape Astra, entering the Strait of Gulls.

And so, eventually, back into the Sea of Bakre.

As the *Sun Queen* sailed clear of the overcast that seemed to be perpetually present over the Strait of Gulls, Jules looked up to see how the sails were drawing. Not far above the mast, a bird that wasn't a sea gull was flying overhead.

She saw the bird's wing slice through the edge of a high cloud and realized that it wasn't small. It was high, and very large, and the shape of the bird brought up unpleasant memories. "Trouble up high," Jules told Ang.

He followed her gaze, his face hardening. "You should get below before you're seen."

"Let me know if it comes lower and stays over us," Jules said, heading for the ladder down to the main deck.

Reaching her cabin, she shut the door with an odd sense of relief. It wasn't as if that wooden door could stop the beak and claws of the huge Mage birds she'd encountered before. But she still felt safer. If the Mage riding atop that bird hadn't seen her, it might not realize that this was her ship and she was aboard.

She'd gotten out of the habit of wearing the Mechanic weapon. That clearly had to change now that they'd returned to the Sea of Bakre. Jules slid the "holster" the Mechanics had given her onto her belt, then brought out both Mechanic revolvers. She had a total of three cartridges left, so Jules put all three into one weapon and put away the second weapon, which without cartridges was only useful as a bludgeon.

And then could only sit in her cabin, hoping the Mage wouldn't attack her ship.

Eventually Ang came down from the quarterdeck. "The Mage bird flew on north. Maybe it's heading to Altis."

"Maybe." Jules remembered something she'd heard a Mechanic say. "You could explore like that, couldn't you? I mean, if you could fly."

"Sure," Ang said, rubbing his chin. "I guess you could see a long ways from that high up. Do you think the Mages are exploring?"

"Or maybe they're trying to find out where new settlements have been established in the west," Jules said.

"Why would Mages care about that?" Ang asked, then answered himself. "They want to keep us scared of them, so they want to know where we are. That way they can show up wherever we go."

"Maybe," Jules said.

The *Sun Queen* kept on to the east, aiming for the trade routes off of Landfall where rich merchant ships might be found. There'd be greater risk of encountering Imperial warships close to the Empire, but the last place Jules would be expected was back around the area where she'd narrowly escaped.

Jules avoided looking toward Dor's Castle as they sailed past without stopping.

The winds and the weather cooperated as the *Sun Queen* beat her way east. Whether that was a good omen or a bad one offered the subject for many a debate. On two consecutive days ships passed them heading west, their decks covered with escapees from the Empire. Neither seemed likely to have much money aboard, so the *Queen* let them pass.

They were only about a day out of Landfall, if the winds held, when another ship was sighted. "Sloop three points off the port bow!" the lookout called.

"We've captured three of those sloops," Ang said, "but odds are he's an Imperial warship."

Jules checked the sails and the wind, then looked off to port where the tips of the sloop's masts were coming into sight. "He's got the weather gage on us. If the winds don't shift, we won't be able to outrun him.

"Get the crew ready for a fight."

CHAPTER EIGHT

The sloop had gotten close enough for the hull to be visible from *Sun Queen*'s quarterdeck. "We can't outrun him," Jules said. Usually nervous and excited before a fight, she was feeling uncommonly tired, perhaps because this was a fight to be avoided if at all possible. The *Sun Queen* couldn't take on an Imperial sloop by herself. "We'll try to draw out the engagement until night so we can slip away from him under cover of the dark."

"That's our best choice," Ang agreed.

But a moment later the lookout called down again. "She's the *Storm Queen!*"

"Why isn't that idiot flying his flag?" Jules grumbled, relieved and annoyed.

Instead of a fight, the crew of the *Sun Queen* waved as the *Storm Queen* came close, the two ships loosing their sails to drift alongside each other. *Storm Queen* put a boat in the water that rowed across the gap between the ships, Liv supervising dropping the Jaykob ladder of rope and wood to allow Captain Lars to climb up to the deck of the *Sun Queen.*

"How's hunting?" Jules asked Lars as he reached the deck.

"Mixed bag these days," he said, smiling. "I heard you'd been captured. I'm glad to hear that the rumor was wrong."

"I was captured," Jules said. "Long story. Why the personal visit?"

"I have a message for you," Lars said, offering her an unmarked, sealed envelope. "From the Mechanics."

"The Mechanics?" Jules took the envelope as cautiously as if it were a knife with a poisoned blade.

"We were in Jacksport and some Mechanics showed up, gave me that, and told me to give it to you when I saw you. I didn't bother telling them that I'd heard you'd been captured, because they wouldn't have cared. You know Mechanics. 'Just do as you're told.' I ran into Captain Erin on the *Storm Rider* a week ago and found out she'd been given the same orders and maybe the same letter."

Jules drew her dagger and slit open the envelope, pulling out a single sheet of paper that had been folded over. Unfolding it, she saw only her name and a single line of text. "Go to Caer Lyn, anchor in the harbor, and wait for instructions," she read.

"They want you at Caer Lyn?" Lars frowned. "But they want you to anchor out rather than tie up?"

"There are Mages in Caer Lyn," Liv said. "As we all remember all too painfully."

"Yes," Jules said, not trusting herself to say more. It had been at Caer Lyn that two Mages had snuck aboard the *Sun Queen*, some-how invisible until they revealed themselves, and killed Captain Mak. She'd killed both Mages afterwards, but that couldn't bring back Mak. "Maybe that's why the Mechanics want us to anchor out."

"It's still very risky," Liv said.

"So would be ignoring orders from the Mechanics," Jules said. "Could you tell how the Mechanics felt when they gave you this message?" she asked Lars. "Did it seem like they wanted to talk, or like they wanted to kill me?"

"It was like they could barely force themselves to talk to a common," Lars said. "Just the usual *do this or else* Mechanic attitude. I can't tell you more than that."

Jules rubbed her neck, gazing at the letter and remembering what Mechanic Hal had said at Julesport. "I think I know what this is about. If I'm right, we should do as they ask. Lars, how is Caer Lyn doing? Are the Imperials trying to take over?"

"No," Lars said. "From what I've heard, Imperial warships are gathered near Landfall and Sandurin, or else scattered through the Sea of Bakre searching for a certain woman of the prophecy." He eyed her with a speculative look. "Erin slipped ashore in one town along the coast. From what she heard in the taverns, you've got the Imperials chasing their tails. But their attempts to guard their major ports and search for you farther out are leaving the rest of the Imperial coast open, making it easier for people to flee for the west. We were waiting around here for a couple of ships that have paid us for a safe escort as far as Dor's. That's why we ran down on you. We thought you might be one of them."

"Making money the honest way?" Ang asked.

"Not entirely, since the people on those ships are breaking Imperial law by leaving the Empire," Lars said. "A lot of trade along the coast seems to have broken down because of all the ships that are being hired to haul people west. If you're looking for money, either carrying people yourself or serving as an escort is a safer bet than trying to find someone hauling cargo between Landfall and Sandurin."

"We'll keep that in mind," Jules said. "Oh, there are some updates to the chart of the western waters. You should copy them so you can pass them on to Dor when you get there."

Lars watched with interest as a copy of the newest chart was brought out and shown to him. "Pretty big islands out there. But mostly rocks?"

"That's what they look like from the coast," Ang said. "There's a decent harbor here on the south tip of the big one, though."

"The mainland coast from the top of the islands down to Cape Astra didn't offer any natural harbors," Jules said. "If people don't head for the west coast inside the Sea of Bakre, I'd still recommend the south coast near the straits and on down."

"I'll pass that on," Lars said. "Is there anyone at Julesport yet?"

"Yes," Jules said. "There's a settlement."

"Congratulations, Jules of Landfall."

She grinned. "As of now, it's officially Jules of Julesport."

* * *

After *Storm Queen* had headed back out to wait for the ships she'd be escorting west, Jules called the crew together for a vote. "This is risky, so I'm asking for a vote before we do it," she explained to the crew gathered on the main deck and lower spars of the masts. "The Mechanics want me to bring this ship into the harbor at Caer Lyn and anchor out, waiting for them to do something. All of us who were aboard the last time this ship was at Caer Lyn know why I'm reluctant to return. But this meeting might be very important not only for our safety, but for the safety of the settlements in the west. And if we stay anchored out, and only allow any Mechanic boats alongside, no Mages should be able to sneak aboard. So I'm asking your approval to run this risk."

"None of us are going ashore?" Gord asked.

"Not as far as I know," Jules said.

"There will be Mages in Caer Lyn," Ang said. "They don't need to board the ship to harm those aboard it."

"That's true," Jules said. "But it's also true that the only one on this ship that they want dead is me. They don't care about the rest of you."

"Why do I feel insulted instead of relieved?" Marta said, drawing laughs.

Keli cleared his throat, gaining everyone's attention before speaking. "If one of those metal Mechanic ships is there, and if they want our captain kept alive, they'll have a lot of weapons to use against any Mages that try anything."

"I thought you'd be against going there," Liv said.

"If the captain is right that this is about the safety of the settlements in the west, then I'm all for it. We can't pretend the Mechanics don't have a say in things, and so far our captain has convinced them to do what benefits us."

"Another thing," Cori said, "is that if we don't go, the Mechanics are going to run us down with one of their ships sooner or later. I don't think it'd be a good idea to have them mad when that happens because we never went to Caer Lyn like they told us to."

Gord nodded. "It's risky to go, but it's risky to not go."

"I only have three cartridges left for the Mechanic weapons," Jules said. "That's another reason. If the Mechanics give me a few more cartridges it'll help defend us against Mages the next time they make a try at us. And it'll help deal with any Imperial warship that comes to close quarters."

"We can deal with Mages," Mad announced from where she stood with the other guards.

"Oh, we can, huh?" Cori asked. "You ever dealt with a Mage?"

"I have! Stared him down on the road to Landfall while he stood right in front of me!"

"She did," Jules said. "I think I was more scared for her than she was."

"This is a pretty straightforward matter," Ang said. "I think Cori has the right of it, that not running this risk sets us up for more danger in the future. Does anyone else have anything to say? No? Then I call the vote. Do we proceed to Caer Lyn as the Mechanics have ordered the captain to do, taking all precautions we can while there to ensure no Mage gets aboard our ship?"

"As long as we anchor well out in the harbor," Gord said.

"Aye. We'll anchor well out from the piers. All in favor?"

Jules saw almost every hand raised in agreement and felt herself smiling. "Thank you. Let's head north for the Sharr Isles."

* * *

Wary of Mages seeing them, Jules kept the *Sun Queen* loitering outside of Caer Lyn until the afternoon was well along.

They finally made their way into the harbor as the sun was setting, a flaming beacon flaring to life on Meg's Point to help guide ships entering and leaving. From what Jules could see, Meg herself didn't live there anymore, her fishing shack gone. The lumber from the shack had probably been reused somewhere else in the buildings of the Caer Lyn. "I hope Meg didn't die," Jules said, remembering the elderly woman who'd lived on the point long enough to give her name to it.

Liv shrugged, leaning on the quarterdeck railing as she looked over the harbor. "Why? She was old, that one. Hers wasn't a life cut short. And if she died, she did so doing what she loved in the place she loved. Can't ask for more than that, I say."

"You're pretty wise sometimes," Jules said as the *Sun Queen* glided over the waters of the harbor. The sun, well down in the sky, was already blocked by the heights inland, casting the harbor into shadow.

"Does that mean you'll listen to me next time I tell you that you're being stupid?"

"Probably not," Jules said, wondering what Liv would think when she found out about that night with Ian. As she probably soon would. Jules had been feeling more tired than she should, and what had been a fairly regular monthly event was overdue. But those things didn't add up to a certainty. Not yet.

Every other ship entering the harbor at Caer Lyn tried to tie up at one of the piers or anchor as close in as possible. That left plenty of room farther out in the harbor for the *Sun Queen* to drop her hook. But before they did so, Jules took the ship past the piers, where one of the metal Mechanic ships was tied up. As the *Sun Queen* sailed past, Jules stood on the quarterdeck rail facing the Mechanic ship, holding a lit lantern in one hand, the Mechanic revolver on her hip easy to see.

As soon as they were past the Mechanic ship, Jules jumped down and went to her cabin. It felt wrong to be hiding, but the risk of being seen by Mages and having them attack the ship wasn't worth any amount of her pride.

She had the stern windows open, and heard Ang shout the command to let go the anchor.

There weren't any other ships within a hundred lances of them. The nearest land, on the opposite side of the harbor from where the town of Caer Lyn had first sprung up, hadn't yet been built on.

Figuring that the Mechanics were unlikely to bestir themselves this late in the day for the convenience of a common person, Jules decided to get a meal and try to sleep so she'd be ready for anything in the morning, even if the Mechanics showed up really early.

Those tentative plans went out the window as Ang knocked on her cabin door. "There's a boat heading for us, Cap'n. Looks like everyone aboard it is a Mechanic."

"Blazes." The Mechanics wanted to see her that quickly? In a way, that was reassuring. If they'd decided to kill her then they'd probably have just waited until tomorrow to do that.

Jules hastily donned her best shirt and pants, gave her boots a quick buffing, and washed her face. After making sure the Mechanic revolver was secure in its holster at her belt, she got out the second revolver in its holster. The Mechanics might well want that weapon back, or at least would want to be sure she still had possession of it.

"They're coming alongside," Ang called. "We've already got the ladder down."

Jules came out of her cabin into a harbor where darkness was falling rapidly now. Ang stood at the head of the rope-and-wood Jaykob ladder, a lantern in hand as he looked down.

"You know who we're here for," Jules heard in the superior tones of a Mechanic. "Send her down."

She walked to the head of the ladder, nodding to Ang and others seeing her off. Artem and Mad stood off to one side, looking unhappy at not being able to accompany her. "I'll be back," Jules said. "Keep the ship and everyone on it safe."

She went down the ladder, pausing at the bottom to check the boat. Eight Mechanics sat in it, but no oars were in use. One of the Mechanics gestured to her, pointing to the middle of the center seat. Jules dropped down into the boat, sitting where directed, and was startled when two Mechanics sat down on either side of her. Two of the remaining Mechanics sat on the seat in front of her, and three behind, while the last sat at the very stern.

This looked like the sort of Mechanic boat she'd seen at Western Port, moving somehow under its own, mysterious power.

All of the Mechanics were armed, four of them wearing revolvers at their waists and four with the longer weapons Jules had heard called "rifles." They all seemed to be young adults, not a middle-aged face among them.

She took in those details as the boat moved away from the *Sun Queen*, curving in a wide arc to head back to the piers.

"Put this on," one of the Mechanics said as he shoved a dark Mechanic jacket at Jules.

She took it without thinking, staring at it. "Put it on?" Jules finally said.

"Is that complicated?"

Jules swallowed nervously before replying. "It's death for a common to wear the jacket of a Mechanic. That's a rule of your Guild."

"Oh, for—"

"Hold on," another Mechanic said, his eyes on Jules. "She's worried about breaking our rules. We shouldn't give her a hard time for that."

"Fine." The first Mechanic pointed at Jules, then at the jacket. "I'm ordering you to put on that jacket. Which makes it all right. Put it on."

Jules pulled on the jacket, a crawling sensation going up her spine as the garment settled about her shoulders. Wearing Mage robes in Landfall had felt odd but at least she'd also felt hidden with the hood up. Wearing a Mechanics jacket, her face fully exposed, felt like draping a target over herself, inviting death from all directions. No. Not just death. She hated the idea of common people seeing her, seeing her face clearly, and thinking she really was a Mechanic.

"Think it'll fool any Mages who see her?" one of the female Mechanics said.

"It'd better," one of the men replied. "Listen, common. You're pretending to be a Mechanic. When we get to their pier, we'll form a group with you in the middle. You stay in the middle of us while we all walk to the Guild Hall. Understand?"

"Yes, Sir Mechanic," Jules said.

"Is that revolver loaded?"

"I have three cartridges left in it, Sir Mechanic."

"Don't use it. We're not supposed to attract attention from Mages. If any try to stop us, let us bluff our way through while you keep in the back and avoid being seen."

"What if they do try to kill her?" another female Mechanic asked.

"Our orders are to get her to the Guild Hall without starting a war with the Mages. If it comes to that, we run, keeping her in the middle so they can't get to her."

The Mechanics all nodded.

Jules felt herself hunching down as the boat moved across the water. She could feel it shaking slightly in a steady way and hear a low humming. But as the boat wended between anchored ships Jules felt the shaking and the humming stutter twice before smoothing out again.

"That thing's not going to fail again, is it?" one of the female Mechanics asked.

"It better not," one of the male Mechanics replied. "I hate rowing. I thought they were going to replace that unit."

"Can't get a new one," the Mechanic at the stern said. "I don't know why not. We were told to keep this one working as long as possible."

The pier, well-lit by lanterns down its length, loomed ahead of them. The boat came close past the squared-off stern of the big metal Mechanic ship, coming alongside the pier in the shadow of the ship. Two Mechanics waiting on the pier grabbed lines from the boat, looping them around ties.

The Mechanics stood up to leave the boat, Jules staying with them. Up on the pier they formed a rough circle, Jules inside, and began walking at a brisk but not hurried pace along the pier and toward the town.

"Mages at ten o'clock," one of the Mechanics said in a low voice.

Ten Oh Klock? What did that mean? Jules noticed the Mechanics around her glancing quickly to their left. She did the same, catching a glimpse of Mage robes well down the street and a little to the left of their group.

The Mechanics angled right to the other side of the street, Jules doing her best to stay in the center.

Aside from being crowded by the Mechanics on all sides of her, the experience felt oddly like being back in Mage robes in Landfall. The common people hastily made way for the Mechanics, who walked on as if not even aware of how others got out of their path. Perhaps they were so used to such treatment that they no longer noticed it.

Jules didn't need any encouragement to try to stay hidden among the Mechanics. Aside from not wanting any Mages to spot her, she didn't want any commons seeing her wearing this jacket.

She noticed that Caer Lyn had grown a lot in the time since she'd last been here. More buildings, bigger buildings, more lanterns on the streets, and more people. Not everyone escaping the Empire was going far to the west. Some were just coming as far as the Sharr Isles, counting on the Great Guilds to keep the hand of the Emperor from following them here.

The buildings on either side fell away as the group entered a large open area. Glancing between the Mechanics around her, Jules saw they'd reached the plaza around the new Guild Hall. Like other Mechanic Guild Halls, it was a massive structure, about four stories high, a long and wide rectangle, the outside bearing windows higher up but the bottom level almost fortress-like. Bright, steady Mechanic lights blazed inside and outside the structure, letting her see that it was still far from finished. A number of large tents were still set up around the building, and Jules assumed one of those would be their destination.

To her surprise, the group went up the broad stairs leading to the massive double doors at the main entrance.

They were going inside. Jules felt the way she had when she was being chained in the brig of an Imperial sloop. Commons didn't go into Mechanic Guild Halls, or Mage Guild Halls for that matter. Or if they did go in, they didn't come out again. She had to fight down a panicky instinct to flee as the group stepped through one of the partially-opened main doors into the interior.

Once inside, they stopped before an older Mechanic who was waiting. "Any problems?" that man asked.

"No, Sir Senior Mechanic," one of Jules' escort replied. "We spotted a few Mages but none of them took notice of us." He looked at Jules.

Guessing what he wanted, Jules started to take off the Mechanics jacket.

"Leave it on," the Senior Mechanic ordered her. "We don't want anyone who sees you questioning what's going on. You all wait here," he told the Mechanics who'd brought Jules. "Don't talk to anyone else about what you're doing."

"Yes, Sir Senior Mechanic," the Mechanics all replied.

"Come along," the Senior Mechanic told Jules, beckoning to her. He walked off without looking to see if she was following.

She hastened to catch up, staying with the Senior Mechanic as the two of them walked deeper into the Guild Hall, through a section that was still only rough walls with blindingly bright Mechanic lights hanging from hooks, then into a more finished area. Jules heard noises, ranging from conversations in the distance to occasional strange deep rumbles, and high-pitched whines that didn't seem to come from any natural source. As they passed gratings in the wall, cool air flowed out, startling her.

Reaching a broad, important-looking door, the Senior Mechanic knocked, then cracked it enough to look inside. "She's here." Nodding in response to some reply Jules couldn't see or hear, the Senior Mechanic stepped back and waved Jules inside.

Nerving herself and trying to keep her breathing steady, Jules stepped through that door, hearing it close behind her.

She was in a large room, three or four lances to a side, the ceiling maybe a lance and a half over her head. Lights set into the ceiling provided bright illumination. Wooden paneling had been partially installed on two walls.

A couple of utilitarian desks made not of wood as Jules had always seen but of metal sat in the middle of the room. Behind those desks sat four Mechanics.

At least two Senior Mechanics, Jules corrected herself as she looked at them. She'd met them all before. The older woman whom Jules had seen once on a Mechanic ship, the older man who'd met her twice, once on the *Sun Queen* and once on a Mechanic ship, and the middle-aged man and woman Jules had met on a merchant ship they were taking to the Sharr Isles. Now here they were all together, plainly waiting for her.

Jules walked to the center of the room, heart pounding and more than a little worried but trying not to show it, acutely aware once more of the Mechanic jacket she was wearing.

"She looks natural in that jacket, doesn't she?" the younger of the women remarked to the others.

"Very natural, Rhian," the oldest male Senior Mechanic replied. "But she may have a more important role to play as a common."

"What have you been up to?" the younger of the men asked Jules. "The Mages are as frantic as we've ever seen them, and the Emperor is throwing tantrums. All apparently because of you."

"I was captured by an Imperial ship," Jules said, "but was able to escape when Mages attacked it to try to kill me, Sir... Senior Mechanic." He hadn't insisted on that title when last they'd met, but he and the others seemed to be on an equal basis.

"There was more than one recent incident in Landfall where Mages attacked Imperial soldiers," the older woman said. "Did all of those involve you?"

"As far as I know, yes, Lady Senior Mechanic."

"The Empire still doesn't know where you are," the younger man said. "Where have you been?"

"In the west, Sir Senior Mechanic."

"Exploring?"

"That and overseeing the establishment of..." What was the term that Mechanic Hal had used? "Of stable, free governments in new settlements."

Her last words held their attention, all four watching her intently in silence for a long moment. "You might have been right, Uri," the older woman finally commented to the younger man.

"It was your idea first, Grace," he replied. "You're the one who convinced the other Grand Masters to give her that revolver."

"How much do you know about what's going on right now?" Senior Mechanic Grace asked Jules.

"I know the Empire and the Mages are still searching for me, Lady Senior Mechanic," Jules said, "and that the flow of people out of the Empire has gotten heavier because Imperial forces are concentrating on trying to find me."

"Why do you think common people are leaving the Empire in such numbers?" Senior Mechanic Uri asked.

"Because it feels like a dead end, Sir Senior Mechanic. Too many people, too few jobs, too much corruption, those highest in the hierarchy like senior Imperial officials and members of the royal family taking whatever they want. The west offers a chance to escape all of that."

"But it's only possible for them to leave in such numbers because of you," Uri said. "You've destabilized the situation, and inspired more instability. One common isn't supposed to be able to do that."

They wanted her to reply to that, Jules could tell. But what should she say? She took a deep breath, trying to draw on the only metaphor she could think of. "Sir Senior Mechanic, sometimes when cargo is stacked in the hold of a ship, it seems to be stable and firm. But it's actually just balanced, ready to fall if something happens. Just a little shifting of some of it, or just a little weight to one side, and the whole pile comes down. I think the Empire, the world, may have been like that, of have become like that, sort of perilously balanced. And then the prophecy unbalanced things that were already on the verge of falling."

The older man slapped the desk before him, the sound sharp enough to startle Jules. "If we had her as Empress in Marandur, instead of that idiot Emperor, we wouldn't be facing these problems! Isn't there a way we can get her on the throne? The Emperor would marry her because the prophecy, and then we could arrange a fatal accident for the Emperor, leaving her as Empress to start fixing things!"

Senior Mechanic Grace shook her head, grimacing. "I think it's gone too far for her to be able to put things back together. Besides, from what our sources say, the Imperial family and senior bureaucracy would never accept her as Empress. What's the matter, girl?" she asked Jules, having noticed her reaction.

Jules, shocked by the direction the conversation had gone, had to swallow before she could speak. "I... I... I'm an orphan. The Imperial family would never..."

"An orphan." Grace sighed. "Girl, the Mechanics Guild has its faults, but bias based on origin isn't one of them. What counts is ability. Both of my parents were commons, but that hasn't stopped me from becoming one of the Guild's grand masters."

"I think you're right that she'd never be accepted as Empress," Senior Mechanic Rhian said. "If we're going to regain stability, we need to think of... well, like she said, restacking things in a way that'll hold up for the long term."

"What you said earlier," Uri asked Jules, "about setting up stable governments. You're already doing that?"

"Yes, Sir Senior Mechanic," Jules said. "Using the model of the free ships, where the crew can vote on who the captain is and on important courses of action. In Western Port I have a... loyal follower who's running the place and getting the people there to think that way. Dor at Dor's Castle is the leader there but he has popular support. At Julesport someone was trying to set himself up as sole ruler and I got rid of him."

"And what," the older senior mechanic asked, his eyes in Jules, "do you think these individual settlements will accomplish? That sounds like a recipe for lots of weak actors constantly fighting among themselves."

"No, sir," Jules said. "I'm getting everyone to think of working together. There are already ties among them. Like, when an Imperial ship tried to enforce the Emperor's will at Dor's, I had a ship there that was beholden to me and did what I asked, and there was another ship present whose captain has learned to trust me, and while we were fighting the Imperial ship a third ship, my own, showed up. Individually, none of our ships could've beaten that Imperial ship. But together the three of us captured it. I want the individual settlements and towns, as they grow into cities, to be the same, supporting each other and working together. Not because some Emperor demands it, but because the people of those places trust each other."

"You initiated an attack on Imperial forces?" Grace asked.

"A defensive action, Lady Senior Mechanic."

"And you won? By using allies you've already accumulated?"

"Yes, Lady Senior Mechanic."

Uri nodded to his companions. "There's our long-term fix. We let people flood out of the Empire to relieve the pressure and give it time to reform itself a little, and she forms those people into a counter-force to the Empire so it will never again think it's strong enough to challenge the dominance of our Guild."

"Why are they listening to you?" Rhian asked Jules. "Why are the commons doing what you say? Just because of the prophecy? Sooner or later they'll realize that's Mage nonsense."

"At first the prophecy had a lot to do with it," Jules said. "It still does, I guess. But they're listening to me because of what I'm doing. They know I keep my word, and can be trusted, and… I don't know. I've killed Mages, and captured some Imperial warships, and Western Port, and I've survived so far, and I'm trying to learn as much as I can. People respect that. And… to be honest, you Mechanics haven't killed me yet. I guess that impresses common people, too."

Grace looked to her companions. "She had the prophecy as leverage, and she's used it very effectively. That's the kind of tool we need." Her gaze went back to Jules. "You cooperated well at Western Port. What are you telling the commons elsewhere about cooperating with the Guild?"

154 ✧ *Fate of the Free Lands*

"Lady Senior Mechanic, I'm telling them to do what the Mechanics say. I'm telling them the Mechanics will show up at their settlements someday, and when they do to cooperate." Jules was glad she didn't have to try to carry off a lie about that. And was glad that the Mechanics didn't follow up Senior Mechanic Grace's question by asking about the prophecy's role in that. Because the truth was, Jules was advising cooperation only to ensure her people grew strong enough in the future for the daughter of her line to overthrow the Guilds' rule.

The oldest senior mechanic leaned forward, both elbows on the desk before him, resting his chin on his clasped hands as he gazed at Jules. "The Empire has never faced a real challenge. It's going to keep doing what it thinks should work, which means trying to catch you. Our sources within the Imperial court tell us that the court's reaction to those leaving is that the Empire is better off without them. But at some point, probably in about a year because it'll take that long for the extent of the Empire's problems to sink in at the Imperial court, they'll realize they've been out-thought. At that point, we think the Empire will openly defy the Mechanics Guild by launching an invasion of the settlements to the west—challenging the Guild to either look aside, or risk a war that the Guild will certainly win but at a cost of destroying the Empire. Such a victory wouldn't be cheap for the Guild, either. As a common familiar with the Imperial military, what do you think they'll try?"

Jules didn't have to hesitate or think, because she'd already considered that question. "They'll attack Dor's Castle first. They have to. That's where we, the free commons, will have to meet them and beat them."

"Dor's Castle?" Senior Mechanic Grace said. "Why there?"

"Because of where it is, Lady Senior Mechanic. Dor's Castle sits on the coast along the path to anywhere west of it. If the Empire tries to bypass Dor's, ships operating out of the harbor there will be able to attack the Imperial line of communications, destroying supplies and reinforcements. Dor's Castle is the fortified gate to the west. Take it, and the rest of the west is exposed. If it stands, the rest of the west is beyond the Empire's grasp."

"They're building a wall at Dor's, aren't they?" Uri asked.

"Yes, Sir Senior Mechanic. A very strong wall. If that wall is properly defended, if it has enough men and women atop it ready to fight, even the legions won't be able to take it."

"That's your plan?" Grace asked.

"Yes, Lady Senior Mechanic. Convince every free settlement that when Dor's is threatened they need to send people to help defend that wall, and get every free ship to gather in the waters off of Dor's Castle to defeat the Imperial invasion."

The senior mechanics all smiled. "And while that force of commons defeats the Imperial attack," Rhian said, "the Guild can sit back, applaud, and afterwards deal with a chastened and weakened Emperor. We won't have to risk open confrontation and war."

"We can't just sit back," Grace said. "The stakes are too high. We have to do what we can to ensure that this girl survives and convinces the other commons to support her plan. Here." Senior Mechanic Grace pushed a small wooden box across her desk toward Jules.

Jules stepped forward to pick up the box. Opening the lid, she saw inside the box a wooden shelf with large holes in a regular array. Set into each hole, nose down, was cartridge.

She counted them in disbelief. "Twenty? You've giving me twenty cartridges?"

"You're going to need them," Senior Mechanic Uri said. "The Mages are growing desperate."

"Keep the second revolver as well," Grace told Jules.

Jules nodded in reply, momentarily lost for words. They were giving her twenty more cartridges, an unbelievable arsenal for a common. They accepted her reasoning, agreed with her on what the Empire would do, and liked her plan.

She felt herself relaxing, no longer as frightened, thinking perhaps she could work with these people rather than covertly fighting them every step of the way.

And then her memory conjured up the sight of Mechanic Hal on the beach at Julesport, despairingly describing how Mechanic Gayl had disappeared, and how he had been forced to run for his life.

These Senior Mechanics were among the leaders of the Mechanics Guild. Only Senior Mechanic Grace had been referred to as a "grand master," but the others were clearly important. Which meant they were important parts of the system that caused the disappearance of Mechanics who said the wrong things. Grace herself might have given the order for Hal's arrest, and for Gayl's disappearance. And that was how they treated other Mechanics.

She could never forget who these Mechanics were, Jules told herself. Never forget that while they were happy to use her, to praise her for doing what they wanted, they'd never regard her as an equal. If she crossed them, outright refused their orders or defied the Mechanics Guild, she might disappear as well. To them, every common was merely a tool, something to be used. Jules had been a particularly useful tool, but that was all she would ever be to them. And other commons were far less. Even now their plans weren't about freedom for people oppressed by the Empire, but about creating stability so that their rule of the world wouldn't be challenged.

It was a great pity, Jules thought, that none of these Senior Mechanics would be alive to see the daughter of her line break their Guild.

"I think we've resolved all of the important issues," Senior Mechanic Grace said, looking at the others.

Her voice came back as Jules realized there was another problem she hadn't brought up. "Lady Senior Mechanic, there's something I'm concerned about."

Had she pushed her luck too far? Grace and the others eyed her for a moment before Grace finally nodded. "What is it?"

"The Mages, Lady Senior Mechanic. You've figured out how to support me with your devices, the revolver, I mean. What if the Mages decide to begin supporting the Empire directly?"

"By doing what?" Senior Mechanic Uri asked.

"By having Mages operate alongside legionaries," Jules said. "Using their abilities in direct support of the Imperial forces."

Rhian shook her head. "That would risk exposing the Mages as frauds. All of the Imperial forces would see that the Mage tricks didn't actually produce any real results."

At least Mechanics were consistent in their willful blindness when it came to Mages, Jules thought. But that wouldn't help her or the free commons if her fears came to pass.

To her relief, the oldest male senior mechanic frowned. "But it would have an impact on the commons fighting the Imperial forces. Their superstitious fear of the Mages might make it hard for them to stand against legionaries alongside Mages."

"We'll have to keep that possibility in mind," Grace agreed. "If the Mages do weigh in that way, we'll have to provide more of our weapons to the other side to balance it out."

"And so they can kill more Mages," Uri said with a smile.

"You know what to do," Senior Mechanic Grace said with another smile at Jules. "Keep it up and maybe several years from now you can earn the right to wear that jacket."

Another vague offer to be a Mechanic herself someday. What should she say? *I'll see you dead first* probably would be a mistake. "Thank you, Lady Senior Mechanic," Jules said, trying to sound grateful rather than repulsed.

Uri went to the door, opening it and speaking to the Senior Mechanic who'd waited outside. "Take her back— No, wait. Get her two new revolvers and take those ones she has. They probably need maintenance and cleaning. Then have her taken back to her ship. Same orders, but this time if Mages try to attack, our Mechanics are authorized to shoot."

None of those in the room said goodbye to Jules, just as none of them had made any polite greeting when she arrived. They were, after all, Mechanics, and she was a common. The senior mechanic took Jules to another room where a massive door protected ranks of shelves. A Mechanic on duty there took her two revolvers, shaking her head in disgust at their condition, and returned with two new ones. "She has to sign for them," the Mechanic told the Senior Mechanic. It was only at that point that Jules realized the Mechanic on duty had mistaken her for a real Mechanic because of the jacket.

The senior mechanic shook his head. "No written records of this, by order of Grand Master Grace."

Heading back toward the entrance, Jules and the senior mechanic passed a column of boys and girls of various ages marching through a hallway wearing serious expressions. How many of them had been born to Mechanics, and how many had been stolen from common families because they passed the Mechanics Guild tests? Jules looked away, not wanting to know, because she could do nothing about it.

When they passed other Mechanics, Jules took quick glances to see if any were Lady Mechanic Verona, Mak's lost daughter, but saw no sign of her.

The eight younger Mechanics were all waiting at the main entrance. "Take her back. Same procedure," the senior mechanic told them. "Except this time if attacked you can shoot."

Seeming more intimidated than enthused about the chance to engage in a fight with Mages, the young Mechanics once again made a circle with Jules in the center as they headed out of the Guild Hall and down the stairs.

Full night had fallen, the Guild Hall blazing with light behind them, scattered lanterns on the streets ahead, and patches of darkness on all sides. "Do any of you guys have any experience fighting Mages?" one of the Mechanics muttered to the others as they made their way across the wide plaza.

"I do, Sir Mechanic," Jules said, not certain if she should have answered or not.

"Oh, that's great. The common does."

"Shut up, idiot," another Mechanic said. "She's that one."

They headed down a wide street with too few lanterns for either its width or its length. Ahead, long before the waterfront, their path was shrouded in darkness. Their footsteps sounded unnaturally loud on the empty street. The Mechanics looked about, the ones with the "rifles" fingering them nervously.

Something was wrong, Jules realized. "Um, Sir Mechanic, Lady Mechanic—"

"What?" one of the women growled at her.

"Shouldn't there be a lot of people on this street? Commons?"

The group stumbled to a halt, the Mechanics searching the night. "The lanterns up ahead have been put out," one of them said. "You, girl, why wouldn't there be commons on this street?"

"They'd be avoiding it," Jules said, "if they saw signs of trouble. Or Mages."

"Blazes," another Mechanic muttered, his hands tight on his weapon.

Ahead and around them, the darkness seemed to press in.

CHAPTER NINE

"We'll see them coming, won't we?" the Mechanic in the lead whispered.

"Not necessarily, Sir Mechanic," Jules said.

He looked back at her. "You said you'd fought Mages. More than once?"

"Yes, Sir Mechanic."

"Suppose we wanted to avoid fighting Mages. What should we do?"

One of the women spoke up in incredulous tones. "You're asking a common for advice?"

"This common is the subject matter expert! Am I wrong? Come on, what's your advice?"

Jules looked ahead into the deep darkness. "Do something different. Unpredictable. Mages sometimes know what people are planning. I don't know how. Like now, waiting on this road for us."

"So if we go another route we'll throw them off?"

"That's what I'd do, Sir Mechanic." Jules sensed the hesitation in the Mechanics around her. "Mages chased me all through Landfall, and out, and back again. I'm still alive."

"All right. Wendi, left or right?"

"Ummm... right," one of the Mechanics said.

"Let's go." The Mechanic led the way back a short distance and then down a side road, the entire group moving quickly. "Myke, left, right, or straight ahead?"

"Straight."

They kept it up, wending through the town using random choices until the group reached another wide street, this one well lit. "Let's head for the pier," the leader ordered. "Double-time, people."

The Mechanics broke into a trot, Jules staying in the center.

They'd gone perhaps halfway when Jules spotted something out of the corner of her eye. "Mages to our left," she gasped between breaths.

The Mechanics on the left looked that way. "I see them."

"What're they doing?" the leader asked.

"Just standing there."

Jules managed a better look. "They're looking inland. With their hoods up they can't see us from this angle."

"How do you know that?" the Mechanic leader demanded.

"I stole a Mage's robes and wore them to get away one time," Jules said.

"How'd you steal a Mage's robes?" one of the women asked.

"I knocked her out."

"You… Why are we protecting her again?"

They'd kept moving, and as the Mages to the left were lost to sight behind buildings the leader slowed their pace, which was attracting attention from the commons.

"There's one Mage up ahead," the leader said. "Crossing from our right to our left. Doesn't seem to notice us. Everybody keep on. Common, stay low so they can't see you."

Resentful at the tone and the orders, Jules nonetheless saw the wisdom in what the leader of the Mechanic group said. She hunched over a bit, losing any ability to see past the Mechanics crowded around her.

Jules was surprised soon after when she realized they'd turned onto a pier. The Mechanics were relaxing a bit as they walked, audibly sighing with relief as they came even with the big Mechanic ship tied up there. Jules stole a glance at it, seeing how the metal structure rose above the deck in tier upon tier.

"You go down first," the leader told Jules.

She grasped the second revolver firmly as she went down the wooden ladder to the boat astern of the ship. The box of cartridges had barely fit into one of her pockets, but the revolver would have only fit inside one of the pockets of the Mechanic jacket, and she didn't expect to be wearing that much longer.

Jules had barely taken the middle of the center seat when the Mechanics came down the ladder quickly, once again taking seats around her. "What's this chest?" the leader asked the Mechanics on the pier, pointing to a small chest resting next to the middle seat.

"We don't know," one replied. "They brought it from the ship and said to give it to her," he added, pointing to Jules. "Orders from a Guild Master. We weren't told anything else."

"Fine. Let's get going."

She couldn't see what was happening behind her in the stern of the boat, but it began shaking gently again, the lines were cast off, and the boat curved out into the harbor. They were quickly in among anchored ships with one or two lanterns marking them, the dark water showing rippling reflections of the lights.

"It should be easy from here on out," the leader commented.

"Hey," another of the male Mechanics said, looking at Jules, "have you got a boyfriend?"

Before Jules could recover from her surprise enough to answer, realizing with a shock that a male Mechanic hitting on her wouldn't be doing so because of the prophecy, a female Mechanic laughed. "Seriously, Myke?"

"Hey," the male Mechanic protested, "they said it's all right to look outside Mechanic ranks for partners. They're encouraging it!"

"Yeah, but her?"

"What? She's smart."

Another female Mechanic joined in. "Sure she is. Have you been listening to her? She's also dangerous. A shorted power line sends off nice sparks, but you probably don't want to grab it."

"I don't know," another male Mechanic said. "Sometimes that kind of danger is pretty attractive in a girl."

"Stars above! What is wrong with guys?" The female Mechanic who'd spoken last noticed Jules watching and listening. "You look surprised. Why?"

Jules weighed whether to be candid, and decided to risk it. "It was just, listening to you, you seemed like any other group of people. Not Mechanics. Just people."

Instead of being offended, the woman grinned and pointed to the second man who'd spoken. "Don't let looks fool you. That guy is an architect. He's not like other people."

"And proud of it," the male Mechanic replied. "Why does that surprise you?" he asked Jules. "That we sound like people?"

"Common folk like me rarely see that side of Mechanics," Jules said.

After a brief pause, one of the women shook her head at Jules. "You're getting into Guild politics there. Better we don't start that debate."

"People are people," one of the men said.

"Not Mages," Jules said. "They're different when you talk to them."

Another pause, then the first female Mechanic leaned close to Jules. "You've talked to a Mage?"

"More than one, Lady Mechanic," Jules said.

"Why did they talk to you instead of ignoring you or trying to kill you?"

"They were dying."

Another, longer pause before the first female Mechanic spoke again. "You really have killed Mages?"

"Yes," Jules said. "They... they think differently."

"Any idea why?" one of the men asked. His voice sounded genuinely curious rather than mocking.

"I think it has something to do with the scars."

"Scars?"

"They all have scars on them. Not recent. As if they were the result of a lot of beatings when they were young."

"Mages," another Mechanic muttered in disgust. "Why do you sound like you're sorry for them?"

"I am sorry for them," Jules said. "For whatever was done to them to make them Mages."

"But you've killed Mages," the first woman said.

"Yes. And I'll kill more if I have to. I'll kill anyone I have to."

The Mechanics exchanged looks. "She's not a downed power line," one finally said. "She's an over-pressurized boiler. Still want her as a girlfriend, Myke?"

"Maybe," Mechanic Myke said.

The other Mechanics laughed.

Jules listened, wondering what these Mechanics would do or say if she told them of Mechanic Hal and Mechanic Gayl. If they knew nothing of such things, they'd be sure she was lying. And if they did know of them, they wouldn't be eager to risk the same fate for themselves by doing or saying the wrong thing.

Maybe that also made them just like other people.

The boat finally reached the *Sun Queen*, coasting along to the bottom of the Jaykob ladder with effortless ease. "Jacket," the Mechanic leader said, holding out his hand to Jules.

She pulled off the Mechanics jacket, trying not to show how relieved she was to rid herself of it.

"Chest," he said, pointing.

Jules tried hefting it, finding it surprisingly heavy for its size. "Somebody up there drop a line so we can haul up this chest!" Jules called to those on the deck of the *Sun Queen*.

A line came down, she knotted it securely about the chest, checked that the small wooden box was still securely in her pocket, grasped the second revolver firmly, and reached for the ladder.

But paused to look around at the Mechanics who'd escorted her. "Thank you, Sir Mechanics, Lady Mechanics."

"We were just following orders," one of the women said. "Go kill some more Mages for us."

Jules climbed the ladder while the chest was hauled up beside her.

By the time she reached the deck the Mechanic boat had already left and was being lost to sight as it wended among the anchored ships between the *Sun Queen* and the pier.

"Is everything all right, Cap'n?" Ang asked as other crew members crowded around.

"I think so," Jules said. "But Mages may have been looking for me in town. Let's get back out to sea and head north to Marida's."

"Aye. Gord, help the cap'n get that chest into her cabin. The rest of you get on the capstan to raise the anchor and get ready to make sail."

Jules paused in her cabin only long enough to stow the extra revolver and tell Gord where to set down the chest. She went back on deck as the *Sun Queen*'s anchor cleared the water and the sails were unfurled to catch the mild wind inside the harbor. Coming about, the ship tacked across the gentle waters, Jules and Ang watching closely to ensure the ship remained in the safe channel with enough water under keel. The *Sun Queen* sailed past the still-glowing beacon on Meg's Point, and out into the rougher swells of the sea.

"Captain Lars said we could find ships in need of escort west in the waters around Marida's," Jules told Ang. "We'll pick up some easy money that way. But we have to be sure we don't get too close to Sandurin, where the Imperial patrols are thick."

"No problem, Cap'n."

Jules went back down to her cabin, yawning, thinking it must be nearly the middle of the night. Liv followed her. "So, no difficulties with the Mechanics?"

"No," Jules said. "They were…" She sat down, rubbing her forehead. "It was strange. A couple of times it felt like the Mechanics I was with were just regular people. Like other commons I was working with or talking to. Only for a few moments, though, and then I'd remember who and what they were and it'd be over."

"What, like they were friends of yours?" Liv said, taking another chair and kicking back.

"Almost. Strange, huh?" Jules looked out the stern window, where little could be seen of the dark, restless waters. "The prophecy says the daughter of my line will have Mechanics helping her. I wondered how she could do that, but I think I caught glimpses of it tonight. I can't do it, though. The Mechanics will never respect me enough, and when I think about what they've done I hate them."

"Of course. You're a common." Liv pointed to the small wooden box. "What's in that?"

"You'll never believe it." Jules opened the box, canting it so Liv could see inside. "Twenty cartridges. These are worth an Emperor's ransom. Or they would be if I tried selling them."

"Twenty? And you still had, what, three others you said?"

"Yes," Jules said, suddenly realizing that she'd turned in those three cartridges along with her original revolver. "Blazes, I *had* three more." She pulled out the new weapon, looking to see if it had any cartridges.

And stared. "This is a new weapon," she told Liv. "They had me swap them out. It's got five cartridges in it." Jules dug out the second new revolver and checked it. "This one has five, too. Stars above, Liv, I've got *thirty* cartridges and two Mechanic revolvers!"

"You're practically a legion all by yourself," Liv said dryly, acting unimpressed. "Why do you suppose the Mechanics were so generous?"

"They need me, Liv. They need us. They need what we can do." Jules glanced at the small chest. It was sturdy, with metal strapping over what looked like thick hardwood. "I never did find out what was in that. Senior Mechanic Grace had the ship give it to me." She leaned over, working the latch and opening the top.

And stared again.

Liv, looking as well, let out a low whistle at the sight of the gold coins. "Imperial eagles. How much is in there?"

"A lot." Jules put one hand in among the gold eagles, moving them to see if all of the coins were the same. "There aren't any silver galleys. They're all eagles."

"What are you going to do with it?" Liv asked.

"What do you mean? It belongs to the ship."

"The ship didn't earn it," Liv said. "You were given it. I wouldn't want to consult a lawyer in the matter, but I think most would say you're under no obligation to share."

"Then most would be wrong." Jules shut the chest. "I'll count it later, but some will be shared with the crew. They've foregone other chances at gold on my account, and run risks on my account as well. I won't withhold this from them."

"What do you suppose the Mechanics think you'll do with it?" Liv gave Jules a concerned look. "You didn't promise anything, did you?"

"No," Jules said. "I just talked about doing what I was going to do anyway. I did make it sound like I was doing it for their benefit, though." She paused, remembering the conversation. "They think we've got about a year before the Emperor snaps and orders an attack on the western settlements. That's just enough time for me to get something important done."

"What's that?"

"I think I'll be able to tell you soon."

* * *

The next morning she counted the gold, finding enough to share an eagle with every member of the crew with plenty left over for future needs. The crew lined up to receive their eagles, cheerful at the unexpected pay and at the prospect of a stop at Marida's, whose waterfront bars were gaining a reputation among sailors for good times.

Marida's harbor had added two more piers and a lot of buildings, as well as some defensive fortifications facing east toward the Empire. The *Sun Queen* anchored out, her crew taking the boats in for some good times ashore while Ang sought business from anyone wanting an escort west. Jules stayed on the ship, trying to remain out of sight to anyone on other ships or ashore. Aside from not wanting to attract Mage attention, her escape from the Empire still wasn't widely known, including to Imperial authorities who were still searching for her inland as well as at sea. There wasn't any sense in advertising where she was. The crew had been told not to mention ashore that she was back, and hopefully would keep their mouths shut even after downing a number of beers and other forms of booze.

Ang found a merchant ship packed with escapees from the Empire that was willing to pay for protection and guidance to Western Port. The *Sun Queen* left Marida's harbor after a day and half, her crew poorer but happier, Jules relieved to get out without being noticed.

The day before they got to Western Port, Jules threw up again.

She sat in her cabin, gazing morosely at her chamber pot.

"Problem?" Liv asked when she stopped by.

"I'm sick again this morning," Jules said, reluctant to come right out and say it.

"I'll get Keli. Maybe it's something you ate. You stayed aboard at Marida's so you shouldn't have picked up any bugs there."

"It's not something I ate," Jules said.

"You sound like you know what it is," Liv said, giving her a curious glance.

"It's been about seven weeks since we left Dor's last."

"Seven weeks?" Liv stared at her. "Are you saying—"

"Get Keli and Ang. We need to talk."

When Liv came back with the other two, they sat around the table. Jules looked down at the table, facing a moment that she'd dreaded. "I'm having morning sickness," she said. "I'm sure of it. There are some things we need to plan out."

Keli looked at Liv, who nodded. "If one of the men on the ship also needs to be involved…"

"It wasn't one of the men on the ship," Jules said.

"Ah. Do you know who he was, then?"

She glared at him. "Of course I know who he is! Blazes, Keli, who do you think I am?"

"A woman facing a very unique set of problems," he said, "as well as a common condition. This needs to be kept quiet. If word gets out, the whole Sea of Bakre will boil."

"Yes," Jules said. "That's one thing. We need to try to keep as many people as possible in the dark, including every Mage and Mechanic and servant of the Empire." She was trying to sound as if this was just one more voyage being planned. Nothing too difficult, and nothing to get alarmed about. "Liv, how long before I start to show, do you think?"

"Most women, it's three to four months the first time," Liv said. "With your build, you should match that."

"So we've got at least a month and a half before I start showing," Jules said. "We have to ensure people see me until then."

"Loose clothes, a long coat left open, will help hide it for a while after that," Liv said. "But there'll come a time when it'll be obvious to the most casual observer."

"Maybe a long voyage might be a good idea," Ang said. "Say you're exploring. The crew would know. But we don't have any among us who'd betray you."

"It's not just me personally," Jules said. "Any child of mine will be a target for a lot of people. We have to minimize the number who even know a child is coming."

"You could go to that Pacta Servanda place for the last few months," Keli said. "No Mages, no Mechanics, and no way for the news to spread."

"That's a good idea," Jules said. "But that's the other thing we have to plan. The hardest thing. When I get close, I'll need to be back in these waters." She paused, unable to force the words out.

"Why?" Ang asked.

"It's a good idea to be where good midwives can be found," Keli said.

"I don't think that's her reason," Liv said. "What is it, Jules? You look like you're watching a loved one die."

"That's how it feels," Jules said. She looked toward the drawing of Severun that was her sole memento of Mak, unable to meet their eyes. "The child, when it comes, will only have one chance to survive. There's only one way to give my child a chance at life. Because if anyone knows who that child's mother is, the Mages will not stop until they find it and kill the child. As a young adult, I've barely survived. A baby wouldn't stand a chance."

"A foster family?" Keli said.

"A foster family would know," Ang said. "You don't mean an orphanage?"

"No!" Jules said, remembering her own harsh upbringing in an Imperial orphanage. "I want a family. But… I can't know. They can't know. No one can know. If anyone knows, the Mages might find out. Even I can't know."

Silence, finally broken by Liv. "Even you?"

"You know I'm right. I need you guys to set it up. The moment the child is born and safe, you need to take him or her, and pass the baby somehow through enough people that no one can trace the path afterwards and the family who ends up with the child has no idea who the mother is. So no one looking for that child can ever find him or her."

"The moment the child is born?" Keli said. "Don't you want to—?"

"Of course I want to!" Jules fought to control herself. "Don't you understand? If I hold the child, if I even see the child, I won't be able to do it. I'll never let him or her go. And that means they'll die." Silence again. "You know I'm right. I have to do this to save my child's life."

"Girl…" Liv said, sounding as if she was about to cry.

Keli nodded slowly, his expression tragic. "You're braver than even I thought. I'm sorry, girl. I'm sorry the prophecy did this to you. But you're right. It's the only chance. Otherwise the Mages, or someone else who means the child ill, will find him or her and then it'll be the end." He paused. "You know who the father is. What of him?"

"He doesn't know," Jules said. "He won't know."

"But—"

"It's my responsibility. The decision is mine. I will bear the blame and the guilt for it. He shouldn't have to endure either of those."

"I think you're wrong about that," Keli said.

"Your disapproval is noted," Jules said. "Can we do this?"

Ang nodded with clear reluctance. "Anything that people want, there's an underground market for it. There'll be people who trade in getting babies to those who want them badly enough."

"A fake mother, a fake history," Keli said. "What do they call it when you pass something through more than one person?"

"A cutout," Ang said. "Like when we want to sell a special bit of cargo whose origin we don't want traced. It passes through more than one set of hands, each set knowing less of its origin that the one before."

"But we're talking of doing this to a baby," Liv said. "Your baby, Jules."

"Do you think I'm happy about it?" she whispered. "Please think of an alternative that offers that child a chance at survival. I'd be very, very grateful if you did."

Silence, in which only the muffled sounds of sailors on deck could be heard.

"Why did you decide to go ahead with it?" Keli asked. "Why now?"

"Because events convinced me I might not live long enough to get it done if I kept putting it off," Jules said. "And I wanted to be in control of who the father was. Can we do this?"

"It can be done, I think," Keli said. "Ang and I will share our collective knowledge and start to work on the second part of things."

After Keli and Ang left, Liv lingered, eying Jules. "This is hitting you hard. I understand, and yet I think there's something more behind it."

Jules clenched her fist on the surface of the table, feeling the pain as she tightened it, her fingernails digging into her palm. "While I was growing up in that Imperial orphanage, I vowed that if I ever had a child, I'd be the best mother any kid could ever want. I'd never leave them and I'd never see them hurt. And now I have to plan to send my child to strangers, unable to ever know their fate."

"That was a foolish vow," Liv said. "I'm a child of the orphanages as well, so it's easy for me to see how a young girl there would've made such a promise. But no woman, no mother, can count on keeping such a promise. We can't keep hurt from those we love, and our own mothers didn't leave us because they wanted to. They had no choice. Just as you have none."

"That's true," Jules said. "But it still hurts. I'm afraid for how much it'll hurt when I actually have to give up the child."

Liv sighed. "We'll be here for you. What about the man? Having him here might offer comfort as well."

"Why do you think he's someone I'd want here?" Jules scoffed.

"Because I know you. You would've waited a dozen more years if you hadn't known a man you thought would be a worthy father."

"I'm not telling him, Liv. It's best for him this way."

Liv shook her head. "Girl, he was man enough for you to choose him. Do you think such a man will accept you deciding for him what's best? You owe him a voice in it."

"The world owes me a child to raise," Jules said. "People don't always get what they're owed in life."

* * *

The next morning they reached Western Port, Jules throwing up early enough that she could be on the quarterdeck as the *Sun Queen* reached the pier with no one the wiser. The merchant ship they'd brought this far, the *Fair Dani*, tied up on the other side of the pier. As soon as the *Dani*'s boarding plank was down, escapees from the Empire began streaming off, gazing with hope at the town.

Jules saw the stream of refugees reach the end of the pier and encounter not only some members of the new town militia who got them lined up, but also what appeared to be various officials of the town.

She came down onto the pier to find Shin waiting, smiling broadly.

"Jules! Welcome back!" he cried, engulfing her hand in two of his. "I've been doing as you ask. Can you see?"

"I see," Jules said. "What's your official title?"

"Mayor of Western Port." He turned to point to those meeting the escapees from the Empire. "Police, of course. And she is head of the town schools. And he arranges places to stay. And she keeps track of skilled artisans or apprentices so we know what we have and use it best."

"That's a lot more than I would've thought of," Jules said.

"You would've done the same," Shin said with a laugh. "Experience in the legions, you know. If we don't learn anything else, we learn how to organize, right?" He looked up onto the deck of the *Sun Queen*, his smile growing broader. "Marta!"

Marta leaned on the railing, grinning at Shin. "Are you busy tonight?"

"That's up to your captain. She might have jobs for me," Shin said.

"I don't need Marta sulking around," Jules said. "Go ahead and make a date."

After Shin had made social arrangements for that night, he and Jules walked down the pier. "You need to see how things have come since you were here last," Shin said. "We've finished many of the buildings, thanks to the foresight of the Imperial planners who provided precut lumber and everything else we needed."

"Have you had any problems?" They were walking past where the new arrivals were lined up, and Jules was trying not to notice how many of them were looking at her and speaking excitedly to each other. She heard a few words. *Prophecy. Great Guilds. Daughter.* To many commons, those defined her.

But she also heard words like *pirate, explorer,* and *captain.* It was nice to know she'd managed to make those words stick.

"Problems? A few," Shin said with a dismissive wave of his hand as they left the pier, their boots crunching on the gravel of the waterfront streets. "Mostly people not understanding that being free doesn't mean no rules exist. We're not trying to use the Imperial legal code, but we do have laws because we need laws."

"I hope you don't have any laws against piracy," Jules said.

"Why?" Shin asked with a grin. "I don't know any pirates. Oh, there's someone you must meet. Your guess that the people who came through the Northern Ramparts from Kelsi's might have settled somewhere up this same river was correct. They sent a boat down to explore. It got here three days ago. Over there. See?"

Jules looked at the craft drawn up on one bank of the river. It had a frame of bent wooden branches, over which leather hides had been stitched together to form a watertight hull. "I'm guessing they don't have much lumber north of here. That boat'd be pretty light, though."

"Very light," Shin said. "Three people came down the river in it, riding the current. They are going to walk back, carrying the boat to use as shelter each night by overturning it."

"Clever."

"They should be waiting for us in the mayor's home, which right now is my home," Shin said as he and Jules reached the former town commander's house. He opened the door and led Jules inside. "When we saw the *Sun Queen* coming into port, I asked those who came in the boat to be here to see you."

Two men and one woman stood in the reception room on the ground floor, looking awkward and anxious. Their clothing was worn by long use, except for leather articles that were clearly newer. As their eyes fell on Jules, she heard gasps of recognition.

"Lady," the older of the men said, smiling. "I am T'mos. This is Jani, and Bors," he added, indicating the woman and the younger man. "We haven't forgotten you from Sandurin. How is Captain Mak?"

"Captain Mak died a while back," Jules said. "Killed by Mages."

"Oh." T'mos' face fell. "We're very sorry."

"It wasn't anything you could have helped," Jules said. "So you did found a settlement on those plains to the west of the Northern Ramparts?"

"Yes, Lady," the woman named Jani said. "We named it Ihris, after one of our leaders. She died not long after we reached the spot."

"Ihris." Jules remembered that woman, tall and willowy, but with the shadow of some serious illness on her. Mak had guessed she didn't have much longer to live. "I'm sorry to hear that. How are you governed?"

"Governed?"

"Is your settlement ruled by all of the people there making decisions, or does one person rule?"

The visitors from Ihris exchanged looks. "We've been using a group of people who everyone respects to make decisions," T'mos said. "But it's still sort of informal. Shin has been telling us about voting. I think our leaders will be happy to hear of that."

"Good." Jules smiled at them. "I'm glad you escaped the Empire. You know a lot of other people are doing the same these days. We just brought another group of them here."

She was surprised to see wariness appear in the eyes of the visitors from Ihris. "We don't know much of what has been happening outside Ihris," Jani said.

"A lot of new settlements are being founded in the west," Jules said. "That's good for you. Markets for whatever goods your town can produce, and other free people to support you in the face of danger."

"We have leather, and livestock herds," Bors said eagerly. "Cattle. Horses. We've been gathering them from wild herds. And planting crops."

"That's good," Jules said. "There'll be ready markets for those. Can you provide any support to Western Port if danger threatens?"

"Why would danger threaten us?" T'mos asked.

Why did these people seem to be drawing back from her even though they weren't actually moving? "The hand of the Emperor has tried reaching beyond the borders of the Empire," Jules said. "Western Port was going to be an Imperial outpost. If that had succeeded, you would've had legionaries controlling this river."

"But it didn't succeed," T'mos said. "The people here are free."

Jules glanced at Shin, who was frowning in puzzlement at the altered attitudes he was seeing. "You do know that this town was freed by fighting, don't you?" she said. "Three free ships came here and defeated the legionaries. My ship was one of them."

The three from Ihris nodded politely, but said nothing.

Jules decided to be as direct as possible. "If the Empire attacks Western Port, will Ihris send men and women to help defend this town?"

"We cannot make such a commitment," Jani said.

"But you can tell us the sentiment of your people," Shin said. "And you can carry our proposal for mutual assistance back with you."

T'mos seemed to be looking everywhere in the room but at Jules and Shin. "We are not soldiers," he said. "We have no soldiers among us."

Shin frowned. "What if the Empire captures Kelsi's and sends legionaries through the pass to your city? What if Western Port is captured? What will you do?"

"There is much land to the west," Jani said. "We'll head that way and found another settlement."

"You'll hit the ocean eventually if you keep fleeing west," Jules said. "What about the towns being founded in the Northern Ramparts? And Kelsi's? Do you have any agreements with them?"

"We haven't contacted anyone to the east since we left Kelsi's," Jani said.

"I'm confused," Shin said. "Do you think you can live separate from all others? All of us in the west have common interests in freedom."

"Then no one should object to us doing what we want."

Jules looked at the three. "Do I understand that if your free neighbors are in need of help, you will not offer any aid?"

"We... have a policy of... not getting involved in the disputes of others. That seems safest for us," T'mos said, unable to meet Jules' eyes.

She gazed coldly at him. "How fortunate for you that I didn't follow that kind of policy when you were locked up in Sandurin."

T'mos didn't answer.

"It was nice meeting you again," Jules said, hearing the ice in her voice. "If you'll excuse us, Shin and I have other matters to discuss."

Mumbling farewells, T'mos and Jani left.

The younger man, Bors, hesitated at the door. "Lady," he blurted out, "not everyone in Ihris agrees with those ideas. The older ones fear being caught again, hauled back to slavery in the Empire, and want to avoid anything that might risk that. Do you remember Aron?"

"Of course I remember Aron," Jules said. "Are he and Lil all right?"

"Yes, Lady. And they speak of you! They remind others of what risks you ran for us, and shame those who want to hide rather than help others. Don't judge our town too harshly. Not yet. Ihris may always stand apart, but not all of us have forgotten what we owe a stranger who came to our aid when all seemed lost." Ducking his head in apology, Bors ran off after the other two.

"So much for gratitude," Jules said, hearing the bitterness in her voice.

Shin shook his head, his mouth tight. "They were indentured laborers on an agricultural estate, you said? The older ones must have been beaten down by such a life."

"I know all about being beaten down. So do you, because we were raised in the same Imperial orphanage. But being beaten down doesn't make you beaten in life."

"Are you sorry you saved them from that prince at Sandurin?"

Shin had a way of asking just the right question. Jules shook her head in turn. "No. I had to do it for reasons that had a lot to do with me, not them. I know that. And the example of their escape has motivated a lot of others to flee the Empire. It was the right thing to do. But I'm still disappointed."

"When you make someone free to act as they wish, they may act in ways you wish they would not," Shin said.

"Look at you," Jules said. "The orphan legionary philosopher. I hope you're writing down things like that." She ran one hand through her hair, her mood darkening at the memory of causing the death of Ian's father in this building. "Shin, how about you and Western Port? Will you send help if I call?"

"Why do you even ask this?" Shin said. "Of course we will send you aid if you call for it. Do you have any idea yet where and when that aid will be needed?"

Jules walked to one side of the room, where Shin had posted one of the new charts. "I think *where* is pretty definite. Ultimately, the Emperor wants access to all the lands in the west, especially those in the rich southern lands. That means the Empire will attack Dor's Castle."

"To secure his lines of communication," Shin said, nodding. "Yes.

His eye will be on Julesport, because you have frustrated him so often, but getting to Julesport means taking Dor's Castle."

"Which won't happen," Jules said. "Because we're going to defend it."

"When do you think the Emperor's patience will end?"

"The Mechanics think it'll take about a year. The Empire isn't used to failure mattering, so the Emperor and his advisers will keep trying to capture me while protecting their main port cities of Landfall and Sandurin. And no one is going to want to tell the Emperor it's not working, because they'll fear taking the blame. But the Emperor will eventually realize his advisers are lying to him about what I'm doing and where I am, and that while he's been chasing me his Empire has been bleeding refugees to found new, free cities in the west."

Shin made a face. "I would not want to be one of the advisers when the Emperor's patience finally runs out. But after he has them killed, he will look at a map and see Julesport on it."

"And that's when Dor's Castle will need help," Jules said. "Have any Mechanics or Mages shown up around here?"

"One of the big metal Mechanic ships sailed past one day," Shin said. "But it didn't stop and no one got off. No Mages have been seen, either."

"That's strange," Jules said, looking at the chart. "The Mechanics have some kind of internal dispute going on that's taking a lot of their attention, but the Mages know I'm spending a lot of time in the west. And before this they've shown an occasional ability to know where I am and when I'll be there. Where are the Mages?"

Shin had no answer.

CHAPTER TEN

Wherever the Mages were, Jules knew she had to keep moving. But she had other reasons to travel from place to place for as long as she could.

The founders of the settlement north of the Strait of Gulls were calling it Farland. The town was less than a month old when Jules brought the *Sun Queen* by for a visit. As she dressed to see Farland's leaders, Jules received another daily reminder that she herself was now five months along.

"Girl," Liv warned when Jules walked up to the *Sun Queen*'s quarterdeck, "you're showing. Keep that long coat on and don't stretch or stand in a way that makes your belly obvious."

"I know. It's probably time to be thinking of that long voyage to Pacta Servanda," Jules said, leaning on the railing and reluctant to move her feet.

"Can you handle not having much to do while you're there?"

"Liv, I've spent the last few months bouncing all over the Sea of Bakre, and out of it a few times, showing my face everywhere, never stopping anywhere long enough for Mages to show up, and talking to every new settlement and the older ones about standing together when the Emperor finally realizes what he's doing isn't working. I'm exhausted."

"You have seemed really tired at times."

"Yeah. Having nothing to do for a while sounds like fun." Jules winced as she straightened. "And that's not counting this. My feet hurt, my back hurts, and it feels like my guts are slowly being pushed up into my stomach, which does not like that, by the way."

"It's only going to get worse," Liv said.

"Thank you. I really needed to hear that."

She'd scheduled the meeting for after dark, just to make it a little harder for anyone to spot the swelling of her mid-section. For now, Farland consisted of a few tents, some improvised shelters, and a couple of half-finished buildings of wood cut from the seemingly inexhaustible forest stretching inland. The population of a couple of hundred were settling down for the night around outside fires where dinner was being cooked. "We'll have an oven soon," one of Farland's leaders told Jules. "And that means bread!"

"Is everything else going well?" Jules had declined an offer to take a seat around the fire where the "town leaders" were gathered, fearing that sitting on the ground would expose her awkwardness. Behind her stood four of her guards, wearing the better armor that she'd bought for them using Mechanic gold. She'd feared at first that common people might be intimidated by the presence of her guards, but they instead seemed to find them reassuring.

"It's a little spooky at times," one of the women said, waving toward the darkness gathered under the dense woods outside the area cleared for the town. "That forest is so big, and full of eyes. Animals. A lot of them. It's easy to imagine legionaries or Mages lurking in there ready to pounce."

"Or Mara the Undying," one of the men said with a grin.

"You probably know why I'm here," Jules said. "The Emperor is going to reach his hand this way sooner or later. When he does, will you send aid if I call for it?"

The leaders of the town exchanged glances, their emotions hard to read in the flickering light of the fire. "What kind of aid?" one asked Jules.

"A ship if you have one. Men and women who can help crew ships, or help fight the Emperor's legionaries."

"We don't have that many," the woman who'd spoken earlier said. "We couldn't send much."

"And don't we need them here?" the man said. "If the legions come, we'll need our defenders here."

Jules, having heard that argument in every new settlement in the west, nodded in understanding. "The Emperor will have to attack Dor's Castle first before he can risk attacking anywhere else in the west. If Dor's Castle holds, the Empire can't threaten you here. And if Dor's Castle doesn't hold, ask yourselves this. Suppose a couple of Imperial galleys sail to this spot and put a century of legionaries ashore. What could you do?"

A pause, then the woman answered. "We couldn't beat a hundred legionaries. We'd either have to surrender or try to escape inland."

"How about fifty legionaries?" Jules said. "Same answer, right? Because the few fighters that you have can't, on their own, stop such a force of soldiers. But," she said, pointing to the southeast, "some of your fighters, added in to fighters from other towns throughout the west, can hold the wall that Dor is building. It's big and strong. If occupied by enough defenders, even the Emperor's legions won't be able to take it. And then the legions will never come to Farland."

The town leaders looked at each other again. "If we defend Dor's Castle, we'll be defending Farland," one said. "I see what you mean. But how do we know Dor will make good use of our people? That they won't be needlessly sacrificed? And if Dor becomes powerful enough, what if he sends soldiers here to make Farland part of a new empire?"

Once again, she'd heard those worries before. "Because I'll be there, and I'll never let Dor, or anyone else in the west, try to gain that kind of power over others. The west is free, and it will remain free," Jules said. "That's my promise to you. I can't finish the job. I can't stop the Great Guilds. That'll be up to the daughter of my line when she comes. But I'll do all I can to smooth the waters for her."

They heard her out, nodding. "Your promise is worth more than gold eagles," the man said.

"That went well," Artem said as they walked back to the beach to take their boat to the *Sun Queen*. The night sky seemed filled with stars, the forests on either side murky and filled with eyes, the water washing up on the pale beach dark and mysterious.

"Unless something happens to me before the Empire attacks," Jules said. "No one else can rally the free lands. There's something wrong when this is all dependent on me being there."

"That's how things are in the Empire," Artem said. "The Emperor or the Empress makes things happen."

"I don't want the west to be like the Empire," Jules said. "I don't want one person to be in charge, or one person able to do whatever they want. Like on a free ship. Elect the captain, and let the captain make a lot of decisions, but if the captain is wrong, or dies, someone else can be elected captain."

"Can cities work that way, though?"

"I hope so," Jules said, looking across the water to the dark silhouette of the *Sun Queen* riding at anchor. "I really hope so."

"Where are we going from here?" Gord asked as the rowers drove the longboat back to the ship.

Jules looked down at herself. "Dor's. There's someone I have to see."

* * *

The day before the ship reached Dor's, with nothing but empty sea visible around them, Jules called the crew to a meeting. Everyone gathered on deck or the lowest spars and rigging, looking toward the quarterdeck where Jules stood. "There's an open secret on this ship," Jules said. "One all of you surely already know from the looks of me. You know how important this is to the future of our people. I have to establish a line or the prophecy can't come true. But if word gets out that I'm expecting, the Mages will go berserk, and the Emperor will likely do the same. The Mechanics might also try to kill my child, or take it for their own uses."

She paused, hating to think of the possible futures her child might face. "That's why it's so important that none of you breathe a word of this to anyone. This has to be a secret kept to the crew of the *Sun Queen*. Don't speak of it to others. Don't speak of it among yourselves if you're off the ship, or where any others could hear. I can't demand this of you, but I beg that you do as I ask. I know it'll be hard to stay quiet about such a thing, but if you do, you'll be able to someday tell people that each of you, personally, had an important part in helping the prophecy to come to pass. That daughter of my line when she comes will owe her life to you as much as to me. Keep your silence, and someday when it comes out you'll be able to boast of your part in it."

For a long moment no one said anything, the only sounds the waves alongside the ship's hull, the creaking of wood, and the sigh of wind through the rigging.

Then they cheered and applauded, while Jules felt her face warming with embarrassment.

"We all knew," Marta called out. "And we've been quiet, because we're smart enough to know what you just said, that it has to stay a secret. But there's one question we all have. Is the man responsible among us?"

Her first instinct was to tell Marta and the crew that it was none of their business, but that would just set the rumors flying. "No," Jules said. "No disrespect intended to the men of the *Sun Queen*, but I never considered any of you for that."

"I told you!" Liv said. "She has too much good sense to fish for a man in these waters!"

The men in the crew let out a groan of disappointment that was so loud and theatrical that even Jules couldn't help laughing. "Sorry. You'll do it, then? Hold your words?"

Kyle shouted a reply. "For our hatred of the Great Guilds, for the sake of our children, for our loyalty to our ship and our crew mates, and for the honor of our captain, we'll keep it among ourselves!"

"Thank you," Jules said, her voice nearly breaking on the last word. She watched the crew talk and laugh, happy to have their suspicions confirmed, and happy to know the prophecy was being safeguarded and that they had a role in it.

Liv sighed. "They see only the good sides of it. Just as well they don't think about what it means for you."

"You're right," Jules said. "Bad enough I have to think of it. We've got a great crew, don't we?"

"They're not bad," Ang said. "Even if none of the men are worthy."

Ang joked so rarely that Jules had to look at him to be sure he was making fun of himself and the others.

"I had my money on Keli being the one," Ang added, unable to suppress a smile.

"Keli?" Jules said. "Keli? Say that again and I'll knife you!"

* * *

Maeve of Marandur had been one of the most sought-after midwives in the Imperial capitol, serving the highest as well as the lowest levels of society. Until the day one of her patients, the wife of a prince, suffered an unforeseen complication. It wasn't the sort of thing anyone could've prevented given the state of the healing arts on the world of Dematr, but the prince (as princes can and sometimes do) blamed Maeve anyway.

Luckily for Maeve, some of her other high level and more grateful clients warned her that her arrest, show trial, and certain conviction were imminent, and then helped her escape Marandur and the Empire. As with other skilled men and women, the Empire's loss had been Dor's Castle's gain.

And since Maeve was well-known among other healers for both her skill and her ability to keep her patients' secrets, Keli had sought her out to work with Jules. Maeve had seen her once before, but Keli thought it wise to get another check before Jules headed south.

The *Sun Queen* slipped into the harbor at Dor's Castle just after sunset, dropping anchor not too far from one of the piers. Keli was rowed to the pier to collect Maeve and return with her. The primary reason for the stealthy arrival was to avoid any Mages who might be watching for Jules, but there was another person Jules wanted to avoid. It would be very awkward if Ian were to show up now.

The stars and the moon told of midnight by the time Keli returned.

Maeve looked over Jules carefully, touching her gently and asking her questions which Jules did her best to answer truthfully. At one point Maeve brought out a sort of tube with flared ends, placing it against Jules' midsection and listening intently. Keli watched from one corner of the cabin. When Maeve was done Liv and Ang were summoned into the cabin to hear the results. Jules sat on her bunk while the others stood around the cabin, the three lanterns lit for the examination providing an unusual amount of light.

"You're disgustingly healthy," Maeve said to Jules. "I can't see any grounds for concern as long as you take care of yourself. That's no guarantee, of course. How many children did your mother have?"

"Two," Jules said, surprised that she could discuss it so calmly. "She died in childbirth with the second. The child also didn't survive."

Maeve sighed. "It happens too often. Do you know exactly what happened?"

"No. No one told me. I was five years old."

"Did your mother ever mention any difficulties giving birth to you?"

Jules made a helpless gesture with both hands. "I don't remember. I was five when she died."

Maeve shook her head. "You don't show any signs that your birth caused you any problems, so if there were complications they must have been minor. I've given you a list of what to expect, and what to see as warning signs. Pay attention to that list. If you experience the warning signs, get to me or another midwife as soon as you can."

"All right," Jules said. "Is there any reason I can't continue to fulfill my responsibilities as captain of this ship?"

"That depends on what you consider your responsibilities," the midwife said. "Giving orders on the quarterdeck? Fine. Running up the rigging to the maintop? Could get to be a bit risky."

"What of the Mechanic weapons?" Keli asked, indicating the revolver that Jules had set on the table. "Can she safely use those?"

"Of that I have no idea," Maeve confessed. "No one except Mechanics know how they work. Is there anything about them that would worry you?"

"They've got a kick when I shoot one," Jules said. "A lot more than a crossbow. But that's in the arm. And there's an acrid odor from something burning."

"Has the odor ever made you feel ill?"

"No."

"When do you use that thing?" the midwife asked.

"It's mainly for fighting Mages, though I've also used it against legionaries," Jules said. "Pretty close-in fighting situations."

"Ah." Maeve nodded. "As a rule, I do recommend that women as far along as you are try to avoid getting into hand-to-hand combat, especially so when Mages are involved."

"I'll keep that in mind," Jules said. "It's often not a choice for me, though."

"Do you have any other questions or problems?" Maeve asked.

"Yeah," Jules said. "When's that glow supposed to start? I've been looking forward to being able to walk around in the dark without a lantern."

"The glow's only in your head, and those of your friends," Maeve said, smiling.

"You sound like a Mage," Jules grumbled.

"What?"

"Nothing. I'll see you again in a few months."

Maeve paused, looking down soberly at Jules. "I don't know how far off you're going, or how far you'll have to sail to get back here, but I hope you understand that you can't time these things to the day. When the baby decides to come, that's it."

"So I've heard," Jules said. She studied Maeve. "Do you disapprove of what I'm doing?"

Maeve sighed. "It's risky to be away during the last months. Things can happen to you and things can happen to the baby. But if you're asking me whether I disapprove of your need to hide your condition from as much of the world as you can, and for your need to think foremost of that baby's life and safety, I'm in no position to judge that or to judge you. I'm only glad that I don't face the need for such choices. And I'll be honest that my ability to spot a problem is limited to what I can see and feel and hear from the outside, which is why we sometimes lose mothers, and babies. There'd be a risk no matter what you do."

She paused again, looking at Jules. "Because of your plans, there's something you should know. You said you've been extremely tired at times, and had some pretty severe morning sickness. And at the moment you seem to be pretty large for a first-time mother. Those are signs that there may be twins."

"*Twins?*" Jules sighed. "Twins. I have to give up not one child but two."

"I'd say there's a real chance of that."

"If it was twins, couldn't you hear two heartbeats with that horn?" Keli asked.

"Not this early," Maeve said. "I have to go with my experience and my instincts on this, and those say twins are likely."

Jules stared down at herself, her heart sinking. "Then we need to…" Blazes, it was hard to say. "We need to prepare for two children who need to be… hidden."

"As much as I hate to say it," Maeve said, "if you want the highest possible chance that both will live, they should be separated. Sent to different families, neither ever knowing of the other."

"You're right," Jules said, surprised that she was able to say it.

"We'll take care of it," Keli said in a somber voice, looking at Ang and Liv, who nodded.

"I'll help," Maeve said. "Sorry I can't be certain. There're legends that the Mechanics once shared with commons devices that allowed a healer to see inside a person, to actually see what problems might be inside, or to see if you were carrying two instead of one."

"I've heard such stories," Keli said. "But I think they're just wild tales. How could anyone see inside someone?"

"I don't know," Maeve said. "If the Mechanics could do it at one time, and shared it with us, that hasn't happened in living memory.

And they may not have it anymore even if they once did. When I was still in Marandur I got called into their Guild Hall to assist a difficult birth." She grimaced. "We lost the baby on that one, though we saved the mother. If the Mechanics had such devices, surely they would've known what to do before that night."

Jules looked south, remembering different things she'd heard. "Mak thought over time the Mechanics would lose some of their devices. Mechanic devices can break, you know. Or just not work. And I've heard… never mind where… that sometimes the Mechanics will kill their own because of their Guild politics."

"I wouldn't put anything past Mechanics," Keli said. "But if they end up killing the wrong people, ones that might know special things, that could hurt them, couldn't it?"

"I certainly hope so." Jules thought of Mechanic Hal and Mechanic Gayl. "It'd be ironic if the things the Guild did to maintain its power turned out to weaken it, wouldn't it? Justice will slowly sap the strength of the Mechanics, while our people grow stronger. Mak told me that. I think he's right."

Maeve smiled at her. "Is this Mak a friend who'll be with you the next few months?"

"Mak is always with me," Jules said.

* * *

The midwife was taken ashore, the boat picking up some supplies that had been delivered to the pier by a grumpy, sleepy merchant. Before dawn lit the sky, the *Sun Queen* was clearing the harbor and turning to head west.

"The guy who delivered our supplies said he saw three Mages walking the streets of Dor's," Ang said.

"Three Mages?" Jules looked back toward Dor's Castle. "Did he say how they were acting?"

"Like Mages. But walking around at an odd hour, like they were looking for someone."

"I wonder who they were looking for," Jules said sarcastically. "Why did they think I'd be in the town?"

Ang rubbed his chin, looking east and south over the water toward Dor's. "The last couple of months you've been going into every settlement and town we stopped at. Showing your face and talking to people. The Mages might've taken note of that."

Jules nodded. "This just happened to be the first port visit in months where I didn't go ashore. The Mages were ready for me to visit Dor's, but expected me to act like I have everywhere else recently."

"Are we going to stop at Julesport?"

"Let's get through the Strait of Gulls and then decide," Jules said. She looked west. "The weather looks fine. Let's hope it's an easy voyage."

The fine weather held as day followed day. Sailors, always alert to omens, were cheered by that.

Until the fine weather became a strange thing.

"That's very odd." As they approached the strait, Ang had been gazing ahead, and then gone up to the maintop to see farther. As he dropped back down to the deck, he gestured toward the west. "It's clear as far as I can see."

"The Strait of Gulls is clear?" Jules asked.

"No fog, no mist, no clouds. Clear weather," Ang said.

"Anywhere else I'd be happy," Jules said. "What could cause the strait to be clear?"

"I've never heard of any ship passing through the strait without encountering some fog or rain," Ang said. "Of course, ships haven't been using the strait for that long. But, still, this is odd."

The perfect weather held as the *Sun Queen* entered the Strait of Gulls and turned south. Jules, walking about the ship in defiance of her aching back and sore feet, noticed the crew looking about with worried expressions, muttering among themselves. "The first time we went through the strait, you guys were unhappy when faced with fog and rain and all the other bad weather," she commented to Marta as they both stood in the bow looking forward. "Now you're unhappy because the weather is great."

"These waters aren't kind to sailors," Marta said. "When they act all nice and pleasant, it makes a person wonder what's going on. Just like when some guy who's been nasty to you every day suddenly acts like he's your best friend and admirer."

"Yeah," Jules said, because she also distrusted this perfect weather in the strait. "But maybe sailors are so used to being mistreated that we can't handle it when the sea is nice to us."

"If I knew what the sea was thinking, I'd be happier about this," Marta said.

The fine weather held as the *Sun Queen* cleared the strait before noon, angling south-southwest toward Julesport.

The sun had passed its highest in the sky when the crew of the *Sun Queen* learned that they'd been right to be wary.

"Stars above," Liv whispered. "Look at that."

Sweeping in from the south and west, clouds were piling up with amazing swiftness. As Jules watched, they filled the sky before the *Sun Queen* from one side to the other. Big, dark clouds, rising high into a sky that was rapidly darkening from the brightest part of the day to what felt like an early night, but a night without stars or moon to illuminate it. Whatever this was, it was bad.

"All hands get aloft and take in sails!" she shouted. "Take in everything except the main, and reef the main! Gord! I want you doubling up on the helm. You and Marta tie yourselves to the helm. Anyone not in the rigging get everything loose below decks! Move it! We've got until that hits us, and it's coming on fast!"

Jules waited, watching as her crew raced up into the rigging, bringing in the sails with frantic haste.

"It looks like a fist as big as the world taking a swing at us," Liv said, out of breath from rushing about. "Here, you fool," she told Jules. "I know you won't do the common-sense thing and go below yourself, so you need to be tied down as well." Instead of wrapping the line about her midsection as was usually done, Liv raised it to sit just above Jules' breasts and under her arms. "That should be a lot more comfortable than having it tied about that belly of yours." She tied the line securely before wrapping the other end about one of the posts for the helm and knotting it off.

Ang paused in tying himself off to stare ahead. "Should we meet it bow on or stern first?" he asked Jules.

"Bow on, I think. It's stronger than the stern if hit dead on hard."

The dark mass of cloud swept overhead, plunging the ship into night. But the wind at sea level had dropped to almost nothing, the seas eerily calm about the *Sun Queen*. "Get on deck!" Jules shouted to those sailors still in the rigging. "Get below or tie yourselves in place! Lookout! You, too! Get down here!"

She stared past the bow, past the weird stillness of the air and gentleness of the sea, seeing a maelstrom of water and wind racing at the *Sun Queen* and her crew. "BRACE FOR IT!" Jules shouted as loudly as she could.

The storm hit the bow with a shock that rattled the *Sun Queen*, Gord and Marta on the helm holding on with grim expressions. The storm swept across the ship, a gale of wind and water that knocked Jules from her feet. She staggered up again against the force of the tempest, nearly blinded by the darkness and the wind blown spray and rain that pummeled her. Lightning flared on all sides, tracing lines of fire across the dark, the boom of thunder almost lost amidst the other noise of the storm.

Taken aback by the wind hitting from off the bow, the ship shuddered, the reefed mainsail pressed back against the mast. Her forward motion halted, the *Sun Queen* began staggering backwards, gathering sternway.

Ang pulled himself next to her, shouting near her ear, his voice barely loud enough to be heard over the tumult of the storm. "We can't face this! We've got to turn about!"

Jules reeled as another gust tore at her, trying to sense the feel of the ship through the chaos. Ang was right. The ship was sliding backwards, fighting the efforts of the helm to maintain her on a steady course. Jules could barely make out Gord and Marta straining to keep the helm from flying loose. Forcing herself step by step against the storm, Jules got close to the helm. "Come about! Stern on to the seas and the winds!"

Gord nodded, his face twisted with effort. Together, he and Marta fought to control the wheel as it threatened to spin uncontrollably. Ang staggered up to the helm and joined his efforts to theirs as the *Sun Queen* swung wildly to starboard.

For a terrifying moment as she came about, the seas were on the ship's beam, coming straight at her side, threatening to shove the *Sun Queen* far over and bury her masts in the water. But then the ship swung past the midpoint of her turn, the wind suddenly helping to push her about, the reefed mainsail billowing out taut away from the mast, Gord, Marta, and Ang fighting to stop the swing before the *Sun Queen* spun about too far.

Sun Queen yawed wildly as she fought the helm, the ferocious wind now shrieking from aft and the seas pummeling the stern. Normally, following seas made for smooth sailing, but not when those seas were this high and moving this fast. Jules had to grab onto the railing, holding tightly as the deck shifted under her feet in an erratic dance.

The rain cleared a little for a moment, giving her a look at the main-mast as lightning flared overhead, the reefed mainsail stretched tight with strain. If the sail ripped, they'd be at the mercy of the sea. But if the pressure on it and the mast were too great and the sail held, they might lose the mast. That would also doom them. And sending sailors aloft in this weather would mean a high risk of losing some of them over the side.

Spray broke over the stern, the impact of the wave driving the *Sun Queen* down into the trough before it, the ship shuddering again as her bow dug in and water foamed over the deck.

Jules worked her way hand over hand on the railing until she was close to the helm again, letting go and reeling step by step like a drunkard barely able to walk as the storm and the ship's motion tested her sea legs. "Can we keep on this course?" she shouted at Ang, her voice thin and small over the tumult of the storm.

His face and body rigid with the strain of helping to hold the helm,

Ang blinked against the rain as he stared ahead. "We weren't far south of Cape Astra when this hit! If we hold this course we'll be run onto the land to the north!"

Jules nearly lost her feet again as the *Sun Queen* jerked and dropped into another trough. She gazed into the murk ahead, breathing heavily from the effort of just staying standing. "Cape Astra! This storm might be the death of us unless we can make the harbor there!"

"The harbor?" Ang flinched as what felt like a solid wall of rain washed over them. "We'll have to try!"

They needed someone up forward watching for the coast and signs of the harbor, Jules knew. But posting someone on the bowsprit in this weather would be insane, and passing the word back from there would require a line of sailors, all of them also risking death every moment.

The wind veered suddenly, whipping about to the west and slapping the *Sun Queen* so she reeled. Gord, Marta, and Ang struggled to hold the ship on course, the helm jerking under their hands, as the wind howled and swung back to coming from nearly astern of the ship. A bolt of lightning hit the water so close that the crash of thunder came at seemingly the same moment, producing an instant of heart-stopping fear.

Jules made it to the front railing of the quarterdeck, holding on against the blows of the storm, trying to see ahead. The rain and spray filling the unnaturally dark sky was ripped by frequent lightning that made the murk between the bolts seem all the gloomier. Maybe the dark was lifting a bit, or maybe her eyes were just growing accustomed to it, but she thought she could see a little farther. She held on and gazed ahead, hoping for the sight of land ahead, and dreading the possibility that her first view of land might be of a jagged coast too close for the ship to avoid.

The bowsprit jumped skyward as another high swell rolled past the stern and dropped the aft end of the ship in the trough. *Sun Queen* tried to veer to starboard again, Gord, Marta, and Ang straining to shift the rudder to port.

There was no way to mark the passage of time when the sun was masked and the storm was raging at them. Every moment seemed an eternity, yet each came and went so quickly in the welter of the storm that no moment could be held onto.

She had no idea how long they'd been running with the storm when Jules thought she saw something. Risking removing one hand from the railing to try to shield her eyes. she stared into the gloom ahead as more lightning raced down to the sea or tore among the clouds.

Yes. There was a darker mass rising into the sky, fitfully lit by the glow of the lightning.

"Ang! Heights ahead!"

Bent over the helm, Ang raised his head, gazing at the dimly seen land as more lightning popped above them, very briefly showing a little more detail of the coast. "It's Cape Astra! We need to come left to reach the harbor!"

Together, he, Marta, and Gord wrestled the helm, forcing the *Sun Queen* to port, the shadow of land ahead now just to starboard of the bow as the ship jerked wildly.

Jules hung on, measuring their odds and not liking them. They'd sailed into the harbor at Cape Astra twice before this. It was a beautiful, well-protected harbor, but the entrance was narrow. Would they be able to spot it in the midst of this storm? And if they did see the entrance, would they be able to maneuver the *Sun Queen* into it?

The barely-seen black bulk of Cape Astra loomed ever closer and higher as the *Sun Queen* raced toward the land ahead. Now, when they needed it the most, the lightning grew erratic, only a few bolts flaring amid the clouds. Ang forced the helm over a little more, bringing the ship a bit farther to port, the heights of Cape Astra now seeming far too close and menacing off the starboard bow.

Twin threads of white spray appeared off the bow, a slim band of open water between them. "That's it!" Ang roared. "Head for it!" he ordered Gord and Marta.

Together the three threw their weight against the helm, the *Sun Queen* fighting to break free and smash herself against the rocks. The white spray grew closer, easier to see, the storm-driven waves hurling themselves against the land with a thunder that matched that of the lightning overhead. Shadowy land came into sight rising above the spray. The bow jerked first toward the land to starboard and then abruptly swung to point to the surf to port, while Ang, Marta, and Gord struggled to aim for the narrow channel that would mean the ship's and the crew's salvation.

Perhaps no one else could've done it, perhaps no one else had the combined experience and skill of years at sea to hit that mark, but together Ang, Marta, and Gord brought the *Sun Queen* into the channel, the waves from the south shoving the ship in. The darker masses of land were on either side now, and then falling away as the ship made the harbor. Ang ordered the helm to starboard to swing behind the curving headland that sheltered the harbor, the water suddenly choppy but no longer massive swells, the fury of the wind dropping off as the living rock of the heights blocked it. Above, thunder still echoed from the land as lightning danced madly among the storm.

"Liv!" Jules shouted, her voice carrying better now. "We need to get the crew ready to drop anchor and bring in the mainsail!"

"I got it!" Liv yelled back. She struggled for a moment with the sodden knot holding her line about her before bringing out her sailor's knife and sawing through it. Reeling across the quarterdeck, she made it to the ladder and down onto the main deck.

The ship's speed had slowed as wind and wave ceased battering her, but ahead a scattering of dimly-seen lights marked lanterns inside the new buildings of Cape Astra. They could still run aground if they didn't get the anchor down.

Jules looked about, trying to judge their position in the harbor amidst the rain still falling in torrents.

Liv had come back to the foot of the quarterdeck, ready to pass on Jules' orders.

Jules continuously blinked away rain as she gazed at what little could be seen of the land around the harbor. Lightning rippled down to hit the heights to starboard, giving her a decent look for a moment. "Drop anchor! Bring in the mainsail!"

Liv shouted the commands as well, running forward in a staggering dash.

Sailors went up the rigging, the journey no longer insanely dangerous with the ship inside the harbor. Others ran forward to the anchor to let it go.

As the mainsail flapped in feeble imitation of the thunder rumbling overhead, the anchor dropped, splashing into the water, the thick cable attached to it running out.

The *Sun Queen* jerked as the anchor reached the bottom and sought purchase. But though the ship slowed, she kept moving.

"The anchor's not holding!" Ang shouted.

"We've still got room!" Jules yelled back.

Sun Queen jerked again, slid, shuddered, then with a jolt came to a stop as the anchor found purchase on something hard enough to hold. The thick, hemp rope anchor cable emitted a squeaking, crackling grumble as it came under strain, a few terrifying pops marking fibers snapping inside it. But as the *Sun Queen* settled the strain on the cable lessened, and the warning noises subsided as the risk of the cable parting faded.

Everyone on the quarterdeck simply stood still for a long moment, exhausted, as the rain fell on them and the wind gusted across the ship. Jules saw Marta and Gord straining to unlock their hands from the spokes of the wheel that they'd been holding in death grips.

Ang came away from the helm, his feet unsteady. "No problem, Cap'n," he said to Jules, smiling broadly as the rain ran down his face, his breath still coming in deep gasps.

She laughed, amazed to still be alive, and wrapped Ang in a hug, then released him to clap Gord and Marta on their shoulders. "You are sailors!" Jules shouted. "The best the sea has ever seen or will ever see!"

Marta winced as she tried to flex her hands. "How about backing up those words with a shot of rum for us?"

"You've got it," Jules said. She looked about at the land, checking the barely visible landmarks to make sure the anchor wasn't dragging.

Keli the healer came up the ladder, peering at everyone on the quarterdeck through the rain. "Anyone hurt up here?"

"We're good," Jules said. "How about the rest of the crew?"

"Some bad bruises and a sprain or two, but otherwise we're in good shape for men and women who ought to be dead."

"That's great," Jules said, trying to gather her thoughts. "Ang, we need to—"

"You need to get below, Captain," Keli interrupted as Liv rejoined them.

Jules shook her head at him. "I need to set up a watch to keep an eye on the anchor, the hull and rigging need to be checked for damage, the… the…" Her thoughts suddenly ran out, leaving her groping for words.

Keli stepped closer, wiping rain from his face. "Captain. You're worn out. You're wet through. And you're shaking with cold. Hold your hand out! See? Your hand is shivering like a flag in a stiff breeze. Get below, get dry, get warm, and get rest."

"I can handle anything the rest of the crew can," Jules insisted.

"Sure, you can," Keli said. He pointed to her midsection. "But those in there might not. Do you want to lose them? You could, if you don't do as I say."

"Keli's right," Liv said. "Let me help you down the ladder to your cabin."

"But—" Jules protested.

"We can handle things," Ang told her. "If we have need of you, we'll let you know."

She glowered at them, unwilling to give in.

Keli looked south. "So that's what the Jules Sea is like when it gets a mad on," he said. "Sudden and furious, and any man with any smarts better get to a safe harbor. I'm thinking it was well-named. Takes after its namesake, doesn't it?"

"That it does," Liv said.

"You're all so very funny," Jules said. But she felt a cramp in her abdomen and realized that she'd better listen to Keli. Grumbling, Jules headed for the ladder, Liv right with her. Suddenly dizzy, she had to grab on to Liv as they went down the steps. She realized that both her back and her feet hurt like blazes.

Liv half-supported her to the cabin and inside, pausing to look about.

Some of the stern windows had been broken by the storm, a mix of rain and seawater washing about on the deck. "I'll get some crew in here to sweep and swab this out," Liv said. "We'll put some planks over the broken windows until we can get the glass replaced. Your bunk's dry, though. Let's get those clothes off you. Is your nose bleeding?"

Jules wiped under her nose, looking at the pinkish water on her hand. "I guess it is. I don't remember hitting it."

"No, a nosebleed is just one more gift from the cargo you're carrying," Liv said, pointing to Jules' midsection. "Come on, then."

Jules managed to peel off her clothing, though her back hurt so badly she needed Liv's help to get her boots off. Liv wrapped her in a blanket and helped Jules fall into the bunk. "I'm not an invalid," Jules growled even though she was shaking so hard the blanket nearly fell off.

"Of course you're not. Try to rest. Ang and I'll look after things. We can do that, you know. Handled everything ourselves while you were vacationing around Landfall."

"Vacation? Was that what it was?" Jules clutched the blanket, resolving to stay awake until her cabin had been swabbed out, and then…

* * *

She woke to see the grayness outside the stern windows had lightened. Rain still fell, but in a steady drumming rather than a lashing downpour. The ship was still shifting in the choppy water of the harbor, but less than before.

Sitting up, Jules stiffened with pain. Everything hurt. It took her a few moments of sitting on the bunk before she could start dressing.

Almost immediately, Jules discovered that she'd grown again. She'd always thought a woman grew slowly and steadily bigger through a pregnancy, but her bulge seemed to expand in sudden bursts. Her former set of pants wouldn't close anymore, so she had to dig out a larger pair Liv had acquired for her.

But once in the pants, Jules discovered that her feet were so swollen she couldn't get her boots on. Fortunately, the cabin still held a pair of Mak's old boots that Jules had hung onto for sentimental reasons. Those boots were a bit large even with her feet swelled up, but they'd do.

Outside the cabin, Jules paused to look up at the sky, the rain falling on her face cold but also refreshing. Spare sails had been strung up as awnings over part of the deck and the quarterdeck, providing shelter from the rain.

"Good day, Captain!" Mad said.

Jules looked over at her, seeing Mad and another one of her guards dressed in their armor, swords at their sides. "What are you doing guarding my cabin?"

"We're in port, Captain," Mad said. "Artem said that means we guard you."

"I guess so," Jules said, having accepted that the guards made sense for her even if they also made her a bit uncomfortable at the special treatment. "You can wait here. I'm just going up there." She went up to the quarterdeck, finding Liv leaning against the helm and yawning. "How long have you been here?"

Liv shook her head. "Not that long. I took over from Ang a little while back. How are you doing?"

"I'll live, but I hope every day for the next four months doesn't feel like this."

"They won't be like this," Liv said. "It gets worse."

"I really wish you'd stop telling me that," Jules said. "How's the ship?"

"We've got some rigging that parted during the storm and needs fixing, some hull planks that need looking to, and a fair amount of caulking to plug up small leaks. The anchor cable is holding the strain but Ang thinks it'd be a good idea to get a new one next time we're back east. Both Marida's and Kelsi's should have some for sale. Otherwise, we're good. Ang and I both think we should spend a few days in port here to do the fixing."

"There's no reason we can't stay a few days," Jules said, squinting toward the town. The rain partially obscured the wooden buildings and a couple of masonry structures that were being constructed. Like other settlements in the west started near good harbors or the mouths of large rivers, Cape Astra was growing fast. "We can let the crew ashore for some time off, too." Among the first buildings thrown up in any harbor were waterfront taverns, because where sailors went taverns followed like gulls seeking out schools of fish. "We need to know if there are any Mages about, though."

"We've got both boats in the water," Liv said. "I can send Gord ashore to talk to folks."

"Make it Marta," Jules said. "Gord might decide to gather information at the nearest bar and indulge too much." She looked about the harbor. Two other ships rode at anchor, both appearing to be merchant ships.

"That one came in this morning," Liv said, pointing to one of the ships. "They've already sent some people ashore. Looks like new settlers. The other ship was already here when we came in, but we were a bit too busy to notice it."

"All right." Jules leaned on the railing to ease her back, wincing. "You and Ang work up a schedule. I want to make sure everyone gets some time off the ship."

"Everyone but you," Liv said. "Because I don't know if you've noticed, but you're big enough now that a blind man could see it."

"Yeah, I've noticed," Jules said. "People might wonder why I'm not going ashore as well, though." She paused, thinking. "We'll tell the crew to tell anyone who asks that I hurt my leg during the storm. Nothing that won't heal, but it hurts and I can't walk well, and that has me in an awful mood, so visitors would be a bad idea."

"People will believe that," Liv said. "About the mood, I mean."

"Do you guys really think I'm like what Keli said last night? I mean, I'm not that bad, am I?" Jules remembered the Mechanics who'd described her as dangerous among themselves. Even though she hadn't recognized the terms they used, the meaning had been clear enough.

"Not usually," Liv said. "To be honest, though, there are probably a few people who've moved on from this world thanks to you who likely felt like we did when we saw that storm coming for us."

"But they deserved what they got," Jules said.

"I won't argue that. I will say that just as folks are wary of crossing you, I'll be respecting the mood of the Jules Sea a bit more from now on."

Marta came back with a report that no Mages had been seen about Cape Astra. Jules wondered about that again, why the Mages didn't seem to be moving aggressively into the west in search of her. Were they in their own way like the Empire, so unaccustomed to challenges that their response was slow and fixed on whatever had worked in the past?

Whatever the reason, it freed up the crew to work on repairs to the *Sun Queen* during the day and to go ashore to drink and gamble in the evenings. Jules, unable to spend much time on deck where someone might notice her, chafed at her confinement to her cabin but endured it for the sake of her crew. They'd sacrificed before for her, and would do so again. The least she could do was to let them have breaks when possible.

Two guards remained around her at all times, the eleven men and women dedicated to that taking turns at the duty. It seemed unnecessary to Jules, but everyone else was happy with it, so she kept quiet on the subject.

Two nights later, Jules stood on deck talking to Ang. Most of the crew were ashore. Only about ten remained on the ship in case of emergency, plus the two guards watching Jules tonight.

Her conversation broke off as Jules heard a bell being rung, and shouts. She went to the bow of the *Sun Queen*, gazing across the bowsprit toward the town of Cape Astra. Flames lit the town, leaping high from one of the buildings, bright enough for the light to illuminate the parts of the *Sun Queen* facing the blaze. "Looks bad," Ang said as he arrived beside her.

"If it spreads they could lose most of the town. They'll need everyone they can get to fight that fire," Jules said. "Take the crew that's still aboard."

Ang shook his head. "It wouldn't be wise to leave you aboard alone."

"I've got two guards on duty. I'll post them at the ladder so no one can get aboard. Now get our people ashore to help the town fight that fire!"

Ang hesitated, but one of the unwritten laws of the sea was that anyone who saw someone in trouble would offer whatever assistance they could, and Ang had such rules written into his blood by now. "Yes, Cap'n!"

He and the other nine sailors tumbled down the Jaykob ladder into the small boat and began rowing to the pier.

Jules beckoned to her guards. "Alons, Kala, post yourselves by the head of the ladder so you'll see anyone trying to get aboard. I'm going to go up to the bow to see what I can of the firefighting."

"All right, Captain," Kala said. She and Alons took up positions at the gap in the railing leading to the ladder down, standing casually and chatting with each other, but also keeping an eye on things around them.

Jules went forward, blinking against the brilliance of the flames devouring one of Cape Astra's buildings. She could see the shapes of men and women racing around, grabbing buckets and anything else that would carry water to hurl it onto the fire.

"What's that?" she heard Alons say.

Jules looked aft, seeing both Kala and Alons looking down at the water, but neither showing any sign of alarm.

"I can't see—" Kala began.

"Hey," Alons interrupted, "where did that—"

The blades of long knives appeared out of the air, slashing and stabbing, firelight reflecting on the deadly steel.

Alons and Kala didn't stand a chance.

As both fell to the deck, Jules stared at the place where they'd fallen, belatedly realizing something she of all people should have known. Just because no one had seen a Mage didn't mean there were no Mages about.

Feeling safe, she'd left her Mechanic revolvers in her cabin. The only weapon she had was her dagger.

And she was standing sideways, looking aft, her shape silhouetted perfectly by the fire in the town. The Mages who'd killed Alons and Kara could see that she was expecting. The Mages had surely seen her, had surely seen that she was pregnant. They wouldn't let her leave this ship alive.

And she couldn't afford to let any of the Mages leave the ship alive, because if any of them did with news that her children were on the way, their Guild would hunt down her children with single-minded, cold-blooded determination as soon as they were born.

But how did she alone fight an unknown number of Mages, who couldn't be seen, when her only weapon was a dagger?

Shouting for help would be useless. She was too far from anyone who might hear amid the noise made by the fire and those fighting it.

Standing still would only make her an easier target for the Mages.

All of these thoughts tumbled through Jules' mind in a single moment as she watched her guards die.

CHAPTER ELEVEN

Drawing her dagger, Jules quickly moved a few steps aft and toward the port side. She felt awkward, her weight off- balance, the borrowed a-little-too-big boots not firm on her feet. Jules barely sidestepped a bucket of water waiting to be used for cleaning the deck the next morning.

A bucket of water.

Once before when she'd fought a Mage who couldn't be seen, she'd spotted movement in the dust particles of a beam of light. Even if Mages couldn't be seen, they were still there, still interacting with things around them.

Sheathing her dagger, she grabbed the bucket with both hands and splashed an arc of water onto the deck for about a lance in front of her.

Dropping the bucket, Jules drew her dagger again. She went into a crouch near the port rail, her eyes not searching the ship but fixed on the wetted portion of the deck, reflected firelight dancing on it.

She tried to calm her pounding heart, tried to control her breathing, listening for any sound made by the Mages and trying to balance herself ready to move or fight, a task made more difficult by the unaccustomed weight she carried in front of her.

Sudden splashes erupted on the surface of the spilled water. Two sets of them, one along the port side, the other coming in from the ship's starboard side. The two Mages charging her were far enough apart that defending against one would leave her fully exposed to attack by the other.

Jules barely had time to realize that before her legs pumped, hurling her forward along a line about midway between the attacking Mages. She caught a glimpse of a long knife blade slashing toward her from her right as she went between them, staggered off-balance, then got her feet under her and ran for her cabin. A revolver would not only help even the odds, but the sound of it shooting would draw help back to the ship.

The run gave her just long enough to realize that she didn't know there were only two Mages, and that if there was at least one more the best place for that Mage to wait for her would be at the door to the cabin where Jules would sprint for safety and weapons.

Not knowing how far behind her the first two Mages were, Jules risked grabbing onto the ladder up to the quarterdeck just before she reached the door to her cabin, jerking herself to a momentary halt and nearly falling.

In that instant, Jules saw a long knife blade appear out of the air before her, slashing across where her body would've been if she hadn't pulled herself to a sudden stop.

The door to her cabin was guarded by at least one Mage. Jules knew she had no chance of making it up the ladder to the quarterdeck without being caught and killed, and running to another part of the main deck would only trap her against another rail or leave her exposed to attack from any direction. Barely having time to think, she pushed off, lunging for the ladder down to the second deck, nearly falling again as an unexpected bout of dizziness hit. She turned the stumble into a drop over the edge of the opening to below deck, her feet hitting one of the steps on the ladder as her free hand tried to grab the edge.

Instead, Jules fell forward, turning the fall into a roll, her side hitting the stair rail with a jolt of pain as she rolled over the side of the ladder, her hand catching the edge and braking her fall. The moment she'd halted her drop, Jules let go again, knowing there wasn't far to go. Her boots hit the deck with a thump that sounded far too loud on the deserted second deck.

A single storm lantern burned against the aft bulkhead. Jules darted that way, limping a bit, extinguishing the lantern and plunging the second deck into nearly total darkness. Backing cautiously and quietly away from the lantern, her dagger ready, she listened for any sound of the Mages, cursing her heavy breathing for masking other sounds and possibly giving away her location. Now in addition to her back and feet hurting, her side also hurt. Hopefully it wouldn't stiffen and hinder her movements, which were already awkward.

But it was dark down here. She couldn't see the Mages, but they couldn't see her. She'd evened the odds that much.

She heard footsteps on the ladder down, the ladder itself still dimly visible in the distant firelight filtering down from the main deck.

Two shapes suddenly appeared: Mages in robes, their knives held close to their bodies. They were coming down the ladder. A moment later a third Mage joined them. Their hoods were lowered, allowing the Mages to see well around them, but that wouldn't help them in the dark below deck.

The third Mage stayed by the ladder, knife out, clearly guarding Jules' means of escape. The other two faded into the darkness beyond it, leaving Jules with little idea where they were.

She'd gotten her breathing under control, her back to the bulkhead, straining her ears for any hint of the location of the two Mages searching the second deck. Aside from the area at the ladder, the rest of the deck was pitch black.

Jules nearly gasped when a sudden skittering noise came from the left, but managed to stay silent. She knew that sound from sleeping below deck. A rat, running along the edge of the deck.

At least one of the Mages didn't know the noise, though. Jules heard fast footsteps moving from her right to a little to her left, passing front of her.

How far in front?

There was one way to find out.

Jules moved as quickly and quietly as she could, her free hand sweeping before her. Her fingertips brushed against fabric. The back of a Mage's robes, she hoped. Stepping closer before the Mage could turn, Jules grabbed at where the Mage's shoulder should be, getting a good enough grip to halt the Mage's move. Her other hand brought the dagger up and forward, past where the Mage's neck should be, then back with a brutal slash.

She felt the dagger blade bite in, felt warm blood gush onto her dagger hand.

Dropping her grip on the Mage, Jules stepped back quickly.

She heard movement in front of her, the stumbling of feet, and a whisper of air past her face as the Mage's knife swung wildly at her. His throat cut, the Mage had still managed to turn and make a slash at where she might be.

Jules kept moving back, the sounds of her feet masked by the sound of the Mage falling to the deck.

She stopped moving and listened. In the very dim glow near the ladder, Jules could see the Mage there looking about in her general direction, but betraying no sign of having located her.

Where was the other Mage?

Jules edged carefully sideways and back, mentally mapping out the deck in her head. Tables should be there. Chests over there—

A *thunk* drew Jules' attention to a spot directly to starboard of her. She knew that sound, too, the noise of someone who'd forgotten to bend enough to avoid hitting their head on one of the wooden beams overhead. Tall sailors learned to crouch down a little without even thinking about it, but people unaccustomed to the low overhead below deck often hit their heads even when the area was lighted.

That gave her an idea. If she was right, there should be a post supporting the deck above, right about... here. There it was, her hand encountering the stout wooden post.

And the second Mage was over there.

Jules set herself against the post, nerving herself. She brought one boot down a little too hard, making an audible thump, following up with a couple of lighter thumps like someone trying to regain their balance. The moment she finished, Jules silently stepped back to one side of the post, knowing the area there should be open.

Swift steps, barely able to be heard, coming in fast from her right.

The thud of a body hitting the post.

Jules stepped in, her free hand pinning the stunned Mage to the post he'd just bounced off of, her other hand driving her dagger repeatedly into his back, guessing by touch where his vitals should be.

A half dozen stabs and Jules stepped away, her eyes going back to the ladder to reassure herself that the third Mage was still there.

The second Mage staggered past not far from Jules, his breathing heavy and labored. He fell, the sound echoing in the below deck.

Jules waited to see what the third Mage would do, trying to figure out how to kill her without being badly hurt herself.

As she watched, the third Mage turned and raced up the ladder.

She was trying to escape. To get word back to the Mage Guild that Jules was pregnant.

Jules broke into a run for the ladder, hitting her shin on the bottom hard enough to send a jolt of agony up her leg. Ignoring the pain, she went up the ladder, the dagger held high to parry a blow in case the third Mage was waiting at the top to attack Jules when she pursued.

But she reached the main deck, which almost seemed bright after the black pit of the second deck, without being attacked. Jules spun about, searching, and saw the third Mage almost to the Jaykob ladder.

She couldn't afford to hesitate, but she couldn't catch the third Mage in her condition. Instead Jules lunged for her cabin, yanking open the door and grabbing the Mechanic revolver kept ready nearby.

Lurching back onto the main deck, Jules ran for the Jaykob ladder, reaching the gap in the rail and seeing the third Mage climbing into a small punt that in a pinch could barely have held three Mages.

Jules leaned out, extending her arm toward the Mage, her finger tightening on the trigger.

Noise bellowed from the revolver.

A fountain of water splashed high next to the third Mage.

Jules adjusted her aim a little, pulling the trigger quickly once more.

Another roar of thunder from the Mechanic weapon.

The Mage jerked from the impact of the blow, dropping to the bottom of the punt.

Jules waited, breathing hard again, her weapon pointed down.

The Mage didn't move.

Cautiously swinging over the side, Jules came down the Jaykob ladder one step at a time, keeping the Mechanic revolver pointed at the Mage all the way.

Reaching the bottom of the ladder, the waters of the harbor right beneath her boots, Jules hung onto the rope with her free hand, crouching and leaning out to see if the Mage was still alive, her weapon almost touching the Mage who still lay huddled in the bottom of the punt.

The punt swung a little as the harbor water moved beneath it, bringing the Mage's face to where Jules could see it.

The Mage's eyes were open, unfeeling as they focused on Jules.

Jules looked back at the Mage, coldness filling her. Kill or be killed. She had no other choice, not against opponents like this female Mage who showed no emotion even as she prepared to die.

Jules leveled the revolver at the Mage's face. "Any last words?"

The Mage startled Jules with a reply, her voice thin but still carrying no feeling. "Why?"

"Why?" Jules shook her head. "There is no answer to why, and there are countless answers to why."

A trace of surprise entered the Mage's eyes. "Wis… dom?"

"Another Mage told me that."

"Oh." The word held no interest. But the Mage kept her eyes fixed on Jules. "I see… this…"

Jules listened, dread filling her. That was what the Mage in Jacksport had said before pronouncing the prophecy that had upended her life. Was this Mage about the repeat that prophecy, or speak another?

"…son of… Ihris… a… Mage…" The weak voice faded out completely, the Mage's eyes taking on the star of death, her mouth going slack.

Jules lowered the Mechanic weapon, staring at the dead Mage with mingled frustration and anger. What kind of person could die without showing any feeling? And what had those few cryptic words meant?

She sat on the bottom rung of the Jaykob ladder, worn out, holding the revolver, waiting for the noise of the shots to bring crew back to the ship.

* * *

"You shouldn't have left her alone!" Liv berated Ang, who stood glowering.

"He didn't," Jules said. They were in the stern cabin while the crew cleaned up the remains of the Mages. She'd managed to regain her mental and emotional balance while waiting for the crew to return to the *Sun Queen*. "I thought it was safe. I told him to go and take the others with him. I had two guards left with me."

"And you!" Liv said to Jules. "What did the midwife say about hand-to-hand combat?"

"She advised against it," Jules said. "Which is not the same as prohibiting it."

"It's not like she had a choice," Ang said. "They would've killed her."

"Three Mages." Artem had been mostly silent since returning to the ship and finding the bodies of Kara and Alons. "They could not be seen?"

"No," Jules said. "I was looking that way when they struck. Alons and Kara were doing their jobs well. But the Mages couldn't be seen."

Ang frowned. "The punt could have carried only three Mages. There wasn't enough room for more. Why didn't Kara and Alons see the punt?"

"I think they saw something," Jules said. "But it wasn't anything to alarm them. I think the punt may have been hidden by whatever the Mages used to hide themselves. I'm sorry, Artem."

He nodded, his mouth a tight line. "Captain Jules, both Kara and

Alons owed every day of their lives since we escaped the Empire to you. You gave them that time."

"I wish I could've given them more." Jules looked toward the town. "It was a clever plan. Start the fire to distract and draw away anyone protecting me, then come out and kill me under cover of the commotion."

"No one had seen Mages," Liv said. "No one in Cape Astra."

"They've been hiding from the people here, hoping to get a chance at me," Jules said. "We have to assume the same might be true of other places out west. We haven't been seeing Mages, but that doesn't mean there aren't any."

"There won't be Mages at Pacta Servanda," Keli said. "You seem to be all right, Captain."

"I've got a nasty bruise on my side," Jules said. "And I felt dizzy during the fight."

"Occasional dizziness is normal." She pulled up her shirt and he looked at her side. "It doesn't seem like a deep injury. I don't think the bruise indicates any problem inside."

Jules nodded, feeling morose. "I'd like to speak to Keli alone, please."

The others left, Keli watching Jules with concern. "What's bothering you? Is there some other injury you didn't want to speak to the others about?"

"No injury. Just a worry. Am I like a Mage, Keli?"

He raised both eyebrows at her. "You? Like a Mage?"

She made an angry, confused gesture. "I watched that last Mage die, and I didn't care. And I thought, how could she not care about killing and dying, and then I thought aren't I the same way?"

"I see." Keli sat down opposite Jules. "It doesn't bother you to kill?"

"Not if they deserve it."

"Have you ever killed when you didn't have to?"

"Maybe," Jules said. "I get angry."

"Because of what they've done?"

"Yes."

Keli shrugged. "Then at least you have a reason. If your reasons were poor ones, if you killed because someone sneezed at the wrong moment or because someone bumped into you on the street, that'd be bad for certain. But I haven't seen that in you. If you see the need, you don't hesitate, and that does worry me sometimes. But I haven't seen you misuse that. So, if it's a wrong in you, it's one you control. Would you kill Mages if they weren't trying to kill you?"

"If a Mage was hurting someone else—"

"Still a reason," Keli said. "What about those Mages who died on this ship tonight? Would they kill someone for no reason at all?"

"Yes," Jules said. "That's what Mages do. I don't think they see us as people. I don't think they see anyone who's not a Mage as people. As bad as the Mechanics are, the Mages are worse that way."

"You say you've asked Mages why, and they give you an answer you can't understand."

"Yes," Jules said. "I mean, it may have some deep meaning, but nothing I can figure out."

"And yet I've asked you why you killed and you gave me straight answers. Jules, you know why you're doing it, and you're questioning whether you should. Do you think that's true of Mages?"

"No," Jules said, looking at Keli. "Thank you."

He shrugged, gazing at the deck with a distressed look. "Maybe you have to be capable of that, Jules. Maybe that's the only way you could've survived, and lived to have that child."

She looked away, angry. "That makes it sound like I didn't have a choice in the matter."

"You had a choice every step of the way," Keli said. "Don't sell yourself short, and don't give yourself an all-purpose excuse that it was destiny forcing your hand. You made the decisions. Take credit for those that were right, forgive yourself for those that were wrong, but learn from them, and never stop questioning the right or wrong of what you do. That's the difference between you and the Emperor. And if that daughter of your line inherits that questioning from you, the world will be in good hands."

She looked at him again, smiling. "Liar."

"Not this time." Keli got to his feet. "As for your worries, I don't know any other common person who would've questioned the morality of killing a Mage. You do what you have to. Don't blame yourself for that."

"Kara and Alons are dead," Jules said, the smile fading from her lips. "Because of me."

"Not because of you," Keli said. "Because there are those who don't want the world to be free. Kara and Alons died because making the world free someday mattered to them. Don't deny them the right to be proud of what they gave their lives for."

"I won't. Keli, the last Mage said something just before she died. I don't know what it meant, and I really don't want people hearing about it and thinking it was another prophecy."

"What's that? What did she say?"

"Something about a man from Ihris. And a Mage. Maybe the man from Ihris will be a Mage. And nothing else. She died."

Keli scratched his head. "That could mean anything or nothing. Certainly since Ihris was just founded there are no Mages from there. Maybe that man will be a special danger to the daughter of your line when she comes."

"Maybe, but we have no idea, do we? Do you think I should mention this to anyone else?"

He hesitated, then shook his head. "No. It's so vague that those who mean mischief could interpret it in any way they wish, and those who think they're helping you could interpret it in any way that *they* wish. Maybe it never did mean anything. A dying person sometimes says things that are just random thoughts from a mind approaching its end."

"Thank you," Jules said. "I was thinking the same thing, but I wanted to ask at least one other person what they thought. Let this be a secret between us."

"A healer has to know how to keep secrets," Keli said. "I will not speak of it."

"Why did it have to be twins, Keli? It was going to be hard enough for me to send away one. But two…"

"Maeve wasn't certain it'd be twins," he said.

"I think she was right."

After Keli left, Jules sat watching the dark harbor waters outside the stern windows.

Why? No answer, and answers without number.

Why twins? Had the prophecy wanted to ensure it would come true by having two children, not one, to carry on her line? It was scary to think something like the prophecy could've done that.

But maybe she'd have had twins regardless. There was no way to know.

Why? Because she wouldn't give up, because she wouldn't let people like the Mechanics and the Mages rule over the common people forever, because sometimes right was right and worth fighting for. *You'd better be grateful,* she thought to the daughter of her line, somewhere in the future. *I'm going to give you everything I can.*

* * *

The next morning the *Sun Queen* stood out of Cape Astra into a sea whose tranquility almost caused everyone to question their memories of the furious storm that had driven them into the safety of the port. They rode the winds down past Julesport and on south, following the curves of the shore down through the Jules Sea until the slow, majestic swells passing under the *Sun Queen* told them they'd reached the Umbari Ocean. Down farther, the land bending west before turning south again, they reached the broad river where a man named Edin had begun a settlement a short time before.

The *Sun Queen* followed the coast as it bent east, even turning a bit north of east for a while, swinging back to the south. And there, partway down that south bearing coast, they found the old walled town of Pacta Servanda, set up here long ago by the Mechanics for reasons the few hundred remaining inhabitants knew nothing of.

Jules brought the *Sun Queen* alongside the pier this time, knowing there was sufficient depth of water to accommodate the ship's draft. Some of those in the oddly named town were still wary, but most of the inhabitants of Pacta Servanda believed Jules to be a Mechanic and didn't question her arrival. Former mayor Terrance, who knew the truth about her, welcomed Jules. "I need a place to stay for a few months," she told him. "A place where there is no chance of Mages finding me."

"I still don't know what a Mage is," Terrance confessed. "No one here does."

"Be glad for that," Jules said.

Terrance eyed Jules' belly. "A few months? Do you mean to have the child here?"

"No. Sorry," Jules said.

On her previous stop at Pacta Servanda, the *Sun Queen* had loaded some exotic wood which had fetched truly astounding prices when smuggled inside the Empire. The rich and powerful couldn't get enough of something uniquely beautiful that they could flaunt. Jules, as she had promised, brought back the town's share of that money, even though it would be of little use to the town until the rest of the world reached Pacta Servanda. Meanwhile, the *Sun Queen* took on more wood harvested in the ship's absence, planning to deliver it to eager Imperial buyers who would be indirectly and unknowingly helping to bankroll the western settlements defying the Emperor.

"Try to make everyone think I'm still aboard," Jules told Ang as they sat in her cabin. "Mages, Mechanics, the Empire, and every common in every port. Unless it's dangerous, and then tell them I'm somewhere else. Just keep changing where that somewhere is."

"Aside from this ship, no one knows this town exists," Ang said. "You asked to meet with Cori," he added. "She's outside."

"Good. Bring her in."

Ang got up, opened the door, ushered a worried-looking Cori inside, and sat down again.

"Cori," Jules said, smiling at her. "Have a seat."

She sat down facing both Jules and Ang, looking from one of them to the other as if expecting a sudden attack. "I haven't done anything."

"No!" Jules said. "This isn't that kind of meeting. I wanted to say that you did a great job pretending to be me when we attacked and captured Western Port."

"Aye," Cori said, her wary eyes going from Ang to Jules and back again.

"How'd you like to do that again?"

"No, thanks, Captain."

"It's an important task," Ang said, leaning toward her. "You have the right height and build for it, and your hair color is close as well."

"I'd be greedy to keep such important tasks to myself," Cori said. "Someone else in the crew should have a chance to show how well they can pretend to be the captain. How about Marta?"

"Marta's build is nothing like the captain's," Ang said.

"Cori," Jules said, leaning forward as well and smiling again. "How'd you like to carry one of these for a while?" She placed a Mechanic revolver on the table.

"One of those?" Cori stared at the revolver. "I'd have it? I could use it?"

"You shouldn't have to use it," Jules said. "But you could wear it around, impress every man who sees you…"

"I don't need that to impress a man," Cori said, but her eyes stayed on the weapon. "I… um…"

"And you'd have some of my guards with you whenever you were pretending to be me," Jules said. "Artem and Mad will be staying here with me, but the others will guard you just as if you were me."

"Personal guards? With their armor and all?" Cori frowned, obviously tempted. "What would I be doing?"

"Just pretending to be me for anyone watching from a distance," Jules said. "When the *Sun Queen* is in port, you'd walk around the quarterdeck and look important."

"No one would get close enough to endanger you," Ang said.

"Those Mages off the Bleak Coast weren't all that close when they threw lightning at the captain," Cori pointed out. "And the Mages at Cape Astra were really close."

"That's because they were all close enough to tell it was me when they saw me," Jules said. "Mages can tell. If they get close enough to endanger you, they'll be close enough to know you're not me."

"And then they'd have no reason to harm you," Ang said. "Of course, since you'd be pretending to be the captain, you wouldn't have to work the ship when we're entering or leaving port. You'd just stand on the quarterdeck and look like you're running things."

"Really?" Cori bit her lip. "Me with that weapon, and guards and all?"

"That's right."

"And the Mages won't try to kill me once they know I'm not the captain?"

"They wouldn't have any reason to do that," Jules said. "It's only for a couple of months, until I rejoin the ship."

"Well… I guess I could do that," Cori said, still a little hesitant.

"Since this is an extra duty," Ang said, "you'd get a little bonus out of it as well."

"A bonus?" Cori took a deep breath and nodded. "All right. I can do that."

"Great," Jules said. "I'll go over how the weapon works with you later. Thank you, Cori."

"No problem, Captain."

After she'd left, Jules sat looking at the closed door. "You know, if Cori does get killed I'm going to feel really bad."

"Don't worry about Cori," Ang said with a laugh. "She's the fastest runner on the ship. Any Mages who come after her are going to find themselves left in the dust while she sets a record for the thousand-lance run." He took on a thoughtful look. "Why, if the Mages sent lightning at her like they did at you, I'd bet that Cori could outrun it."

"You think?" Jules asked, imagining Cori running for her life from Mages while the rest of the crew watched and made wagers on the outcome. "Try to keep her out of trouble, anyway."

"I am a little worried about Cori having that weapon," Ang said, nodding toward the revolver.

"Don't worry about that. I said I'd let her have the weapon. I didn't say it'd have any cartridges in it. The last thing I'd want is for Cori to goof around with that thing and accidentally shoot someone else in the crew."

"She'll never live down that incident with the crossbow, will she?"

"Not as long as I'm captain." Jules paused. "Ang, take care of the ship and crew while I'm here. I know I don't have to say that. You've acted as captain before and proven you're good at it."

He smiled. "If this is a warmup to asking me to become a captain, you can save your breath, Cap'n."

"No," Jules said. "Well, in a way. I'm just want you to know that I'm happy that you'll be in charge of the *Sun Queen*."

"But you will be back. I'll just be acting captain."

"Right." Jules sat back, looking around her cabin. "But if something happens to me, take care of things, all right?"

Ang nodded.

* * *

A few days later, Jules stood on the pier, watching the *Sun Queen* leaving port without her. It felt incredibly strange, wrong in some fundamental way.

"They'll be all right," Artem said, misreading her mood.

"With Ang and Liv watching out for them, they should be," Jules said. "But the Empire is still trying to get their hands on me, and the Mages still want to kill me, and the Mechanics don't know I'm down here hiding."

"What are we going to be doing?" Artem asked as he, Mad, and Jules walked into the town, escorted by former mayor Terrance and a few other citizens of the town.

"All you guys have to do is keep an eye on me," Jules said. "I'm going to be... thinking."

"That's a dangerous pastime," Terrance said. "I hope you're not planning on digging for anything the Mechanics might have left around here."

"No. Nothing like that," Jules said. "This isn't about the past. I need to think about the future."

* * *

It felt odd waking up every day in a comfortable bed, the floor steady underfoot rather than rolling to the motion of the sea. The two and three story homes the Mechanics had built here were in good shape for their age, and nice inside. Nothing like a palace, or like what Jules imagined a palace would be like, but the sort of place that was pleasant to live in. Plenty of air, natural light, windows looking out on courtyards and gardens. A lot of homes in Pacta Servanda were empty, built for the use of the departed Mechanics and commons who'd worked for them, so the only problem with finding housing was deciding which one.

Jules sat in the room she'd taken as her own in the house where she, Artem, and Mad were staying. It had that comfortable bed, and a desk big enough for her to spread out papers as she thought and painstakingly wrote down ideas. At times she'd pause, looking out the room's window at what could be seen of the street below.

"You're forgetting lunch again, Captain," Artem said as he opened the door after a polite knock. He brought in a plate of cold chicken, bread, and cheese, setting it carefully on an uncluttered part of the desk.

"Thanks," Jules said. "You shouldn't have to bring me meals."

"Not a problem," he said. "It's not like we're being worked hard." He glanced at the window. "I noticed when I came in you looking that way and seeming sad."

"Not really sad," Jules said. "Do you have time to talk? Sit down. What do you think of this town?"

"It's nice," Artem said as he took the room's other chair. "Real nice."

"The Mechanics built it. Or they had commons build it for them." She grimaced. "The whole world could be like this, if the Mechanics had shared their devices with commons."

"That'd be something." Artem glanced toward her for a moment. "The daughter of your line, when she overthrows the Great Guilds, she'll make that happen, won't she?"

"It might be a long time before that happens," Jules said. "You and Mad aren't bored here, are you?"

"No, Captain. Just keeping an eye out for you is enough to keep us occupied. After what happened at Cape Astra we want to be sure Mages don't surprise us again."

"I don't think the Mages have any idea where Pacta Servanda is. Not yet, anyway. Hopefully I'm right."

"The captain is always right," Artem said with a grin, quoting an old sailor saying.

Jules smiled at him. "Not always. I thought for the longest time that you and Mad were a couple."

Artem laughed. "People often do. But that's not us. Truth is, I grew up with three sisters, and I've missed them since leaving home. The first time I met Mad I said to myself, that girl's just like your sisters. And it feels like that. I couldn't even kiss Mad without feeling strange about it, if you know what I mean."

"I know," Jules said. "You saw Shin up at Western Port. He's like that for me, a brother. Is Mad all right with being a sister to you?"

"Sure is." He paused, frowning down at the floor. "Mad won't talk about her past much, or her family. Might have been some bad things in there, I think. She's happy to have me around and never asking more of her than she wants to give."

"Then she has what she needs." Jules sighed, looking at the papers on her desk. "I ought to talk to you and Mad about what I'm doing. I've talked a lot with Terrance, but I think you two might have some good ideas."

"What is it?" Artem asked. "I only had basic schooling."

"It's not about schooling," Jules said. "It's about experience. Things you've seen and learned." She picked up a paper, looking at her attempts to write neatly. Her pen work had been the despair of everyone who'd ever taught her, and everyone who'd had to read her reports. "I'm trying to get ahead of a big problem. I've been telling every new town and settlement to set things up like on a free ship, with voting for who's going to run things and everyone being part of that."

Artem laughed. "I remember being that surprised when I first came to a free ship. What? Voting? But it works better than the Empire, doesn't it?"

"It does," Jules said. "But the way we run free ships doesn't work perfectly in a town. On a ship everyone has their job to do, and if anyone doesn't do their job the whole ship suffers. We're focused on sailing and trade and piracy. Towns might have lots of different other things they're doing, so keeping order and what rules and laws are needed is different for them."

"The folks where we've been seem to be working it out," Artem said. "They're listening to you."

"Yeah, but it shouldn't be about me! I won't be around all the time. I might not be around next year if the Mages get me. So I'm trying to write down some rules and ideas that people can use to run towns, and…" She paused, a little reluctant to share her dream for fear speaking of it might jinx it. "I want those towns, those cities, to work together. Not like in the Empire, where a city does what the Emperor says because there's a legion nearby. But like free ships working together. Supporting each other, not because they're being forced to but because it helps them all when they stand together."

She hesitated again, trying to order her words right. "We're going to have to fight. The Empire won't let us be free if the Emperor can put his chains on us. But after we win, I want people in the different towns and settlements to think about how to maybe form their own… empire. There must be another word for that, for a group of cities and people that choose to be part of the same government. So I'm trying to write down ideas, kind of a framework, working from the model of the free ships."

"Thinking of the future," Artem said. "That's why you're the woman of the prophecy."

"Think so, huh?" Jules said with a laugh, putting the paper back on the desk. "There are plenty of times I don't want to think of the future. But this, these ideas, I want to be able to offer them as soon as we win the fight at Dor's, the fight I know is coming, but while everyone is still together, while the memory of what we can do together is still fresh. I'm sure everyone will have other ideas and different ways to do things, but I want something ready that we can all build on."

After Artem had left, Jules sat, her thoughts tangled. They had about one more month before the *Sun Queen* was due to return. What if the ship didn't show up? What would she do? Because within a couple of weeks after that, something else was due.

A kick inside her made Jules wince. "Stop fighting, you two," she grumbled.

She'd tried not to talk to them, not to bond with them, in the hopes that losing them wouldn't hurt so much, but it had been impossible.

One more month. A lot of time. And very little time.

CHAPTER TWELVE

The *Sun Queen* showed up one day before the date they'd been aiming for. Jules, who'd been growing more tense by the day, met the ship with a smile of relief. "How did it go?" she asked after boarding, settling down carefully into one of the chairs in the stern cabin.

"Well enough," Ang said. "Cori's nerves are a bit ragged because of a couple of minor incidents, but she'll be fine."

"The Mage missed," Liv said. "Sure, Cori's coat caught on fire but we got it off and the fire out before she got much more than a singe. Plenty of people have been burned worse than that while making a meal. And that second thing with the kidnappers hoping for the Imperial reward, well, we got her back right away." Liv paused. "Almost right away. Nothing a good sailor shouldn't be able to handle. The girl's just too high-strung if you ask me, so she's probably going to be a little reluctant to pretend to be you again. How are you doing? A lot bigger, I see."

"Bloated, uncomfortable, always tired, and my hips feel like they're about to fall off," Jules said. "Otherwise, never been better. How'd trade go?"

"Very good," Ang said, smiling. "The first batch of exotic wood we sold in the Empire got the attention of everyone with money. Our contacts tell us every prince and princess wants some of that wood for their own use or to make things to gift the Emperor to get on his good side. And of course all the richest merchants and high-level officials want some, as well. You see those money chests? Full of gold eagles. Even with the swords, crossbows, and armor we stocked up on we turned a very nice profit on the voyage."

"How soon do we need to get back to Dor's?" Liv asked.

"As fast as possible," Jules said. "I don't know how much longer it'll be, and I doubt Keli wants to handle it at sea."

They departed Pacta Servanda the next morning, Jules wondering if she'd ever see the town again. It held a lot of memories now, and she wasn't sure she'd want to revisit those moments since they were so bound up with her expecting the twins.

Maybe the prophecy eased their way north and west, the seas brisk but not rough, the winds strong but not harsh. The Strait of Gulls proved to be comfortingly gloomy, banks of fog limiting view of the land to either side and a drizzling rain putting a chill in the air. Inside the Sea of Bakre once more, the *Sun Queen* raced for Dor's Castle on a broad reach, every sail set, the ship bounding over the swells like a horse sensing the barn ahead.

"Dor's is in sight," Ang told Jules one afternoon. "Do you want us to hold off until nightfall?"

"No," Jules got out between clenched teeth. She hated not being able to captain the ship as it entered port, but she'd been forced to stay below in her bunk this entire day, trying to will the twins to wait a little while longer as contractions grew stronger. "Head on in."

She waited it out, feeling sweat dripping down her face, as the *Sun Queen* entered the harbor at Dor's Castle, feeling the ship finally thudding gently against a pier, hearing feet rushing about and orders shouted as lines were put over and the ship securely fastened to the pier. "I'm sorry," she whispered to the twins for what must be the thousandth time.

"We've sent Gord and Marta for the midwife," Liv told Jules after the ship had tied up. "The two ships are here that'll… take care of things."

"How much are those ships charging?" Jules managed to say between the pain roiling her abdomen.

"With the money we've made from the wood we can swing it without any problem." Liv sat down next to Jules' bunk, grasping one of Jules' hands in both of hers. "Hang on. It's almost over."

"I know."

Her feelings must have come through clearly in those two words, because Liv's hands tightened on hers.

Keli came in with Maeve, the midwife quickly checking Jules. "Stars above, how'd you hold it this long? Do you want a blue pill for the pain?"

"No," Jules gasped. "I need to feel it. Every bit of pain. It's what I deserve."

"All right, then. It's your choice. Bite this." Maeve shoved a leather strap into Jules' mouth.

She bit down hard on it.

"Are you washed up?" Maeve asked Keli. "Let's do this."

The contractions continued, growing worse. She had no idea how much time was passing. It just went on and on. Jules thought she knew what pain was, but the cramping inside her almost made her pass out.

There came a moment when the burden inside her suddenly lessened, a pause, then again.

She lay on the bunk, spent, keeping her eyes tightly closed, as the wail of first one baby and then a second announced their arrival in the world. As she heard those cries, Jules' hands reached out as if of their own accord, trying to touch and hold and comfort.

But others grabbed her hands, holding them firmly.

Jules fought, trying to shove away those holding her, trying to get up, trying to get to those cries.

Strong hands pinned her down. "Let me go!" she screamed.

The sound of crying faded fast as the babies were carried out and the door to the cabin shut.

"No."

Jules realized that she'd said that, realized that the emptiness inside her would never be filled, her hands tightening on the hands holding them so hard that she heard gasps of pain.

"Jules," Maeve said, her voice gentle. "There are wet nurses waiting. We've done all we can to ensure the children are safe and find good homes."

"But we'll never know for sure," Jules whispered.

No one answered her.

"I need to get on deck," Jules said, not knowing why, but feeling an urgency to act. "Are all sails set?"

"Everything's fine, Captain."

"No. No…" Jules surged up again, fighting against those restraining her, her exhaustion momentarily forgotten.

A cup poured liquid into her mouth and she had to swallow it. There was something in that drink, some sedative that stole what strength she had left.

She fell asleep, the screams locked inside her forever, hating the prophecy.

* * *

In the night, Jules found herself back in Sandurin, years ago. The railing had vanished as the Mages stood watching her. She was falling, not into the water of Sandurin's harbor, but into a bottomless pit of blackness.

Mak was there, looking just as he had, reaching out to her.

But she didn't reach back, didn't try to grasp the offered hand. Her arms hung limp beside her as she fell.

Mak jumped after her, grasping her hand in his to comfort them both as they fell. "Don't give up. I didn't."

"I know," Jules said.

They fell into the endless dark together, joined by a now-shared pain.

* * *

When Jules awoke the ship was clearly still tied up. Sunlight lanced in through the stern windows. She stared up at the wooden planks and beams above her bunk, seeing the darkness tainting the wood above her, trying to feel something, anything, and failing.

They were gone. Nothing would ever matter again.

Liv looked in, coming inside when she saw Jules was awake. "How are you, Captain darling?" she said in an exaggeratedly cheerful voice.

Jules took a moment to reply. "Where's my dagger?"

"You don't need your dagger," Liv said.

"Yes, I do."

"You're not getting your dagger, Captain," she said.

"Liv, nothing matters anymore. I've given the world, I've given the future, my children. My bloodline is in them. What reason do I have to keep on?"

"What of the west, Jules?" Liv asked, standing by the bunk, her expression saddening despite her efforts to seem upbeat. "What of growing the free lands in the west to give that daughter of your line the strength she'll need behind her?"

"The daughter of my line? The bitch who took my children from me to ensure her future? It doesn't matter what I'll do. She'll win. It's prophesized."

Liv pulled a chair over and sat down, shaking her head. "So that's it? She gets all the glory and you get the pain? Where is that prophesized?"

"What's that supposed to mean?"

"The prophecy has brought you so much pain, Jules. Do you think it won't bring her the same? She won't know who she is. But at some point, she'll find out. Just like you, she'll learn that her life is no longer her own. And she won't know what will happen to her, will she? Win, yes. Survive? Have children of her own? What if she has children and they have to be sacrificed to that victory? Will you envy her, Jules? What if that victory, what if the prophecy, causes her a lifetime of pain?"

Jules stared at Liv, unable to form a clear thought.

"You haven't thought of that, have you? Jules, I don't blame you for that. The pain you're feeling is something no mother should have to endure. But think of that girl. That daughter of your line. Think of how you felt the day that Mage told you, and think how she'll feel the day she learns her life also belongs to that prophecy, not to her."

"Blazes." Jules clenched her eyes closed tightly, trying to shut out everything. "Why are you telling me this?"

"Because before you give up you need to think of her, too. And about the rest of us. You're not alone. We'll help all we can."

Jules opened her eyes, remembering her dream. "That's what it meant. I can't give up."

"It? What do you mean?"

"Mak was here last night."

"Mak? Jules, darling, Mak has long since gone to the place where the dead go."

Jules shook her head. "In my dreams. Mak came back to me, Liv."

"Ah," Liv said. "I've heard they do that sometimes. What happened?"

"He offered help and I refused it and…" Jules swallowed, her mouth suddenly too dry to speak.

"Hold on." Liv held up a mug she'd brought in. "Here you go."

Jules' hands shook so badly she couldn't hold the cup, so Liv held it as she drank. "I wouldn't take his help," Jules finally said. "And he came with me, falling, because he wouldn't let me face it alone."

"That's Mak all right," Liv said. "So, are you going to listen to him?"

"I don't know. The world is so dark, Liv."

"Jules, I don't mean to compare what you're facing to others, but women who've given birth can see the world as very dark for a while. Keli can give you something to drink that'll help."

"I don't want any of the blue pills," Jules insisted.

"I'm not talking blue pills. There are herbs that help. I'll have Keli make up some. It's up to you if you drink it."

"No. Not yet." A wave of misery washed through her. "They're gone."

"They're alive," Liv said, grasping Jules firmly by the shoulder. "Look at me, girl. They're alive. And they'll stay alive, because you did what you had no choice but to do. Try to center your mind on that. You need strength. There's food on the table. Do you want any?"

"No. Give me some time. Please."

"Since you ask nicely, I will. But I'll be back."

After Liv left, Jules berated herself. Mak had come to help her, and she was still refusing anyone's help. And she was captain of the *Sun Queen* and shouldn't be lying abed.

Easier said than done. She forced herself out of the bed, wincing. Walking a few steps to the table was as hard as walking had been during the storm south of Cape Astra. She couldn't motivate herself to get dressed, and probably couldn't manage it if she tried, so Jules draped a large blanket around her and dropped into a chair at the table. That almost made her cry out in pain as her bottom hit the uncushioned seat of the chair. Jules sat, gazing at the food placed there but feeling no urge to eat. Her breasts hurt, filled with milk and no baby to drink of them, that physical pain also feeding her despair.

Voices outside, raised in argument.

Liv stuck her head in again. "You've a visitor."

"I don't want—"

"Here he is." Someone came in, the door closing again afterwards.

After a long moment of silence, Jules looked that way.

Ian stood there, his eyes on her both puzzled and concerned. "I finally find you again, and you're like this. What happened?"

"Nothing," Jules said, her eyes going back to the plate on the table.

"Nothing? This ship feels like a house where something terrible happened and no one will speak of it." He came to the table and sat down opposite her.

The last thing she wanted was to talk about it. To anyone. "Do you want some of this?" Jules asked, nodding toward the untouched food.

"No, thank you." Ian studied her. "You've done a great job of avoiding me since that night. I tried to catch this ship, and you, more than once, but I'd always get to the next place too late. You'd already gone."

"I've got this urge not to be killed," Jules said. "For me, that means staying on the move."

"A couple of months ago, your ship stopped here at Dor's, but when I came aboard I was told you'd stayed at Julesport. Your ship wouldn't give me passage there, but I found another, and when I arrived you weren't in Julesport. I only got back to Dor's a short time ago. Imagine my surprise when I woke up this morning to find the *Sun Queen* in the harbor, and when I came to the ship, to be told you were aboard."

Jules shrugged, the blanket shifting on her shoulders. "How did you do all that traveling while looking after your mother and sister?"

Ian made a face. "They're not my responsibility any more. By their choice. My sister got involved with a character named Synda."

"Synda?" Jules looked at Ian. "Big man?"

"Yes." Ian gave her a measuring look in return. "He hates you almost as much as my sister does, so I guess you two have met."

"I kicked him out of Julesport," Jules said. "I'm sorry to hear he's settled at Dor's."

"He was for a while," Ian said. "But he, along with some followers and my mother and sister, left a few months ago to found another settlement. One where you would not be welcome."

"Where at?" Jules said, trying to muster interest in the conversation.

"The bigger of the two islands on the other side of the strait," Ian said. "My mother and sister were nagging Synda to name the settlement after our father Dar'n. I'm not sure my father would have been pleased by that dubious honor."

"Sorry," Jules said. She finally reached out for the mug on the table, finding it filled with coffee mixed with a generous amount of rum. It was cold, but it still felt good going down into the emptiness inside her.

She could try that, try to fill the emptiness with rum. But as Jules thought of that, misery almost choking her, she sat down the mug. That would be the easy way out. "I don't deserve any easy answers," she muttered.

"What did you say?" Ian shook his head in distress. "Jules, I've never seen you like this. Please tell me what happened. Have you been hurt?"

Jules tried another shrug. "I've suffered some physical pain and struggle, but it's nothing many, many other women haven't endured." She sighed, her eyes not leaving the food that stirred no hunger in her. "You deserve to know, I guess."

"Know *what*? What happened?"

"First you must promise to tell no one off of this ship. Not a word."

He gazed at her, finally nodding. "I promise. Not a word. Now, what happened?"

"Count the months, Ian. How long has it been since you saw me last?"

He paused. "Eight... about nine months... what does..."

This time the silence lasted so long that she finally looked at him again, dreading what his eyes might reveal of his feelings. But all she could see at the moment was shock.

"Nine months. Are you saying...?" He looked around the cabin, his eyes searching it, initial surprise giving way to concern. His hands were moving about as if trying to grasp something that eluded them. "There's a child?"

"Twins," Jules said.

"Twins." He stared at her, dread in his gaze. "Did they...? Something went wrong?"

"Everything went as well as it could. They're both healthy."

"But then where—?"

"I don't know."

"What?"

"*I don't know!*" She heard the despair and pain in her voice, and struggled to get it under control again.

Ian stared at her, confusion and anger appearing, his hands clenching into fists. "The twins were definitely mine?"

Her own anger stirred. She welcomed it, embracing the heat it brought. "I can't believe you asked me that."

He got mad in turn. "I'm the father? I can't believe that I wasn't told! I deserve to know where the children are!"

"I don't care what you think you deserve!" She closed her eyes, too tired to keep arguing. "Beside, I can't tell you. Not won't tell you, *can't.*"

"Jules, I don't understand any of this."

"The prophecy, Ian. Any child born to me is doomed. You know that! I had to do it! There was only one way to save the twins, Ian. Only one way to give them a chance at life. Because if anyone knew I was the mother, they'd die."

"What did you do?" Ian asked, his voice low.

She knew she had to tell him. "As soon as they were born, they were… taken. Ships left here last night. I never… never saw… Never touched…" Jules inhaled deeply, the words suddenly spilling out. "The ships will take the children somewhere, different somewheres, and transfer the children to someone else, who will transfer the child to someone else, and… I don't know how many. Enough that no one will know who the child's mother is, no one can ever trace the chains afterwards to the end. At the end of it all, there're supposed to be good families for both. But I don't know. I *can't* know. No one can know who the mother of those children is."

Ian stood up abruptly and walked to one side of the cabin, then turned and walked across to the other, moving like a man who wasn't seeing where he went. He stopped, turned and sat down again, his mouth working but no words coming. "Why didn't you tell me?" he finally got out, his voice holding grief as well as reproach. "I'm the father."

"Because this way the guilt is on me," Jules said. "You didn't deserve any of the pain, Ian. It's mine. Go ahead and hate me. You can't possibly hate me more than I do myself."

He didn't answer for a long time, his hands on the table before him twitching, his expression that of a man slowly taking in something he hadn't sought or expected.

"I'm sorry," Jules finally said. "I shouldn't have done this to you. I know why you hate me now."

He looked at her, his eyes filled with struggle and concern. "I don't hate you."

"Why not?"

"How can I hate you?" he said, his voice barely above a whisper. "Yes, I hurt, but I can see how much having to do this hurt you."

"I'm fine," Jules said, trying to push aside his sympathy.

"Are you? Then why do I see your heart lying on the table between us, ripped from you and bleeding?" He looked toward the door to the cabin, his expression torn, his voice filled with yearning. "If I left right away… tried to catch one of the ships…"

"What, Ian?" Jules asked. "Suppose you did catch the ships, find the children. Then what?"

He grimaced in pain, clenching his fists again. "The children would die. Eventually. Before then they might be traded as pawns or prizes among those wanting in on the prophecy. They'd never have peace and they'd die young, probably very young. I hate to admit it, but I understand your reasons. I understand the terrible logic that leaves only one choice if our children are to live. But you should have let me share in the decision. I had a right to be part of it."

"No. The prophecy lies on me. The decision was one I had to make," Jules said, her own voice faint. "It's my fault."

"I wasn't so drunk that night that I didn't know what might come of it! And I knew the danger any child of ours would face. But I didn't listen to my own conscience. The guilt is mine as well."

She looked away, not wanting to share the pain. "It's done now. I used you. You can leave with a clear conscience." There. That should get him out of here.

"You used me? You have no feelings for me?"

"No. Nothing."

"Liar. Do you think I'd let you off that easily?" Ian reached to pick up the mug on the table, offering it to her for another drink. She took a swallow rather than turn her head away, the rum-laced coffee once more feeling both cool and warm, welcome in her dry mouth and throat. "I'm facing things I want to avoid. You should do the same. My memories of that night with you are vague in part, but I do remember some things very clearly. I remember you saying 'I love you' to me."

"That was just passion," Jules said. "I didn't mean it."

"You said it more than once, and it sounded like you meant it."

"Well, there, you see what a fool you are?"

"Jules." Ian extended one hand toward her. She saw it was shaking. "I want to stay with you."

"Why?" she asked, ignoring the gesture. Why wouldn't he go? "Do you like being mistreated? Or do you like being in constant fear of your life?"

"Maybe both," Ian said. "Why does your crew stay with you?"

"I honestly don't know." The longer he was here, the more part of her wanted him to stay, the more part of her wanted that comfort. But the prophecy looming over her life would destroy anyone who became too close to her. "If you stayed on this ship, nothing would come of it. Don't think it'd be a way to get close to me."

"Closer than we were nine months ago?"

She felt her face warming at the memory. "Um… that… Why? Why would you want to stay?"

Ian laughed, slow and quiet, the tones sad rather than humorous, his voice afterwards still strained. "Jules, you do realize that most people have to figure out what their goals in life are, right? That most of us have to search for what we want to do and what we want to become?"

"What are you talking about?" Jules asked, wondering why Ian was speaking so oddly.

He looked at her. "You told me about growing up, about how you decided early on that you wouldn't be forced into the usual paths of orphans and instead become an officer in the Emperor's service. You had that goal for so long that you have no memory of deciding on it. And then the prophecy happened, and your goals in life were suddenly bent in a very different direction. You fought it, but you've had to live with the reality of the prophecy that sets your life on a certain road.

"But the rest of us, Jules. We have to look at many different paths, trying to choose one."

She shook her head at him. "You told me that it was expected that you'd become an officer, following in your father's footsteps. You didn't really decide that."

"I did decide it," Ian said. "I could've walked away, but there wasn't anything else I knew of that I wanted more, so I went along with it. Then you... you captured me, and told me my mother and sister were here, and that set my goals for me again. I had no choice but to look after them, until they decided to go off in a direction I would not follow. I didn't fully realize how much my life had lacked a goal I really wanted until I was left alone here in Dor's Castle."

"I can't help you find a purpose in life, Ian," Jules said.

"You already have."

She made a face. "Stop that. Don't give me that junk about me giving your life meaning."

"It's only partly about being in love with you," Ian said, looking back at her with a serious expression. "And, yes, I do love you. I still love you even though I don't know why. I've loved you for some time, and I finally freely confess that to you now."

"Ian, stars above, I am not in the mood—"

"But there's something else," he went on. "I went to a lot of places looking for you, and everywhere when you come up they speak of not just the prophecy, not just what you've done, but also what you're saying about keeping these new lands free. As free as the Great Guilds will permit, anyway."

"That's right," Jules said, surprised at the turn in the conversation. "I'm going to make that happen. If I can. Keep the free lands as free as possible, until whenever the Great Guilds are overthrown."

"Will you let me help?" Ian said. "I'd also like to see that happen."

"You... what?"

"I don't want the system that betrayed my father after a lifetime of loyal service, the system that corrupted the soul of my sister so she can only think of social advancement, the system that sentenced my mother to hard labor for a crime she didn't commit, I don't want that to take over these lands. I want something better here, and you seem to know what that better thing is. I want to help you." He took a deep breath. "And… I have a new reason as of today. It's the only way I can help… our children." His voice cracked on the last two words. "Make their world, wherever they are in it, a better place, and hope they benefit from that."

She stared at him, anxious and confused by his offer. "What if I still said no? What would you do?"

He frowned at the deck. "Work toward that goal another way. They need people with military knowledge here at Dor's. I could do that. Help defend that wall."

"You could die on that wall," she said, knowing as the words left her how much that would hurt her. The emptiness inside her still had room for more pain.

He shook his head, his face working. "At the moment, that doesn't seem that awful a thing."

"Ian…" She sat back, closing her eyes. Could someone else help fill the void inside her? Did she want to let anyone fill that even a little? "Ian," Jules said again, keeping her eyes closed because she couldn't look at him, "if that's how you truly feel, we can make room on the *Sun Queen* for you."

"Such a generous offer." She could feel Ian's eyes on her before he spoke again. "Why me, Jules?" he demanded, his voice harsh. "Why did you choose me to be the father?"

She tried to shrug once more, but that almost made the blanket fall. "I thought you'd be good in bed."

"Jules, don't I deserve the truth from you?"

Not really a question, more of another demand, but that didn't raise the resistance it usually would in her. Because he had a right to make this demand. She finally looked at him again. "I wanted the father of my children to be my choice. And I wanted them to be strong, and brave, and smart. That's why I chose you. And I wanted you to live. That's why I sailed away the next day, because having you close to me will kill you. I have enough on my conscience without adding your death to it."

"So you do care for me."

She shifted her look to a glare. "Were you listening? Where did I say that? Everything I said was selfish. Things I wanted. Why can't you see that?"

"Different people see different things," Ian said, his eyes on her.

"Stop sounding like a Mage."

"I have no idea what sounding like a Mage means." He stared into the distance. "What were they? A boy and a girl? Or…?"

"I don't know," Jules said. "I can't know, or I might give it away to people watching me for clues as to who they are and where they are."

"I see. You're right." His voice sounded dull, like someone trying to tamp down all feelings. Ian stood up abruptly. "If you're going to let me join the crew, I should report to your first officer. Is it the big man who didn't want to let me in here or the woman who insisted I be let in?"

"Either one." Jules looked down at the table again, suddenly afraid of being alone in this cabin with only the memories of what had happened yesterday to keep her company. "Um… Ian… if you'd like to stay a little longer, we could talk."

"We could?" His voice, his eyes, still held anger and remorse. "What could we talk about?"

"I don't know. I…" Emotions overwhelmed her for a moment. "I have to… I'm the captain. I have to…" Jules gritted her teeth, trying to power through her grief and failing. Too soon. Too soon.

His eyes held worry, too, as Ian nodded and sat back down. "Maybe you could tell me about the people in the crew. Who they are and all."

"Yes. I could do that." Jules hesitated, something tight inside her blocking her throat for a moment. "Ian, it hurt so bad. I don't mean my body. I mean…"

"I know what you mean. As it sinks in for me, it's hurting, too. I think later it's going to hurt a lot worse, once some of the numbness inside me wears off. At least we can hurt together."

He'd also lost them. She reached out, grasping his near hand with her own. "Thanks."

* * *

"No Mages in town," Dor said to her, looking about the *Sun Queen's* stern cabin curiously. "For a while we had three or four pretty constantly, but they left over a week before you got here this time."

"Are you sure they left?" Jules said. She was wearing her usual clothing after having her midsection wrapped to hold it in until her body could recover more. To those who didn't know, she didn't look like a woman who'd recently given birth. Keli's herbal drink had helped lift her spirits a little, and as Mak had reminded her in the dream, having others around had also helped her pull partway out of the pit of depression. "I didn't see any Mages in Cape Astra before three tried to kill me."

"We saw two of the Mages board a ship and leave. The other two…" Dor shook his head in amazement. "They went out into a field and suddenly there was a huge bird, and they both climbed on it and flew away. I admit I had trouble believing your crew when they told me about being attacked by Mages riding huge birds. Maybe I simply didn't want to believe they could do that. But they can."

"I wonder what's up this time?" Jules muttered, looking east.

"Speaking of something being up, I heard Maeve was called to your ship a couple of days ago," Dor said.

"She checked out one of the girls in the crew," Jules said, having readied that lie and shared it with Maeve by a message sent with Liv. "The girl'd had too good a time ashore and it looked like she'd acquired an extra souvenir as a result. But it turned out to be a false alarm."

"Ah. I'll tell anyone who asks. You know how it is. A midwife coming out to your ship, people talk."

"Do you see any babies in here?" Jules said, amazed inside that she could say those words without breaking down. But she'd sealed that away, an unhealed wound that no one but those closest to her could see or would ever see.

"No, of course not! Why did you want to see me?"

Jules looked east again. "The Mechanics guessed we'd have about a year before the Emperor realized how futile his efforts to catch me were, and how badly the Empire was rupturing citizens who were heading west to new settlements. They told me that nearly eight months ago."

Dor nodded, his mood suddenly grim. "Leaving us maybe four more months to prepare."

"Have you heard anything from any of the newest escapees?"

"Not about an attack, no. Pretty much the same news as for months. Tight security around Sandurin and Landfall, and whatever's left sailing the sea in search of you. No one's mentioned legions being gathered or extra ships being prepared to transport them."

"Good. I've been doing what I can to get people in the new settlements to commit to sending aid here when the Empire comes knocking on Dor's Castle," Jules said. "How are your preparations?"

"Coming along," Dor said. "Building a wall takes time. It should be done in two more months. Three at the outside. Funny thing about walls, isn't it?"

"What's that?"

"I've had plenty of time to think about it. You know, if this wall was being built in the Empire, it'd be all about the Emperor. The reasons for building the wall wouldn't even have to make sense. They'd do it because the Emperor said so. And if building the wall did make sense, it'd be about controlling people: keeping them in, keeping them out, forcing them to do what they're told. But my wall isn't to force people to do anything. It's not to keep out refugees fleeing their old lives in search of a better future. It's to defend them, and that better future, for all of us." Dor scratched his head. "That's funny, isn't it? You could have two walls that might look the same, might be built the same, but serve totally different purposes."

"Mak used to tell me that why something is done matters," Jules said. "I think that's why your wall will hold. It's being built for the best of reasons, to help instead of hurt, to serve hope instead of fear. If the things we build take anything from us, I'm sure the wall will draw strength from that."

"That's good," Dor said, a smile appearing on him. "Give me enough defenders, and we'll hold it."

"I'm going to do my best. *Sun Queen* will be leaving port tomorrow," Jules added. "We'll be going to the Sharr Isles to drop off some cargo and see what we can hear about events in the Empire."

"It still surprises me that you're willing to risk being that close to the Empire."

"The Empire thinks I'm still engaging in frequent piracy," Jules said. "I hear they've got decoy ships sailing around looking like rich, helpless merchants that are actually crammed with legionaries ready to nab me when I attack. But since the *Sun Queen* and I are engaged in other forms of commerce at the moment, those ships aren't seeing any action."

"What about other pirates?" Dor said. "Aren't those decoys snaring other ships?"

"They got one before word got out," Jules said. "Now all pirates are avoiding obvious targets and making money escorting ships full of refugees to the west, or carrying the refugees themselves."

Dor smiled. "Meaning the Empire's attempt to stop piracy has helped cause the numbers of its citizens escaping to increase dramatically. Good sailing. I'll be looking forward to seeing you again."

After Dor left, Ian came by. "I'm going to go ashore and get my things," he said. "I don't have much. You're not going to sail off and leave me here while I'm gone, are you?"

"No. Of course not," Jules said, realizing as she did so that in the back of her mind just that thought had been lurking, to leave Ian on the pier and spare him the risk of being close to her. "How did you know I'd consider that?"

"Because as brave as you are, sometimes you want to run," Ian said.

"I can't blame you for that. It's why you're still alive. But I do take it personally when I'm what you're running from."

"You are pretty dangerous," Jules said, amazed that she could muster even that weak a joke. "Be careful. There may still be Mages in town, and if Imperial agents find out you've joined this crew they might go after you."

"See? You do care about me."

"No, I just don't want you to die." She looked at him, thinking of how much harder the last few days would've been without him. "Having you around would be… a big help. There's a lot left for me to do, and not much time left for me to do it. "

* * *

They'd be leaving Dor's Castle today. Jules couldn't wait to get underway and clear the harbor, wondering if she'd ever again feel comfortable in this place.

She'd woken up several times last night, imagining she'd heard a baby crying. Hopefully that would stop once the ship left here. If not, she'd have to learn to live with it.

Jules stood on the quarterdeck as final preparations were made to sail, grateful for the railing to lean on. She looked up at the masts, checking the rigging, and felt herself tense as she saw something beyond the highest mast.

"What is it?" Liv asked, looking up as well. "One of those monster birds. Is it coming lower?"

"I don't think so," Jules said, watching the creature fly, wondering if there was a Mage on its back, and surprised to feel a slight yearning to know what flying felt like. "It looks like it came from the west and is heading east."

"Back toward the Empire," Liv said, shading her eyes to continue tracking the movement of the bird. "Yeah, he's keeping on steady to the east."

"Dor said the Mages who were here all left a little while ago, heading east."

"Huh." Liv gave Jules a questioning look. "Like they're being called in, maybe? You've said the Mechanics were calling their people in because of some Guild politics. Could the Mages be doing the same?"

"Do Mages have politics?" Jules wondered, then answered herself. "They're still people, deep inside, so they must have politics. I hope you're right, Liv." The shape of the bird dwindled quickly as it flew east, showing no sign of changing its path.

"I hope I'm right, too." She leaned on the rail next to Jules. "Speaking of men…"

"We were not speaking of men," Jules said.

"I was thinking the timing of our new shipmate is a good thing."

"Why?"

"Well, assuming you take up with him—"

"I am not taking up with him," Jules insisted.

"If you did," Liv went on, "anyone watching would think that anything that came of you and him becoming friends wouldn't show up for at least another year."

"Oh." Liv was right, Jules realized. "That'll help hide the babies, and throw off people trying to guess the age if anyone realizes they exist."

"You know he's devoted to you."

"Ian? No, he isn't," Jules said. "He'd be better off without me. He'll realize that and find someone else eventually."

"Him?" Liv said with exaggerated incredulity. "That man? I've known plenty of men who would find another. But not him. I can already see it. He's one of those who loves only one. You attract such men, Jules. Like a bright flame that devours them."

"You make me sound like such a great catch," Jules said, not sure whether to be amused or annoyed at Liv's words. "The only reason men have been attracted to me is because they want in on the prophecy."

"Oh, nonsense. You're a dangerous girl," Liv said. "Men like that."

"Why are you sounding like a Mechanic?"

"Mechanics said that to you?"

"Female Mechanics," Jules said.

"And why did the female Mechanics say that?"

"Because some male Mechanics... were... hitting on me."

"I rest my case and await with confidence the judgment of my peers," Liv said.

Jules looked over at her. "Hey, Liv. Thank you for what you said to me a few days ago, the morning after... that happened. I've been resentful of the daughter of my line almost since the moment the prophecy was spoken, because she took my life. I'd never thought about what the prophecy would do to her. Now I realize that we're both victims of it, sisters in battling fate despite the fact that we'll never meet."

"I'm glad I said it, then," Liv said. She looked east. "Our friend the monster bird has flown out of sight. I wish I knew what the Mages were up to."

"You and me both," Jules said. She straightened, wincing. "And I wish my body would get back to normal." Walking to the front railing, she called across the ship. "On the *Sun Queen*! Prepare to get underway! Ang, is anyone left ashore?"

He shook his head. "We're ready to go when you are."

"Then let's start taking in lines!"

The familiar routine comforted her, and the tasks of calling commands and feeling the winds required her full attention. By the time the ship cleared the harbor and tacked to the east Jules could almost pretend she was no longer haunted.

She'd worried that being up here might be exhausting, but found herself standing, watching the sea and the sails. Pacta Servanda had been comfortable. Someday Julesport would be comfortable. But this... this was home.

Keli came up onto the quarterdeck, looking her over. "That's the first smile I've seen on you in a good while."

"A smile?" Jules realized he was right. There was a smile on her face, a slight one, but still a smile. And then she realized the reason for it. "No offense, Keli. Being around friends has helped, and your draughts have helped, but what's lifted my spirits is being underway again. There's nothing like being underway, sails set, with a fine wind and a following sea. That's why I'm feeling good again."

"No offense taken," Keli said. "There's many a sailor who'd agree that there's no better treatment for sorrow than sailing, and no better medicine than the feel and smell of the sea. As a healer, I recommend you continue sailing."

"You've finally told me to do something that I want to do," Jules said. "I'll follow your advice."

On subsequent days as they passed ships heading west, their decks crowded, Jules wondered if among them might be...

It'd be like that for the rest of her life, she realized. Every time she saw a baby, and then as years passed a child, and then a teen or a young adult, she'd look at them, trying to spot any resemblance, and wondering. But never knowing.

As they passed south of the Sharr Isles, drawing close to Imperial waters, Jules saw a big merchant ship gliding slowly over the water with only a few sails set. The ship, riding low in the water, looked laden with cargo and an easy mark for pirates. It flew the flag of a rich merchant family in Landfall that every sailor knew had close and lucrative ties to an Imperial prince. "One of the decoy ships?" Jules asked Ang as the *Sun Queen* sailed past a few thousand lances distant.

"Not a very good trap, is it?" Ang said. "Too obvious."

"What do you think the legionaries sweating below deck on that ship would say if they knew they were this close to the woman their Emperor wants so badly?"

"They'd probably say a few choice words even sailors might not have heard."

The next morning *Sun Queen* finally approached Caer Lyn from the south, having timed her approach for near sunset. The longboat was put into the water, Ang and several sailors climbing down afterwards. Jules watched the longboat disappear into the growing darkness as it headed for shore. "Ang says this isn't risky," she commented to Liv.

"We've done it before," she said. "He'll find our contact, arrange for a boat to come out and pick up our wood, and then we'll go on to other business while the lumber is sold for a very nice sum to rich Imperials who want to impress others. Ang won't be back until after midnight, even assuming everything goes perfectly. You might as well go down and get some food in you."

"That's a good idea. Maybe I'll eat below deck tonight with the rest of the crew."

"That'll disappoint your man," Liv said in an innocent voice.

"I don't have a man."

"Then who's been going to your cabin to share dinner the last few days?" Liv asked with mock surprise.

Jules gave her an exasperated shove. "Ian and I have a lot to catch up on. That's what we do. Talk. Nothing else."

"Certainly. I believe you."

"Liv! I don't have time or energy for a relationship, and if you or anyone else spreads rumors that Ian is my man his life won't be worth a dollop of warm spit."

Liv turned away, patting Jules' arm. "Relax, Captain. No one on this ship is going to breathe a word about you and any man to anyone not on this ship. We know the stakes."

"Thanks," Jules mumbled.

As if to further darken her mood, Ian was waiting at the foot of the ladder leading to the main deck, his brow furrowed with unhappiness. "Captain," he began, "request permission to—"

"Knock it off, Ian," Jules said wearily. "This is a free ship, not an Imperial warship. What do you need?"

His mouth tightened. "I volunteered to go along with Ang. I'd like to know why I was told to stay on the ship. Is it because I'm not trusted?"

"It's because until less than a year ago you were an officer in the Imperial fleet," Jules said. "Which means if there are any Imperial ships in Caer Lyn you might well be recognized by someone on them. Which would be bad for you and for Ang's job of lining up the buyer for our cargo."

"Oh." Ian had the grace to look embarrassed. "I'm sorry. I should have realized."

"What's really bothering you?" Full night had fallen, the stars out above, easily seen framed by the masts and spars overhead that stood out black against the vault of the sky. *Sun Queen* rolled gently in the swells, the darker bulk of the island to the north and west looming off the starboard side, the wind sighing through the rigging. Members of the crew were speaking in low voices, though an occasional laugh pierced the night.

"I don't think I'm contributing as much to the ship as I could," Ian said.

"Meaning you were trained as an officer and can do an officer's tasks, but are working pretty much as an ordinary sailor," Jules said. "I'm sorry. I can't displace someone like Ang or Liv. There'll come a time I need another officer, and I promise your skills will be used."

"You have much bigger things to worry about than my happiness," Ian said.

"Maybe," Jules said.

* * *

Ang got back about the middle of the night, and just after dawn a small ship was sighted coming to meet the *Sun Queen*. The *Sun Queen* off-loaded her exotic lumber onto the small ship, which then sailed back toward Caer Lyn. "We're to meet them back here in two weeks," Ang told Jules. "They'll pass on our share of the profits, and the arms and armor we've asked them to pick up."

"They'll need those arms at Dor's," Jules said. "Two weeks? That's about right to escort a refugee ship west, isn't it?"

Well north of Landfall on the Imperial coast, a small town named Balmer boasted a single pier and Imperial officials who were even more easily bribed than usual. Little watched by those creating fortresses at the big ports of Landfall and Sandurin, Balmer had become a common way station for citizens escaping the Empire. The *Sun Queen* sailed to Balmer, finding a large merchant ship waiting there to pick up its human cargo and eager for an escort against pirates. "Do you think any of those hiring ships like us to escort them against the threat of pirates know that the ships they're hiring are all pirates?" Keli asked Jules as both ships stood out from Balmer en route to Kelsi's.

"It's all good as far as they're concerned," Jules said. "And there's much less danger of anyone getting hurt."

"How are you doing?"

"I'll live."

Sun Queen only stood into Kelsi's long enough to pick up fresh water and food, as well as local news. "No Mages in town," Ang said. "There were usually five or ten around, but they all headed east back to the Empire."

"Someone's expecting something to happen soon," Jules said.

They made it back to the waters south of Caer Lyn one day shy of the two weeks, planning to drift while waiting.

But those plans changed as one of the big metal Mechanic ships came sailing their way, plainly aiming to intercept the *Sun Queen*.

CHAPTER THIRTEEN

The Mechanic ship maneuvered close alongside the *Sun Queen*, dwarfing the wooden sailing ship and paying no attention to the winds as it slowed. Jules stood on the quarterdeck, wondering whether Mechanics Guild internal politics had settled on a course that would be hostile to her. She couldn't tell whether it was the same as one of the Mechanic ships she'd been on already. The Mechanic ships bore no numbers or names or other distinguishing marks, and flew only the Guild flag, probably to make it hard for commons to keep track of them or even to be sure how many there were.

As the Mechanic ship glided to a halt, plainly waiting, Jules told Ang to put a boat in the water. "I'll go over and see what they want."

"How dangerous is this?" Ian asked.

"They haven't killed me yet," Jules said. "I'm trying to keep that record intact."

"I should—"

"I'm the only one they'll let come aboard."

Jules hastily changed into her best pants and shirt, buffed her boots, and settled one of the revolvers in its holster at her waist. By the time she was done, the boat was in the water, several sailors already waiting at the oars. Feeling Ian's worried gaze on her, Jules went down the Jaykob ladder, grateful that she'd recovered enough physically to be able to handle the descent without any problem.

"Let's get on over there before they get impatient," Jules told Gord, who was in charge of the boat. The other sailors bent to their oars as Gord steered the boat toward the looming mass of the Mechanic ship.

"How does it float?" Gord called to Jules as they neared the high metal side of the ship. "I mean, it's all steel or iron, right? How does that float?"

"If the Mechanics ever tell me, I'll let you know," Jules said. The boat came alongside the Mechanic ship, the metal of the hull rising beside it. The Mechanics had also dropped a Jaykob ladder, a reassuringly normal thing about their ship.

Jules breathed in and out slowly to calm herself, then began climbing up the ladder. This was the first time she'd confronted Mechanics since giving birth. Would they be able to see anything that would betray what had happened?

Several Mechanics were waiting on deck. None of them seemed to notice anything different about Jules. She was, after all, just a common. Even though all of the Mechanics had revolvers in holsters, none of them had the weapons in hand. One of them beckoned to Jules and led the way wordlessly inside the ship.

She tried to keep track this time of the turns and passageways and ladders they used until reaching a door. The Mechanic leading the way opened the door, revealing a room lined with wood paneling, a large wooden desk fastened to the deck near one wall. It resembled a similar room that Jules had been in on a Mechanic ship, but she thought a few small details might be different. Behind the desk, a single older Mechanic waited, his eyes on her.

After a pause in which Jules felt increasingly awkward, she decided to risk speaking first. "Good afternoon, Sir Senior Mechanic." It seemed safe to call him a senior mechanic. Every Mechanic she'd encountered who was in charge had been a senior Mechanic.

He didn't correct her, so she must have guessed right. "You have about five weeks," the Senior Mechanic said.

"Five weeks?"

"We have very recently received word from Marandur. The Emperor has executed all of his senior advisers for treason and ordered an attack to seize all settlements along the south coast, on through the strait. The Guild has learned that the Empire's plan calls for four weeks to gather the soldiers and ships at Landfall. Our understanding is that sailing from Landfall to... what's the name of that place?"

"Dor's Castle, Sir Senior Mechanic?" Jules, reeling internally at the news that the long-dreaded Imperial attack was coming, was surprised that she could speak so calmly.

"Yes. That place. Sailing there will take about another week. So, five weeks. The plan places particular emphasis on ultimately seizing Julesport because the Emperor thinks that you will be certain to defend it in person, and he still wants your person."

"We'll stop the Imperial attack at Dor's Castle," Jules said. "The Emperor's hand will never reach Julesport."

He eyed her for a moment. "There's something else. The Mages are providing assistance to the Imperial attack."

"Mages?" Another worst fear confirmed.

The Senior Mechanic walked in front of the desk and sat down against it, watching Jules. "It's a clever move, since it would make any direct attack by the Mechanics Guild on the Imperial force also an attack on the Mage Guild. We can tell the Mages are worried. They've pulled Mages back into the Empire and stationed them at their Guild Halls in the big cities, ready to defend them if the Final War breaks out. That means the Imperial forces that attack Dor's Castle will have a limited number of Mages among them, though it's not hard to guess how superstitious commons will react to facing even a few."

"We will fight, Sir Senior Mechanic," Jules said.

He looked her over as if skeptical of her words. "I understand that you've been loaned two revolvers. How many cartridges remain for them?"

"I've had to use two since my last meeting," Jules said. "I still have twenty-eight cartridges."

"Oh? I hope that means at least one more Mage is dead."

"I killed three that night, Sir Senior Mechanic."

One of the Senior Mechanic's eyebrows raised skeptically. "Three Mages with two bullets?"

"I stabbed two of the Mages," Jules said. "I had to use the two shots to kill the third."

"I'm glad that you're working for *our* Guild," the Senior Mechanic said. "But we want to give you something to help counterbalance the support of the Mages for the Empire's actions. And something that will make it clear how much support we're throwing your way." Walking back behind the desk, he picked up a long, heavy bag and set it on top of the desk. Untying the line holding the top closed, the senior mechanic drew out a Mechanic weapon. Not a revolver, but one of the long weapons. "This is a rifle. Watch how this is done." He picked up a cartridge that looked like those for the revolvers, but perhaps twice as long. Setting the cartridge in a groove on one side of the weapon, he slid the cartridge in until it disappeared. "Load cartridges until it's full. Like this. To shoot, you pull down this part," he swung down a lever on the bottom, "and pull it back up. Do it each time. This," he added, pointing to a small, flat piece of metal, "is the safety. Push it like this and you can't fire the weapon."

"Fire?" Jules asked, surprised by the word.

The senior mechanic looked annoyed. "I meant shoot the weapon. Move the safety like this and you can shoot again. Keep the safety on unless you're ready to use the weapon. Did you get all of that?"

"Yes, Sir Senior Mechanic," Jules said.

"Doris!" the senior mechanic called. One of the Mechanics who'd brought Jules and had been waiting outside came into the room. The senior mechanic pushed the rifle at the Mechanic. "Show this common how to hold the rifle and aim it."

"Yes, Sir Senior Mechanic," the Mechanic said. She checked the setting of the safety, then raised the weapon in both hands, the back end against her shoulder. "This is how you hold it. Make sure the butt rests firmly against your shoulder. If you don't, it'll hurt. You've got two sights, here and here. Line them up on the target." Mechanic Doris held the weapon out to Jules. "Show me."

"Yes, Lady Mechanic," Jules said, amazed that she was being allowed to touch the weapon. She placed her hands as the Mechanic had done, raising the weapon.

"Hard against your shoulder," Mechanic Doris said, grabbing the rifle and pushing it back hard enough to stagger Jules. "Try aiming."

Jules looked along the long barrel just as she had seen Mechanic Doris doing, seeing the two sights line up.

"Rifles have longer range than pistols," the senior mechanic said. "These are insurance for the Guild that you'll win, and something to stiffen the spines of gullible commons facing the superstitious threat of Mages. Unload that," he told Doris.

Once she'd done so, the senior mechanic pushed the rifle back into the long bag. "There are four rifles in here, along with ten cartridges for each. Use them wisely. On the bottom are two more revolvers and a box of cartridges for them."

"Don't try to use rifle cartridges in the revolvers, or revolver cartridges in the rifles," Mechanic Doris said. "They're not the same."

"Yes, Lady Mechanic," Jules said, stunned that the Mechanics were providing her with such an arsenal of Mechanic weapons. They must want her to win very badly, or else lacked confidence in her, or wanted to make sure the fight cost the Mages no matter what happened. Maybe all of those reasons were true.

"Five weeks," the senior mechanic said. "We understand you're calling yourself the Empress of the west."

"No, Sir Senior Mechanic, I am not calling myself that," Jules said. "There will be no empress or emperors in the west. I've been called an empress only on the seas of this world."

"Really?" The senior mechanic gave her another long look. "As long as you get the job done, you can give yourself any common title you want." He gave her a brusque wave-off, turning away.

Jules approached the bag on the desk warily, not surprised at how heavy it was to lift. With the long rifles inside, it was also awkward to carry, especially through the passages inside the ship. None of the Mechanics offered to help, of course.

Once outside on deck again, Jules paused to look grimly down the ladder to the boat. Getting it down safely would be a major problem, especially if she overstrained her body.

Help came from an unexpected source. "Get over here, apprentices." One of the Mechanics watching Jules beckoned to two boys whose jackets differed from those of the Mechanics. "Fasten that line to that bag and lower it into the boat after this common gets down into it."

"She doesn't need help, Ken," Mechanic Doris said.

"The Guild wants her to have that stuff," Mechanic Ken said. "Which means the Guild wants us to make sure she gets it into that boat. This isn't about how much fun you'd have watching her try to make it down that ladder."

Lady Mechanic Doris shrugged and leaned against the metal side of the structure rising from the deck of the ship. The two apprentices hastened over, tying a stout line to the bag. Jules watched, worried about how strong the result would be, but apparently Mechanics did a decent job of teaching knot-tying to their trainees.

Before heading down, she faced Mechanic Ken. "Thank you, Sir Mechanic."

It was his turn to shrug. "I didn't do it for you."

She made her way down the ladder, wondering why Mechanics who acted decently toward a common always felt the need to disavow what they'd done.

And yet, Jules thought as she caught the bag being lowered to her, the Mechanics had given her an awesome number of their weapons to use against the Empire and the Mages. For all their contempt of her, they also needed her.

The boat had barely cleared the side of the Mechanic ship before the ship began moving ahead, going faster at such a rate that the stern wake rocked the *Sun Queen*'s boat when it hit. By the time the boat made it back to the *Sun Queen*, the Mechanic ship was well on its way back to Caer Lyn.

Jules supervised hauling the bag aboard, terrified of losing it. "Conference," she said to Ang and Liv, then nodded to Ian as well. "In my cabin."

Ang picked up the bag, displaying surprise at how heavy it was, but had no trouble hauling it into the stern cabin. Jules pulled out the chart, slapping it onto the table. "The Mechanics say we have five weeks before the Empire hits Dor's Castle. We have to alert every settlement in the west to send any ships and men and women they can spare, and we need to do it fast."

Ang and Liv were momentarily speechless, but Ian frowned at the chart. "Do the Mechanics know how much the Empire is bringing to the fight? How many legionaries, how many ships?"

"No," Jules said. She paused, trying to decide whether to tell the others about the Mages.

No. Not yet. They were already rattled by the news of the Imperial plans.

"Five weeks," Ang said, shaking his head. "We can't do it with one ship. By the time we made it around the entire sea, and south through the Strait of Gulls, the Emperor's forces would already be at Dor's."

"Ang," Liv said, "are there any ships in port at Caer Lyn who'd help? Someone we can count on?"

"Caer Lyn has gotten too hot for pirates to drop anchor," Ang said. "But... *Prosper* is in port. I saw her."

"We can count on Captain Aravind," Jules said. "*Sun Queen* can take the south settlements. I can write a message that Captain Aravind can take around to settlements on the northern shores of the sea and..." She saw the skeptical looks on the others. "Why wouldn't that work?"

"Who'd believe him?" Liv said. "Who'd believe he's really coming from you? And even if they believe him, would they send forces if you're not there to urge them on?"

Jules ran one hand through her hair, staring down at the chart. "All right, then. Give me another idea. We know there's not enough time for me to go everywhere."

A long pause as everyone considered the problem, abruptly broken by Ian. "I could take the message around. A personal representative of Captain Jules. Wouldn't that make a difference?"

"It might," Ang said. "But how does anyone know you are who you claim to be?"

"I'm not sure it's a good idea anyway," Jules said, reluctance rising in her at the proposal. "For you to be gone from the ship so long," she said to Ian. "And you'll be going through waters where the Imperials might catch you."

"If what the Mechanics said is true," Ian said, "then the Imperial warships that have been searching for you will be withdrawing to Landfall to prepare for the attack on the free settlements. Jules, I can do this."

"I know you can. I just…" She glanced at Liv and Ang, who were giving her level looks that clearly conveyed a message. "I… it'll be dangerous."

"Aren't we planning on all meeting at Dor's Castle to fight an attack by the Imperial fleet and legionaries?" Ian asked. "That's going to be a little dangerous, too, I think."

"But…"

Ang nodded at Ian. "Cap'n, I think your man has the right of it."

"He's not my man!" She clenched her fist, trying to come up with reasons why it was a bad idea and instead realizing what could make it work. "He'll have one of the Mechanic revolvers with him. Every common knows the only common entrusted with those weapons is me or someone working with me. If he has the revolver, people will believe him." Jules slammed a fist down on the chart, knowing this was her only halfway decent option and hating it. "That's what we'll do! We need to get word to *Prosper* and get that ship out here as fast as possible. Ang, take care of that. Liv, help him. Ian, get your things ready to transfer to *Prosper*. I'll write a message for you to carry along with you."

Ang and Ian began to go, but Liv stood firm. "What's in the bag, Captain?"

Jules glowered at her. "Mechanic weapons. Six more Mechanic weapons. Those should help inspire settlements to send aid to Dor's. Any more questions?"

"No, Captain." They left her alone. Jules stared at the chart, unhappy at the idea of Ian leaving and realizing she never had mentioned the Mages.

Should she tell anyone about them?

* * *

Ang made it into Caer Lyn that afternoon, running an extra risk. By evening *Prosper* and the small ship of their trade contact had come out to meet *Sun Queen*.

As the swords, crossbows, spears, shields, and armor that had been purchased with the profits from the lumber sales were transferred to the *Sun Queen* and lowered into the cargo hold, Jules brought Ian into her cabin.

"Here's the letter I wrote," she said, handing him the envelope. "Let the leaders of each settlement read it, and try to get them to commit to sending help to defend Dor's Castle."

Ian opened the envelope, looking over the letter. "All right. You make your plea well. Your handwriting is still terrible, though."

"Thanks."

"Signed, Jules of Julesport." Ian looked at her. "You're not signing it the woman of the prophecy?"

"They all know who I am, and I don't want to be known just as that," Jules said. "Let me give you one of the Mechanic revolvers. With that, you can protect yourself better, and people will know you're my representative. No other commons have had Mechanics weapons but those working with me."

"Yes, you said that before."

"I want to be sure you remember it. Take off your belt," Jules said as she got out a second revolver and its holder. "The Mechanics call this a holster," she added as she slid it onto Ian's belt. "See how you can tie it closed? That's important. You don't want it falling out." Her mind preoccupied with worries, she threaded his belt back on, fastening it in front for him and not really noticing his surprised look at her. "Here's how the weapon works. Well, no common knows how the weapon *works*, but this what we do to shoot it. These are for aiming, like with a crossbow, and this is the trigger, also like on a crossbow."

She opened the weapon, dropping the cartridges onto the table. "Each of these is worth the same as a jewel of that size. Don't waste them. Each only works once. See how they go in? You pull the trigger, nice and easy, and just like a crossbow you don't want to jerk it, and see this goes back and then whams forward and the revolver shoots. It's going to feel like… Remember in training when they fired crossbows at shields we were holding so we'd know how that shock felt? It's kind of like that. A real kick. And, see, this turns when you pull the trigger, so the next cartridge is lined up. That's really all there is to it, except the same rules as with a loaded crossbow."

He'd been watching, listening, eyes intent. Ian nodded. "Don't point it at anyone you don't want to shoot at, and keep your finger off the trigger until you want to shoot someone. It's heavy for its size, isn't it?"

"Yes. Oh, sometimes the cartridges don't work. I don't know why that is, but if you try to shoot and nothing happens, just try to shoot again." She looked it over as Ian gingerly lowered the weapon into its holster, biting her lip, trying to think what else to say. "If any Mechanics see you with this weapon, they might get upset and worried .
Tell them that the weapon was loaned to Captain Jules by Lady Senior Mechanic Guild Master Grace so we can carry out an important task for the Mechanics Guild. That should prevent any Mechanics from attacking you. At the very worst they might take you into custody while they use whatever device they have to talk across long distances to check with Grace."

"Got it." Ian frowning, concentrating. "The weapon was loaned to Captain Jules by Lady Mechanic—"

"Lady Senior Mechanic."

"Lady Senior Mechanic Guild Master Grace so we can do an important task for the Mechanics Guild."

"That's it." She hesitated, feeling a need to say more, but unsure of what that should be. "Thank you for volunteering for this. You know how important it is."

"I'm glad that I can help," Ian said. He hesitated as well, began to say something, but stopped, his eyes on her.

He might die, or she might die, before they could meet again. She knew that, and so did he.

She didn't know which of them moved first, maybe they both did at the same time, but they leaned in and their lips met for a long moment.

Pulling back, Ian stared at her. "I guess I should get going."

"Yes." Jules said, her heart pounding. She led them out onto the deck, walking past members of the crew resting after bringing aboard and stowing the weapons. "Go to Marida's first, Ian, then work your way west. Also try to tell any ships you encounter along the way, but be careful not to get too close to any that might be Imperial decoy ships hunting for me. If any Mages come after you, use that revolver. It will kill them. When you've finished coming down the west coast of the sea, come back east to Dor's Castle. I should be back there by then after visiting the southern settlements like Gull Haven and Julesport."

"I won't take more than a month," Ian said. They reached the gap in the railing, the Jaykob ladder leading down to the boat from the *Prosper* waiting for him. "All right. Um, I'll get it done."

"Thank you," Jules said again, feeling the force of unsaid words pushing against her throat. She wanted to kiss him again, but something held her back.

Another moment of hesitation, then Ian nodded to her and started down the ladder.

She watched him go, feeling something of herself going with him, her mouth opening to speak but then closing again.

"Girl, say something," Liv murmured from close beside Jules.

Jules looked at her helplessly. "Liv, everyone I've ever loved has been taken from me. If I admit it, if I say it, will he be taken from me, too?"

"If you already have those feelings, then anything fate holds is already fixed. You can still do what you feel you should."

"But what do I say?"

"If he doesn't come back," Liv said, "what will you wish you'd said right now?"

Jules stared down at Ian. She quickly leaned out, calling. "Ian!"

He looked up at her.

"Ian, do your best not to get killed!" Jules told him. "You… you're the finest man I've ever known, and I don't want to face the future without you!"

One foot still on the Jaykob ladder, Ian stared up at her, a smiling forming on his face. "I'll see you at Dor's Castle in less than a month!"

"You'd better!" She settled back on her feet as Ian climbed into the boat, watching as it began heading back to the *Prosper*. Finally turning, Jules discovered that what seemed to be the entire crew was looking at her with a variety of grins and amused expressions. "What's so funny?" she yelled at them. "Why is everyone standing around gawking and listening in to private conversations, when there is work to be done?"

In the night, the three ships separated. The small one headed back to Caer Lyn, the *Prosper* sailed north, and the *Sun Queen* sailed south.

Jules stood on the quarterdeck, looking aft over the sea, as the *Prosper*'s sails faded from sight.

* * *

They stopped at Dor's only long enough to offload the arms and armor, take on more food and water, and warn Dor.

"Five weeks?" Dor stared at her in horror. "That's all the time left?"

"It was five weeks when we left the Sharr Isles," Jules said. "Now we're closer to four weeks. How's your wall?"

"Close to done." Dor collapsed into one of Jules' chairs, staring at one bulkhead of the stern cabin. "It will be done in time. But I don't have enough men and women to hold it."

"Leave that to me. All of the settlements in the free lands are being told, and asked to send help here."

"That leaves very little time, Jules." Dor wiped his face with one hand. "But I'll do what I can. May I ask a favor?"

"Of course."

"My daughters. If I don't make it through, please help look after them."

"I will," Jules said.

They cleared the harbor before night fell, tacking west with a strong wind urging them on as if the sea itself wanted to ensure their voyage was a fast one.

Sun Queen stopped at each port and settlement in turn. First the new one at Gull's Haven, then another at Lar's Harbor where the Strait of Gulls opened into the Jules Sea. Then down to Julesport, Jules counting the days and risking a dash to Edin's Town. In each place she passed on the news and urged the people to send help to Dor's. Jules met with the captains of every ship they encountered, doing the same, and asking that they pass on the warning and the plea for help.

Finally a quick stop at Cape Astra, a final entreaty for whatever help they could send, and they headed back through the strait to the Sea of Bakre. If the winds held, they should reach Dor's again a day beyond the end of the fourth week.

And the whole time at sea she brooded, worrying about the fight to come, and how much time was left, and many other things.

"Captain?" Liv said as she came into the stern cabin, closing the door behind her. "Can we talk?"

"Sure," Jules said, pushing away a plate of food that she hadn't eaten much of. "What's bothering you?"

"I'm worried about whatever it is that's bothering you," Liv said.

Jules gasped a short laugh. "You mean with the Imperial attack coming at Dor's? What could possibly be bothering me?"

Liv sat down opposite Jules, leaning back and watching her. "There's something else, and I finally figured out what it is from watching you at every port. What are you not telling people?"

"What?" Jules looked away before she could stop herself, realizing that was exactly what a guilty person would do. And also realizing that she couldn't outright lie to Liv. "I'm… I have to."

"Have to what?"

Jules rested her elbows on the table, her head in her hands. "I couldn't let everyone know that the Imperial attack will be accompanied by Mages."

"Mages?" Liv demanded, bolting upright in surprise. "With the Imperials?"

"Yes. To help them."

"How many Mages?"

"I don't know," Jules said, keeping her eyes on the table rather than look at Liv. "Limited numbers, the Mechanics guessed. I don't know how many."

"Jules, how the blazes can you not tell people that?" Liv demanded, sounding as angry as Jules had ever heard her. "How can you not tell them they'll be fighting Mages as well as legionaries?"

"Because if I did they wouldn't come!" Jules shot back, raising her head to glare at Liv. "They wouldn't fight, they wouldn't try to fight, they'd lose before they even tried, because they'd be afraid to face Mages and legionaries!"

"You can't—"

"I have to!" She paused to try to regain control, but the repressed anger and guilt inside overrode her attempts. "Don't you understand? All their lives these people, all of us, have been told we're inferior. Inferior to Mechanics, and Mages, and Imperial officials, and princes, and anyone who's a little better off than we are! And we all believe it. The people in the free lands believe it. They don't think they can win. But they can. If I can get them to Dor's Castle, I will show them they can win, and we will. But first I have to get them to Dor's Castle."

Liv returned Jules' glare. "By lying to them."

"Yes! Because I know they can win, and if we can win just once they'll know it, too!"

"And if you're wrong?" Liv asked in a low voice.

"Then the free lands will fall to the Empire, and I will die at Dor's Castle."

* * *

And so they came to Dor's Castle again, for possibly the last time. Jules wondered how many of those with her would ever leave again. Would she? The prophecy, after all, was done with her now.

The wall was visible well behind the houses of the town, inland at a place where the valley narrowed enough that a substantial structure could be built from one sheer side of the valley to the next, each end of the wall anchored in the living rock rising almost straight up. People were carrying things north, trying to get their valuables behind the wall before the Empire arrived. Already, the town was emptied of the old and very young, all of them moved to temporary shelter behind the barrier. Food was being moved as well—anything a person could eat or drink. None of it would be within reach of the Imperial invaders.

"You're back," Dor said, looking tired. He'd come to the *Sun Queen* soon after she tied up, and now sat in the stern cabin across the table from Jules. "Some people doubted you'd return. I reminded them that Captain Jules was a woman of her word. Just having you here will lift spirits immensely."

"There aren't any other ships in the harbor," Jules said.

"No. None have come. Only you." Dor turned a haunted gaze to the east. "The ships of citizens escaping the Empire have also stopped coming. The Empire is probably scooping up every ship it can get its hands on to carry legionaries."

"Other ships will come," Jules said, hiding the doubt that made her gut tighten. "Listen, I have something else I didn't tell you about, something that'll help a lot in defending this place." She went to the long, large bag and began drawing out the Mechanic weapons, laying them out carefully one by one on the table.

"The Mechanics gave you these?" Dor asked, gazing in amazement at the rifles and revolvers. "All of these? What are these long ones called?"

"The Mechanics call them rifles," Jules said. "They can shoot much farther than the revolvers."

"That's wonderful! They use the same, um, cartridges?"

"Different ones than the revolvers," Jules said.

"All right. We'll just have to choose which targets are worth shooting with them." Dor smiled with delight as he looked at the rifles.

"It probably won't be hard to decide on the targets," Jules said.

"Why?"

She took a deep breath, knowing she couldn't keep this secret from him any longer. "We'll want to kill the Mages first."

"Mages?" Dor blinked, confused. "What Mages?"

"They're helping the Empire. Some Mages will accompany the legionaries and assist them in the attack."

Dor stared at her, his mouth open but no words coming out.

Jules leaned over and grabbed his shoulder. "Listen to me! We can beat them! Every single Mage has been trying to kill me for years and I'm still alive. We have these rifles, and four revolvers. And the Mages will still be coming for me, first and foremost."

"But…" Dor finally got his voice back, his gaze terrified. "Mages. They're…"

"I've killed them! They're not invincible! Stay on that wall, hold it, and we can beat them."

Dor lowered his face into one hand, visibly calming himself. When he finally looked back at Jules, his mouth had firmed up and his eyes were dark. "All right, then. Mages. We'll stop them, too."

"That's it," Jules said. "We'll have to tell the others at some point, and they'll be scared, but if we're confident, they'll hold the line."

"I hope you're right," Dor said. He looked at the weapons again. "If you hadn't brought these, our people wouldn't stand. They'd be too frightened. But with these, we can hold that wall." He rubbed his forehead. "If we get more people to defend it. Do you still think everyone will send help?"

"No," Jules said. "I'm hoping at least half of them will. If we get that, we'll stand a chance."

Dor reached to touch one of the rifles. "Why are the Mechanics giving us these? Because we'll use them to kill Mages?"

"The Mechanics are loaning them to us," Jules said. "Why? As you said, they're happy every time we kill a Mage. But also because they need this battle to be fought, and they don't want to fight it."

"Why don't they want to fight it?"

"The Mechanics are afraid of something I heard one of them call the Final War. They're afraid if they get into direct fighting with the Empire, the world will be devastated."

"So they want us to do the fighting," Dor said, his mouth tight. "We're just more tools for them, aren't we?"

"That's what they think," Jules said. "What they don't realize is that we're fighting this battle not for them, but for us. They think they're using us, but we're using them. Mak told me that was how to handle things, and it's served me well. It'll work here, too."

"But if we win using these things, doesn't that make us dependent on them?"

"They're going to move into the west," Jules said. "We commons can't stop them, and the common people need whatever devices the Mechanics will share with us. If we can stay out from under the Emperor's hand, the free commons will keep getting stronger. Someday, they'll be strong enough."

"Then they'll need that daughter of your line," Dor objected. "Shouldn't you... I mean... this coming battle will be risky. You can't—"

"I decide what I can do." Jules kept tight control of her voice and her expression to keep from revealing anything. "The prophecy is up to me," she said. "It'll be taken care of."

"But…" Dor saw the warning in her eyes and stopped speaking. "As you say. It's up to you. No one can force you."

"The Emperor wants to." Jules smiled. "But he's going to be disappointed."

* * *

The next morning Jules went out on deck as the sun began to rise, a slight chill in the air as the red rose of dawn grew in the east. The Mechanics had delivered their warning of the looming Imperial attack to her four weeks and two days before. Dor could not hope to hold this town without help, and she could not hope to stop the Imperial fleet on her own.

If the Mechanics were right, there were only five days at most left before the Imperial attack reached here.

Jules stood on the deck, viewing the harbor of Dor's Castle, empty except for her own ship.

CHAPTER FOURTEEN

Not even *Prosper* was here. Had the Imperials managed to capture or sink *Prosper*? And, if they had, what had been the fate of Lieutenant Ian, deserter? The Imperials wouldn't have waited for a trial to hang him.

In the growing light of this morning's sun, nothing could be seen to inspire hope. Had everything she'd done been for nothing? The twins were out there somewhere, separate and not knowing of their true parents or that each had a sibling, but at least she'd managed that. Everything else, though, looked destined to fall into ruin here at Dor's Castle.

"They'll come." Keli had walked up on deck as well, a cup of hot coffee held in one hand.

"How can you be sure of that?" Jules said.

"Because I would've come, if I hadn't already been on your ship. Because you're this world's hope."

"You're thinking of that daughter of my line," Jules said.

"No, I'm not." Keli took a drink of coffee, looking to the west where the last remnants of the night were surrendering to the rising sun. "That prophecy set things in motion, didn't it? I've been thinking on that. If the prophecy had never been spoken, the last few years would've been a lot different, wouldn't they? But once people knew what the future was supposed to hold, they started acting differently. Maybe a prophecy like that doesn't simply predict the future. Maybe that sort of prophecy helps bring about the future it says will come."

"I've wondered about that myself. Where does anything begin or end, then?"

"Maybe there are no real beginnings or endings." Keli took another drink. "Maybe we just see things that way because it's easier." He nodded to the north. "Speaking of seeing things."

Jules looked, seeing the masts of three ships approaching the port as the light grew stronger.

There were moments when she'd despaired, when the prophecy seemed impossible to fulfill, when her own role seemed destined to be short and involve a violent ending.

But then there were moments like this.

The three ships came parading into the harbor, the morning sun gilding their sails with gold, a three-master like *Sun Queen* in the lead. Behind came two sloops equipped with ballistae. *Storm Rider, Second Chance,* and *Storm Queen.*

Before noon, *Star Seeker* showed up, carrying militia from Western Port.

In the afternoon, three more ships arrived, one of them *Prosper,* their decks crammed with more volunteers to swell the ranks of defenders.

The volunteers came ashore, determined and enthusiastic, cheering when they caught sight of Jules.

Ian boarded the *Sun Queen,* nodding to Jules and smiling. "I managed not to get killed," he told Jules.

She smiled back, no longer trying to suppress her feelings for him. "I'm glad." If she might die soon in defense of this city, she would take this much from life, at least. Taking another step forward, she grasped his hand tightly. "I can't tell you how happy and relieved I am that you're back, but I can't show it on deck in front of the world. I can say welcome back, my man."

"Your man? Don't I get a say in whether I want that?"

"You do," Jules said. "And I wouldn't blame you for refusing it."

Another smile quickly came and went on his face. "I can't. I could pretend not to want that, but I'd be lying to myself." He looked about as if seeking something else, then back down at her, sadness in him.

She knew who he'd been searching for. "I'm always looking for them, too. Ian, you understand if we're together, we can never have more. They'd be born with death marks."

"I know." Ian lightly squeezed her hand. "Even though no Mage ever made a prophecy about me, I guess it was always my fate to stand with you. If the worst happens here, we'll face it together."

"Yes." Jules turned to face the boarding plank as others arrived.

"You're going to be impossible to live with after this, aren't you?" Captain Erin said to Jules as she came aboard *Sun Queen*.

"She already has been," Liv said.

With Erin were Captain Hachi, Captain Lars, and Captain Kat. Jules led them along with Ian into her cabin, the other captains looking impressed by the sight of two of Jules' guards in armor standing post at the cabin door. Once inside, though, she found herself without enough chairs for everyone. "Introductions," she said, standing while the others sat in the mismatched collection of chairs the cabin boasted. "This is Ian of Marandur. Ian, this is Hachi, Lars, Kat, and Erin. They look like ruffians because they are ruffians. I guess the first thing we have to decide is who'll be in charge of the effort at sea."

"We get to decide that, do we?" Erin said.

"It's been decided," Captain Lars said, waving toward the town. "Everyone knows the pirate of the prophecy is leading this effort."

"I'm not—" Jules began.

"You're the only one the rest of us will all listen to," Captain Kat said. "I mean, I like these guys, but I don't want them giving me orders. Especially that one," she added, pointing at Hachi.

"Aren't you the Empress of the Seas?" Hachi asked Jules.

"I've never called myself that," Jules said.

"A lot of other people are calling you that," Lars said. "Your fellow captains consider it a title of honor. And as far as the sailors are concerned, destiny gives you special strength to stand against the Empire and the Great Guilds."

"So," Erin said, leaning forward and resting her arms on the table, "what's the plan, Empress?"

Jules shook her head at them, trying not to feel overwhelmed by her responsibility, as well as by the trust these others were granting her. "Uh… the Imperial force will have warships, and other ships carrying legionaries. I was thinking we have to let the legionaries come ashore. If we try storming ships full of legionaries we'll be the ones getting overrun."

She pointed at the chart. "We can post a sloop east of Dor's Castle, to spot the Imperial force before it gets here and give us a little advance notice of what it's like and how big it is. If they've got heavily laden ships with them, they'll be slower than the sloop, so it can warn us before the Imperial forces get here."

"But you don't want to engage them right off?" Kat asked. "I agree with you there."

"What's going to change, though, to make it any easier for us?" Erin said, leaning forward in her seat. "The war galleys won't put ashore their legionaries."

"I think they will," Jules said. "I thought our ships would withdraw as the Imperials approach. Make it look like we're fleeing, which is what they'll expect to see, a bunch of pirates afraid to confront an Imperial fleet."

"They're not all that wrong when it comes to the afraid part," Lars said. "Taking on one isolated Imperial warship is one thing. A fleet'll be a much tougher bite."

"Hear me out," Jules said. "We sail just over the horizon and wait. If they chase us then, they'll get strung out and we can hit them one by one. But I don't think they'll chase us, even though the Empire's commander will be over-confident."

"It's Prince Ostin," Kat said. "We swung by the Sharr Isles just before heading west and everyone was talking about it."

"Prince Ostin?" Jules thought of Sandurin and what had happened there. "I still owe him payback."

"When he learns you're here, he'll be all that more eager to win," Erin said.

"Good. That'll make it easier to beat him." Jules pointed inland. "The Imperials will put their legionaries ashore, probably not all of them at first, and they'll run into Dor's wall. With the men and women who've already come to help hold that wall, the legionaries won't be able to crack it. They'll land more legionaries, all they've got, and they still won't take it."

"Ah." Captain Hachi nodded in understanding. "And defeat is unacceptable. So the prince will strip his remaining ships of all legionaries to put maximum force against the wall and finally capture it."

Erin nodded as well, smiling. "And that's when we sail in and hit them, while their crews are their weakest."

"Yes!" Jules said. "After we capture or drive off the Imperial ships, the legionaries ashore will be trapped, without any means of getting more food or other supplies. They'll have to surrender. We'll be able to avoid a fight to the death that could cost us very dearly."

Hachi pursed his lips as he thought, finally nodding. "It sounds easier than it will be to carry out, but that's a plan as good as any I could have thought of. You're to be congratulated."

"Thank you," Jules said. "Sometimes you sound like a Mechanic, Hachi."

"There's no call for insults." Hachi rubbed his mouth. "Do we have enough ships to carry this off, though?"

"I don't know," Jules said. "We've inflicted some losses on the Imperial fleet, but it depends on how much the Emperor sends."

"His advisors will want to hold plenty back to defend the Empire," Kat observed.

"I hear that his former advisors are dead," Hachi said. "The new advisors may hesitate to contradict the Emperor's wishes."

"He's worried about the Mechanics," Jules said. "They've made it clear they don't want him to do this. The Emperor has to be scared that the

Mechanics Guild will hit the Empire at home when they learn about this invasion. That might make him hold back both legions and ships."

"As if his legions and ships could do much against the Mechanics Guild," Erin scoffed. "But I think he will be worried, and want the imaginary security those offer him."

"The Mechanics are worried about fighting the Empire," Jules said, drawing surprised looks. "They're sure that they'll win, but they think the cost could be immense. That's why they don't want to directly confront the Empire and risk all-out war between the Empire and the Mechanics Guild. And that's why they gave me these."

She brought out the extra revolvers, and then the four rifles, one by one, drawing looks of astonishment and glee from the other captains.

"The Mechanics gave you these?" Hachi said. "That guarantees our victory, I think."

She had to tell them. "No," Jules said. "They make victory possible. They give us a means to counteract the Mages."

Silence suddenly filled the cabin. "Mages?" Erin finally asked, her voice deathly calm in a way that spoke of emotions barely being held in check.

"The Mechanics tell me that the Mages will assist the Imperial attack. There will be Mages with the legionaries."

Lars sat back, looking stunned. "Mages? How many?"

"Limited numbers," Jules said. "That's what the Mechanics think."

"Exactly how many is limited numbers?" Lars demanded.

"Does exactly how many matter?" Kat asked.

"You just heard this?" Erin asked, giving Jules a hard look.

"No," Jules said. "The Mechanics gave me these weapons so we could deal with any Mages helping the legion attack."

"Jules, you had no right to withhold that from us until now!" Erin looked ready to get up and storm out of the cabin.

"You're right," Jules said. "But I held off saying it until now because I know that we can stop them. I've faced Mages and I've killed them. With these rifles any common person can do the same."

"They have to believe they can do that," Erin said, shaking her head. "And even I have trouble believing it. Just because you've taken on Mages one at a time—"

"I killed three at Cape Astra. Fighting them by myself."

"If anyone else said that, I'd know they were lying," Erin said. She sighed heavily, looking at the others. "We're here, and committed to it, and that's what you wanted, isn't it?"

Hachi, who had either taken the news more calmly than the others, or had been much better at hiding his reaction, spoke in a pensive voice. "Captain Jules, I know you say there's nothing special about you, no powers beyond that of other commons, but the rest of us see you as different. Other common folk think the same. We will follow if you lead us against Mages. And, if you're there, sailors will rally about you and hold. But we have to hold the wall if we're to win using your plan, and you can't be on Dor's wall and with our ships at the same time. The defenders on that wall will not hold against Mages without you there."

"I can be on Dor's wall," Ian said, startling Jules.

She stared at him, surprised and unhappy. "That's not—"

"And exactly who are you in relation to Jules?" Erin asked.

"He's my man," she said. "My chosen partner."

"If I'm on that wall," Ian said, "and the other defenders know who I am to Jules, they'll know she believes we can win. Maybe they'll think she's given me some of her own luck. I can ensure that the wall holds while Jules wins the battle at sea."

The others had sat up, startled. "You've promised yourselves?" Kat said.

"Not yet," Jules said, realizing that Ian had seen what had to be done. "We will. After the battle is won." Inside, her heart hammered at her in denial of her decision to do this. She'd sacrificed the twins for the prophecy, and now it seemed she might have to sacrifice Ian as well.

Erin shook her head in wonderment at Ian. "Do you know what you're committing to, man? The Mages there and every legionary will bend every effort to kill the chosen man of the woman of the prophecy. There'll be so many spells and crossbow bolts and spears and daggers flying at you that it'll seem like a hard rain."

"If they come at me," Ian said, trying to look confident, "it'll make it easier for me to kill them with those Mechanic weapons."

Hachi had sat back, his eyes on Ian as if measuring him. "If Prince Ostin hears that the chosen man of the Pirate Jules is on that wall, he'll throw everything he can at it. That's what we want."

"Are we going to paint a big target on him?" Kat asked, looking appalled. "Jules, you're willing to do this?"

"I have to do this," Jules said. "Just like all of the other things I've had to do since that Mage looked at me and spoke the prophecy." She tried to summon the cold inside her that would give her the strength to ignore her fears, but for the first time it wouldn't come. "Ian is right. If he's on that wall, and the defenders know who he is to me, we'll be able to hold because it will show how confident we are that we'll win, and how confident I am in him."

"If he dies on that wall, that same confidence could vanish in an instant," Hachi warned. "We will have that risk."

Erin sighed again, her mouth a tight line. "We couldn't ask this of you, but since you've volunteered it I will agree to it. What if he dies, though, Jules? Who else will father the children needed to carry on the prophecy?"

Jules braced herself, looking at them with defiance. She needed these people to fight without hesitating. "Why are you so certain that hasn't already happened?"

That floored them, every captain gaping at Jules.

"This can't leave this room," Jules said. "But, if I fall, if Ian and I both fall, the prophecy is already assured."

"Blazes, you're a sneaky one," Kat said. "How'd you manage that with the whole world watching?"

"Where—?" Lars began, then sat back, shamefaced. "Of course you wouldn't tell anyone that."

"So," Erin said to Ian, "have you fought Mages before? Was that part of your courtship?"

"Not exactly," Ian said. "The courtship, I mean. I fought Mages in Landfall, including one of their troll monsters."

"At Landfall. Where that Imperial ship was destroyed?"

"Yes," Ian said. "I was on that ship."

"Ah, so you're a former Imperial officer as well?" Erin said. "How'd you stop the troll?"

"It was very hard," Ian said. "Very strong. Crossbow bolts mostly bounced off, swords only scratched it. Fire worked, though. That's how we ultimately killed it, by confusing it and keeping it amid the ruins of the pier as fire consumed everything."

"How do we make that work here?" Hachi asked himself as much as the others. His eyes opened wider as an answer came to him. "Lamp oil."

"Lamp oil?" Lars asked.

Jules got it. "If the Mages send trolls against the wall, pour lamp oil on them and set it afire. There must be barrels of lamp oil in town."

"That would harm a troll like the one I fought," Ian said.

"What about a dragon?" Lars asked Jules. "Do you think it'd work on a dragon?"

Jules rubbed her mouth as she thought, remembering the monster that had pursued her outside of Jacksport. "I don't know," she finally said. "The dragon that chased me moved a lot faster than the troll I encountered in Landfall. It had… scales. Like armor. They were shiny, so maybe lamp oil would just roll off them. But a wall as stout as Dor's will stop a dragon. They seem more capable of killing people in the open and less capable of smashing than a troll does. I mean, I wouldn't want to be in a wooden building with a dragon after me, but I think it'd have trouble getting through a wall like the one Dor has built."

"You're the expert," Lars said. "I doubt any other common has encountered a dragon and a troll and survived both." He looked at Ian. "Although you may soon have that distinction as well."

"Hopefully the survival part, too," Ian said.

"How tall was the troll you fought?" Erin asked.

Ian frowned as he thought. "About a lance and a half, about the height of a tall person with a child on their back. But it was about that wide as well. Massive, like a stone wall brought to life."

"The dragon that attacked Jules near Jacksport was, what, three lances tall?" Lars said.

"About that," Jules said. "But supposedly dragons come in different heights. You told me that."

"Right. No one knows why."

Ian nodded. "All right. We won't have to worry about trolls reaching the top of the wall, but we'll have to keep them from battering their way through the gate. Dragons we'll just have to hope won't be too tall. And, if they are, that these Mechanic rifles can harm them."

"We have a lot of cartridges for the weapons," Jules said, wanting to keep the conversation centered on their ability to defeat Mages. "Ten each for the rifles, so forty total. And fifty-eight total for the four revolvers."

"Almost a hundred?" Erin asked in astonishment.

"The Mechanics really do want us to win," Hachi said. "You know, if you happened to misplace a few of those cartridges during the fight, I could probably get an emperor's ransom for them on the black market."

"I'd rather save them all for killing Mages and legionaries," Jules said. She tapped one of the rifles. "These can hit a target a lot farther off than the revolvers can. I wouldn't be surprised if they can hit something at a longer range than crossbows manage."

"How do we find out?" Erin said.

Jules sighed. "The only way is to shoot one, and if we don't want to waste any cartridges, that means waiting until we have someone we want to kill to try it out on."

Kat scratched the side of her face. "I can think of a few people I dislike fairly intensely. How about trying it on one of them?"

"You see why we only trust *you* in command," Erin told Jules. "If these rifles are like crossbows, then we should find the best crossbow shooters we have and let them use the weapons, I think."

"Good idea," Jules said. "I was going to send three of the rifles and two of the revolvers with Ian." No, she wasn't. She'd planned on sending those weapons to Dor, not to Ian standing on the wall facing an Imperial horde fixed on killing him. "The defenders on the wall are more likely to face Mages and their monsters, and the hardest push by the legionaries."

"That seems wise," Lars said. "Strange. Part of me just thought that doesn't leave much for us on the ships, but it leaves one rifle and two of the Mechanic revolvers, which is a mightier arsenal than any commons have ever wielded before."

"Aye," Erin said. "Lars, Kat, you two have the sloops, so one of your ships will have to take sentry duty as Jules said."

"When do we want to start that?" Lars asked.

"I'd say as soon as we can get one of you out there."

"Erin's right," Jules said. "Can one of you get resupplied and back out to sea? We should wait for dawn tomorrow, I think. We don't want the Imperial fleet surrounding you in the night."

"I'll take out *Second Chance*," Kat said. "We'll clear the harbor as the sun rises."

"If the Imperials don't show up for a few more days, we'll have *Storm Queen* take over sentry duty," Jules said. "All right, Lars?"

"Of course," Lars said. He stood up, looking at the others, a small smile on his face. "Only a few years ago no one would've dreamed of doing what we're about to try. I don't know how many of us will survive, but I'm glad we can now dream together of greater things."

"Aye!" Erin said, grinning. "Have you got any rum, Jules? This is mighty poor hospitality, if you ask me."

She didn't have enough glasses, so Jules got out a bottle and took a slug from the neck before passing it to Ian. He took a drink, passing it to Erin, and so on around the group. "To victory!" Jules cried.

* * *

More ships came in the next morning, their crews swelled by volunteers ready to fight. *Fair Dani*, *Gallant Mike*, *Bright Star*, *Moon Chaser*, and *Sky Dancer*. Not the top of the line ships owned by wealthy merchants or princes or princesses in the Empire, but the ships that had gotten by on the wits and the labors of their crews and their captains. The ships that had eagerly fed the flow of people to the west and already traded between the new settlements. Having tasted the opportunities rising in the west, they were ready to fight to keep them.

Kelsi's Pride arrived about noon, the first ship built in the town increasingly known only as Kelsi.

Another sloop showed up, the *Western Pride*, which had been taken at Western Port when that Imperial settlement was captured. Her captain, an older man named Rik, seemed to be as hard as a piece of salt pork and nearly as grizzled. "I've been waiting for the chance to bop the Emperor on the nose ever since I was a kid," he told Jules. "I won't miss the chance to do it, even if it's my last fight."

And with every new ship that showed up, the spirits of the defenders rose higher. It felt less and less like a desperate struggle of isolated refugees and more and more like the joining of hands in a common fight.

Late that afternoon the *Bright Morning* showed up, her new captain offering Jules a rigid salute. "Captain Ross of the *Bright Morning*," he introduced himself.

"I didn't think the *Bright Morning* would come," Jules said.

"If Tora had still been in command we probably wouldn't have. But we hear there's a fight to be had, and we don't want to miss it."

"It might be as early as tomorrow. Get your ship ready."

Late in the afternoon she walked ashore with Ian, through the rush of preparations as the defenders of Dor's Castle hauled everything they could to the other side of the wall. By the time Jules reached the wall, the sun had dipped below the western bank of cliffs penning in the river valley that Dor's Castle occupied. She went up onto one of the stone battlements beside the main gate, looking down at the defenders who came to see her. The pungent odor of lamp oil rose from barrels placed on the platform inside the wall where the defenders would stand. Torches were lit along the wall, giving her light as the day faded, and Ian came to stand by her.

"This is my chosen man!" Jules cried, grasping Ian's hand in her own and raising them together. "He will be on this wall with you when the legionaries come! He is a sign of my trust in your bravery and your commitment to keep our lands free!"

That brought an enthusiastic response that Jules had to let die down before she could speak again. "You may face Mages!" she cried. "And their monsters!" A ripple of fear ran through the crowd watching and listening to her, so she went on quickly before it could take root and grow bigger. "I've fought Mages, face to face, and their monsters, and I stand here before you. And those of you defending this wall will have weapons such as I have not had before!"

Ian handed her a rifle and she held it high, the light of the torches reflecting off the metal of the weapon. "Mechanic weapons!" Jules shouted. "Three of these rifles! And two of their revolvers! Mages and legionaries cannot stand against them! If your hearts stay strong, you can hold this wall while I lead our ships to defeat the Imperial fleet! Will you do it? Will you stand firm so that these lands remain free of the Empire's heavy hand?"

Another eruption of shouts, merging into a mass of sound in which one word dominated. "YES!"

Jules turned to Dor. "Let's hope they stay firm when the legionaries come."

"We're fighting for our homes," Dor said. "I didn't think you could do it, didn't think so many would come. Thank you."

"Thank that prophecy. At least it helped one good thing happen in this world." Jules clapped Dor on the shoulder. "I'll see you after the battle is won."

"Yes. Remember your promise for my daughters."

"I will. And I'd like you to do something for me." Jules handed him a thick envelope. "I wrote down some ideas. Ways for the free settlements to get along and support each other. If I'm not able to meet with representatives of everyone who came to help here, please discuss my ideas with them. They're not meant to be take it or leave it. Just things to think about."

"You have my promise," Dor said, taking the envelope.

She and Ian walked back to the pier, through a town grown dark and quiet with so many moved beyond the wall. The pier was crowded and busy, swords and armor being handed out to sailors, food and water being brought aboard the ships, and sailors from different ships meeting old friends for what might be their final reunions.

Jules boarded the *Sun Queen*, seeing her guards in full armor practicing against each other, Artem leading one side and Mad the other. After losing Alons and Kara at Cape Astra their numbers had been reduced to nine, but Artem had recruited another sailor to step in and bring them back up to ten, which seemed a solid enough sum.

"Are we all right?" Jules asked Ang and Liv, who were talking to each other.

"Ready as we will be, Cap'n," Ang said. He had the somber bearing of someone expecting hard times ahead.

"We're ready," Liv agreed. "The air has a funny feel to it tonight, doesn't it? Not like a storm coming. Just funny."

"Yeah," Jules said. "Thank you, both of you." She walked on to her cabin, letting Ian walk in before she closed the door. A couple of steps took her to the table. She leaned on it, both arms tight with tension, and closed her eyes, her head lowered. "It's going to be tomorrow," she said to Ian. "I can feel it."

He nodded. "We should eat. I'll get something from the tables below deck."

"Thanks." Jules sat down and waited, her eyes on the drawing of Lake Bellad that was her sole memento of Mak.

Ian came in with two plates of broiled chicken. "The locals are getting rid of some of their livestock before the Empire gets here, so there's plenty of meat."

Jules ate, savoring the greasy chicken, trying not to think.

"Where's home?" Ian said.

"Home?" Jules asked, startled by the question.

"I mean, if we're going to be together, I was wondering where that would be," Ian said. "Julesport is a great spot, if that's where you feel home is."

"Home is right here," Jules said, flicking her fingers to indicate the cabin. "This is where I live."

"I should've guessed." Ian looked about. "It might be a little crowded for two of us."

"Oh, did you think you were going to get to stay in here after we were married?" Jules asked, surprised that she could joke. She saw Ian's face and laughed. "It'll be fine. But we can build a place in Julesport, too."

"Good." Ian looked toward one bulkhead, his eyes distant. "Every settlement sent someone. Even a few volunteers from Ihris. Every place except the settlement Synda set up on the big island west of the Strait of Gulls."

"I didn't expect help from there," Jules said, chomping on a chicken leg.

"You know, you never actually proposed to me. You just told the other captains that we'd be getting married." He carefully took apart a chicken wing as he waited for her reply.

"Are you sure?" Jules said.

"Yes. Very sure. Which means I get to propose first. Jules, will you—"

"I already proposed! You're doing it second!"

"Telling me we're going to get married isn't a proposal. It has to be asked and an answer given. So I'm first," Ian said. "Jules, will—"

"Yes." She smiled at him, the light of the single lantern in the cabin tracing flickering patterns on his face. "How about you?"

"Yes." He looked at the bulkhead again, his sad gaze once more somewhere beyond it. "They'll understand why they had to be hidden. Or she'll understand, that daughter of your line, if the others never learn."

"I hope you're right," Jules said. "Will you stay with me tonight?"

Ian raised his eyebrows at her. "You're not getting me drunk first this time?"

"I want us both to remember all of it," she said, staying serious.

He knew why she said that, so he only nodded in reply, because neither of them wanted to say out loud that this night might be their last.

* * *

Dawn had barely broken the next morning when shouts sounded. "The signal fire has been lit on the height! *Second Chance* is on her way back. The Imperial fleet has been sighted!"

The word raced through the harbor and on beyond to the defenders waiting at the wall. Jules dressed carefully, making sure her boots were polished and settling her Mechanic revolver in its holster at her waist. She made sure Ian's holster and revolver were also ready.

She'd already delivered the last revolver to Captain Erin, trusting her to use it wisely. That would leave the *Sun Queen* with only Jules' revolver and one rifle.

"I'll do everything I can to ensure the wall is held," Ian said. "I have to be sure, when the battle is done, will you sail away and leave me again?"

Jules reached out to touch his face. "Even after last night you have every right to ask me that. The answer is no. When this fight is won, I'll say my promise to you. And don't you try to sail away without me, because if you do I will hunt you down no matter where you hide."

"I suppose I'll have to stay with you, then," Ian said, his voice suddenly rough. "Do you think the prophecy will allow us any happiness?"

"It had better. I've done what it needed." She stepped back, her eyes on his. "Don't die."

He nodded, serious. "Don't die," he told her.

She nodded, watching as he picked up the bag holding three rifles and another revolver, and walked quickly from the cabin.

After a short pause, Jules followed, climbing up to the quarterdeck. Ian was already off the ship, heading inland. She tried not to think about whether she'd ever see him again. Stepping up onto the railing, she grabbed onto the rigging to stand high where everyone could see. "All hands!" she shouted, bringing the frantic preparations on the ship to a pause as everyone stopped to listen. Activity on nearby ships slowed as well, sailors stopping to look her way and listen. "We're going to win this fight! We're going to beat the servants of the Empire! We're going to show the Emperor that these lands and these people are free, and will remain free! And we will show the Mages as well! Here is where the Empire learns that it will not rule the west! And someday, the Great Guilds will be overthrown by the daughter of my line, and all will be free, because of the battle you first fought and won today! Don't hesitate! Never falter! Go on with firm hearts and strong arms to win the freedom we and our children deserve!"

Jules thrust her hand high, the cutlass she held flashing in the light of the sun.

A roar answered her, the shouts of men and women whose hearts were in the fight. It cheered her, dispelling her own doubts and fears.

Ships were letting go lines, moving away from the pier. "No one's crowding anybody else," Ang noted. "That's a good sign that everyone is keeping their heads."

"Liv, you and your team take in all lines," Jules called. "The rest of you get aloft and make sail. The Emperor's servants are coming to visit and I'd hate to disappoint them by being late for the party!"

Sun Queen joined the line of ships heading out of port. Jules leaned on the quarterdeck's forward rail, feeling the wind, as the sun rose above the cliffs to the east of Dor's Castle. "This has never happened before."

"What's that?" Liv asked, wiping her mouth with the back of her hand.

"A fleet of free ships, going to battle with a fleet of Imperial ships. Going to face the absolute authority that has ruled common people for as far back as history goes."

"There's that," Liv said. "But we'll still be subject to the absolute authority of the Great Guilds no matter how many times we beat the Empire."

"I have to leave something for that daughter of my line to do," Jules said. "On deck! Let's hoist my flag so these Imperials know who they're dealing with!"

They'd sewn a special flag, nearly two lances long and more than a lance tall, the crossed swords of Jules in silver thread clear against the dark blue fabric. The flag was hooked to the halyard and hauled up fast, the wind catching it. As the flag unfurled at the top of the main-mast, Jules heard cheers coming from the other ships.

She stood on the quarterdeck, cutlass in hand, as the *Sun Queen* cleared the harbor and met the waters of the Sea of Bakre. All around the *Sun Queen* the other free ships were riding the swells, their sails billowing in the breeze, their crews on deck with cutlasses and cross-bows at the ready. The sloop *Second Chance* was gliding over the water from the east to join them, behind her on the horizon the tops of a forest of masts beginning to appear as the Imperial fleet approached.

She'd never been more scared, and she'd never felt more exhilarated. "There'll never be another day like this," she said to Liv. "As long as I live, there'll never again be a day like this."

CHAPTER FIFTEEN

By the time *Second Chance* reached the other free ships, the sun was backlighting the masts of the Imperial fleet, some of the nearer ships beginning to show their hulls over the horizon.

"Should we head west?" Ang asked Jules.

She shook her head. "Not yet. We're supposed to look like we lose our nerve as the Imperials approach, so let's allow them a little closer."

The winds were a bit erratic this morning, shifting about unpredictably. The free ships had been tacking slowly to the north-west, but as the Imperial ships drew closer Jules brought the *Sun Queen* about onto the opposite tack.

A few special flags had been made up to allow simple signals, but the general rule for the free ships was to follow the movement of the *Sun Queen* flying Jules' banner.

Finally, Jules judged the Imperials were close enough. "All right. Let's head west like we're afraid to meet them."

The *Sun Queen*'s helm went over, her crew went to the braces to shift her sails, and the ship came about to head west along the coast. The other ships followed, staying in a loose group about the *Sun Queen*.

"This is harder than I thought it'd be," Jules said to Liv as the free ships sailed away from Dor's Castle, allowing the Imperial fleet free access to the harbor. Somewhere beyond her sight Ian would be on the wall, ready to meet the Imperial forces and the Mages with them. "I want to fight *now*."

"But you're smart enough to wait," Liv said. "If you can keep these ships together as we avoid a fight, we'll be fine."

"It's the pirate ships you might have to worry about wandering," Ang said. "But their captains know to fight smart. You'll have no problem there."

"Except maybe *Star Seeker*," Liv said, frowning. "Why's she falling behind the rest?"

"That's part of the plan," Jules told her. "Captain Hachi is playing the lame bird, trying to see if we can lure an Imperial ship or two into chasing him. If we could get one or two Imperial ships separated from the rest, we could overwhelm them before help could come for them."

"It doesn't look like the Imperials are going after the bait, though," Ang said, squinting toward the east.

"It was a long shot," Jules said. "Imperial discipline was likely to keep their ships together. But worth a try."

When the Imperial ships reached the harbor they stopped moving east. Jules brought the free ships onto another tack to remain about the same distance from the harbor, then went up the shrouds to the maintop to get a better look at the Empire's forces.

Old Kurt was on lookout duty. He moved aside to give Jules room as she stood, leaning out a little, one hand grasping a stay and the other shading her eyes. "Looks like the sloops and war galleys are staying outside the harbor while the ships carrying legionaries are going in," Jules said. "Looks like… four sloops? And ten war galleys?" Those wouldn't be great odds, but they wouldn't be terrible, either, especially not if many of the legionaries could be lured off those warships.

"That's what I'd counted. There may be more to the rear that haven't come close enough to count yet, though." Kurt nodded, eyeing the distant Imperial ships distrustfully. "Those warships might come after us once the others are all safe in the harbor."

"I don't think so," Jules said. "Imperial commanders like to keep their entire force together so they can exercise personal control of everything. Princes and princesses were the worst that way. Besides, Prince Ostin is going to want to claim personal credit for capturing the town, and personal credit for defeating our ships." She sighed. "We won't be able to see them landing legionaries from here."

Jules shifted her gaze to the cliff tops west of the valley that held Dor's Castle. Men and women who were too old to fight had been brought up the cliffs and stationed along them to provide reports of what was happening. Sure enough, Jules saw the flash of a mirror as someone with a view of the port sent a quick series of long and short flashes. "The first ships have reached the piers and are sending legionaries ashore."

She could visualize it easily in her mind, having been part of a practice drill for such an attack: the legionaries quickly spilling onto the pier, forming into ranks and advancing inland. It had felt exciting when she was part of it, even though the older officers present had complained that they'd never have to actually attack a town from the sea, because there weren't any towns that didn't belong to the Empire and no town would ever revolt. Things had changed a lot in the years since then.

The legionaries would be in the town by now, advancing quickly while watching for ambushes. They'd be wary, but very confident.

Where were the Mages? Would some of them come ashore right after the legionaries, or would they wait to see if they were needed?

Ian would be by the main gate, stiffening the defenders at the spot that would be the aim of the Imperial attack.

"Keep on eye on them, Kurt," Jules said. "But also check the north and even the west. We don't want to be surprised by any new Imperial ships sneaking in from an unexpected direction."

She went back down to the main deck, trying to relax herself. After the rush of leaving harbor, there'd be a long period of waiting now.

A quick *bang* rolled across the water, made faint by distance, but clearly coming from the direction of Dor's Castle. Everyone on the *Sun Queen* and the free ships around her turned to look, even though nothing could be seen. "Hopefully that shot means one less Mage to deal with," Jules said to Keli the healer, who was standing nearby.

Keli nodded. "Normally I don't cheer for harm to come to others, but for Mages even I have to make an exception."

"They shouldn't have shot this quickly unless it was a Mage," Jules said.

Mirrors on top of the cliffs flashed messages toward the free ships. The first attack on the wall was underway. Jules watched them, trying to stay calm, dreading the sight of a rapid series of quick flashes that would mean the wall had fallen.

Occasional distant thunder claps told of more shots, sometimes singly, sometimes two close together. Jules hoped the defenders were being careful, not using their cartridges too quickly. But the sound of every shot served as a reassurance that the defenders were continuing to hold out.

She wondered how the Imperial force had reacted to the discovery that they were facing more than one Mechanic weapon. And how the Mages had reacted, if Mages with their lack of emotions could be said to react.

"Look there," Keli said, pointing.

Off to the southeast, in the direction of the battle, Jules saw a thin column of dark smoke rising into the sky.

"A building on fire?" Keli wondered.

"More likely a troll," Jules said. As awful as the troll was that she'd seen at Landfall, she was glad she couldn't see one doused with lamp oil and burning. Or hear any screams it might be making. "I wonder where they come from? Trolls, I mean. Why do they do what Mages say?"

"What's bothering you?" Keli asked, leaning on the rail to look across the swells toward the harbor. "You're getting ready to fight a big battle that'll probably cost a lot of lives, and you're worrying about trolls?"

"What if they're like us, Keli? What if they're some other form of common people?"

He paused. "It's a credit to you that you thought of that. I never heard anyone else think of what the monsters might be like inside.

But I have heard that you can't talk to them. Troll or dragon, they just keep killing until they're stopped."

"That's what I've seen," Jules said.

"If they won't listen to our words, if they won't stop doing what the Mages command them to do, it doesn't matter what they are, does it? They don't leave us any choice but to stop them in any way we can."

Another pillar of dark smoke began rising from the direction of the battle for Dor's Castle. Another pop of distant thunder came from that way. How many had that been already? She should've been counting. Too late to start now.

At the site of the fighting, the air would be filled with shouts and cries, the clang of metal on metal as swords crossed and crossbow bolts met armor or shield. But none of those sounds could carry far, nor would the screams of the wounded or the final breaths of the dying.

It felt so odd to know that fighting was going on there, but to be standing on the quiet deck of a ship riding the waves of a peaceful ocean. The harsh cry of a sea gull swooping past startled her, the bird winging on toward the harbor, not caring about the wars of humans.

"Sometimes," Keli said, his eyes looking across the water, "someone who's hurt bad will tell me to let them die if the only way to save them is to take a leg off. A sailor can work without a hand, maybe, and sometimes even without an arm. But a sailor needs both legs to get up the rigging and out along a spar. They fear they'll lose the sea, lose their means of living, if I take the leg."

"What do you do?" Jules said.

"Sometimes I take the leg anyway, sometimes I let them die as they wish. I never know before what I'll decide. All I can do is try to respect their wishes but also save lives if I can." Keli straightened, looking at Jules. "Mostly, I save them. Because that's what a healer does."

"Thank you," Jules said, and knew that he understood those words were about much more than this one conversation.

"Try not to give me too much work," Keli said. "That's all the thanks I need."

* * *

The smoke and the erratic sound of shots stopped as the morning wore on.

Light flashed on the cliff tops, everyone looking that way. "They're putting more legionaries ashore," Ang said.

In the middle of the afternoon, two distant sounds of thunder announced the next Imperial attack going in and the defenders shooting back. Jules stared toward the town, wishing again that she could see more. Three more columns of dirty smoke rose into the sky, one first and then two in quick succession.

Marta, like the others, stood watching and listening as the group of free ships slowly tacked back and forth west of the harbor, only the tops of the masts of the closest Imperial ships in sight from the deck of the *Sun Queen*. "I can tell when each attack goes in," she said to Jules. "Funny, huh? I only had a few weeks of legion training before I deserted." She shook her head, frowning. "I could be there, one of the legionaries storming that wall. Instead of here, hoping they don't take it."

"Choices matter," Jules said.

"I suppose. Though when I deserted I wasn't thinking of any future like this."

"Who's the best crossbow shot on the ship, Marta?"

"Not me." She nodded toward the forward part of the ship. "I'd say Gord."

"Gord?"

"Yeah. He doesn't let on much, because then he might get extra work, but he's a good shot. A really good shot."

Through the rest of the afternoon they waited, listening and wondering, dreading the sight of the rapid flashes that would report the wall had fallen. But all through the afternoon the occasional sounds of a Mechanic weapon told of the fight continuing.

The sounds of battle had once more subsided, the sun sinking in the western sky, when Kyle, who'd taken over as lookout, called down. "Captain! Those Imperial warships are doing something!"

Jules went up the rigging fast, stopping only when she reached the maintop, gazing to the east.

"See?" Kyle said. "The sloops are coming alongside the galleys."

Jules looked, hoping this meant her plan was working. "We're too far off to tell if they're transferring legionaries to the galleys. Watch to see if any of the galleys go into the harbor."

"Sure thing, Captain. Once the sun sets I doubt I'll be able to tell, though."

Jules went back down the rigging, looking about at the ships surrounding the *Sun Queen*. The closest sloop was *Storm Queen*, which suited her fine. She went onto the quarterdeck. "Bring us closer to the *Storm Queen*," she told the sailor at the helm. "Within hailing distance."

Sun Queen angled slightly to port, closing the distance at a steady pace until the ships were less than ten lances apart.

"Captain Lars!" Jules shouted, cupping her hands about her mouth. "I have need of a ship to sneak closer to the harbor once it gets dark. I need to know if the war galleys have gone into the harbor or are still outside."

Lars listened, then raised one hand in acknowledgment. "We'll find out!"

Clouds had gathered during the afternoon, light patches of rain falling over the water and inland. As the sun neared the horizon and light faded, one rain storm wandered over the free ships, lowering visibility a bit more. *Storm Queen* took advantage of that to head east toward the harbor.

Jules looked around again, seeing *Star Seeker* not far off. "Captain Hachi! Pass the word to other ships! If *Storm Queen* finds the Imperial galleys are inside the harbor, we're going to move east tonight and attack at dawn!"

As it grew darker, three lanterns were lit and fastened to posts on the *Sun Queen*'s quarterdeck, so other ships would know this was Jules' ship in the night. Another lantern was set high near the bow. The other free ships also lit lanterns, one forward and one aft, so they could stay together in the dark and not risk running into each other.

There were no more sounds of fighting, and no more pillars of smoke could be seen rising against the starlit night sky. With no distractions left, Jules went into her cabin, standing at the stern windows, fear for Ian and fear for what might happen tomorrow gripping her.

Someone came in. "I brought you something to eat," Liv said.

"Thanks," Jules said without turning around.

"You need to eat and then if we're to attack at dawn you need to try to rest," Liv said. She gripped Jules' arm and steered her to the table. "Go ahead."

"I'm not really hungry," Jules said, sitting down and picking at the plate. "Liv, what if we lose? What if tomorrow is a disaster and everything was for nothing?"

Liv sat down as well, leaning her elbows on the table. "For nothing? Those twins are out there somewhere. The prophecy will come to pass some day. As for now…" She paused to think. "I'm no farmer, but I've listened to them. They talk about planting seeds, but sometimes that doesn't mean farming. Sometimes they mean thinking of something new. And you've done that. Not just any seeds. Weeds. Weeds that the Great Guilds and the Emperors and the Empresses won't be able to ever pull up. You've cast them far and wide and this world will never be the same, no matter what happens tomorrow."

Jules looked at Liv, thinking. "What sort of weeds?"

Liv sat back, her eyes distant. "For as long as anyone knows, the commons of this world have accepted their fate. The Great Guilds ruled all, and the Emperor ruled beneath them. That'll never happen again, Jules. Common people here in the west will never again simply accept being ruled. They'll demand a voice in things. They'll fight in every way they can. Oh, they won't go to war with the Great Guilds. They'll know they need that daughter of your line to win. But they'll resist. And it's because of the ideas you've planted."

"I didn't come up with any of that on my own," Jules protested. "The free ships, the different ways of ruling a city using votes, lots of people have given me their ideas."

"But you put them together and you showed them to everyone," Liv said. She looked east. "Now the Empire, whoever's left there might keep the old bargain, trading any trace of freedom for the chance to feel safer, but I think even the Empire is going to have its problems at some point. The world has changed, and it changed before this night."

"I hope you're right." Jules looked east as well. "What if Ian is dead?"

"Then we will go on," Liv said in a soft voice. "As you and I and Ang went on after our mothers and fathers died, and as we all went on after Mak died. What else can we do? You won't stop fighting, will you?"

"No," Jules said. Suddenly feeling hunger, she stabbed a piece of meat. "I'll never stop fighting."

* * *

She'd lain down in her bunk, not expecting to get any sleep, but was awakened by Ang. The ship felt quiet, the wood creaking gently as swells rolled under it, deep night showing outside the stern windows. "Cap'n, *Storm Queen* is back. Captain Lars says as near as he could tell, all of the war galleys are inside the harbor, alongside the piers. All he saw outside were Imperial sloops, and they all seemed to mistake his ship for one of their own."

Jules sat up, breathing deeply. "Let's start moving slowly east. I want to be right on top of the Imperial sloops when it starts to get light. Tell the crew to be ready for a fight at dawn, and pass word to other ships."

"Aye, Cap'n."

As she came out on deck, Jules could hear word of her plans being shouted from ship to ship. She glanced at the sky, seeing that it was just past midnight.

The rest of the *Sun Queen*'s crew came on deck and swarmed up into the rigging, setting more sail, the ship turning to tack eastward.

All around her, lights floating above the water that marked other ships kept pace with the *Sun Queen*, the three lanterns still burning on the stern providing a clear marker. In the night, the free ships might've been a ghost fleet, their shapes vague and little seen except for the phantom lights of their lanterns.

An early meal was prepared so everyone could eat before dawn, Jules approving a serving of rum for the whole crew.

Artem and her other guards had put on their armor again, ready early for the fight.

Jules got the rifle from her cabin. "Gord!"

He came over, squinting at her in the low light. "Yes, Captain?"

"I hear you're our best shot with a crossbow."

"Well, I wouldn't—"

"I want you to use this during the fight," Jules said, offering the weapon to him. "It's a Mechanic rifle."

"Me?" Gord stared at the weapon, his eyes so wide the whites could be easily seen.

"This is the trigger. Don't put your finger on it until you're ready to shoot."

"Just like a crossbow," Gord said.

"Just like a crossbow," Jules repeated. She showed him the workings of the weapon, as much as she'd been shown by the Mechanics anyway. "Practice aiming it. Steady it on a railing or against a mast, as you would a crossbow. If we see Mages, try to hit them."

"Mages." Gord inhaled sharply. "Yes, Captain. Never thought I'd take aim at a Mage."

"Can you do it?"

"Sure thing. I've done a lot dumber things in my time than threaten Mages, or try to kill them. They do die?"

"Gord, you've seen the bodies of the Mages I've killed on this ship," Jules said.

"That's so. I'll go practice my aim."

"Don't drop the weapon," Jules added as Gord turned to go. "You only have ten shots."

She'd long known a night could pass very slowly. Those first nights in the orphanage had lasted eternities, as she wondered where her mother had gone. Much later, nights spent on the helm or on watch, as nothing happened for so long it felt as if the world had ceased to move. But this was the longest night of all, adjusting the sails, bringing the *Sun Queen* and all of the ships guiding on her onto another tack, trying to adjust their progress just right so that as the sun neared dawn and morning twilight began to lighten the dark, the free ships would be in perfect position to pounce on the Imperial sloops.

As the night began to lighten almost imperceptibly, Jules stood on the quarterdeck, her revolver at her hip, extra cartridges in her pockets, her dagger in its sheath in the small of her back and a cutlass riding on her other hip. Her hair, tied back, drifted in the breeze. She looked down at her hand, barely able to make out the strange flower pattern of her Mage lightning scar that began there. *Hold on, Ian. We're on the way to end this fight.*

Near her stood Gord, the rifle held tightly in both hands.

Around the edges of the quarterdeck were five of her guards, armor on and swords ready. Five more stood on the main deck. Every sailor on the *Sun Queen* had a weapon ready to hand except for Keli the healer, his knife intended not for fighting but for trying to save lives.

Jules could barely make out the dark shapes of the ships around the *Sun Queen*, sails pale against the stars. Lanterns had been put out except for the three at the stern of the *Sun Queen*, which were now shielded so they could be seen only from astern and the sides. But she knew every other ship was ready as well. Only the sloops had real distance weapons, the single ballista each carried, so everyone knew that this fight would be decided hand to hand on decks that would soon run wet with blood.

"I'm glad that you didn't go away," Ang suddenly said, his voice low but easy to hear in the hush covering the sea.

"When was that?" Jules said.

"When you tried to come aboard in Jacksport, saying you had to speak to the cap'n, and I told you to go away. Instead, you insisted on speaking to Cap'n Mak."

"I've brought a lot of trouble to this ship," Jules said.

"Yes," Ang said. "You have. But I'm glad that you didn't go away."

The sky was definitely growing a little lighter, though the stars still fought for dominance overhead. The partial moon had long since set, the twins racing it themselves near the horizon.

"I can see masts ahead," Gord whispered.

Jules strained her eyes, seeing straight, dark lines rising against the sky. And then along them, the paler shapes of sails.

The air grew a little lighter.

The free ships had spread out a bit as they approached the harbor, the three pirate sloops off to port of the *Sun Queen*. Jules heard the sudden thunk of ballistae shooting to port, followed quickly by the crash of a rock striking wood.

She heard faint shouts erupt ahead as the crews of the Imperial sloops awoke to their peril. The crews of the free ships stayed silent, grasping their weapons, waiting.

Another volley of ballistae, followed this time by the sustained cracking of a mast giving way. She hoped that was the mast of an Imperial sloop and not one of her ships.

The light kept growing. One moment she could barely make out the vague shapes of masts and sails, the next she could see ahead three Imperial sloops, crew running about their decks and into the rigging to make more sail. Off to port was the fourth enemy sloop, its mainmast lying across the deck in a ruin of rigging.

Jules jumped up on the railing. "*At them!*" she shouted as loudly as she could.

A full-throated roar answered her as the sailors shouted their defiance of the Empire that had once ruled unquestioned.

The free ships swept down on the three sloops ahead as they tried to turn away, penning them in and chasing them toward the harbor entrance.

Two free ships came alongside the fourth Imperial sloop, wallowing helplessly with its mainmast down, and the sound of swords clashing carried across the water.

The surprised Imperial sloops were trying to get up more speed, but had been forced to turn away, slowing them and allowing the free ships to sweep around them. Jules saw *Storm Rider* sliding even with one the sloops ahead, then coming over hard. The sloop got off a ballista shot that passed harmlessly above the *Storm Rider's* deck, then the two ships collided with a thump and screech of wood. As the crew of the sloop tried to stave off the *Storm Rider*, the *Bright Morning* came in from its other side, smashing side to side into the sloop.

"Get that one!" Jules ordered Ang, pointing to a second sloop ahead that was veering off to avoid the tangle where its comrade was fighting off *Storm Rider* and *Bright Morning*. The mass of ships was approaching the harbor mouth, ships swerving to avoid each other and avoid running aground, but Ang took the *Sun Queen* cleanly through the chaos. *Sun Queen* rammed into the starboard quarter of the sloop, jarring both ships. As they spun into the waters of the harbor, *Star Seeker* came from port and hit the sloop as well, crew pouring over the bows of both ships and onto the sloop, cutlasses clashing on Imperial short swords, crossbows shooting at close range.

Jules held herself on the quarterdeck despite a powerful urge to race forward and join the attack. That wasn't her job this day, at least not yet.

Western Pride, which like the other pirate sloops had bypassed the Imperial sloop whose mast had been knocked down, came in fast on the last Imperial ship. The Imperial warship managed to come about just in time to avoid *Western Pride*'s dash, but that slowed him so much that *Storm Queen*, *Second Chance*, and *Moon Chaser* surrounded him.

"Here they come!" Liv called, pointing toward the town.

Jules looked, seeing the Imperial galleys casting off from the pier, their oars rising into the air to come down and strike the water. "They didn't wait to get any of their legionaries back aboard," she said, grinning viciously. "And in the restricted waters of the harbor, they won't be able to get up speed to ram."

She heard the *boom* of a Mechanic weapon, realizing that it had come from inland. The legionaries ashore, perhaps still unaware of the peril facing their ships, were launching another attack on the wall.

She couldn't spare any attention for worries about Ian. This fight had to be won if he was to live. Jules jumped onto the rail again, waving her cutlass so it caught the light of the sun that had just risen above the cliffs to the east. "The galleys! Get them!"

One of the galleys was racing toward *Sun Queen*'s starboard side, away from where she was locked to one of the sloops. In the light of the sun's rays lancing across the harbor, Jules saw a cluster of Mage robes on the galley's quarterdeck. "Gord! On deck!"

Gord knelt by the rail, resting the rifle on it. The *Sun Queen* was rocking and twisting a bit, but with so many ships locked together as their crews fought she wasn't moving much.

The rifle thundered, the sound carrying across the harbor.

One of the Mages fell backwards.

Gord had already worked the lever of the rifle and was aiming again. Another thunder, but this time nothing could be seen of a hit.

He worked the lever again, shot again.

A second Mage fell as the galley neared the *Sun Queen*. Jules could only see one other Mage standing on the galley's quarterdeck.

And the front half of Gord's rifle disappeared as if it had never been.

He stared at it in shock as the galley's oars rose straight up to allow it to smash into the *Sun Queen*.

Jules pulled out her revolver and pointed it at the last Mage, who was still gazing fixedly toward Gord. She aimed, pulled the trigger, aimed, pulled the trigger, and aimed and shot a third time just before the galley slammed into the side of the *Sun Queen*, rocking everyone on their feet. The last Mage reeled backwards, falling to the deck.

With a collective shout, the oar handlers on the galley grabbed swords and climbed aboard the *Sun Queen*. With many of her crew already fighting the sloop's crew forward, the *Sun Queen* didn't have a lot of defenders left aft.

Jules' five guards on the main deck retreated up the ladder to the quarterdeck. Gord had dropped the useless half-rifle and picked up a sword, as did Ang and Liv and Cori, who'd been on the helm. Together with Jules' other five guards, they formed a shell about Jules, fighting viciously as scores of Imperial sailors from the galley crew swarmed onto the quarterdeck.

Her revolver already in hand, Jules aimed and shot a galley crew-member who looked like a leader, then holstered that weapon.

Drawing her dagger and readying her cutlass, she joined the others in defending the quarterdeck as the galley crew tried to swamp the defenders.

Jules' dagger went into the side of an Imperial thrusting at Liv. Bringing her cutlass up, she parried a blow from an Imperial.

The *Sun Queen* rocked again as another galley rammed into the mass of ships inside the entrance to the harbor. The free ships at the back of the locked-together fighters were lashing themselves to their nearest compatriots and sending their crews over the decks of ships already locked in combat to reach the Imperials.

One of Jules' guards fell to a blow by a powerful Imperial. Jules pulled out her revolver and shot that Imperial in the face before he could recover. But she and her defenders were being pushed into one corner of the quarterdeck by the mass of attackers.

Two more *booms* of a Mechanic weapon, this time from elsewhere in the tangled mass of ships.

A wave of sailors and volunteers from the *Proud Mari* and the *Bright Star* came charging onto the *Sun Queen* and hit the Imperial attackers, driving them back.

As the Imperials on the quarterdeck fled to avoid being hit from behind, Jules took a moment to look around.

There'd been ten war galleys. At least eight were locked into the mass of ships, using their oar handlers in their only chance to try to overwhelm the free ships. A ninth galley was coming around, as if trying to reach the harbor entrance past the fighting, but as Jules watched, *Fair Dani* collided with the galley on its port side, oars splintering and rowers howling with pain. Before the galley could get free, *Gallant Mike* came along the other side, sandwiching the Imperial warship, crossbows on both free ships shooting down into the galley.

Where was the tenth galley? There. Backing down using its oars, trying to get some distance from the fighting.

But *Prosper* came across the galley's stern. Before the oars could halt or turn the galley, it struck the stout side of the larger ship. The two spun about, drifting into contact with the larger mass of ships.

Another *boom* of a Mechanic weapon. Jules looked across the tangle of ships and masts and rigging, guessing that the shot had come from almost opposite where *Sun Queen* lay. She hoped Captain Erin was taking down any Mages on that side of the fight. The last of the free ships were coming in, throwing grapnels to tie themselves to the other ships so their crews could get into the fight.

As another wave of free ship volunteers reached the *Sun Queen*, charging onto her deck to hit the Imperial fighters who were trying to hold their ground, Jules, her heart pounding, raised her cutlass as high as she could. "With me!" she shouted, her throat feeling raw. She ran for the ladder to the main deck, her guards following, joining with the other free ship sailors and volunteers to push back the Imperials, clear the deck of the *Sun Queen*, and board the galleys and sloops.

She saw an Imperial officer urging on her fighters. Jules brought out her revolver and shot the officer, realizing she'd have to reload, then used her cutlass to cut down a centurion.

Dropping down to the deck of a galley, Jules saw a single Mage standing against the opposite railing, long knife raised, facing a semi-circle of wary free ship sailors reluctant to risk attacking a Mage. Pausing to pull out the empty cartridges from her revolver and shove in six more that hadn't been shot, Jules stepped forward.

The Mage looked at Jules, his face streaked with sweat. She was shocked to see fear in his eyes, remembering that when Mages were dying or badly hurt they would display some emotion. But this Mage showed no sign of injury, just of being at the end of his strength.

She raised the revolver to point it at him.

Before she could shoot the Mage dropped his long knife and fell backwards, over the side and into the water.

Astonished, Jules ran to the side and looked down, seeing the Mage slowly swimming toward shore.

She should shoot him.

She didn't.

Instead, as a small group of Imperials launched a desperate counter-attack, Jules turned and shot twice into them, dropping the two in the lead.

The others faltered, dropping their weapons and raising empty hands.

Jules joined the rush forward, clearing deck after deck, meeting up with Captain Erin and then Captain Hachi as they reached the last Imperial warship that still remained uncaptured.

A massive volley of crossbow bolts arced across the sky and tore into the surviving Imperial defenders.

Jules raised her cutlass again and led the others onto the deck of the galley, resistance melting away as she charged aft.

A small cluster of Imperials remained on the quarterdeck, some of them exhausted crewmembers grasping swords in hands slick with sweat, their eyes wide with fear. Behind them stood an older Imperial officer with a golden eagle on his collar, and beside him a junior officer holding a straight sword in a hand that shook with fatigue.

Jules stopped, holding back the others with her, her cutlass raised to point at the senior officer. "Surrender your ships and prevent further loss of life."

He glared back at her, proud and apparently unruffled. "Who demands the surrender of the Emperor's ships?"

"Captain Jules of Julesport, the woman of the prophecy," Jules said.

The officer shook his head. "I'd prefer to die quickly with honor to dying slowly of the Emperor's displeasure." He drew his dagger, holding it before him. "But I see no sense in permitting the slaughter of those loyal to the Emperor. Lieutenant Wil," he said to the junior officer beside him. "I order you to surrender these ships once I am dead."

Without another word, the officer plunged the dagger into his chest. He staggered sideways, fell against the railing, then went over it to splash into the waters of the harbor.

Lieutenant Wil stared at Jules, his sword tip lowering, tears of frustration on his face. "As ordered, I surrender these ships and their crews."

"Disarm him and the others," Jules said. "Pass the word. The Imperial ships have yielded to us."

Suddenly, she felt immensely tired. Looking down at her hands, she saw the cutlass in one, the blade notched by the fighting, and her dagger in the other. Both blades were streaked with blood.

"Jules." Captain Erin came up, also looking exhausted. "We need to check all ships for leaks. I think a lot of the Imperial galleys can't be saved."

"The sides of their hulls aren't that strong," Jules said. "To keep the galley lighter so the oars can drive it faster."

"I know that." Erin peered at her. "Are you all right?"

"I don't know." Jules looked about her, listening. "I can't hear any Mechanic weapons."

"No," Erin said. "The attack on the wall must've stopped when the Imperials realized what was happening here. Jules—we need to check all ships for leaks."

"Yes." Jules inhaled deeply, centering her mind. "Find every captain you can and detail sailors to check. If any of the galleys are so low in the water they threaten to pull down the ships tied to them, cut them loose."

"Aye." Erin went off, shouting orders.

Jules looked around her, seeing seven of her guards, as well as Ang and Cori. "Where's Liv?"

"A couple decks back," Ang said. "Her leg took a cut, I think. She told us to go on."

"Her leg? Go check on her, Ang. What about Artem? Mad, where's Artem?"

"Don't know, Captain," Mad said, tears on her face.

"Find him. Make sure he's being taken care of."

"Yes, Captain." Mad ran off.

Where was Ian? she wondered, blinking in momentary confusion. Somewhere ashore. She had to make sure the Imperial attacks on the wall stopped.

Jules looked aft again, where Lieutenant Wil stood, his face that of a man unable to comprehend events. She walked up to him, her boots thumping on the wooden deck, leaving red stains behind from the blood they'd trodden through. "We're going to get a boat in the water," she said. "Are you listening to me?"

Wil looked at her, nodding. "Boat in the water."

"You'll be taken ashore under a parley flag. You'll find Prince Ostin and inform him that his fleet is destroyed or captured, and that he and every Imperial servant ashore are trapped. We can stand off and destroy the cargo ships at the piers with the ballistae on our sloops. There'll be no more food." She paused, knowing that Imperial pride would never allow a prince to surrender, no matter how many other lives that cost. "If the prince agrees to abandon the attack, take his remaining soldiers back to Imperial territory, and respect the independence of the western settlements, he and his legionaries will be allowed to depart in peace. I want them out of this town as fast as they can go. But if he refuses, if he continues the fight," Jules said, thinking of the dead, "it won't matter what happens to the legionaries. I will personally kill him, slowly, a cut for every life lost here. Tell him that."

It only took a little while to get the boat into the water, crew it with some captured Imperial oar handlers, and send it rowing toward the piers.

Jules looked about her at the mass of ships lashed together into one wooden island. Sailors rushed around, trying to save damaged ships. Others slumped against masts and decks and rails, tired out or injured. Where bodies lay, often others knelt nearby, the lines of their grief easy to see.

She watched the boat head for the pier, hoping that what had been done this day would be worth the price paid.

CHAPTER SIXTEEN

Exhausted but restless, worried about Ian but unable to do anything else to help him, Jules went onto other captured Imperial ships, helping to check them for wounded who needed treatment.

Keli said he thought he could save Liv's leg.

Artem had been more badly hurt. Mad was staying with him.

Jules stepped onto one of the wrecked Imperial sloops.

"She's taking on a lot of water," Marta told Jules. "I don't think we can save it. Maybe keep it afloat until we can ground it."

"Do that," Jules said. "Some of the ships have cut free of the mess. There. The *Kelsi's Pride*. Tell her I'd like them to put over a tow line and pull this sloop over to the shallow water near the breakwater."

"Aye, Captain."

Jules walked along the deck, checking, stepping over a fallen mast and seeing something under a sail that had dropped along with the mast. She used her cutlass to draw back the sail, wary of vengeful Imperials or lurking Mages.

It took Jules a moment to recognize the figure who lay on the deck, her legs pinned beneath the fallen mast. Captain Kathrin of Law. Her sword lay on the deck, just out of reach of her grasp. She glared at Jules through eyes glazed with pain. "Give me my sword! I want to die with honor, fighting you!"

Jules shook her head and kicked Kathrin's sword farther away. "Enough have died today. It's over. Your fleet has been taken."

"Liar!"

"Oh, shut up." Jules could understand why Captain Kathrin was so unhappy with her. This was, after all, the third sloop under her command that Jules had been directly responsible for destroying or capturing. "I'm trying to decide whether to let you die there, or get some sailors to help lift that mast enough to get you off this ship before it sinks."

"I'd rather die a thousand deaths than have my one life saved by you," Captain Kathrin spat.

Jules smiled slightly. "And there you've given me my motivation. You'll spend the rest of your life knowing that you owe your life to me. Don't go anywhere."

She walked far enough, trailed by curses hurled at her by the trapped captain, to spot some sailors and wave them over. Captain Kathrin fought back, of course. In the end, despite the agony of her pinned legs, she had to have her arms bound before they could safely get her out from under the mast. Jules flinched at the sight of her legs. "Make sure she gets seen by a healer."

"Captain Jules!" The cry sounded across the still tangled mass of ships. "Captain Jules! The Imperial treaty boat is coming back!"

* * *

Prior to this day, Jules wouldn't have said there were any advantages to dealing with an Imperial prince. But it turned out there was at least one. When an Imperial prince made a decision, he didn't have to worry about convincing anyone else. He could do whatever he wanted.

And, at the moment, Prince Ostin seemed primarily to want to ensure his own safety. He agreed to Jules' terms.

The legions didn't know how to handle defeat. They'd never practiced for it or planned for it or imagined it. Faced with the previously impossible, even Imperial discipline cracked. Jules watched the legionaries who'd been ashore rushing onto the cargo ships still at the piers. She knew how such loading was supposed to be done, in careful order with everyone carrying supplies and tents and other equipment. But the legionaries she saw were racing onto the ships, apparently abandoning any burdens that might slow them down. She saw a few Mages with the legionaries, moving in their usual terrifying isolation. As each ship was filled, wallowing low in the water due to the load, it wended its way through the harbor past the entwined mass of free ships and captured Imperial ships. The three pirate sloops were free of the mess by now, watching each ship closely as it left.

Jules saw on the quarterdeck of the first ship to leave a figure in a brilliant dark red uniform, rows of medals and awards flashing in the sun, himself surrounded by others in perfect uniforms with lesser displays of supposed valor and mock excellence. That had to be Prince Ostin.

She was standing once again on the quarterdeck of the *Sun Queen*. Prince Ostin turned to look at her, and though they were too far apart for her to clearly see his expression, Jules gained an impression of superstitious terror. Certainly, Prince Ostin immediately headed below decks, where he didn't have to face the gaze of a pirate captain.

Volunteers had gone ashore to let those on the wall know that victory had been achieved, and by the time the last legionaries were filing aboard the last cargo ship, many of the wall's defenders had come down to the water to see them off.

Judging it finally safe to leave her ship and find out how Ian was, Jules came ashore on a longboat, still feeling oddly numb, looking at the dwindling line of defeated legionaries. Off to one side stood a small cluster of Mages who seemed to be deciding whether to leave with the legionaries.

Four of her guards followed Jules from the boat.

Dor came to greet her, smiling with the relief of a survivor of what seemed inevitable tragedy. A long cut ran down one side of his face, and one arm was bound against his body to immobilize it, but otherwise he seemed unharmed. "You did it!"

"We did it," Jules said.

She looked over at the Mages, then away, then back again. Hadn't there been one more Mage in that group?

A Mage holding a knife appeared in front of Jules with shocking swiftness, her demeanor that of someone so tired they could barely move. Her arm drew back to plunge the knife into Jules, but the same fatigue that had slowed her steps also slowed her arm. No one else could react in time to stop her, but Jules herself was able to bring her hand up just fast enough to grab the Mage's knife arm and stop the blade, the point nearly touching Jules' skin.

Jules braced herself for a struggle, but instead the Mage froze, her eyes locked on Jules' face.

The Mage's hand opened, the knife falling from it to hit the ground.

Jules let go as the Mage stepped back, her impassive face showing no feeling. "That one has had children."

The people nearest to them heard, Jules seeing their shocked reactions. She herself glared silently at the Mage.

The Mage's voice lacked any emotion, yet somehow still carried a hint of frustration. "How many? Where are they? How old are they?"

Jules laughed at the Mage. "Do you really think I'll tell you any of those things?"

"It will not matter," the Mage said, her dead voice carrying clearly. "That one no longer matters." Having said that, the Mage turned away as if to emphasize her dismissal of Jules.

Anger flooded Jules. Stepping forward, she grabbed the Mage's arm as those watching gasped with shock at seeing someone choose to touch a Mage. The Mage must have been surprised as well, not resisting as she was spun back about to face Jules. "Do you want to hear another prophecy?" Jules snarled at the Mage, her voice carrying even to the legionaries about to board the last ship. "You won't find my children. No one will. They'll live, and have children of their own. And, someday, a daughter born of my descendants will raise an army from the people of the free lands. She will *break* your Guild, and Mages will never again be able to act in any way they want. When that day comes, my spirit will be watching, and laughing. Because I *mattered*. Tell that to every Mage. You've already lost. I've already beaten you."

Shoving the Mage away, Jules walked off, Dor staying with her. "You're not going to kill that Mage?" he asked, bewildered.

"No. I want her to go back and tell her fellow Mages that my children already exist. I want the eyes of the Mages on me, hoping I'll reveal where they are. That'll be different, won't it? They'll want me alive in the hopes I'll betray where my children are." Speaking of the children reminded her of something very important. "Where's Ian? Why isn't he here?"

Dor gazed at her helplessly. "He... was hurt."

"Hurt? Wounded?" Jules tried to get her mind around the word even as it refused to accept it. "How badly?"

"Pretty badly. This morning, during the last Imperial attack on the wall. He's in my home. Getting the best care we can give."

Jules started running, leaving everyone else behind, her guards racing to try to catch up to her.

She ran past piles of trash and debris and supplies left by the hastily departed legionaries, all the way to the house she knew was Dor's, past a pair of startled sentries who weren't expecting visitors. A woman gave Jules a surprised look as she started up the stairs. "Ian of Marandur," Jules gasped. "Where?"

"This way." She turned and led Jules up the stairs to a hallway and door that gave way to a room that must be used by Dor himself in more normal times. The bed had someone lying in it, and a healer Jules didn't recognize standing by the bed along with someone Jules knew.

"Maeve?" Jules got out, struggling for breath.

Maeve turned to see Jules, and after a moment beckoned to her.

Jules walked to the bed, barely noticing her guards finally arriving and halting in the doorway. She reached the bed and stared down at

Ian, whose eyes were closed, his face drawn with pain. A moment of heart-stopping fear eased as she saw his chest was rising and falling. Too shallowly and too slowly, but he was still breathing. "Maeve, tell me true, will he be all right?"

Maeve sighed, exchanging a glance with the other healer. "We owe you honesty, Jules. I don't know. No one could tell you that. He was badly hurt this morning. Not many would've survived this long."

"But he's still alive now!"

"Yes," Maeve said, her voice soothing but not encouraging. "Because he has lived this long, he has a chance. If he lives through the night, he'll probably recover. But… I have to tell you that his chances of living through the night are less than half."

"Less than…" Jules paused to breathe, suddenly aware of her dirty, blood-stained clothes and the weapons at her belt. "There's something I have to do right now. Please stay and witness it, Maeve." Jules knelt beside Ian's bed, gently touching one of his hands. "I made a vow and I'm going to keep it. Now before these witnesses I make my promise to this man, to keep him beside me in all things, to remain faithful and never betray him, for all my life and beyond." She looked at Maeve. "You witnessed it, so it's legal. Whatever happens, he's my husband from this moment on."

"I witnessed it," Maeve said. "And surely he heard you. If anything will get your Ian through the night, it might be those words. Will you come with us now? There's nothing else anyone can do."

"I'm staying here," Jules said. "Until tomorrow. My fight isn't over, and neither is his. I won't leave him while he's still fighting."

"Good luck," Maeve said. She reached to touch Jules' hand. "But we must go. There are other patients to see."

"Yes. Go ahead. I'll be here." Jules looked to her guards. "One of you please tell the *Sun Queen* where I am. I'm going to be here until… until morning." A chair rested near a desk. She pulled it over against the wall next to the bed, and sat down, one hand barely touching Ian's shoulder. Exhausted as she was, Jules knew she wouldn't be able to sleep.

* * *

She had no idea how late it was when someone came into the room. Dor's oldest daughter, still a young child and looking very tired, but also determined. "Captain Jules," she said, "there are some people who need to talk to you. For just a little while. I'll stay here with your man as long as you're gone."

Knowing she had to at least use a chamber pot, Jules yielded to the request. "I'll be right back, Ian," she whispered to him.

Painfully getting to her feet, sore muscles, and bruises, and cuts, and stiffened joints protesting every movement, Jules staggered out the door of the room.

The house's main room was filled with men and women. She blinked at them in the low light of a few candles, recognizing all of them, but her bleary mind not able to pull up their names. There seemed to be people here from every part of the free lands.

"Captain Jules," one of the men said. He was from Edin's Town, and was holding some battered papers. "We know you are engaged in a serious vigil, but if we could have just a few moments of your time."

"What is it?" Jules asked, brushing her hair back with one hand.

"Your proposal," one of the women said. She was from Gull's Haven. "Is this a firm concept for how our settlements can work together?"

"It's a starting point," Jules said. "Something to start from, and talk about, and make changes that people want. You're all here. You've seen firsthand what we can do when we work together."

"Those of us from north of the Strait of Gulls might not want to join ourselves to the places south of the strait," a man from Cape Astra said. "But we'd still like to use these ideas."

"It's not about forcing people," Jules said. "It's not about a new Empire out here. It's about ways to live and work together, and help each other, that will keep these lands free. We won their freedom today. If we're to keep it, we need to try to have peace among us."

"You'll help, though?" a woman from Julesport asked. "If you take charge of meetings to work this out, I think everyone will trust you. You've… well, you've given us freedom from the Empire, and someday the daughter of your line will give us freedom from the Great Guilds."

"I'll help work things out," Jules said. "As long as everyone understands that I gave you nothing. You earned what you have. And, someday, your descendants will join with the daughter of my line to overthrow the Great Guilds, and they will earn complete freedom for our people at last. No one will give it to us. We will earn it. I'm sorry I can't stay. I have to get back."

"But you'll be here for a while," Dor said. There he was, sitting in a corner, his injuries obviously wearing on him. "You'll help us figure it out."

"If you need me," Jules said. "Please, I need to get back to Ian."

* * *

A night could be very long when a life hung balanced on a razor's edge.

Jules watched him, sometimes talking about things they could do and places they'd go someday. "The western continent. I bet there really is one. Maybe we could go looking for it."

But mostly she stayed quiet, because he seemed to be sleeping and she didn't want to disturb his rest.

She watched his face, and the rise and fall of his chest, dreading the moment when it might fall and never rise again.

When it first began to get light outside she refused to believe it, fearing that together they'd get so close to the line and then Ian not cross it with her. But eventually the sky became light enough that it was clear dawn was on its way.

She felt as if her heart stuttered when Ian opened his eyes, looking about, searching, until they rested on her.

"We made it," Jules said to him. "Good morning, Ian. It's morning. They said if you made it through the night, you'd be all right. And you did, so you can't die on me now. Do you understand?"

He didn't try to speak, but she could see the understanding in his eyes.

Jules blinked her weary eyes at the growing light outside. "We won. Did you know? Did you hear me yesterday? I promised myself to you. When you can speak, you can give me your vow. But we already know, don't we? I mean, you already said yes."

His eyes stayed on her as Ian opened his mouth slightly, then closed it. He nodded very slightly, but enough to see, a faint smile slowly forming.

"You need to get well," Jules said. "It turns out there are still some things I have to do. Difficult things. I'm going to need a good man beside me, and there's no better man in this world than you. That daughter of my line will probably never give me my life back, but I think the Mages are going to stop trying to kill me. For a while, at least. They know it's too late to stop the prophecy that way now. So you should be safer from them, too."

Jules smiled at Ian. "The free lands will remain free of the Empire, until the daughter descended from us frees them from the Great Guilds as well. Why don't you sleep some more? I'm also going to rest a little. I'm a bit tired, and there are still a few things that need doing."

Remembering another promise, Jules looked to the west, where his spirit would surely be. "Mak? I got it done. Part of it, anyway. I hope your girl made you proud."

She fell asleep, her hand on Ian's shoulder, her head drooping.

Outside, the sun rose on a new day, its light gradually banishing the stars and chasing the dark from the land.